CHICKEN OF THE SEA

Book III

FREE RANGE CHICKEN

NEIL BARRY

Summary

The first book of the *Chicken of the Sea* series concludes with Victor Joshua Walker's family safely reunited in the Marquesas Islands of French Polynesia after Barkov nearly murdered him. Barkov worked for Zagarovsky (a Russian drug dealer), who wanted vengeance by killing the eldest son.

The second book, *Chicken Too,* begins two weeks later. It ends in Australia with a breathtaking conclusion, after Zagarovsky has personal involvement in Victor's demise. With Victor Joshua returned to his father, and a family he never expected, the mystery seems revealed, except for one question.

Free Range Chicken begins the next morning as Victor Joshua takes a precarious step towards manhood. After an explosion, the Walker family heads north up the Queensland coast, where tragedy and crocodiles lurk. Although it means giving up what he loves, and putting his life in danger, Victor Joshua returns to the USA, discovering something far more precious.

Be advised that in *Free Range Chicken*, Victor Joshua turns 15. Accordingly, the content reflects his age and maturing interests.

Cover

Background: Cropped from 060617-N-7130B-356.jpg, a U.S. Navy photo by Photographer's Mate 2nd Class Aaron Burden.

Chicken: Flying Rooster © by Cory Thoman, graphic designer and illustrator. Modified and used with permission.

ISBN 978-0-9962926-4-1

First Edition, Published in May, 2016

In Appreciation

The author extends his heartfelt appreciation to those people who assisted and supported him in writing the third book of the *Chicken of the Sea* series, and bringing it to public attention. In particular, the author offers his sincere gratitude to Kathryn, who inspired him to finish the trilogy, who reported discrepancies and errors, and who made helpful suggestions. With a lifetime of teaching music, playing, and conducting, Frank's wealth of knowledge was invaluable in sending Victor Joshua Walker to music school.

To readers,

If you enjoy this book, the author would be very grateful if you encourage your friends and others to read it. Please visit the author's website, <u>neilbarrybooks.com</u> for more information and background about *Chicken of the Sea*, *Chicken Too*, and *Free Range Chicken*.

Contents

Chapter 1..1
Chapter 2...18
Chapter 3...27
Chapter 4...32
Chapter 5...43
Chapter 6...48
Chapter 7...64
Chapter 8...74
Chapter 9...84
Chapter 10...91
Chapter 11..101
Chapter 12..114
Chapter 13..124
Chapter 14..133
Chapter 15..142
Chapter 16..151
Chapter 17..159
Chapter 18..166
Chapter 19..172
Chapter 20..177
Chapter 21..190
Chapter 22..197
Chapter 23..204
Chapter 24..211
Chapter 25..220
Chapter 26..226
Chapter 27..238
Chapter 28..244
Chapter 29..251
Chapter 30..258
Chapter 31..264
Chapter 32..271
Chapter 33..276
Chapter 34..290

Chapter 35. 296
Chapter 36. 302
Chapter 37. 308
The Walker Family's *Spray* i
Glossary for sailing beginners ii
About the Author xviii

Please visit neilbarrybooks.com for background
information on many of the places and things in this story.

What Happened in Books I and II of *Chicken of the Sea*

Readers are strongly encouraged to read the first two books in the series before proceeding. For those who want to be reminded of what has already transpired, the following review may be helpful.

Chicken of the Sea is the story of Victor Joshua Walker, seen through his eyes. For most of his life he lived in a trailer on the outskirts of Norfolk, Virginia, believing his mother to be an emergency room nurse at the local hospital. His father was an assistant manager of a nearby supermarket. He was obsessed with Russian composers and Captain Joshua Slocum, the first man to sail alone around the world 100 years earlier. Not only are his kids named after Slocum's children (much to the family's dismay), John Walker planned a similar journey, and built a boat in the barn next door.

After a neighbor's trailer burned to the ground, he launched his boat, a modern replica of Slocum's *Spray*, and the family moved aboard, just in time for Christmas. After nine years, his *Spray* still wasn't finished; it was the dead of winter; the marina was deserted; the boat was the size of a school bus, heads (toilets) didn't work; and no heat! He remedied the situation by bringing aboard a kerosene heater. Josh, (he is Victor only to his father) would not go near it—his parents told him he fell on a heater when he was three. He has unsightly scars on both arms to prove it.

Josh's family slowly adapted to living aboard. His father continued to work on the boat, while providing nautical lessons, a long list of rules, and a rigid routine, which began every morning with Mom homeschooling Josh (now 13), his ten-year-old brother, Ben, and his seven-year-old sister, Jessie.

Three days of rain ended February. After being cooped up in the leaky *Spray*, Josh willingly took the trash to the dumpster. In the parking lot, a stranger (a wimpy man with oblong glasses) told him he was interested in buying the family minivan, even though he was driving a new black Cadillac. Within hours, Josh's father was ready to depart the marina. It didn't matter that the boat wasn't finished, that Josh had an important swim meet in a few days, or that his kids had no time to say goodbye to their friends. Despite telling everyone they would follow Slocum's route across the northern Atlantic, for seemingly no reason at all, his father suddenly decided to head south.

Their journey proceeded along the Intracoastal Waterway, through the rivers, canals, and sounds of North and South Carolina. Josh helped his father sail the boat. For most of the trip, Ben's head was stuck in his *Encyclopedia Britannica*. As the weeks passed, Josh's resentment diminished. Despite a few unpleasant incidents with his father, living on a boat wasn't as awful as he expected. There were interesting side trips, including the time Josh met an elderly man in a sculpture garden in South Carolina. He claimed Zagarovsky ruined his life.

There were also disquieting revelations: his grandparents died in a house fire when he was three, and his aunt and uncle were missing. Rare Russian Christmas ornaments, valuable first-edition books, and a guitar once played by Segovia are just some of the clues to Josh's mysterious past.

They were looking for a place to anchor, with Josh at the steering wheel, when the *Spray* became entangled with a submerged buoy attached to a plastic drum full of house bricks, smelly water, and a small unidentified nut. Two days later, in Beaufort, South Carolina, the family narrowly escaped being hit by a black Cadillac when they crossed the street. In St. Augustine, Florida, the kids were playing hide and seek on the docks when Jessie overheard someone on a big power boat threaten murder. Josh had seen the boat earlier, when it came too close to the *Spray*, and in

Charleston, where the argument was about losing a 'bucket of esnortiar.' It was not the only boat that kept cropping up as the *Spray* headed south; there was also a mock-trawler tagging along when they left West Palm Beach in Florida.

By the time the Walkers arrived in the Bahamas, things definitely weren't what they seemed. Josh's outwardly paranoid father not only went out of his way to avoid other people, but he changed his mind erratically. On desolate Acklins Island in the southern Bahamas, an old man arrived just in time to save Josh and Ben when they encountered a Hammerhead shark while diving for conch. Within days, Josh and Sal were good friends, sharing a love of fishing and ice cream aboard Sal's luxury ship, the *Marionette*. Josh (now nicknamed Sharkbait) reminded Sal of his dead son, Dante, further cementing the unlikely relationship. Not surprisingly, Josh's father distrusted the elderly diamond trader from New York and demanded Josh stay away from him. However, like the men who had followed the Walkers from Norfolk, Virginia, Sal was always nearby.

Two days before leaving the Bahamas, the Walkers met Bruce McKenzie, an Australian sailing around the world. Right away, Bruce confused Josh's father with someone he knew in Australia.

Their arrival in the Dominican Republic was complicated by not having the appropriate clearance forms, yet the problem vanished as soon as the officials realized that the Walkers were friends of Sal, who was due to arrive the next day.

On the way back from a rafting trip, Josh witnessed the exchange of drums from a farmer's truck to a pickup, with Sal and two henchmen standing by. The next day, Josh is kidnapped after discovering the drums are full of drugs, hidden under a layer of macadamia nuts. There were also suitcases full of cash on the *Marionette*—in addition to trading diamonds, Sal laundered money for a Colombian cartel. Josh escaped being fed to the sharks when his father arrived just in time; however, their relationship hit a new low.

Using long-range SSB radio, his father reported Sal to the US Coastguard. Within days, the *Marionette* was scuttled hundreds of miles away. Despite being on the run, Sal soon reappeared to make good the damage he had caused.

Six months later, the *Spray* was sailing off the desolate coast of Brazil, with a boat following in the distance. After a terrible storm that seemed to confirm Josh's father was, in fact, crazy, the Walkers headed to Rio de Janeiro, only to encounter three men who had been following them since departing Norfolk, Virginia. Josh confronted his fear of fire to enable the family's escape, yet a thousand miles later, the mock-trawler was just around the corner. According to his father, the man aboard was an insurance investigator, who was following him because of the fire in Norfolk.

After passing through the Magellan Strait, the family sailed up the west coast of South America. In a storm, Josh suffered severe stomach pains. His mother diagnosed a burst appendix, and performed an emergency operation in a remote cove in Patagonia, not something even a highly trained emergency room nurse could do. While under the influence of morphine, Josh dreamed about an old man who played the piano, and pulled him from a fire.

The next leg of their journey took them across the south-eastern Pacific with a stop at Easter Island. On the way to the Polynesian islands, they listened to a garbled radio message from Sarah, their grandmother. What little they heard suggested bad things had happened. Upon arriving in the Marquesas Islands, Josh's father caught a flight to Tahiti and returned to the US to find out what happened to Sarah. The rest of the family sailed the *Spray* to a remote island and anchored in a small bay to await his return.

After several days of catching up on schoolwork and exploring the bay, they trekked to a nearby village to see the remains of an ancient cannibal culture. Upon their return to the *Spray*, Sarah came on the radio once again. This time she sounded cheerful, yet there was a voice in the background. Josh's mother decided the risk was too great to talk to her.

Shortly after, there was a cryptic message from their father, ending with, 'I'm on it, going a new way.'

The following afternoon, the last thing they expected to find was Sarah reclining in the *Spray's* cockpit when they returned from spearfishing. Sal's sailing yacht, the *Maid Marion*, was anchored nearby. Zagarovsky had struck again, this time burning Sarah's house while she was taking the cat to the vet. With nothing left, she'd fled west to Omaha, Nebraska, where she found a ham-radio operator to send a message to the *Spray*.

Within minutes of meeting Sal's gorgeous granddaughter, Dani, fourteen-year-old Josh was infatuated. Though he had seen her from afar in the Dominican Republic, up close he was speechless. Dani was equally awkward, yet as they scavenged for food, they soon became friends. That night, Sal, his wife, Marion, and Dani had dinner on the *Spray*. No one worried when another boat entered the anchorage.

In the middle of the night, Josh awoke to the smell of gasoline, and a man (Dmitri Barkov) creeping through the cabin. Barkov was one of the men who'd followed them since West Palm Beach. After firing the spear gun at him and missing, Josh was moments from being choked to death, when his brother slammed a volume of the *Encyclopedia Britannica* on his assailant's head, knocking him unconscious. With the *Spray* awash with gasoline and the imminent risk of explosion, the family hastened to shore. The man followed, pursuing them through the jungle.

Just as the man closed in to finish off Josh, his father appeared. His puzzling 'I'm on it, going a new way,' actually meant, 'I'm on it, going Aranui.' He sent the message already aboard the *Aranui*, a tramp steamer going from Tahiti to the Marquesas. The men grappled on the beach until Sal's bodyguard arrived. Barkov was 'ex-KGB, the Bratva's top man.' He worked for Zagarovsky, a Russian drug dealer.

As the sun slowly set over the lagoon... a love-sick Josh played *Dani's Song* on his guitar. By nightfall, he knew his real name was Alexander, named after his Russian grandfather, a composer and musician, and an even more famous great grandfather. His father was one of two brothers, one a musician, the other an undercover FBI agent. His mother had been in the final stage of internship, prior to becoming a doctor, when the family had to change their identity to escape Zagarovsky's vengeance. Zagarovsky gets to the father by killing the eldest son—he had murdered Sal's son, Dante, years earlier. Josh's long repressed memories slowly returned, remembering when he stayed at his grandparents' house on Long Island. Barkov had started the fire that killed Josh's grandparents, and burned him so badly he spent one month in hospital.

Chicken Too: After two weeks of frolicking on tropical Nuku Hiva, the *Spray's* crew set sail again, following Slocum's route west. The sun was a fireball on the horizon when Sarah saw a ship steaming towards them. A near collision left the *Spray* without an engine and drenched from bow to stern. They diverted to Tahiti to make repairs, and cleaned up on the way. They were almost there when Sarah showed the kids a photo of Josh taken by Grandpa Alex a few weeks before the fire, when the extended family was on vacation in Beaufort, South Carolina. Josh is three, a happy kid with his toy fishing rod, standing between his uncle and aunt, who is wearing a billowing T-shirt. When Ben asked, 'Where are you guys', his late-arriving father was quick to say his wife was at the hotel with morning sickness, and that he took the photo.

With the *Spray* docked in Papeete, Tahiti, they went to the local market to replenish supplies. They discovered Sal had already arrived, his *Maid Marion* anchored on the other side of the island in Port Phaeton Bay. As they left the market, Josh's mother spotted Faro, another of Zagarovsky's thugs last seen in Rio de Janeiro. Realizing that Josh was still in great danger, his father swiftly relocated to Vaiare on the nearby island of Moorea. He rebuilt the *Spray's* engine, while the rest of the family stayed at a luxurious tropical resort hotel. It was a farewell present from Sarah, who was planning to jump ship. What should have been very enjoyable turned tragic when Faro aimed his walking stick (a camouflaged high-powered rifle) at Josh as he sunbaked on the dock. A slight gust of air deflected the bullet. It struck Ben in the femoral artery in his thigh.

Close to death from loss of blood, Ben was rushed to the hospital on Tahiti. Josh was unable to give blood because his blood type was wrong. Frustrated and angry, he was interrogated by a police inspector. When Faro passed by the door for the second time, clearly hunting for Josh, his father took action. He handed Josh a 1,000 franc note with veiled instructions to go to Vaiare. Josh escaped down a stairwell into the busy streets of Papeete. Faro and a policeman pursued him until he jumped onto a departing bus. Fortunately, its last stop was Port Phaeton Bay.

With sunset approaching, Josh swam out to the *Maid Marion*. After telling Sal what happened, and bidding Dani a fond farewell, he left with Tony's younger brother, Rick, on an overnight dinghy ride back to Vaiare. While Josh drifted in the lagoon, Rick took care of two Zagarovsky' goons guarding the *Spray*. By the next morning, Rick had completed the engine repairs. As he started the engine, a tousled head appeared from the neighboring boat. It belonged to Bruce, the Australian they'd met in the southern Bahamas.

Despite Sal's instructions to the contrary, Rick sent Josh with the *Spray* to a bay on the opposite side of the island, and returned to wait for Faro to arrive. While listening on the radio for news about Ben, Josh learned that a body had washed ashore near Vaiare, and that the next day, Bruce intended to visit the bay where he was anchored. Suspicious and unable to contact Sal or his father, he followed the alternate plan and sailed through the night to Huahine, some 90 mile west. There, he anchored and waited for his family to join him.

With Ben recovering, his family reunited, and his father considering Sal a good friend for his role in getting the family out of Tahiti, Josh was happy even though Dani had gone back to school in the US. However, an unfortunate incident caused Sal and Josh's father to argue, and the Walkers headed off to Samoa by themselves. Shortly, the course changed to tiny Palmerston Island, no more than a dot in the ocean. Here, the Walkers experienced true island life, primitive, personally satisfying, and safe.

With the supply ship due to arrive, once again the Walkers moved on; this time to Niue, on the way to Tonga. With fuel running short, they sailed to Neiafu, in Tonga. Trying to get a lower price for diesel fuel, Josh's father rented a Jeep and took the family inland. They were walking on a promontory overlooking the sea when Josh's father met Bruce again, discovering that Zagarovsky's people were also on the island. They rushed back to the *Spray* and once again headed off, this time visiting the Fijian Islands.

On Fulaga, a girl from a Filipino fishing boat pursued Josh, worrying his parents enough that they hurriedly departed. However, the fishing boat followed them, claiming a member of the crew needed medical attention. They boarded the *Spray* during a squall, their real goal to capture Josh for a $100,000 reward. Josh remained on board while the rest of his family was put into the dinghy and cast adrift. In a gust, Josh rammed the fishing boat and leaped overboard.

For two days, their dinghy drifted in the current, finally washing ashore on Moala. With only the clothes on their backs, and $100, they survived on handouts until a tramp steamer arrived. Unable to pay for everyone, Josh and his father remained behind. They camped on the beach, with Josh in the throes of dysentery. He was still sick when Bruce arrived to take them to Suva, the likely destination of the stolen *Spray*. After recovering the boat and a few of their belongings, father and son sailed to Sydney, Australia. Once again, the family was reunited, this time sharing a luxurious apartment with Sal's friend, Angelo.

Two weeks before Christmas, the family went to the Sydney Opera House. Confronted by Faro and Zagarovsky's local goons, Josh escaped with the help of stranger who called him Sander, a nickname for Alexander. Josh remembered enough to know the man was his long-lost uncle.

In a now-common pattern, the family fled Sydney, this time into the outback. Faro tracked them to a distant town, and again they escaped. They travelled for a month, before returning to the *Spray* and continuing their journey up the coast of Australia, still with Faro in pursuit.

Ahead of schedule, they found the uncle's restaurant, Sails. A few days later, Josh became a teenage rock star, performing with his uncle's band at the local school fete. The next morning, they visited nearby Fraser Island. This time, Faro and his assistants pursued them in four-wheel-drive vehicles across beaches, sand dunes, and through rainforests. Only luck and the timely intervention of Bruce in a small airplane saved Josh and his uncle.

Late that night, Josh's father awakened him and delivered the news that he was not his father. Josh's 'Uncle Ron' was his real father. Josh and his real father drove to the restaurant, where Sal waited. With the *Spray* tied at the dock, and appearing occupied, they waited for Zagarovsky's men to arrive. A gun battle ensued. Afterwards, Josh realized he'd been used, and asked Sal whether his nickname meant that he was bait for the shark. Question everything, assume nothing triggered Josh's final question, "What happened to my mom?"

FREE RANGE CHICKEN

The *Spray* is modeled on Bruce Roberts-Goodson's
Centennial Spray 38 ©, which is based on Slocum's *Spray*.
Reproduced with permission.

Chapter 1.

With her mouth full of cereal, Jessie stretched across the breakfast table. Out of the blue, she pointed at my nose.

"Josh has a mustache!"

Luckily, no one heard her. There was faint fuzz sprouting on my upper lip. It looked like I hadn't washed my face since the day before. I rolled my eyes in unhurried circles and pretended everything was the same. Jessie crunched cereal and squinted in my face before she leaned on her elbows, tilted her head, and stared.

My mother, only she wasn't my mother, intervened from the kitchen before we crossed eyes. "Jessie, elbows off the table and sit down!"

"I am sitting down!"

Sugar and spice and everything nice seldom applied to Jessie. At nine years old, she preferred slugs and snails, though she could be endearing when she wanted. She stared at me through hazel eyes, defying me to blink first. I pretended to waver before rapidly switching my gaze from side to side. On the verge of giggling, she poked out her tongue, her usual response when she was losing.

"Stop annoying Josh!"

"We're playing a game, Mom."

"Who has the worst table manners?"

Outside the sliding glass door, doves fluffed their feathers under a garden spray, making mist over the swimming pool and a garden blooming with color.

I used to think I spent half my life in the water. At 12 years old, I went to both morning and afternoon practice, endless laps for three hours, six days a week! For the last three days, I'd swum laps in the pool outside, far more enjoyable with a tropical paradise alongside.

'Sexy Pink' *Heliconia* stopped seducing me when Aunt Erin put a platter of toast on the table. Before I could ask what I should call her, she smiled; not a mischievous grin like her daughter, Tanner; a smile that said we'd get along.

"Erin will do just fine, Josh."

I smiled back. At least someone appreciated what I was going through.

"Aunt Erin said my manners are better than Tanner's," Jessie countered, now trying to get my attention by rolling her eyes.

"That's not saying much," Erin laughed.

At 8:00 am, Tanner was on her way to school. It was the first day of the Australian school year, so Jessie walked with her to the corner to wait for the bus to Gympie. Since returning, she'd prattled on about the advantages of regular school, which didn't include being able to spend most of her day reading Ben's *Encyclopedia Britannica*.

"I'm trying to cheer him up," Jessie said.

I was about to say I didn't need cheering up when Ben dropped his spoon in his bowl and scrutinized me like a biology specimen.

I wallowed in misery. Overnight, my entire life changed. Just ten hours earlier, Aunt Erin became my stepmother. Tanner was now my constantly chattering half-sister. It only got worse. Ben and Jessie were my cousins, not my brother and sister. My mother for 12 years was now Aunt Virginia; her real name was Susan. Not that it mattered, I still couldn't say it. My father was my Uncle John. His real name was Peter, named after the great Russian composer, Pyotr Ilyich Tchaikovsky. Uncle Ron was my father. His real name was Nicholai, for Nikolai Rimsky-Korsakov. And my grandmother, Sarah? She wasn't even a branch of my family tree. Altogether, it was a stab through the heart.

2

"Jessie's right. He's got facial hair," Ben declared. "You need to shave, Dude."

I wasn't in the mood for imperfections, not even a single hair on my chin. It had been invisible until I looked in the mirror that morning while brushing my teeth. "I'll be fifteen in three weeks; it's about time."

"I'll get you a razor for a present," he said jauntily.

He jerked back when I flicked at his nose. Our transformed family situation didn't seem to bother him at all.

"Better fuzz on my face than fur everywhere else," I said under my breath.

"Kids have vellus hair."

Ben got defensive about the silvery down on his arms. He had far more than I did when I was his age. Maybe it was one of those genetic things.

"Body hair changes with puberty. Androgenic hair is thicker and darker." If anyone was born to be a doctor, Jessie was. At nine, she knew more about the human body than I did.

Ben stole a sideways glance at his mom making toast. She hadn't said a word to me besides a tactful 'good morning,' both of us happily avoiding the elephant in the room. Ben turned to me, his preteen smirk a sure sign he was about to whisper something he wouldn't dare say in adult company. He stopped just in time as the back door swung open. My father followed Uncle John. They might have been twins; however, a darker tan and sun-bleached hair made it easy to tell them apart.

I could tell from their faces the news wasn't going to be good. My newly acquired father had returned to his restaurant after I was safely back at his house, seven hours ago.

"Everything okay at Sails?"

3

I might've been talking to myself. They crossed to the coffee maker and poured themselves cups.

"Nothing you'd notice if you weren't looking for it," my real father said between sips.

I expected him to call me 'Sander.' When he didn't, it bothered me. "What about Zagarovsky?"

"Skedaddled as soon as he saw Sal kill Faro. I expect he caught the next flight to Los Angeles. The rest, Tony cleaned up."

He sounded peeved. I thought it undeserved. Sal saved my life. It was hard not to like Sal; Tony too.

My newly minted uncle leaned against the counter, clearly avoiding me, coffee cup in one hand, the other hand clenched with *his* thumb pressed on top. Each time *he* rubbed, it sounded like an anchor rode straining when the wind strengthened. Up in the *Spray's* bow, the creaking rode kept me awake at night. Now, as much as how *he* looked at me, it made me feel like I'd done something wrong.

Instead of keeping my mouth shut, I asked, "Cleaned up how?"

My father gave an anemic smile. "It wasn't my first choice. We stuffed two of Zagarovsky's goons in a construction site toilet. It's pretty busy that close to Gympie. Someone will find them by lunchtime."

"Nick, the last time Tony cleaned up, they were stuffed in a trawler. It sank on the way to Hawaii." *His* tone was coldly critical, as much as saying spending even a few hours in a construction toilet fell short of his moral standards.

I studied my cereal bowl, wondering if muesli was uniquely Australian. According to Ben, who chose it over little bricks made from wholegrain wheat, most Aussie kids ate muesli for breakfast. It came in clumpy sugarless lumps of raw oats, seeds, nuts, and dried fruits, with a handful of extra raisins, slices of banana, and soy milk to make it edible. A clever photographer made muesli look appetizing on the recycled, biodegradable box.

"They deserved to die." I sounded heartless; I didn't care. Getting rid of Zagarovsky's hired killers was like putting trash in a can. You didn't care what happened to it afterwards.

"Sander?"

I refused to meet my father's eyes. He called me 'Sander' trying to score points. So what if he'd named me Alexander the day I was born, and called me "Sander" for more than three years?

My uncle stopped creaking. "Josh, we know how difficult this is for you."

"Now, I'm Josh?"

He'd made it clear the night before. I wasn't the Victor Joshua Walker that I'd grown up with. More than my name was different; I wasn't *his* son. I filled my spoon with soy milk, no muesli. I'd never tasted soy milk before. It reminded me of coconut water, sweet yet bland. From Ben's expression, he didn't like it either. He separated out raisins and bananas with his spoon. The rest he pushed to the side.

"What we call you is no big deal. You're still who you are, right Mom?" Ben's voice squeaked at the end.

She exhaled, folded her arms and leaned against the sink. *She* looked at me, blinking. The last time *she* was this unhappy we were in a Tahitian hospital. Ben was unconscious in the emergency room.

"We should've told you when you were seven..." The rest waited until I met *her* gaze. "A boy at school teased you. You came home in tears."

"About being Noah Junior?" My nickname started when word got out that a half-finished boat filled the barn next to our trailer. It made my family sound crazy.

"It was about your scars. You wanted to know how you got them."

"You told me I fell on a heater."

"It was too dangerous to tell you the truth. The accident was all over the news when it happened."

"It wasn't an accident!" *he* interjected.

She went on regardless. "For a couple of years, you always wore a long-sleeve shirt so people couldn't see your arms. You hated the ointment too."

"It made me itch something awful."

"Actually, it helped with the itch. The shirt; there wasn't a choice. If someone remembered and made the connection with you..." *Her* conclusion dangled in silence.

"Forgetting about the fire was the best thing that could happen," *he* said.

"Forget that! I had nightmares every night."

He interrupted me. "They were never about the fire."

"Of course, they were. He suppressed the memory. It was easier to blame Slocum than deal with it," *she* said.

He wasn't about to give up. "The important thing is he forgot."

"He didn't forget *everything*." *Her* emphasis was puzzling. "Every Sunday he insisted on going to church."

He exhaled, his way of backing down from a fight. "He was four. Maybe he liked Sunday school. It doesn't mean he remembered."

"Remembered what?" I asked when he didn't elaborate.

"It doesn't matter," he muttered. "It was too dangerous to keep going."

"It was clear to me you hadn't forgotten some things. You were seven when you asked to join the swim team." *She* nodded at my real father to take over.

"When you were little, you used to go to the Y with me. You'd sit on the edge and watch me swim laps. It's probably why you wanted to join the swim team."

I glared daggers at *him*. I wanted to make *him* squirm for years of lies. "Why didn't you tell me about my parents?"

"We wanted to. However, you needed time to get well. We thought… if you knew we weren't your real mom and dad, and they weren't available, it would be an added complication."

"You were much safer with them, Sander," my father added.

I wanted to ask why that justified abandoning me, yet I kept my eyes in my cereal bowl. Muesli was like trail mix from a health food store, not something you ate for breakfast, or because you liked the taste. The box said it had honey in it. If there was, I couldn't taste it.

"That email about you when you were seven…"

"What about it?" Muesli didn't help my mood.

"I was in Melbourne at the time. Someone who I thought was a friend said he saw a woman who looked like your mom," my father said. "It was a risk worth taking."

I didn't know who or what to believe. Months earlier, *he* had said his sister-in-law was dead. Just the night before, my real father said she'd disappeared the night of the fire. One of them was lying.

"It was a trap?"

Ben put down his spoon, giving up on muesli despite what the box said about healthy high fiber and protein. "Duh; they were going to use him to find you."

"They were still looking for me after three years; yeah, that makes sense."

7

"With people like Zagarovsky…" My father hesitated. "When they say they're going to do something, they follow through. Otherwise, they're seen as weak."

"How come he's not still in prison?"

He answered. "He's got friends."

"He got early parole," my father said. "August 12th, one day after he was sentenced to 25 years, Barkov tried to kill you again. Some bureaucrat in Washington DC decided you weren't eligible for Witness Protection. We had to hide you ourselves."

"In a crappy trailer at Arcadia Park," I finished.

I could tell from the way *he* studied *his* feet that I'd hurt *him*, my father too.

"If Zagarovsky's still looking for you after 12 years, he'll never give up," Ben said.

"What about my mom; you still looking for her?"

"The woman in Melbourne…" My father waited for me to look up. "She was supposed to be playing the organ at a church, not far from where she used to live. It made sense at the time."

With a grunt, *he* got my attention. "Remember when we went camping; Spruce Knob Lake in West Virginia?"

A day after my seventh birthday, *he'd* borrowed a tent and sleeping bags from the O'Neils, who lived across the road from us. We left the same day and spent a miserable week in the middle of a vast pine forest, hiking, reading, and playing cards. Mid-February was too cold to do anything else.

"What about it?" At the time, I thought going camping was a special birthday present. It didn't matter that the tent stank of Jessie's dirty diapers.

"We had to disappear, just in case." *He* glared at my father. It was clear who *he* blamed.

"I told them to leave, Sander. There was a good chance my email was hacked in Melbourne. Going there was a big mistake."

"What happened?" Ben asked.

"I had high hopes. It was the first good lead I'd had. Luckily, I spotted Barkov before he saw me. It still blew up in my face. They were right on my heels for months after that. I didn't stop looking behind me until my car broke down a few miles out of Gympie. I figured a tiny town in the middle of nowhere was the last place they'd look." He smiled at Aunt Erin. "Erin's dad needed help on the farm so I stayed."

"That makes it okay to forget about me?"

"Sander, if I returned, I would've led them to you. There was no choice. I had nothing left. Living on the run; it's exhausting."

"Tell me about it, Nick." *He* beat me to it.

My father went on regardless. "I had three jobs until I saved enough to create a new identity, one that Zagarovsky's people couldn't discover. I always planned to go back for you."

"Instead, you opened a restaurant."

He looked as if I'd slapped him. "You don't understand. The next year, you were doing better. You'd caught up at school. John sent email a few days after your eighth birthday so he could tell me you won the 8 and under 100 yard freestyle at the Southeast District Championships."

"Not that big a deal."

She smeared butter on toast. "It was to us."

She'd been at the swimming pool, cheering for my team. By Sunday, *she* was hoarse, yet I still heard *her* shouts over the roar of applause when my fingers punched the timing pad first.

My father perked up. "It was to me too. He videotaped you so I could watch you on YouTube. Not smart, though definitely worth the risk."

I couldn't help myself. "That changes everything."

"It changed things for me, Sander. You were safe. You had friends. Your teachers were planning to move you up a grade. The next year, things got crazy. I could hardly drag you away."

"You'll always be part of our family, Josh." *She* spoke softly to get my attention.

I looked up at *her*. "I don't even know what to call you."

She came over and hugged me, one hand massaging my shoulders the same way *she* did on the way home from swim practice. "You'll think of something."

I knew I'd always be able to talk to *her*. "How about Aunt Mom?"

She laughed. "I think Aunt Vee will do just fine."

He cleared his throat. "I'm sorry I lied to you for so long."

I wasn't ready to call him Uncle John. "Sal said Grandma gave up everything to be with me; and we're not even related."

"Not by blood," she said from behind me. I spun around in my seat. "By everything else that counts, you're my grandson."

"But you lost everything because of me. I caused all this."

"Dude, you were three!" Ben interrupted.

"A very cute three, I might add." She picked up the muesli box to look at the nutrition label. It was in grams, milligrams, and kilo-joules. She caught Ben's eye.

"It's packed full of fiber, vitamins, and protein, Grandma."

She winked at him as she sat down next to Jessie. "I thought Sal was coming for breakfast?"

My father hesitated. "Sal left an hour ago."

I hid my disappointment. "Tony too?"

"He is Sal's bodyguard," *he* replied haughtily. "It's only for a week or two."

Every time I looked at Uncle John, I still saw my father. Like muesli, it would take time to get used to.

"Sal's taking advantage of the lull to regroup," my father went on.

"We need to as well," I said under my breath.

He let out a tired sigh, perhaps to show what he thought of that idea.

I repeated what Sal said six hours earlier. "We were lucky last night."

He reacted as the words left my mouth. "It depends on how you look at it."

"We've bought some time!" My father and I seemed to agree on that.

My uncle and father swigged coffee and talked about finding a better hiding place. I chewed buttered toast, of the mind that anything was better than muesli, silently resenting that even though Zagarovsky was on his way back to New York, he was still in control.

"Heading north makes the most sense," *he* declared.

"Doesn't it make more sense to do something they don't expect?" Sarah was 61, outspoken and stubborn like a teenager. She'd clearly given our situation thought.

"Something like what?" *he* asked.

She peeled and sliced a mango with a razor-sharp paring knife. She divided slices between herself and Jessie before looking up. "You don't have to be Einstein to realize that repeating the past and expecting a different outcome is nonsense, John."

"Not much else we can do at this point."

"We need to change our names as soon as we can," my father said. "Sal said he'll get us new fake IDs in New York; however, it'll take weeks to set up."

"What we need are new passports. Sal going to fake those too?" *he* grumped.

"Once we have IDs, we'll apply the usual way."

He exhaled. "It'll take months!"

"We'll stay here as long as possible. It'll be safe until Zagarovsky returns," my father added. With coffee cups in hand, they headed into the dining room to sit down.

Her mouth full of mango, Jessie turned her table manners on me, "Are you going to shave after breakfast?"

"I don't plan to."

"Can I watch if you do?" Jessie twisted in her chair. "Josh's growing a mustache, Grandma." She made it sound as if fuzz on my face was peculiar.

"All boys do that when they get older, Honey."

"It's because their testicles produce testosterone." Jessie looked to Ben to make sure she'd pronounced it correctly. "They get hairy all over, and make semen."

Was I the only one in the room with a crimson face? Even my open-minded ex-grandmother had her hand over her face, shaking her head. Erin cocked a stunned eye at Jessie. It was all Ben could do not to laugh out loud.

With surprising calm, Aunt Vee said, "If Josh takes after his mom, he'll never be hairy."

Could it get more embarrassing? I glowered back at her, glad my father and uncle weren't there to hear it.

"Not my fault she's been reading the *Brit*," Ben hedged. "Grandma said it was okay."

"What Grandma said was 'learning new things is good. Sharing it requires insight.'" She brushed back silver-gray curls, her eyes bright with mirth. "Josh, I think you're old enough to call me Sarah."

I smiled and nodded. She always made everything easy.

"Now you're old enough to shave; I have just the thing to get you started."

Sarah went into her room to get whatever it was. She was gone so long I tried eating muesli. Amongst crunchy nuts and grains, were pumpkin seeds, and flakes of wheat that tasted like honey. It was definitely healthier than American cereal.

She returned with a wooden box. "I've been carrying this around since before Christmas." She moved muesli aside, and placed it on the table before me. "When Sal left Sydney; he wasn't sure how things would turn out in New York. He asked me to give this to you when you started shaving."

The box was burled walnut, polished so brightly it mirrored my hands as I opened a tiny gold clasp and lifted back the lid.

"It's a family tradition," she went on. "His father gave him one when he started shaving. He would've given this to his son, but Zagarovsky stopped that."

Ben craned his neck to look inside the box. "No way! He'll cut off his head, like in *Monty Python*."

There were four compartments mosaicked with shiny squares of mother-of-pearl, the same as the iridescent flowers on the fingerboard of my guitar. In one compartment was a straight-blade razor, the old fashioned kind with a translucent horn handle. Beside it were a badger-hair brush, a tarnished silver bowl with a round bar of soap, and a rolled-up cowhide belt.

"Sal said to tell you the bowl is Sicilian, from the 1850s. It used to be a salt cellar, so it symbolizes loyalty and friendship; some kind of macho Mafia thing, I expect."

"More like putting salt on the wounds." Despite *his* smile, I wasn't sure if *he* was joking or not.

She lifted the razor from its compartment, the blade honed to dull grey, not shiny like a boat knife. 'Dante' was incised into the handle.

I looked up. "I can't accept this."

"He said there was no one else he would give it to."

It didn't seem possible that she was no longer my grandmother.

"It's really nice of him, but it belongs in his family, Sarah."

"I'm sure Sal would agree." She smiled oddly. "However, he wants you to have it."

"I'm with Ben. I'll cut my throat." My morbid humor drew a discouraging grin from Ben.

Like a scene out *The Godfather*, my grinning father filled the doorway. "A leetle blood maybe. The tricka is getting the angle just so." He pinched the air. "Thirty degree. Anda move it perpa-dicular to the blade, never sideways."

"No way am I using it!"

Ben added his support with, "Smart move, Bro. Stick with electric."

"You going to tell Sal you're chicken, Vittorio?" *He* clearly didn't mean it.

"A coupla nicks will man you up, Sander."

They were teasing, of course; yet I rose to the challenge. Everyone trooped into the downstairs bathroom to watch, even Erin. While my father stropped blade and leather, his brother puddled soap and hot water in the silver bowl and worked up a thick creamy lather.

"He doesn't look old enough to shave, John," my father scoffed.

"Hard to believe he's almost 15."

I glared at both of them. "No wonder kids leave home as soon as they can!"

He put the foam-filled brush in my reluctant hand. As my moment of manhood arrived, my feet got colder. The tiles were frigid, virginal white like the marble top on the vanity.

"Let's make this a bloodless sacrifice, and appease the gods some other time," Sarah chuckled.

With lather covering my face, I gaped at her. As my grandmother, she'd filled my head with stories about Greek heroes. Not one of them shaved!

"Just go slowly, Sander. You can stop, but don't move the blade sideways." My father pressed the razor into my now-unwilling hand. "I'll show you how if you want me to?"

"On your face or mine?"

"Yours, of course."

Ben and Jessie thought that was hilarious.

I raised my hand, my eyes switching between the mirror and the blade nearing my foamy nose, expecting blood to appear at any moment.

Behind me, I heard, "It looks awfully sharp."

"Sal will love this photo. Stop looking so serious, Josh."

Ben hopped up for a ring-side seat on the vanity. "He ought to practice with a disposable first."

"Tilt the blade a bit more, Sander."

My hand was trembling as I adjusted the blade angle. I was so shaky that I took hold of the tip of the blade between my thumb and first finger of my other hand. After a deep breath, I touched the blade right under my nose and cautiously lifted up my head until it reached my upper lip.

"He'll cut himself if he's not careful."

"Don't bug him, Daddy. He needs to concentrate."

I tilted my head and looked in the mirror. The razor left a path free of soap, and no blood. It felt tingly. With unwarranted confidence, I turned my head slightly right and repeated the process twice before I breathed out again. If there was any difference, I couldn't see it. Everyone crowded closer. Jessie hopped up onto the other side of the vanity to see for herself.

"Do I look different?" I asked no one in particular.

"Still the same." Jessie smirked. "Except you don't have a mustache anymore."

"I didn't have one to begin with."

Ben craned his neck to look at both sides of my face. "You missed a hair, Dude."

"I'll get it next year." I was about to add that I risked my nose for nothing when the phone in the kitchen rang.

"I wonder who that is." Erin stepped past my father and through the doorway. She was saying 'hello' for the fourth time when someone banged on the back door.

"No one ever visits this early in the morning," he said to her back.

I inspected my handiwork, not bad at all, a solitary hair left and no blood. In the mirror, gleeful Ben smirked from beside me.

"It looks like you shaved with your eyes closed."

Boldly, I brushed on lather until I bore a marked resemblance to Santa Claus. I had the razor poised under my chin when the kitchen exploded.

Chapter 2.

I wasn't sure whether it was my father or uncle who shouted, 'Is everyone okay?'

A moment later, someone hauled Ben off me. I clambered to my feet, drums pounding in my left ear. There was shaving foam drooling down my chest.

He loomed over me, clutching my wrist until I relaxed my grip on the razor. It clattered on the vanity. "Seems you're still lucky, Victor."

He was out the door before my father got in my face. "Stay here till I tell you it's safe."

"Is anywhere safe?" It sounded distant, not my voice at all.

He pushed past Ben, glanced into the kitchen, and stopped in his tracks. "Everyone stay put."

It wasn't in Aunt Vee to stay put, especially if there was an emergency underway. She trailed behind him, stepping warily through glass shards and wood slivers. "Mom, I need you out here!" she called.

"Shouldn't I call for help first?"

"No need. After an explosion like that, the neighbors will call the cops right away!" *He* was adamant.

"First, there aren't any cops in 40 miles. Second, most of the houses around here are vacation homes," my father interrupted. "Everyone leaves after the holidays."

The smell from the kitchen was sweet and pungent. It reminded me of July 4th, the smoky haze after the fireworks. Bits and pieces of breakfast, cutlery, plates, cups, and glass crystals littered the floor all the way onto the patio. Erin slumped over the sink. *He* held a bloody washcloth over her face. Her clothes were a mess.

"I... hurt ...my... wrist." She sounded peculiar.

My father was already out the back door, looking around.

I stumbled towards the refrigerator. "I'll get ice."

He spun around. "For once, can you do what you're told?"

Erin's wrist was busted; you could tell from the way her hand bent back. I held *his* gaze while I rubbed my ear. When I looked at my fingers, there was blood on the tips. Suddenly, I needed to sit down; however, the blast had hurled the breakfast table and chairs through the sliding glass door. Of our breakfast, only the muesli box remained. It was upright on the floor.

I took a breath. "You're not in charge of me now."

He mouthed what might've been, 'Victor, stop mumbling' as he approached.

My stomach turned queasy. My eyes watered. The refrigerator slanted sideways. Just in time, *he* grasped my arm and kept me from falling.

Aunt Vee took charge of triage. *He* sat me down on the floor next to her while she dabbed at Erin's forehead with paper towels soaked with lemon juice, nature's antiseptic. Erin's wrist, she splinted with duct tape and cardboard ripped from the muesli box. Then, she examined my ear after carefully swabbing it with wet toilet paper to remove the blood.

"He needs an emergency room," she said to no one in particular.

"His ear looks normal."

She glanced up at *him*. "The damage is inside his head. It's very likely he has a ruptured eardrum."

"The nearest hospital's in Gympie," my father said. It sounded as if he was standing behind me, not in the busted door frame. He was breathing hard.

She grasped my hand when I tried to reach for my ear. "That'll do. If he checks out okay, we'll leave right away. If not, we'll drive him to Brisbane; find somewhere out of the way."

He looked as if he hadn't heard a word. "Today?"

"You think tomorrow makes more sense?" she snapped, glancing around.

Every window was shattered. There were spikes of glass sticking out of walls, cabinet doors hanging on busted hinges, broken crockery spilling across the counter.

"Nick can drive you to Gympie. I'll get the *Spray* shipshape and re-provisioned. It'll take teamwork, but we'll be out of here by tonight," *he* said glumly.

"Whatever!" She peered into my ear again.

"Is he going to be okay?" Ben asked.

"He might lose some hearing. Worse, if his inner ear gets infected."

"I feel dizzy." The buzzing increased when I tilted my head.

"So much for dumping them in the toilet," my father said.

He exhaled loudly. "We don't know it was one of them."

"That construction site; they're blasting rock to rebuild the bridge. You think you might find a box of gelignite in the storeroom?"

"It's possible," *he* wavered.

"Zagarovsky sent a message." My father pointed at the remains of the door. "One stick is enough to do that. We'll take what we can from here and head up the coast. Not much else we can do. Unfortunately, it's what he wants us to do."

"You always have a backup plan," *he* said.

"I do for Erin and Tanner." My father wavered. "They'll be safe without us."

Jessie gripped her grandmother's hand. "We can all fit on the *Spray* if we share our beds."

"That's very generous, Sweetie," my father said. "I think it's safer if we split up."

He reacted the way I expected. "What exactly do you intend to do with Victor?"

"Actually, the very thing Zagarovsky expects. With luck, it'll all work out." He sounded confident.

+ + +

My father rattled off assignments before he rushed off to get Tanner. He hoped to catch up with the bus at Tin Can Bay, the next town on the road to Gympie.

Even before his Jeep, nicknamed *Beastie* hurtled down the street, *he* took command.

"Ben and Jessie, get your stuff packed. Josh's too. Sarah, I want you and Josh to box up any food you think we can use."

"Look at him, John! He can barely stand up!"

Why couldn't Aunt Vee be my real mom?

"I can stand fine." I got to my feet to prove it.

Everything swayed. My stomach cramped, ready to puke. *He* put his arm around my shoulders. I shrugged him off.

"I can manage by myself." I expected a reprimand.

"I can see that," *he* said.

"He's just trying to help, Josh."

"I don't need his help, ever." I almost called her 'Mom.'

Before he could say something, she said, "John, he needs time to adjust. Right now, he's hurt and angry."

She was always the calm one in the family.

They went upstairs with Erin to pack their things. I was certain they were still talking about me as I tottered back and forth, lugging cans and boxes from the kitchen cupboards to the counter. Sarah stuffed what she wanted to take into recycled shopping bags. The rest she shoved aside.

I was emptying the refrigerator as she stacked cans into columns. "Must run in the family," she laughed.

"What must?"

She held up a can of 'Chunky Tuna in Water.' When I smiled, my ear throbbed.

"I shouldn't be surprised; your uncle and father are like two peas in a pod."

I nodded, not at all sure I wanted to talk about either of them.

"I can see both of them in you," she added.

"Because I'm stubborn?"

"You're also resourceful, and very good looking. When you came along, the whole family adored you. Of course, it helped that you were the first grandkid. You were so cute; everyone wanted to hold you. My Thom used to say we should take a number for five minutes apiece."

I thought, but kept back, 'the fire changed all that.'

"We'd go all to your grandparents' house on Long Island for Christmas. The last time, you were nearly three, and into everything. No present was safe from Giggle Boy."

"That'd be me; a laugh a minute."

She gave me a disapproving look. "Your Uncle Peter said he wanted a son like you for Christmas, so your mom gift-wrapped you for a lark. Midnight-blue paper with snow crystals. I don't think I've every laughed as hard as when he unwrapped you. Everyone was so happy. Between you and me..." She lowered her voice. "If ever there was a night to conceive babies, that was it."

"Meaning Ben?"

"The timing is perfect."

I rested against the counter, wanting her to go on, afraid to ask because of what she might say. She made me wait while she put chunky tuna in a separate bag.

"The last time Thom and I were at your grandparents' house was July 4th." From her tone, it was more than just reminiscing. "You were pretending to be a ninja and leaping on the sofa when you fell on the guitar." She tied off the bag. "There we go, a month's supply of tuna fish sandwiches."

"You think it's enough?"

"For John by himself, maybe. We really should stop this name nonsense and call him Peter. Anyway, he said he accidentally sat on it. He insisted on paying for the repair."

"Why?"

"So you wouldn't get in trouble. He doted on you. Of course, everyone knew you'd been showing off for him." She sniffed. "It was three days after that..."

"July 7th was the fire."

She nodded. "You know he ran into the house to get you, don't you?"

I nodded.

"You weren't breathing. They resuscitated you twice on the way to the hospital. You were in Intensive Care for a month, unconscious for a lot of it. Nick stayed with you at night, and when he wasn't investigating the fire. Losing your mom devastated him." She seemed about to say more, but thought better of it.

I wanted to ask about my real mother. Now wasn't the time. "What happened when Barkov tried to kill me the second time?"

"Peter was with you during the day." She hesitated again. "Susan and I filled in the gaps. She was doing her internship at the hospital across the street. She was with you when she got a phone call to help with an emergency, a building collapse or something. It was bogus, of course. Luckily, she asked a nurse to keep an eye on you. Barkov strangled her. After that, your father decided you had to disappear."

"So he dumped me on them and moved here." For a moment, I thought my sarcasm slid by.

She looked me in the eye. "First; he didn't dump you. We planned it the day after Barkov tried to kill you. Second; Peter and Susan were more than willing to take care of you; they love you, same as they love Ben and Jessie. Third, you're still alive, so your dad going to Australia worked."

I didn't believe any of it. "They lied to me."

"It was for your own good. You shouldn't blame anyone except Zagarovsky."

"How could I forget my real parents?"

She folded her arms and leaned against the counter. "You don't call them 'Dad' and 'Mom.' Why is that?"

"I call them Mom and Dad all the time," I protested.

"Not to their faces; not once since I've been on the boat. In fact, you've never said 'Mom' or 'Dad' in my presence."

"It doesn't mean anything," I said, heating up.

"I don't think you forgot your real parents." She touched my cheek. "San-boy."

Only my father called me 'Sander.' I scowled, just for a moment, before I realized.

"You remember, don't you?" she pressed.

"Every night when she put me to bed she sang to me... about a bird that helped a little boy go to sleep... She was Tushka, and I was San-boy."

"After the fire, I think you wanted to forget what happened, so you locked your memories away, deep down, where you felt safe."

"I don't even remember what she looked like."

As she stepped away from the counter, it struck me that she'd been waiting for me to say that. I watched her go into the office, currently her bedroom. She came back with her purse.

"Memories fade; they don't die, Alexander." She unsnapped the gold clasp. "Thom used to say our memories determine who we are."

He said that at the end of our first day of sailing. At the time, I thought *he* was talking about our journey. Now, I wasn't so sure.

"Someday, memories are all you have left," I added.

I was certain she'd heard it before—she fumbled as she opened her purse. "Thom bought this for me in Venice. My first book had just been published so we splurged on a trip to Italy. We were having coffee at the Caffè Florian in the Piazza San Marco when he gave it to me." She blinked and wiped a tear away. It made me uncomfortable. "It was raining so we sat under the arcade."

She withdrew a photo and held it out. It was a photo of me, three years old with a fishing rod, standing between my real mom and dad. Although I'd seen it before on the way to Tahiti, I was still taken aback.

"The first time I showed you this, you stared at it and didn't say a word," she said quietly.

They were an odd match. He was older, tall, and broad-shouldered; she was willowy with a delicate beauty, yet you could tell they loved each other from how they had their hands on my shoulders. Even in an oversized white T-shirt, she was graceful.

"She's beautiful."

"Every time I look at you, I see her. It's not just that you have the same hair and eyes. You think like her too."

"How?" Suddenly, she seemed fragile, like a porcelain statue.

"Right before Thom took this photo, you'd caught a fish. It was tiny. Your dad wanted you to use it for bait to catch a bigger fish, but you let it go."

"You remember that far back?"

"You said it was too young to die. Your mom was the same way."

I glanced up as my father heaved the door off the remaining hinge and carried it outside. Tanner inched past the remains of the door frame. She looked around the kitchen, taking it in, her mouth stuck in the open position.

Chapter 3.

Like pack mules, nine people lugged boxes and bags from the house to the cars, judiciously skirting the mess on the patio. I'd made five trips to my father's Jeep Wrangler when an elderly woman tottered from a junglefied bungalow across the street, no doubt to see what the activity was about.

"Soon as I saw him sneaking through your *Pandanus,* I tried to phone you, Ron. Your number's not in the local directory," she all but shouted at my father.

"It's unlisted. You have to look under 'Sails', Ellen," he explained loudly.

"No need to shout, Dearie. My hearing aid works fine. When that car backfired; it very nearly deafened me…"

I was on my way back to the house for another load when he beckoned me over. "Ms. Masters, this is my son, Victor."

Despite 'Victor,' I said 'G'day' with a smile. I wondered if my ear was still bleeding because she peered at my face after adjusting the thickest spectacles I'd ever seen.

"Looks like his mum, does he?"

He grinned. "I reckon he got her looks. I'm certain he's mine, though. He's not bad on the guitar. He was on stage with me at the school fete last Friday."

I could tell she wasn't impressed.

She went on peering, "He's exactly like she described him."

He pondered that as if he had all the time in the world. Only a few minutes earlier, we needed to leave immediately. "And who might she be?"

"She was with him, of course; the man I saw in your *Pandanus.* A right stickybeak, asking about everything under the sun. She said they were looking for some friends from America, only they didn't sound like you at all."

"And not from here, I assume?"

"Yugoslavian maybe. It's hard to tell with those Eastern Europeans."

That got his interest. "What did they look like?"

"Her, dyed hair, I guarantee it. And sunglasses too, so dark you can't see her eyes, but I could tell she was taking a good look around. Miss Pushy; that's her. Now him, he was Mr. Average, nothing unusual about him, not like he had a wart on his nose or something. He was so polite, I didn't expect to see him sneaking around the back of your house."

My father was about to say something when Erin dragged a suitcase up the path. Tanner was on her heels, still wearing her private school uniform, her arms full of toys. She handed me a packet of her favorite cookies as she passed, as unhappy as Jessie, who lagged a few yards behind with a duffle bag and her mom's handbag slung over her shoulder. My father pointed the other way, to the SUV under the carport.

"They can't be leaving already? They only just arrived," Ms. Masters barked.

"He hurt his ear this morning, so I'm driving him to Brisbane to see a specialist. Then, we'll be on the Gold Coast till Friday." My father lied like his brother, without blinking an eye.

"School starts today," she said, now frowning at me.

"He's home-schooled," he said, so abrupt that he seemed annoyed with the concept. Then, he added, "School never stops for him."

"At his age, he needs to go to a real school or he'll fall behind." She was loud enough to be heard across the street.

When he didn't disagree, I said, "I'm 15 next month and I'm taking college prep courses."

She regarded me as if shaving cream scum stained my front. "I was a teacher for 35 years, young man; I ought to know the benefits of attending school."

"I know *Pandanus gemmifer* grows in rainforests near Cairns. That's why it's on the shady side of the house. It can be male or female, and it produces pups on the trunk, which fall to the ground and take root," I said, confident after hearing Ben say the exact same thing two days before.

That a teenage boy knew anything about plants earned a spinsterish chuckle. "Touché!"

My father smiled too. "While we're gone, Ms. Masters, I'm having a mate redo the kitchen. Bruce McKenzie; he'll be likely driving a VW bus with 'Sunset Air Tours' on the side. You see anyone else hanging about; I'd appreciate it if you called the police right away."

+ + +

We departed as if a tidal wave was bearing down. I rode in the Jeep, my father and *him* in the front, Ben and me squeezed in the back with bags bunched at our feet and boxes in our laps.

No sooner than we'd pulled onto the main road, my father said, "I called Bruce after I picked up Tanner. I'm dropping you and Ben off at the *Spray*. He'll go on the *Bus* with Erin and Tanner. Susan too, so she can get what she needs to take care of him."

He grunted, "Okay."

Ben and I shared a glance. After twelve years of *his* moods, I knew to keep my mouth shut. *He* wasn't happy! Even my father knew to keep quiet. He drove, quietly tapping the steering wheel.

"Gympie Hospital any good?" *he* queried.

29

"Slight change of plans. He's going to Hervey Bay Hospital. It's farther than Gympie, but it's on the way north." My father steered with one hand on the wheel, sure to give *him* cause for consternation. "I'll be in the *Beastie* to make sure they're not followed. They'll arrive before lunch. That should be plenty of time," he added as if thinking aloud.

"Why the change of plans, Nick?"

"We need to keep using our names, John."

"Whatever you say, *Ron*."

"Working undercover, there's no faster way of discovery than being out of disguise."

"That go for you calling him Sander?"

"You're right. I should know better."

They simmered in silence again. Ben shifted beside me, his head down. "What happened to teamwork?" he whispered.

He heard him. "What's the rest of your plan, Ron?"

He wasn't apologetic like *he* should've been, but the emphasis was gone.

"You, Sarah, and the kids load up the *Spray;* leave as soon as you're ready. Follow the channel to Great Sandy Straits. I'm told it's well marked all the way to Hervey Bay. I've already told Susan…" He caught himself. "… Virginia… we'll meet them at the pier. South end of the beach."

"What are you going to do?"

My father slowed down to turn into the marina parking lot. He looked at the cars one by one as we passed them. "It'll take me a few hours to catch up"

"Catch up? How?"

"I just bought a sailboat. It's a bit old, made in 1977, and nowhere as big as your *Spray;* however, it'll do just fine for what I've got in mind."

"What kind of sailboat, exactly?"

"A Cavalier 32; made in New Zealand, so it's got to be good."

I could tell *he* was as confused as I was.

"Bruce said it needs a cleanup." Then, my father noticed the silence. "He assured me it's seaworthy."

"Coming from him, that's debatable!"

Ben and I smothered laughter. From the Bahamas to Australia, Bruce and his boat, *Down Under,* always seemed to be following us. It looked as if it might sink at any moment.

He shrugged it off. "It was cheap, John, and the motor runs fine. With luck, we'll get to Hervey Bay by midnight. If everything's okay, we'll keep going north."

"If not?"

"We'll find a quiet place to hang out until Victor can travel."

"I'm Josh!"

Chapter 4.

It seemed as if I'd just fallen asleep when Aunt Vee woke me. I sat up, groggy, sweaty, and brushing sand and she-oak needles from my face and hair. The moon was a plump crescent in the sky, bright enough to see the beach sweeping to Torquay, a spindly jetty, barely a ripple on the water.

She pointed in the opposite direction, into the darkness beyond the much longer Urangan Jetty and a vast sand bar exposed at low tide. "I think that's them."

There were two red pinpricks creeping from behind Big Woody Island, towards a navigation light flashing every four seconds.

I returned a tired smile. "He said they'd arrive around midnight."

"Right on time." She got her to feet, sending a shower of grit over me. "It's a hike to the end of the pier."

As I shuffled after her, I thought it made more sense to wait for them to anchor and come to get us in the dinghy.

+ + +

I could tell *he* was in a bad mood before *he* puttered up to the jetty. Even though *he* swerved away, the dinghy still bumped into a barnacle-encrusted piling.

The ringing in my ear and warnings to be careful made for a perilous climb down a slippery seaweed-covered ladder. I flopped into the bow, ready to go back to sleep.

He greeted us with a grumpy, "It took forever to get here."

She perched on the side of the dinghy. "Did you know Hervey Bay is the whale watching capital of Australia?" she said brightly.

After a perfunctory examination of my ear in the hospital surgery, we'd spent the afternoon walking the docks and downtown. Wherever we went, there were kiosks taking bookings for whale watching, charter boats, and shops peddling whale paraphernalia.

"I ran aground three times." *He* glared at me as if it was my fault. "He looks awful."

"Probably because his dinner was fried fish and chips from a nasty little take-out restaurant." When *he* didn't react, she continued. "His eardrum is perforated, not too seriously. It might've been a lot worse."

"He's always been lucky."

"Other than some ringing in his ears, he should be back to normal in a couple of weeks," she said.

That seemed to improve the mood all around. *He* motored to the *Spray*, still grumbling about running aground. *He* blamed his crew; they couldn't spot sandbars in time to avoid them. We were abreast of the *Spray*, when *he* suddenly veered towards Bruce's much smaller sloop.

He avoided my eyes. "He thinks we'll be safer if we split up. You'll be on *Down Under* with him."

"Safer," I repeated, certain that *he* wanted me gone. "Right."

"Josh, it's not what you think. You'll be safer with him." It sounded as if they'd already talked about it, and she supported the plan.

"Whatever."

They exchanged glances.

She tried again. "It won't be for very long."

"Just until things settle down," *he* added. "It's better this way."

She exhaled. "We won't be far away, Josh."

"Use his cell phone if you need us..."

33

"I got it," I interrupted.

"They won't expect this." Was it still *his* turn?

"You think Zagarovsky won't expect me to be with my real father, seriously?"

I waited for *him* to snap back. *He* slowed the dinghy to a sputtering crawl towards a rope ladder hanging over the side of *Down Under*.

"We have more important things to do than speculate on what Zagarovsky expects us to do." *He* grabbed a rope trailing in the water and hauled *Squirt* closer.

I kept my thoughts to myself and stepped onto the ladder. The doctor said my ruptured eardrum would affect my balance, and he was right. I missed the next rung. It took both of them to stop me from falling into the water.

When I tried to climb the ladder again, my father loomed above me, one hand extended to steady me, his other hand gripping the stanchion in case I fell.

"Don't forget your clothes." *He* waited until I was aboard before *he* tossed up a bulky plastic bag. "I'm not sure this is a good idea, Ron."

My father ignored him. "How is he?"

She looked at me fondly. "He should be okay if he keeps out of the water."

"We'll leave as soon as you're ready." *His* tone was enough to raise hackles.

"Are you sure he's okay to travel, Virginia?"

"He needs to take it easy for a few days."

Except for a small padded seat behind the steering wheel, there was nowhere to sit down in the cockpit. It looked as if Bruce had departed his boat after tossing everything out of the lockers under the seats. There were tangled piles of grimy rope, boxes of greasy engine parts, tatty lifejackets, moldy rust-stained sail bags, soiled plastic buckets, foul-smelling cloths, and five dinghy oars, none of them matching.

"I have antibiotics if his ear gets infected," she added.

I thought an ear infection would be the least of my health problems.

"Erin called a few minutes ago. She and Tanner are safe and sound," my father said.

He looked up. "The sooner we get underway, the safer we'll be."

"It makes sense if I take him with me, John."

"We've already discussed it. I don't agree."

Aunt Vee sighed loudly. "We don't have the time to argue. We're doing this Ron's way."

Abruptly, *he* shoved the dinghy away from the ladder. "It's 20 miles to Burrum Heads. We need to be anchored by day break."

My father just shrugged and went back to untangling ropes.

+ + +

I watched them motor to the *Spray,* squabbling like roosters. Feeling responsible, I waved, though I doubt they saw me. When I turned around, he was looking at me.

"It's only for a few days, until things settle down."

Still stunned, I stared down the companionway. The mess in the cockpit paled in comparison. "You really bought this wreck?"

Compared to *Down Under*, the *Spray* was pristine. Even on the untidiest of days, our captain insisted on cleanliness.

He smiled. "It's not as bad as it looks, Josh."

"What happened to Sander?"

"Would you rather I called you Victor?"

I shrugged back at him and cleared a space on the cockpit seat only to discover green mold and gobs of sticky goo. It was the final straw.

While he went about starting the engine, I spread the cleanest cloths on the seat and sat down. With a cough, Bruce's antiquated diesel sputtered to life.

"Runs great after it's warmed up," he declared, ignoring smoky fog swirling around the stern.

I wrinkled my nose, trying not to smell when I breathed.

"She needs some spit and polish."

I snorted, 'Right.' His padded seat protected him from infection. "She needs to sink."

He grinned. "Your mom could always see the funny side."

"It stinks below, in case you hadn't noticed."

"Bruce said the head wasn't working properly."

"I reckon he'd know."

"We'll spend tomorrow cleaning downstairs." He stood up. "The windlass is busted. I'll raise the anchor as you motor forward. If I'm not back in time, leave the flashing yellow light to starboard."

+ + +

Cleaning the cockpit began as soon as we set the autopilot on a course to clear Point Vernon. I coiled the cleanest of the ropes; the rest soaked in buckets filled with detergent. We scoured the seats and floor, dragged sails out of bags and spread them across the cabin roof to air, and filled two plastic bags with trash, mostly empty beer cans.

While I wiped grime from spare parts, my father crawled into the hidden recesses of the port locker, tossing out jerry cans, disintegrating fish traps, and more beer cans. Suddenly, he shouted an expletive seldom heard on the *Spray*. A series of thuds followed.

He reappeared, dangling a comatose rat by the tail, a kid's aluminum baseball bat in his other hand. After the rat splashed astern, he submerged the bat and both hands in a bucket until he felt clean again.

"Exactly how much did you pay for it?"

"One dollar."

"About what it's worth," I said.

"However, I loaned him four thousand bucks to buy some sails after he got whacked by a hurricane last year. Once it's cleaned up, it'll be worth ten times that."

I thought 'in your dreams.' Instead, I said, "If I help clean, I expect a share of the profits."

He regarded me. "It won't come to that." He disappeared back into the locker.

I stretched out on the cockpit seat and slept for four hours.

+++

The dim light of dawn revealed distant mudflats and the tree-covered peninsula of Burrum Point. It seemed to go on and on forever; not even South Carolina was this boring. Yet just an hour later, Burrum River was postcard pretty, a jumble of islands, fuzzy white clouds, and brilliant colors from a blazing sun. Chugging upriver astern of the *Spray*, I gorged on Tanner's Tim Tams. As good as they were, I envied Ben and Jessie sitting down to their grandmother's crusty bread rolls and tropical fruit.

A few minutes after turning into a narrow river, the *Spray* drifted in leisurely circles while *he* searched for a passageway through a maze of shallow sandbars. Eventually, *he* got in the dinghy, zigzagging from bank to bank to find a channel.

He beckoned to us to follow *him* into the Gregory River. With a resigned shrug, my father steered a meandering course through tea-colored water, skirting humps tinged yellow. Finally, the water turned green.

"No one's going to find us here," *he* shouted on his way back to the *Spray*.

There was no sign of civilization, no farms, fences, or cell phone towers, just muddy banks and scraggly gumtrees as far as the eye could see.

After scraping the keel on a sandbar, we decided we'd gone far enough. We dropped our anchor close to shore, out of sight behind a small island. I dozed in the now-glowing sun, barely aware of the buzz in my ear.

"Ahoy there!" rudely interrupted my snoozing. *He* leaned out as the *Spray* motored slowly by. "I'll be by to get Victor soon as we're anchored. He's got four days of schoolwork to catch up."

I gestured disinterest, which didn't amuse *him*. Schoolwork could wait when *he* had a higher priority.

Soon, it was too hot to sleep in the cockpit. Instead, we dragged out everything not fixed down in the cabin. In the now-spotless cockpit, we stacked boxes and bags of food carried aboard the previous day. On the cabin roof, we dumped sour-smelling bedding, armfuls of Bruce's dirty detective novels and tatty newspapers from all over the world, food-encrusted dishes, and battered cooking pans. Then, my father turned his attention to fixing the head. I emptied every cupboard and drawer, and sorted out tools and fishing equipment. Bruce's first aid kit was so out-of-date; I tossed most of it in a trash bag.

I was scrubbing teak joinery and grubby plastic-covered bulkheads when *he* thumped on the hull. I went upstairs to see what was so important. Standing up in the dinghy, *he* took in the mess strewn across the boat and grimaced.

"You see the fish? Big ones, all over the place."

"Barramundi," my father said from behind me.

"I thought we could take *Squirt* and fish along the bank after lunch," *he* suggested.

"Maybe tomorrow. Right now, we're bonding."

"I can see. You need a hand?" After a moment, *he* added, "Ron."

My father held up the yellowed plastic pump from the head. Brown stains showed where it leaked. "You know how to fix this?"

I hid my smirk. Both of the *Spray's* heads had leaked for a month until *he* figured out how to fix them.

+ + +

Three days later, we'd scrubbed *Down Under* from bow to stern. Every surface was spotless, the mucky bilge was creamy white, grimy brown seat covers were actually red, and fogged windows were transparent again.

He came to check on our progress after lunch. Even before *he* tied *Squirt* to the rail, *he* said, "It looks seaworthy."

However, I knew what *he* was thinking. My father didn't seem to care either way.

He went on. "You listen to the VHF radio this morning, around 9:15?" *He* looked at me.

"Should I?"

"Someone was asking about an American family on a sailboat."

While they talked, Ben and I loaded *Squirt* with bags of trash. We motored for an hour to reach nearby Buxton, a small fishing village, population 402. We beached the dinghy and deposited our trash in a dumpster conveniently placed at the boat launching ramp, and went to find the only general store in town. Signs outside said it sold bait, beer, and takeaway. It was also the post office and gas station.

He mopped sweat from his brow. "Remember we're up from Brisbane for the holiday weekend." It was the fifth time since *he'd* proposed 'fishing' as our 'cover.'

"Won't be a problem if I do the talkin', mate." My father's faked Australian accent was 'spot on.'

Beyond a screen door was an air-conditioned haven, a cluttered little store that sold the essentials. Ben and I wandered through racks of fishing equipment, garden tools, cooking utensils, magazines, candy, and canned goods. My father went over to a row of refrigerators packed with beer. *He* inspected crates of local melons before moving on to a display case with stale-looking vegetables sheathed in plastic.

My father approached the register with a 12-pack of beer and a hearty, "G'day."

The man who looked up from his newspaper had short red hair and a freckled ruddy complexion. Veins variegated his nose with tangled crimson threads.

"G'day mate. Youse 'ere for 'mundi?" he said as if each word was an effort.

"We've caught a few."

"They're bitin' fer sure. Me mate hooked a whopper this mornin'; 50 kilo, I reckon. Would'a landed it too, except a big sport-fisher came by."

"Too bad fer yer mate."

"Always tomorrow. Start of the season, rivers are full of 'em where it turns brackish."

My father conversed with Blakey, the proprietor, about catching barramundi with lures. *He* told us what to buy while he looked at fishing hats, none of which suited him.

40

Ben and I filled a shopping basket with bread, milk, melons, and vegetables of dubious freshness.

"Get many visitors this time of year?" my father asked casually.

"A few tourists passing through; most of 'ems fishermen like yerselves."

"I was wonderin'; I keep hearing a foreign chap on the VHF radio goin' on about a Yank family living on a boat," my father drawled with the same offhand manner.

"Reckon that'd be the sport-fisher couple. They came in 'ere fer coffee. His wife kept askin' about an old-fashioned sailboat. Like we see sailboats this far up river."

I pushed past Ben and dumped the shopping basket on the counter, hoping he didn't blurt out, 'that's us.' *He* put another melon on the counter, raising an eyebrow when *he* saw that Ben and I had put four packets of Tim Tams in the basket.

"Pushy, huh?" my father said.

"More than me mum, only when she gets 'er knickers in a knot, she ain't polite about it."

"They still around?"

"Took off upstream to meet a mate. There's an airstrip near Wals Camp. I heard 'e run aground. They'll be there fer a while," Blakey chuckled.

My father started taking things out of the basket, yet I could tell he was interested.

"Sounds like a boat to avoid. What's it look like?" He might've been asking about yesterday's weather.

"It was one of them offshore boats. All white with a flybridge. Useless for fishing around here," Blakey said, ringing up prices from memory. "You want a kilo of prawns? Better than mullet for 'mundi."

+ + +

41

Outside, black bushflies swarmed in the late afternoon heat. Without delay, we crossed the empty parking lot to cool our feet on a grassy footpath.

"Bit bloody hot," my father said in Blakey's long-winded way. "Worth the hike though."

"Bad news about the sport-fishing boat," *he* said quietly.

"I expected as much, just not right away."

He handed his shopping bag to Ben. "Guys, take this stuff back to the dinghy. We'll be along shortly."

Ben and I exchanged a glance. It was clear they wanted to talk about me.

Chapter 5.

By sunset, we'd hauled up the anchor and cautiously motored back to what the chart called 'Gregory Islands.' Perched in the bow, I strained my eyes in the dimming light. I pointed out shallow sandbars as we drifted downstream. With slight course corrections, we missed all but one of them. It was bound to happen in the dark. The keel bumped and we stopped. My father backed up and turned to port. The outgoing tide pushed us closer to shore. There was a loud splash ahead, most likely a big barramundi. So far we hadn't seen any crocodiles.

From the opposite shore, we passed the twinkling lights of Burrum Heads and the faint outline of a water tower, and headed out to sea. Then, the sails went up on the *Spray,* gradually widening the gap between us.

"As good a time as any to see how she sails," he said in the darkness.

"Aye, Captain."

Before he could offer to help, I went forward, removed the sail cover, and pulled on the halyard, simple compared to raising the mainsail on the gaff-rigged *Spray*. He unfurled the genoa as soon as I stepped into the cockpit. We hauled in the sheets until the fluttering stopped. Unlike the lumbering *Spray, Down Under* heeled and accelerated until wavelets slapped the bow. He turned off the engine.

I cranked the winch handle to tighten the jib. Within minutes, the distance to the *Spray* was back to a few boat lengths. He changed course a few degrees to windward.

Ready to be lulled to sleep by waves, I settled into the cockpit seat with a pillow and a packet of Tim Tams.

"Where are we going?"

He helped himself to a Tim Tam. "About two days north of here. Find somewhere out of the way and lay low for a while. I'll wake you around midnight, mate."

When he woke me, I had cold feet and a crick in my neck. I peed off the stern and gulped his warm coffee.

He pointed at a hazy glow in the northwest. "Bundaberg." He yawned, stretched, and yawned again. "Forget about using the autopilot. It works for five minutes and conks out. Stay on this course for an hour. Then, 315 degrees. If you see any boats, wake me up."

"Where's the *Spray*?"

He waved at a red pinprick in the east. "It's safer if we don't stick together. If you want to chat on the VHF, keep it short. We're *Victorious*. They're *Fair Haven*."

"Fairhaven is where Joshua Slocum rebuilt the *Spray*."

"John's idea. I figured it had to do with Slocum." He appropriated my seat and two more of my Tim Tams. "We're supposed to be fishing. Practice using your Aussie accent, *mate*."

Without my guitar to keep me company, I spent my watch checking our position on the chart, trimming sails, and watching the speck of light fall farther astern until dawn's feeble light obliterated it.

"*Victorious. Victorious. Victorious. Fair Haven.*"

I scooped up the radio microphone, turned down the volume, and imitated my father so I'd sound Australian. "Victorious, mate."

"How's the fishing? Over."

"Okay," I said, volunteering nothing. *He* always said it was too dangerous to fish at night.

"Everything working out?"

For a moment, I didn't get it. I kept my voice low, the microphone close to my mouth.

"Not bad," I ventured.

I almost said 'better than I expected.' Australians loved litotes, using understatement to emphasize a positive. They made it an art form, with double negatives galore.

"Listen… What I said earlier, I didn't mean it."

The first thing to come into my head wasn't nice. "No big deal, mate."

"I love him, Ron. We all do. I'll check back after breakfast. Fair Haven out."

The *Spray* was a dot on the horizon. With Bruce's fogged-up binoculars, I could see sails, nothing more. I wondered if Ben was already reading his *Encyclopedia Britannica*. Soon, his mom would be making coffee and tidying the cabin. Jessie would still be in bed, likely listening to her grandmother's stories about ancient Greek gods and heroes. *He'd* be in the cockpit, hair disheveled, unshaven, and waiting for coffee. At least *his* self-steering system worked.

+ + +

My father sat up, rubbing bleary eyes. "I should've taken over hours ago."

"You let me sleep past midnight."

He looked around. "When I was your age, my brother and I sailed on Long Island Sound. It was never empty like this. Even in the middle of winter there were other boats."

"At least there are clouds. When we crossed the Pacific, there was nothing for days at a time," I pointed out.

"Being in the middle of nowhere makes you see things from a different perspective."

I nodded and wondered where he was headed.

"Out here, we can catch up on 12 years," he said.

I blurted out, "What happened to my mom?"

He closed his eyes, making each breath an effort. "She disappeared the night of the fire."

"I deserve more than 'she disappeared'."

He hesitated so long I was sure he wasn't going to answer; or if he did, it would be a lie. "I don't know what happened."

"What do you know?"

"Not much. I spent a month investigating and found next to nothing."

I looked him in the eye. There was more. "Tell me."

"When the firemen got to the house, the fire was out of control. It burned for hours. With that much heat, not much is left."

My skin prickled; yet I had to ask. "She was inside?"

"It's the only explanation. She wasn't supposed to be there until ten o'clock. She practiced every night at The Cathedral of the Incarnation for a big wedding that weekend. Friday night after practice, she was supposed to play the *Anniversary Waltz* at a 50th wedding anniversary. She was taking her best violin, because it was so special. Maybe she forgot it. Her car was in the driveway. She'd left the motor running."

All of a sudden, I didn't want to talk about her. "Why was I with my grandparents?"

"Your grandma never charged for babysitting you." When I didn't smile, he went on. "I was flat-out on the Zagarovsky trial; plus our house was a mess, plaster dust everywhere. It made sense for the two of you to stay with my parents."

"Why was *he* there?"

"My brother? He was there most weekends because Susan… Virginia worked the night shift at Good Samaritan

Hospital, a few miles down the road. We're lucky he dropped by on Friday instead of Saturday."

He stood, taking in the bleak grey sea. Anyone could see he was done with talking.

+ + +

Late in the afternoon, we spotted Bustard Bay lighthouse atop a lonely headland. It was welcome relief after endless beaches. An hour later, we rounded Clews Point, dropped the sails, and motored into a broad estuary. The channel was narrow with vast sandbars on one side, and rocks and coral on the other. We anchored among five other boats, barbequed lamb chops, and enjoyed the view. Brilliant gold lit up the sky; Cirrus clouds like streaming mare's tails with vivid pink ringlets. There was rain on the way.

The *Spray* arrived at dusk, motoring past as if we were strangers.

"Don't wave. It's probably safe enough; however, it pays to be careful," my father said.

They anchored in Pancake Creek, so far away that no one would think we were travelling together.

The next day, between bouts of drenching rain and buffeting gusts, we scraped the remnants of '*Down Under*' from the stern. Coming up with a new name for our now-revitalized Cavalier 32 was more difficult. We discarded *Curmudgeon, Carpe Diem, Calamity, and Conundrum. Calypso* was guaranteed not to stand out in a crowd.

Chapter 6.

A week before my fifteenth birthday, we arrived at the entrance to Yeppoon. With waves breaking on the bar, we heaved to, *Calypso* rocking and rolling as we waited three hours for high tide. Finally, we motored up to a tiny break in the rocky foreshore. The channel ahead was so narrow that once committed, there was no turning back.

"What do you reckon?" My father sounded less than sure.

I debated keeping my opinion to myself. "*He* took the *Spray* through smaller gaps in the Bahamas. It's just like going into a crowded marina."

"That sounds like something he'd say. You want to give it a shot, mate?"

"I'll watch, if that's okay?"

He chuckled and checked the chart again. In between waves, the swirling water ahead looked shallow, though the chart said otherwise. However, sandbars shifted and channels became silted. He pointed the bow at the center of the gap, picking up speed as the waves grew larger.

"Just like going into a crowded marina," he repeated.

"He'd play Tchaikovsky's *Marche Slav* when it got scary."

He laughed. "A bit droll for me. The *Festival Coronation March* is much more inspiring."

He turned the steering wheel hard to port, heading straight for the breakwater. I gulped. Ahead, cloudy water churned through a channel no wider than the length of our boat. Within seconds, the breakwater turned into a sand spit requiring a sharp turn to starboard. An even narrower passage branched, one way leading to tiny Fig Tree Creek, the other way ending in a low bridge. He was still deciding which way to go when our keel grated on a sandbar.

"Keep going! We're nearly there!" he urged, coaxing the engine to maximum power.

Running aground at high tide and under full power was never a good idea. Muddy water spewed from our stern. Suddenly, *Calypso* surged forward. He turned into the creek and quickly eased off the throttle.

Sailboats and motorboats lined both sides of the creek. It was so shallow that when the tide went out, boats would be left standing on their keels. We stayed in the middle of the creek, mostly drifting—even an idling motor was too fast. We'd passed the next bend before he pointed at a small unoccupied dock. It was opposite a mosquito-infested mangrove swamp. The only other choice was go back the way we'd just come and try to find a space before the bridge.

After tying up to the dock, we spent the rest of the day replenishing food supplies from the Yeppoon Shopping Center, a few blocks away. We stored what we'd bought, and he went in search of Chinese takeout, and the *Spray*, which should've arrived the previous day. I got on the Internet, responded to five emails from Dani with photos of my own, downloaded school materials, and uploaded three weeks of finished assignments—there was nothing else to do except read Bruce's archaic detective novels.

+ + +

They arrived in *Squirt* while we were still eating breakfast. Ben climbed aboard following some back and forth whispering with his mother. Something unpleasant was in the works; he wore clothes that should've been tossed in the trash.

From the dinghy, *he* grinned up at my father. "Victor knows what's he's doing while we're gone, right?"

During breakfast my father said he was going to hitchhike to Rockhampton, an inland town one hour away. I assumed I'd be doing schoolwork, not babysitting my cousin.

My father smirked at me. "Not yet."

"How's your ear, Josh?" Health was always the first thing Aunt Vee asked about.

"It's good."

"Make sure you keep it out of the water." She nudged *him*. "John, just so you know, I don't agree."

My father hopped into the dinghy, squeezed past Jessie and Sarah, and took Ben's seat in the bow. *He* flipped the gear change into forward, and they took off with a roar.

I confronted Ben. "What's up?"

Still sullen, Ben grumped, "We're cleaning your bottom as soon as the tide goes out enough."

It took a moment to sink in. "What did you do wrong?"

+ + +

An hour later, *Calypso's* keel touched bottom. Armed with scrapers and stiff brushes, we climbed down the ladder and dropped into mud. Spotty barnacles, shaggy weed, and slimy algae covered the hull below the waterline. It wasn't hard to remove, just dirty. Each scrape splattered us until we were covered from head to toe.

"You realize we're destroying an entire ecosystem," I told Ben when we sat down to rest.

Nature Boy wiped weed from his brow and flipped it at me. "Good riddance. Anyway, it'll grow back in a month." He hesitated, squelching bare toes through mud. "How are things going?"

I shrugged. "Okay, I guess."

"It's only been a week, but I miss having you around."

"Me too. I've got no one to pick on."

He grinned back, muddy faced with brilliant white teeth. "Seriously, you're getting on alright with Uncle Ron?"

"I'm guessing *he* wants to know?"

"He said if an opportunity came up, I should ask. Mom and Grandma want to know, too."

"Not Jessie?"

"She gets mopey if we talk about you. She pretends you're at summer camp."

I stood, reached down, and jerked him to his feet. "Tell them it's working out." It wasn't enough. It was a lot better than I thought it would be. "He's cool; we talk about music a lot."

Ben started scraping off barnacles and weed. It was my turn with the brush, scrubbing off whatever he left behind. After a few labored scrapes, he glanced over his shoulder.

"Uncle Ron must've had important stuff to do in Rockhampton?"

"More like he'd do anything to get out of scraping the bottom."

"Dad said something about changing IDs."

"Right! New names all around, repaint the *Spray,* and nobody will recognize us."

"He said you needed to disappear once and for all."

+ + +

Calypso romped up the coast after leaving Yeppoon. Cleaning the bottom added a knot to our speed, enough that the *Spray* was soon far behind despite leaving ten minutes before us. By Port Clinton, the hills seemed to come down to the sea, ending in rocky outcrops and pine-tree-topped headlands. With the autopilot finally functioning properly, we scudded along, heeled and flogging the mainsail in gust after gust. *He* would've reefed the sails before the lee gunwale dipped underwater. Instead, my father delighted in ducking when sheets of spray soaked our cockpit. He was as happy as I'd ever seen him.

He disconnected the autopilot and steered closer to the shore. Ahead, Reef Point earned its name, waves crashing onto inhospitable black rocks, sending up plumes of spray. He veered towards Townshend Island, rugged, uninhabited, and equally hostile. The foreshores prickled with Xanthorrhoea, grassy clumps with spear-like sticks poking straight up.

"Look for somewhere to anchor for a while."

"How long a while?" I asked.

"We might come back for a few weeks, maybe longer," he said with a wink.

I was sure he was joking.

"We need to hang out until Sal gets back from the U.S. with new IDs," he added.

Tiny bays and inlets riddled Townshend Island, all of them suitable for an overnight stay. Any longer required a secluded anchorage, protected from the prevailing winds, with easy access to shore. We spent an hour investigating a promising inlet; however, it meant anchoring near mangrove swamps. We turned around when hordes of mosquitoes descended.

He pored over the chart and decided to check out Quail Island, north of Stanage Bay. It would take us until dark to get there.

+ + +

We entered Stanage Bay with the sunset, tired and hungry, with wind gusts threatening to push *Calypso* onto its side. I was clinging to the wildly swinging boom with one hand and grabbing sailcloth to drag the mainsail down the mast when he suddenly laughed out loud from the cockpit.

"What's so funny?" I shouted over the flapping.

"You're not at all like I expected."

"What did you expect?"

"In his emails, you were always having problems," he ended abruptly. "I shouldn't have mentioned it. You need a hand?"

"I got it." The rest waited until I tied down the sail and I was back in the cockpit. "What did you expect exactly?"

He grinned and leaned back. "I used to think you'd be a wimp. Of course, as soon as I saw you, I knew you weren't."

"That a compliment?"

"Just now, watching you drop the main, you're no chicken, that's for sure."

"This is nothing. Doing it at night with waves coming over the side; that's scary."

He started the engine. Immediately, we started worrying about it quitting. It spluttered erratically with white smoke billowing behind us all the way to the western end of Quail Island. As we turned into a mangrove-lined channel, I spotted the *Spray*, already anchored. However, he wasn't surprised.

It was so late after we changed the fuel filter; we skipped dinner and snacked on salty crackers and cheese.

+ + +

I sat in the cockpit, soaking up the early morning sun and watching seagulls bicker. A charter yacht motored by, staying close to Long Island, likely headed farther up the coast. That early in the day, no one was out of bed on the *Spray*.

My father brought me a cup of coffee and sat down across from me. He looked hopeful, as if waiting for my approval. My mind was made up; I wasn't going to remind him.

After I'd taken a sip, he said, "I arrived two minutes late. The traffic was awful."

I kept my head down, certain he was talking about the fire.

"You were already squawking your head off."

I shrugged, not interested in talking about 15 years earlier.

"And before you say 'no big deal', your birthday is important to me."

"No big deal."

He smiled. "I didn't forget."

Without fanfare, he handed over two plain paper bags. Inside one bag was Monopoly.

"In case we get bored," he said.

"I'm pretty good," I warned. "We played it all the time on the *Spray*."

Inside the other bag was a box covered with brown cloth and mottled black leather. On the spine, in gilt lettering was 'Doktor Faustus' and 'Thomas Mann.'

"There's not a lot to choose from in Rockhampton," he went on, watching intently as I withdrew the book from its slipcase. "I was lucky to find it at a book exchange." Before I could open it, he added. "It's the first edition, in German."

"Um... Thanks."

54

"Your grandma taught you to speak German, the same as she did me. You remember any?"

"No." I flicked through perplexing pages stained yellow on the edges. There was a scribbled inscription in German on the flyleaf. Only '1947' was legible.

"It'll probably come back to you. She was an excellent teacher. It's about a composer who gives his soul to the Devil in return for 24 years of creativity."

"How did that work out for him?"

"Great until 1930. Unfortunately, he revealed the pact and his life fell apart. His decline tracked Nazi Germany."

Happiness all round, I thought.

"We can read it together, if you want?"

"That book exchange have a German-English dictionary?"

He looked past me. I turned to see a big white sport-fishing boat headed down the channel from Stanage Bay. There were two people on the flybridge, a man steering a precarious course through sandbars, a woman scanning the southern end of Long Island with binoculars. If she turned 90 degrees, she would see us.

+ + +

A hurried half hour later, we were underway. From our little anchorage off Quail Island, we motored north at full speed. My father wanted to put as much distance as possible between us and the *Spray*, which headed east, the way we'd come the previous day. When the morning breeze arrived, we raised the sails and took turns threading a course through sandbars and reefs. Long before we reached open water, I was tired of staring at shady patches through sparkling glare, trying to decide whether it was safe to proceed.

When he came up from the galley, he brought lunch on a plate and two water bottles. "Pity the sport-fisher had to show up today. Sarah was going to make you a surprise birthday lunch."

Suddenly, I didn't feel much like talking, or eating his sardines on toast in the middle of the afternoon.

Instead of taking his turn at the helm, he tuned the FM radio to the local ABC station. The Australian Broadcasting Commission delivered news, public service programs, and classical music. Satisfied, he tilted his hat down and dozed for a while. Perhaps he listened to the news, though it was mostly politics. After a story about a large estuarine crocodile nearly overturning a canoe in the Hull River National Park, he sat up and turned off the radio.

"Take a break. I'll steer for a while." He took my place behind the wheel, engaged the autopilot, and studied the chart plotter. "Where should we stop tonight?"

"Not Hull River, that's for sure."

I thought he was smiling as he leaned to switch on the VHF radio, and change from Channel 16 to 73, the channel for chatting to other boaters.

Ahead were dozens of islands, most barren rock outcrops or clumpy grass hillocks. I pointed at a couple of pinpricks on the eastern horizon. At that distance, the islands would be big enough to have trees and hills.

"I need to walk on land for a while."

He nodded agreeably. Only that morning he'd complained about being on the boat for so long. I eased the sheets as he changed course.

"Your mom walked everywhere when she was pregnant with you," he said with a smile.

"You saying it's genetic?"

"Might be, mate. Don't get your ego inflated; with your DNA, we were convinced you'd be musically talented. I wanted to call you Sergei."

"For Prokofieff or Rachmaninoff?"

"You could be either, wildly modern or lusciously romantic. Your mom insisted on naming you after my father. She adored him. They'd play together for hours at a time while you gurgled in your bassinet."

"No wonder I'm weird."

"You definitely have her quirky sense of humor." He looked away. "And her eyes. Sarah used to say they were as 'blue as a Venetian sky'."

"She have blond hair too?"

"Yours is darker," he murmured. "John's right about your hair though."

I bristled. "What's wrong with my hair?"

"It's a dead giveaway."

"I'll get a haircut at the next town we stop at."

"It won't change your appearance enough. Working undercover, you change the most noticeable things first."

"I'll wear a hat, okay?"

He gave me a long hard look. "We might as well get it over with. I need to send Sal a photo for your passport."

He ducked below. I could hear him searching his clothes locker.

"Boring brunette or awesomely auburn, your choice?"

I was sure he was joking. "I like my hair the way it is."

"You won't stand out with brown." He was enjoying this.

"Not funny."

He popped his head through the companionway. "It says it's messy so we'll do it up here."

Before I could ask, he disappeared into the cabin. It sounded like he'd decided to clean up the galley. He returned to the cockpit with a beach towel over his shoulder, a shopping bag, mixing bowl, and kitchen plastic wrap in hand.

"Do what up here?"

Instead of answering, he emptied the shopping bag on the seat, a jar of petroleum jelly salvaged from Bruce's first aid kit, natural henna hair-care package, already opened, purple rubber gloves, and the wooden spatula we used for cooking.

He took one look at my face and said, "We don't have a choice. Think of it as a gag gift for your birthday."

"No thanks."

"No thanks isn't an option."

"I could get my hair cut really short?"

He shook his head, checked the instructions on the back of the package, and mashed a dark clay-like brick into the bowl with the spatula.

"Can we do it at a hair salon?"

"I know what I'm doing. I worked undercover for six years."

He busted up lumps and ground them to grit, splashing in water from my drinking flask before he looked at the instructions again.

"Oops; the water's supposed to be hot." He glanced around, checking the course and making sure it was clear ahead. "Hopefully, the sun will warm it up while I get you ready."

"Do we have to do it right now?"

He draped the towel around my neck, opened the jar of petroleum jelly, and held it in front of me. "This has to go on your face."

He dipped his fingers into the jar and began to smear it over my forehead, around my ears, and on the nape of my neck. Then, he did around my eyebrows, greasing my nose in the process. When I opened my eyes, he was squelching his fingers through thick brown mud in the bowl.

"No way are you putting that in my hair! It looks like poop."

"It smells a bit earthy, that's all." He put his fingers in front of my nose.

I was about to say it stank when he slapped both hands on my head, his fingers massaging my scalp. He scooped out more henna mud.

"Enough already!"

"You want blond streaks?" He plastered my head, rubbing it in with a kind of sadistic delight that might've been *his*. "The instructions say it takes a while for the dye to set."

"How long is a while?" I grumped.

"From one to six hours. It's faster when it's hotter."

Before I could ask, he wound plastic wrap around my head, pulling it tight with every pass. Brown goo squished out and oozed down my cheeks. He wiped it off his finger and smeared it on my eyebrows.

I jerked away. "It's disgusting."

"You're done. Now, you sit in the sun and practice your Australian accent." He grinned and I glowered back. "You think Dani will still like you with brown hair?"

I kept my thoughts to myself.

+ + +

We were a mile south of Middle Percy Island when I went below to clean up, leaving him to drop the sails and the anchor.

Calypso's head was hot and tiny, with a basin, an inadequate toilet, and a spare jib stuffed in the corner. There was scarcely enough room to stand up, let alone undress and take a shower. My bad mood got worse when I looked in the mirror to remove the plastic wrap from my head. Coffee-colored clay clumps stuck in my hair. My eyebrows were conspicuously dark.

He stuck his head through the open bow hatch. "I think there's more protection on the west side."

I closed the door with a bang and grunted, "Whatever."

"How's it look?'

"Bloody awful. I won't forget this birthday, that's for sure."

"It'll take a while to get used to. Make sure you wash it all off with cold water or it'll stink for a week," he added.

+ + +

I thought he was snoozing when I stepped into the cockpit. However, he peeked when he thought I wouldn't see him. I glared back, biding my time.

"Reckon I did an okay job, if I say so myself."

Instead of countering, I looked around. Middle Percy Island was more interesting from a distance. Up close, there were rocky outcrops and spindly Eucalyptus, no different to what I'd already seen of Australia, whether metropolitan Sydney or the outback. Three other boats were anchored in the cove, evenly spaced along the beach. The middle boat was a white sport-fishing boat with a flybridge. I was about to point it out; however, he wasn't finished.

"While your hair is still damp, I need to put in the curlers."

"What curlers?"

He oozed smugness. "I borrowed Sarah's when we were at Yeppoon. By tomorrow morning, you'll look like Jessie's big brother."

"No curlers!"

"No choice, Mister. You're going to look different until I say otherwise."

"Curlers will do that?"

"The goal is to trick the eye and convince the mind."

"Can't be that difficult."

He looked down his nose. "Parla la lingua e ingannare tutti."

There was no mistaking the contrast of consonants, and plentiful vowels that rolled off his tongue.

"You speak Italian now?"

"The particular dialect is from Messina." He was pleased with himself. "What I said was 'Speak the language and fool everyone.' Sounding Sicilian saved my life more than once in New York."

"So will watching where you anchor." I nodded sideways.

He glanced over his shoulder, saw the sport-fishing boat, and muttered under his breath. He seemed to make a habit of cussing, especially that particular expression.

He turned back, not flustered like I thought he would be. "I wonder where he came from."

"We're leaving?"

"Not bloody likely! There's no faster way of drawing attention." He stared at the sport-fishing boat as if committing it to memory. "There's no way to be sure it's the boat following us. Still, we best go below until dark."

"It's like Hades down there." As if I needed to remind him; all he did was complain about the heat in the cabin.

"We'll go over the details while Sarah's curlers do their work."

I followed him down the stairs and cleared a space on the settee. "What details?"

He shuffled through a stack of papers. "For one; Marco Angelo Capra will be the name on your passport."

"Marco as in Polo? No thanks."

"You don't have a choice." He studied a sheet of paper, his untidy scrawl covering both sides. "You're 16 and a half."

It took a moment to sink in. "I don't even look 15, you said so yourself."

"Actually, your uncle said that, not me. Act like you're 16 and you'll be okay. You were born in Sydney and grew up in Drummoyne. That's a suburb on the west side, overlooking the harbor. Lots of Italians in the neighborhood, by the way."

"How many Italians have got eyes like mine?"

"More than you think. However, yours are a giveaway. Starting tomorrow, you'll wear colored contacts." He went on. "We lived over a grocery store on the corner of Gipps and Therry Streets until your mum kicked me out."

"What did she kick you out for?"

"You tell me, smarty pants."

"You drink too much. You chase loose women. You bet on the horses. You're a loser..."

"Enough already! And it's nags, not horses." However, he was smiling.

I took the offense. "What's your name?"

"Mario Capra. You went to school at Drummoyne Public School, then Fort Street High School. You're no dummy, but you dropped out last year…"

He went on and on, reading off details of another life while he figured out how to put curlers in my hair. He went over Marco Capra's background again during dinner, and then we played Monopoly—my quality trumped his quantity.

Chapter 7.

Like any other day of the last two weeks, I began Sunday, March 4th, in front of the mirror, brown eyes staring back at me as I unwound shocking pink curlers. My father made coffee in the galley the same way *he* always did, listening to chatter on the VHF radio. When I woke up, he'd been talking to a fisherman. It was the first time he'd tried getting local knowledge for the waters ahead.

"Get a move on," he called, interrupting a heated discussion about areas closed to fishing. "Che dobbiamo andare."

"Che dobbiamo andare. We have to go," I translated.

"By the way, you don't need the 'che'." He turned down the volume.

"What about breakfast?"

The previous morning we'd eaten breakfast at the marina café: coffee with toasted bagels and cream cheese, and free Internet. We were there for two hours. I studied biology while he downloaded data and caught up on email.

"We'll eat underway. Favorite subject at school, Marco?"

"History," I growled, tired of rehearsing. "I'm starving!"

He stuck his head around the bulkhead and nodded approval as I brushed my now-curly brown hair.

"Even Jessie wouldn't recognize you now."

"Where are we going?"

He inclined his head as if he hadn't heard properly.

I stuffed Sarah's curlers back in their case. "Dove andiamo?"

"Not if you were born here, mate. When you speak Italian, make it sound sloppy, even lazy."

"Dove andiamo?"

"You'll do. There's one more thing; we need to do something about your arms."

"Dye them."

He ignored my sarcasm. "Wearing a long-sleeved shirt will help."

"Bit bloody 'ot."

"You can roll up the sleeves when no one can see you. Practice turning your arms inward so they're less noticeable. If someone asks…"

"Fell on a room 'eater, din' I?"

"You were in a crash. The car caught on fire."

"You were drivin' drunk and we smashed into a truck, huh?"

"Better to say you don't want to talk about it. People will shut up real fast." He took the hair-curler case and closed the zipper. "We'll need these."

I followed him through the cabin, picking up coffee he'd left on the galley counter. "So where are we going?"

"Hull Heads. It's a few hours north."

He turned up the volume on the VHF radio, more meaningless gossip from charter boats cruising the islands along the Great Barrier Reef.

"Why the big rush?"

"We need to arrive a half-hour before high tide."

+ + +

Hull Heads was the last of six rivers interrupting the long scalloped beach stretching from the marina at Oyster

Point to Tam O'Shanter Point. The entrance to Hull River was as hazardous as any entrance I'd seen. There were two exposed sandbars in midstream, likely more under the surface.

I bided my time until we were close enough to see long tails stretching from the sandbars. The slightest mistake and we'd run aground. With the tide about to turn, it couldn't be more dangerous.

"This is crazy."

My father glanced up from the chart plotter where he'd been trying to make sense of his page of handwritten notes purporting to be local knowledge.

"Get the sails down. If anyone comes close, I want you below double quick."

+ + +

Instead of his usual appreciative nod after I'd done duty as deck monkey, my father said, "You take the wheel."

He cranked the engine. Before I could say 'you steer', he climbed onto the cabin roof and was scanning ahead with Bruce's binoculars. Judging from the changing colors of the water, there were more sandbars lurking beneath the surface.

"Stay to starboard. Not too far. There's another sandbar coming from that spit up ahead." He leaned against the mast, calmly taking in the view.

Despite the incoming tide, I could feel *Calypso* slowing down in the current, increasingly strong sideways shoves as freshwater poured into the ocean.

"How about some help here?" I had reason to sound testy.

"If you line up with the trees, you should be okay."

"Should be okay?"

"Don't get stroppy, Marco." He emphasized 'Marco.'

"'e's still sleepin'."

"Lazy bugger, eh?" he chuckled. "Watch out to port. There's another sandbar. You need to be farther over."

"Tell that to the rudder."

"Give her some throttle."

"I already did," I grouched. "You wanna drive?"

He concentrated on scanning the water ahead. "It's way worse than he said."

"No one will ever find us here," I said under my breath.

"That's not the reason… Marco." Yet another reminder.

Calypso lurched into swirling water. "Exactly why are we doing this?" I neglected the accent to annoy him.

I came so close to a sandbar that a school of silvery fish darted out of the way.

"There's a rainforest upstream, really spectacular." He read from his notes. "Where the river splits, make a slow turn to port at the first spit to starboard. That help?"

"Except there's a friggin' sandbar in the way."

"We should be okay. He said the depth is around two meters at high tide."

Calypso's draft was 5'6", dangerously close to 1.5 meters. A half-meter was trivial when sandbars formed or disappeared in hours.

The depth sounder screeched a warning. It stopped beeping in a boat length, though the water looked shallower. Without waiting for his next instruction, I eased back on the throttle and tightened my grip on the wheel, ready for a thump when the keel hit bottom.

"We run aground, don't blame me." It would've been funny under other circumstances.

"Stop grumbling. What's the depth?"

"One-point-eight."

He cussed, his first time that day.

I steered to where the water was slightly darker and called the depth, "Three-point-one. Three-point-four. Three-eight."

"How did you know to come over here?" he asked.

"Color of the water mostly. You can see it's flowing faster too."

"Bloody genius, aren't you? Shallow water was never a problem where I learned to sail."

"When you sail around the world, you learn a lot."

"I assume you mean more than how to sail." He gave a sly wink.

A sandy beach bulged out to meet a submerged sand bar where the river changed direction. I stayed in the center of the channel, wondering if what he meant by his wink was the same thing I was thinking.

"Favor port to the boat ramp. It's deeper after that," he said when we passed a dense thicket of mangroves on the shore. "Time for you to duck below, mate."

He wanted me out of sight in case there was someone at the boat ramp. He called me up as soon as we rounded the next bend.

"You don't want to steer?" I chided, feeling cocky.

"You did a great job coming in, Sander." His grin was as reassuring as being called 'Sander', the first time in weeks.

We motored slowly into Hull River National Park. Soon, the river split again. We turned right, a winding course through shallow sandbars and fallen tree trunks until the river narrowed.

"It's showing six meters now," I said, my relief real.

He ambled to the bow, then back to the cockpit, looking around. Ospreys glided above mangroves. I glimpsed a mountainous backdrop beyond a towering rainforest. Ibis and egrets pecked among tangled roots at the river's edge. The water was a dark mirror, our slow-moving boat fanning ripples behind.

Suddenly, he stopped slathering insect repellant on his legs and pointed. I thought he meant the 'no wake' sign. Beside it was a yellow and red sign nailed on a stump, with 'Warning', 'Achtung,' and 'Crocodiles inhabit this area—attacks may cause injury or death'. It left little doubt it wasn't safe to swim in the deep green water.

"They're around." He sounded hopeful, if not outright happy.

Shortly, a well-used mudslide interrupted the bank. However, if a crocodile resided amongst the mangroves, I didn't see it.

We motored along the meandering river, constantly changing direction. When I tired of turning one way and then the other, I shifted to neutral and *Calypso* drifted among misty shadows, darkening as the trees grew taller and thicker, and dripping water.

Once, when I veered too close to the shore, my father spotted a crimson splash concealed in the undergrowth. At first glance it might've been an orchid among bright yellow flowers and tangled vines. A cassowary stepped timidly from the profusion of ferns, glossy black spiny plumage with a vivid blue, purple, and orange neck. It had the weirdest shaped head I'd ever seen.

"You see the feet on that bird, Dad?"

Cassowaries were modern day velociraptors; its claws were huge.

"I'm too hot to care!" He wiped sweat from his brow.

"Ben would be ecstatic."

"A flora and fauna paradise… except for the bugs." He slapped at mosquito hovering a safe distance from repellant. "You miss having Nature Boy around?"

"He's okay for a know-it-all."

"I'll take that for a yes." He inclined his head. "This last month has been difficult."

"For you or me?"

His smile was a betrayal. "Would you like to go back to the *Spray*?"

I thought about it often, yet I gave an ambivalent shrug.

"They really want you with them," he said after a while.

I could tell he didn't enjoy saying it. "It's too dangerous."

"Not if things work out."

+ + +

We dropped the anchor right before the river branched again. With the engine turned off, and slathered with insect repellent, I stretched out on the cockpit seat and closed my eyes. So close to shore, shadows flitted among the trees. A faint breeze stirred the smell of rotting wood and flatulent mud, mingling with the lush undergrowth. Not pleasant, but full of memories of Brazil's Amazon River.

My father went below to listen to the VHF radio, leaving me with the orchestra of the rainforest, pigeons, thrushes, catbirds, doves, and cicadas, amid calls that even Ben wouldn't recognize.

He awakened my interest with, "We might be here for a couple of days."

"So long as we've got repellant, it's okay by me."

He stood on the stairs, looking smug. "Sooner or later that sport-fisher will turn up, maybe even today. When it does, you need to…"

"Stay out of sight. I got it, Dad."

"You need to wear this." He leaned over and dropped a blond wig on my chest.

It looked like a fur-ball. I tossed it back at him. "You're kidding!"

"They'll be looking for a blond-headed teenager."

My frustration burst out. "He left two weeks ago, in case you haven't noticed."

"You had to get used to being Marco Capra. Until I tell you otherwise, you're Victor Walker again." He threw the wig at my head.

"My hair was never this color."

"It was when you were younger. What matters is it's about the right length. Put it on." He was worried; I could tell by his voice.

I sat up and unrolled the wig. It had an elastic hair net inside. "It's way too curly."

"Stop complaining." He stepped into the cockpit, a small oyster knife in hand.

"You going to stick me with that?"

"I will if I don't hear an American accent from now on."

I put on the wig, knowing I looked ridiculous.

"It has to hide your real hair." He tucked a few loose curls out of sight. "Contacts too, mate."

By the time I got them out, he had the container ready. Blinking, I pushed silvery strands from my eyes. "I look like a dork."

"With luck they won't see you close up." He hesitated, obviously holding something back. "There is one more thing."

"What?"

He nudged my shoulder to make me move over. "I need a piece of your T-shirt?"

"You can have all of it if you ask nicely." It wasn't a favorite; it was black, with Fiji Pineapple Company on the back.

He tugged on my sleeve. "Take it off."

I knew better than to resist when he was like this. I stripped off my T-shirt and handed it over. He inspected it, front and back, tugging the cloth as if trying to decide what to do with it.

"Hurry up. The mosquitoes are having a feeding frenzy over here."

While I slapped at mosquitoes, he spread my shirt over his knees, jabbed the oyster knife through the hem, and dragged it sideways, not cutting, ripping.

"What the hell!"

He poked the blunt-edged blade through my shirt again, ripping through the seam. He did it again and again, yanking threads in every direction until he severed a section of cloth the size of his hand. Then, he handed me what remained of my shirt.

I held it up. "Mauled is the new style, huh?"

He regarded me, unamused, still holding the oyster knife. "We need evidence for this to work. You can put it back on."

Before my head came through the neck, I knew something was wrong. He held the cloth over his left hand. It was blood red.

"Jesus! Dad!"

He lifted off the cloth, exposing a ragged gash in the back of his hand. "Would you fetch what's left of Bruce's first aid kit?

Chapter 8.

My father served dessert in the cockpit; bright yellow pineapple, sautéed on the grill, and topped with a creamy ginger-rum sauce.

"It's Sails' second most popular dish. I created it one evening after we ran out of passionfruit sorbet," he crowed.

I forked a pineapple segment onto my plate and savored my first bite, dripping sweet juice down my front. However, he was looking the other way, at a runabout zipping along, leaving a wake that splashed on the banks.

"Here comes another friendly fisherman. You're up, Victor."

In the last hour, four fishing boats and a tour boat had come up the river. It was my cue to stand and pretend I was checking my fishing rod.

"Keep your shirt tucked in."

I dangled the rod with one hand, shoving shreds of my T-shirt under the waist of my shorts with the other. "Don't blame me; you mangled it."

"Stop acting like a moody teenager. Smile as you wave."

"Who's acting?" I said under my breath, waving reluctantly.

The runabout would pass us in a few moments. The man who steered didn't wave back. Likely, he didn't even notice me, let alone the clothes I was wearing. Then, the boat swerved towards us, slowing down until it was barely making a ripple.

"Like bloody Martin Place this arvo. First, there's a pissed off couple on a big Bertram across from the boat ramp; now youse," the man drawled.

My father got the gist. He gestured at me. "Victor, here, wants to catch a barramundi. We heard there are big ones here."

"Barras around fer sure, mate. Youse Yanks?"

"From New York. You have any advice besides prawns?"

"Prawn's bonzer. Yer better off in a tinny, and closer to shore, only watch out fer salties." He looked right at me. "Crocs don't eat ya right off, y'know. They stuff ya under a log till yer ripe. Rip off an arm or leg when they're 'ungry."

"Thanks for sharing that," I said.

The man grinned. "Just be real careful. No swimmin' and don't go walkin' near the shore."

"We saw a mudslide coming up," my father said.

"That'd be Bazza. He's a whopper. Marge is three meters (10 feet); but she's a cranky one. She rules the roost around here." The man pointed at the bank. "She's got a nest back in there. Middle of the season, so don't go takin' a gander."

"We won't. Hey, I'd like to see Dunk Island while we're here. How would we get there?"

"Take yer dink to the second landing ya come to. Follow the road to the beach and turn left. It's a fair hike to Wongaling Beach, two hours or so. The water taxi departs at ten an' eleven. You'd be better off takin' yer sailboat and savin' the fares."

"Sounds like a plan. Thanks."

"Hooroo, mate."

He waved goodbye. My father was right; everyone in Australia waved. He veered away a moment before he banged into *Calypso*. When he turned to head upriver, I quickly bounced the end of my rod as if getting a bite.

"What was all that about?" I said when he was out of earshot.

"By the sound of it, the sport-fisher's aground," he mused. He glanced up. "He had a good look at you, that's what counts. You notice anything unusual about him?"

I shrugged. "When he talked, it was like his heart wasn't in it."

"Add that to the fact he can barely use his right hand; he probably had a stroke recently."

"So?"

"It pays to keep your eyes open. If you see something unusual, don't blow it off! Assume nothing and question everything. Your life might depend on it."

"Okay."

"Always be aware of your surroundings, other people especially. Figure out what's going on and respond accordingly. End of lecture. Any questions?"

"Are you ever going to tell me what we're doing in the middle of nowhere?"

"Tomorrow." He rubbed his chin with his eyes narrowed, just like *he* did when something concerned him. "Assuming they get unstuck, they'll be here in the morning. We'll put the dinghy in the water as soon as it gets dark."

+ + +

It was still dark when my father woke me. I pulled on my tattered T-shirt and faded board shorts and stumbled from my quarter berth, past the galley. He'd made coffee and burned toast on the propane gas stove.

"We need to go over Marco Capra," he began as soon as he sat down at the table.

After 11 times, I let out a sigh. "I was born on November 20."

"Accent!"

"I'm 16. I lived on the third floor, at…"

"Not the basics; you've got that down. Why did you drop out of school?"

I said the first thing that came to mind. "I hated it."

"Details! And drop the 'h' sometimes."

"Too much 'omework and I didn't like studying."

"Bad answer! You're a teenager. Blame your parents, your teachers, never yourself."

"School's for drongos!"

"Better. When you're unprepared, deflecting usually works. Sometimes, the best thing to do is make them wait. Do it right and they'll think they dragged it out of you. Mostly, you need to lie on the fly. Just remember the best fibs have some truth to them. The more you practice, the better you get at it. Just don't overdo it…You any good at surfing?"

He ate toast overloaded with marmalade until I stopped fabricating. "Not bad for a second generation Italian kid who's never been on a surfboard. Remember, one mistake is enough to get you in trouble."

"What did I say wrong?"

"Always stay calm. Be as careful about what you say as how you say it. Give details if you have to, just make them sound believable. If you go off-script, don't forget to tell me what you said." He opened his wallet and began stuffing notes in a plastic sandwich bag. "Here's two hundred bucks, just in case it doesn't goes according to plan."

"The plan you were going to tell me today?"

"Go put in your contacts first."

We sat in the cockpit and spent 55 minutes going over his plan. The *Spray* was at a marina in Cairns, about 20 hours sail away. By tomorrow, we'd be onboard. I'd be safe once Zagarovsky lost interest; only a few days, he claimed.

"Put on more insect repellant. You're going to need it," he added before I complained.

For the second time that day, I covered myself with it. "What do I do if things go wrong; like we get separated?"

"You follow the plan and keep out of sight. I'll meet you on the south end of the beach as soon as I can. Five pm at the latest."

"What if something happens? What if you're not there in the morning?"

"The *Spray* should be at Dunk Island around midday tomorrow. You take the 10:00 am water taxi from Wongaling Beach."

"What if I miss it?"

"Take the next one. You won't miss it if you start walking as soon as you wake up."

"What if they're not there?"

"Trust me, they'll be there."

"But if they get delayed or something?"

"Improvise!" he snapped. He thought better of it. "Always stay calm. Think it through before you say or do anything. What if you get into trouble, the cops for example?"

"Call Uncle Angelo," I gambled. "He lives in Sydney, at McMahons Point."

I could tell he hadn't expected me to say that; however, he smiled approvingly.

"It took you long enough to figure it out."

I still remembered Angelo's phone number. Just in case he needed it too, he wrote it on a card he kept in his wallet.

+ + +

78

I was in the galley, getting a handful of Tim Tams to snack on when he suddenly stuck his head through the companionway.

"Make sure your wig is on right and get up here. A boat just came around the bend, and it's not a bunch weekend fishermen."

I scrambled up the ladder. A big sport-fishing boat was bearing down rapidly. I was about to say it was going to ram us when it slowed and veered off to pass between *Calypso* and the shore. My father waved unenthusiastically.

A man and woman were on the flybridge, both of them wearing dark sunglasses, yet I could tell they were staring at us. She smirked as they came abreast. My father waved again.

"Bloody amateurs. They might as well hang a sign on the bow," he said.

I waved too, barely lifting my hand. They kept going, taking the left branch. We waited until the sport-fishing boat was out of sight.

"That's the easy part." My father sounded tense. "They'll be back any minute. You got Sarah's curlers, right?"

"They're in the bag."

He scrambled for the galley. "I forgot something. Shirt off and jump in the dinghy. Now!"

I was bare to the waist and trying to start the outboard when he reappeared. He tossed my flip-flops into the dinghy and handed me what was left of the packet of Tim Tams and a long-sleeved T-shirt still in its plastic package. It was stone-washed blue with a foamy wave breaking on the front.

"Surfin'?"

He jerked the starter rope, thumped the gear lever into forward, and opened the throttle. "Why do you wear long sleeves in summer, Marco?"

"Get a rash from lotion, don't I?"

"Good answer. You got everything?" He looked in my bag, frowning when he saw *Doktor Faustus* wrapped in a plastic shopping bag.

I glared back, daring him to try to stop me. "I'm taking it."

"Don't judge a cover by the book," he said.

"What's that supposed to mean?"

"You think Marco Capra would read it?"

I stuffed the Tim Tams in the bag. "Found it in the trash, din' I? Old as shit, must be worth somethin', right?"

He gave me a second look. "Can you judge a cover from the shoes?"

"What's wrong with my shoes?"

"Surfers wear cloth slip-ons, not leather boat shoes."

+ + +

I'd taken off my shoes and put on the T-shirt with the sleeves shoved up my forearms before he reached the shore. He made a gut-churning loop and bounced the bow into a rotted tree trunk. I leaped, clutching my bag and flip-flops to my chest, my free hand flailing for a branch sticking straight up. It snapped off in my hands. The trunk was so slippery I fell into waist-deep water, scraping my legs on mangrove roots. Every time I tried to climb out, I slid back.

"Get a move on!" He stuffed my torn shirt down his front.

"I'm doing my absolute best, Dad."

He wasn't amused. "Stay in character ! Always!"

"Something's around my foot."

"Something will bite it off if you don't bloody hurry."

I grabbed the branch stump and hauled myself onto the trunk. I crawled to the bank, spurred on by his 'hurry ups.' When I looked back, he was wedging the 'evidence' between two mangrove roots.

"Go thataway!" He pointed into the rainforest. "Stay away from the river!" It was an order. "Keep your eyes open. I'll find you as soon as I can."

I was about to say 'good luck' back, but he jerked the gear lever and rocketed away. I watched him all the way back to *Calypso* before I put on my flip-flops and began clawing my way through mangroves, shoving aside cobwebbed branches infested with spiders, some as big as my hand. He said not to leave footprints, so I stayed in ankle-deep orange water, my flip-flops squelching in mud as I headed away from the river.

Smelly water seemed to bubble up through rotting leaves and ooze through my toes. Each cautious footstep brought another horde of mosquitoes buzzing my face. I slapped and fretted about catching malaria. I veered left, to go upstream. It didn't feel right. The sun was north, not south. Suddenly, spindly trees with bark like cream-colored paper surrounded me. Through a gap, I saw *Calypso,* a haze of exhaust smoke billowing around the dinghy tied to the stern. It picked up speed, heading downstream. The sport-fishing boat was right behind. The woman was in the bow, now with a bright yellow sunhat, her black-headed companion steering from the flybridge.

My father had hauled up the anchor and was hurrying back to the wheel. From the cockpit, he stared up at the woman in the bow. She pointed a bright orange flare gun at him. A moment later, he turned to look down the companionway. I could tell it wasn't going according to plan.

I was too far away to hear, though my father's abrupt headshake was unambiguous. Suddenly, he stepped onto the cockpit seat and over the coaming.

I heard the flare gun, a crack like a firework going off. *Calypso* exploded, though not the way he said it would, in a ball of fire. Instead, there was a brilliant flash and a very loud boom. The entire coach roof blew off, flinging splinters of plywood and fiberglass all around. Several chunks of coach roof crashed onto the dinghy, sinking it. Then, the mast toppled forward. It crushed the bow pulpit and flipped into the water. Smoke billowed up, hiding the remnants.

The woman clambered to her feet. She gripped the rail, put her sunhat and sunglasses back on, and peered down into the wrecked hull. The man scanned the water from the flybridge.

Expecting to see my father's head break the surface any moment, I crept closer. A dozen paces away, a big mottled green and black crocodile interrupted its lumbering march to the bank. It looked directly at me. Mangrove trees and a waist-high pile of sticks stacked on bare mud separated us. I backed away slowly, ready to fling *Faustus* and run zigzags—every TV show on crocodiles said that was the only way to escape.

I was back among the paperbark trees before the crocodile resumed its journey. I circled back to watch, my heart thumping. It paused at the mud bank, its tail swishing side-to-side; then, with a sudden loud splash, it was gone.

Hidden behind the mangroves and pandanus palm, I watched the sport-fishing boat bump up against the listing, scarred shell of *Calypso*.

"Grigore, nici o urmă de ele, " the woman shouted over her shoulder.

"Don't worry about him. Look for the boy!"

"Boy not in boat."

"He's not in the water. Must've gone under."

The boat backed off. The man scanned the water again. She watched Marge, like a slow moving log crossing the river. She cackled and pointed it out. Within seconds, the sport-fishing boat was underway, headed down river.

I worried about Marge until I saw my father emerge on the opposite bank. He looked worried as he signaled what he wanted me to do. He turned away, trudging in ankle-deep mud to find a way through the mangrove barricade. So much for things going according to plan.

Chapter 9.

Hours later, I stumbled onto a dirt track. Within minutes, I was out of the rainforest, exhausted, filthy, and peppered with insect bites and scratches. The track led to a boat ramp with an adjoining landing jutting into the river. Another 'Crocodiles inhabit this area' sign on the landing filled me with dread— this was where my father would try to swim across if I didn't warn him. Cautiously, I filled a discarded beer can with water and backed away to find a safe place to sit down and wash off the mud.

When I took off my flip-flops to wash them, there were nine fat leeches attached to my feet. I pulled them off and watched my feet bleed. It was Monday, no weekend fishermen, yet I waited, concealed in the shade while mosquitoes buzzed constantly. Having about the same distance to travel, but without a dirt track, I figured my father would appear on the opposite side of the river within a couple of hours. When he didn't, it was time to 'improvise.'

The road from the boat ramp turned into Jackey Jackey Street. I dawdled, hoping my father would catch up at the last moment. Only a few houses had cars parked in the driveway. An elderly man took time off from mowing his grass to watch me pass. I did my best to look like a surfer kid.

Jackey Jackey Street ended in Kennedy Esplanade, a pristine beach, turquoise water, and distant islands on one side; palm trees, lush gardens and holiday homes on the other. To the left was Wongaling Beach, far in the distance, where people and beach umbrellas dotted the beach. I walked the other way, hoping that I'd somehow missed him and he was waiting for me. The sandy beach turned into a narrow boardwalk winding through the trees, along a rocky foreshore. I went all the way to the end, just in case, and soaked in a warm rock pool festooned with seaweed and periwinkles.

Shadows darkened the beach before I finally decided he wasn't going to meet me. By then, 5:00 pm was long gone. I ate five of the Tim Tams, arranged the least offensive palm fronds into a bed, and primed myself for a miserable night.

+ + +

A flock of red and green parrots picking seeds from palm trees roused me at dawn's first light. I wasn't in the mood for noisy squabbles. I dusted off grit; I was hungry, sore, and increasingly anxious about finding my father. I had more mosquito bites on my legs. My eyes itched from wearing contact lenses all night. I ate two Tim Tams and started on the long walk to Wongaling Beach.

My aching stomach made breakfast a priority. I diverted through the village of South Mission Beach. No one was up at that time in the morning. The only shop was a pharmacy, the only restaurant was Thai, both closed for vacation.

When Kennedy Esplanade ended in forest, I walked on the beach, skirting driftwood, lumps of coral, palm fronds, coconuts, and mutilated fish. By the time I reached Wongaling Beach, the sun blazed and my stomach gnawed; however, instead of hiking to the center of town to find something to eat, I waited for the water taxi.

+ + +

The water-taxi was loading early arrivals; and I was staring down the beach, hoping to see my father trudging north; when a white SUV stopped beside me. It had a checkered blue stripe down the side, red and blue lights strapped to the roof, and a push bar with spotlights at the front. The policeman inside beckoned me over.

"What's your name, lad?"

I glared at him, as much as saying my name was none of his business. When he inhaled deeply, I mumbled, "Marco." I stretched his patience. "Marco Capra."

85

"You going somewhere, Marco?"

I looked him in the eye. "Dunk. Ain't nothin' worth doin' 'round 'ere."

"You going by yourself?"

"A mate of me uncle is stayin' there. 'is son's 'bout my age."

"You a runaway, Marco?"

"I'm 'ere with me dad. 'e's lookin' fer a job 'cause Mum kicked 'im out." I said it the same way I'd practiced.

The policeman glanced down the beach. "Where is he?"

"Reckon 'e's still in bed," I said with a smirk. "'e picked up a sheila at the bar 'n grill last night."

He gave me a guarded look. My father said 'give details if you have to; just make them sound believable.'

"'e made me sleep in the bloody car."

It seemed to satisfy him—after sleeping on palm fronds, I looked like a beach bum.

"Where are you staying?"

"Some caravan park." I jerked my thumb towards town.

"What's his cell phone number, Marco?"

"Up to you, but I wouldn't be callin' 'im till after lunch."

The policeman finally caught my drift. "There someone else I can call?"

"Not Mum, that's fer sure. Uncle Angelo, I s'pose." I smirked again. "Only 'e's in Sydney."

He eyed my bag suspiciously. Before he could ask, I opened it wide enough to see the remains of my packet of Tim Tams, nothing else. His eyes mirrored doubt.

"You got his number, Marco?"

"On me cell, only I ain't got it on me."

"How about his last name and address?"

"Romano." I made him wait. It worked just like my father said it would. "McMahon's Point; it's really posh."

The policeman stared at me as he made the phone call. I heard the phone buzz twice before Angelo picked up.

"Hello. Angelo Romano, please... This is Officer Cramer from Mission Beach in Queensland. I believe I have your nephew with me. He says his name is Marco Capra."

I mentally crossed my fingers. Likely, Angelo was in his pristine white living room, gazing at Sydney Harbour. It seemed longer than two months ago when we packed our belongings and sailed off in the *Spray*.

"No Sir, he's not in trouble. I'm just checking to make sure he's not a runaway... His dad's not available... No Sir, no problem. Like I said, I'm just being careful. We get a lot of teens through here. Thank you." The policeman switched his phone to speaker-mode and held it out the window. "He wants to speak with you."

It was all I could do not to smile. "Ciao Zio. Sono io." (Hi Uncle. It's me.)

"Ciao, chiaro di luna."

I got 'luna' and guessed 'chiaro.' The first time we met, I'd played *Clair de Lune* for him.

"It's good, Uncle Angelo."

"Your papa doing okay, Marco?"

"About the same."

"Sal's here." Angelo paused. "How about you keep in touch from now on?"

I heard Sal laugh in the background. "Try to stay out of the news."

"Hurry up, Marco," the policeman said abruptly.

"I got to go, Uncle Angelo," I said.

The policeman ended the call and put his phone on the dashboard. "What was that about staying out of the news?"

I had no idea what Sal was talking about. "I was in the local paper last month. Said I smashed a coupla car windows, only it weren't me."

"You can go, Marco. Don't be smashing any windows around here. You better start running or you'll miss the boat."

+ + +

I was still thinking about Sal's message when the water taxi slowed down. The Dunk Island wharf extended from a low scalloped peninsula lined with palm trees, all with stunted fronds. According to the water-taxi crew, Brammo Bay had been hit hard by a cyclone almost a year earlier.

First off the ferry, I sauntered down the wharf and sat on a bench, waiting until every tourist disembarked. There were Germans, Japanese, and a handful of garrulous Australians loaded with backpacks. Not one was out of the ordinary.

A few minutes later, a dinghy puttered along the shore. There was no mistaking Ben in the stern, goggles and snorkel pushed back on his head. He steered an uncertain course, following the beach as he peered over the side. He veered closer, too occupied with coral formations and fish to notice. He looked up at the last minute, shoved the tiller to port, and cut the motor. *Squirt* ground onto shells and driftwood. He hopped out, glanced at the bored-looking teenager sitting on the bench, and shoved at the bow.

He spun around when I whacked his butt with my bag. "What the..." His eyes went wide and his mouth gaped. "What did you do to your hair, Dude?" He lowered his voice.

"Now, you look like you're really my bro. You're really you, right?"

I wanted to hug him. Instead, I dumped my bag in the dinghy. "I'm Marco from now on."

"Who?"

"Marco Capra. You need me to spell it?"

Ben grinned.

"I'm from Sydney, visitin' with me dad."

"Your accent is right on, mate." No matter how hard Ben tried, his bogus accent made me smile.

"Angelo's me uncle, y'know."

"Gotcha. You know you're dead, right?"

It was my turn to gape.

"It was all over the news last night. They said your boat exploded and you were thrown overboard. Then, they found a piece of your shirt with blood on. Some park ranger said you got eaten by a Crocodylus porosus." Ben grinned. "That's a saltwater crocodile. Australian's call them salties."

"I didn't know that."

I squandered sarcasm on Ben.

"Uncle Ron cried when they interviewed him."

"He was on TV?"

"Only for a minute. I didn't hear what else he said because Jessie was bawling her eyes out."

I tossed my flip-flops in the dinghy, heaved it off the beach, and waded it into deeper water. "No one else?"

"Nah!" Ben hauled himself over the side and started the outboard. "Dad said Uncle Ron faked it so you could disappear."

"He thinks Zagarovsky will lose interest if I'm dead."

"That's what Dad said. You'll be with us until things quieten down. My job is to smuggle you aboard," Ben confided.

My goggles, snorkel, and fins were wrapped in a beach towel. I stripped off my shirt as Ben zigzagged into the bay. When he wasn't gazing over the side, he babbled about every species he'd seen since we were together. I told him about Marge and her nest, cutting the distance between us in half. Nature Boy hadn't seen a saltwater crocodile, except in the Cairns Tropical Zoo.

We followed a ribbon of palm trees along the beach, all the way to the other side of the bay. Three times, we stopped at granite outcrops, snorkeling in waist-deep water for Ben to collect shells. Anyone watching us would've soon lost interest.

Chapter 10.

The *Spray* was anchored in the lee of a tree-covered promontory, a dozen boat lengths from shore. Tired of Ben enthusing about finding a perfect spotted cowrie, I stayed in the water and followed him back to the *Spray*.

He was oiling teak trim in the cockpit, head down and outwardly busy, yet I could tell *he* was waiting for me. *He* glanced up again and again as Ben rowed closer. Soon, *he* stood and casually surveyed the shore, as much enjoying the sun as taking in the view. Then, certain that no one was watching the *Spray*, *he* beckoned Ben to bring *Squirt* to the port side, away from Dunk Island.

When the dinghy bumped the ladder, *he* caught the painter and tied it to the rail, staring down at me.

"Hey, Dad; this is my friend, Marco Capra," Ben said cheekily.

I shoved back my goggles and swiped sodden dark hair from my face. "G'day, Mr. Walker."

"Good Lord!"

From *his* scowl, *he* definitely didn't like me calling him that. Fortunately, Sarah leaned over the rail. The expression on her face was worth wearing her curlers for a year.

"It's nice to meet you, Marco," she said earnestly, compelling me to grin back. "Such beautiful brown eyes, just like your father's."

"G'day. Pleased to meet ya." I climbed the ladder, dripping seawater, swim fins in hand.

"His eyes fooled me too, Grandma," Ben chimed in.

"This might actually work." However, *he* didn't sound convinced.

"He's Angelo's nephew, visiting from Sydney," Ben added.

Jessie stuck her head through the companionway. I watched her frown turn into joy. "Josh... Mommy, it's Josh! Mommy come quick! "

She flung herself across the cockpit. Only the rail saved us from falling into the water. She hugged me, giggling, muttering, and crying, all at the same time.

"Josh, I missed you so much."

"Jessie, we have to call him Marco Capra from now on," Sarah said.

"He's Josh!"

"We gotta act like I'm not 'im though, no matter what, Jess," I said as she squirmed all over me.

"Cop the awesome accent," Ben mimicked.

Jessie shook her head. "Uh uh. You're still Josh."

"It ain't easy bein' Marco. I keep forgettin'. You can 'elp remind me, if you want?" It sounded like I was speaking through my nose.

Aunt Vee looked on, not saying a word, just smiling. However, she blinked again and again. *He* blinked too, though *he* hid it much better. It made me feel awful.

Sarah looked me over before she turned to *him*. "All things considered, it turned out better than I expected."

+ + +

They fed me chunks of roast beef and cheese on Sarah's crusty homemade bread, two glasses of milk, and a bowl of fruit salad. Then, they confined me to the aft cabin with a fresh towel and surfer clothes they'd bought for me in Cairns. After the longest shower I'd ever taken onboard the *Spray*, I put in Sarah's curlers, wrapped an old towel around my head, and stretched out on the bed. It didn't matter that

92

I'd been gone for weeks, Jag came to visit, meowing loudly, not for food, but to be rubbed behind the ears and tickled under the chin. He curled up beside me. I saw Jessie frown from the doorway.

"Jag's been tellin' me about you. 'e ain't really missed me 'cause you're so nice to 'im," I said.

"Jagie's happy you're back, even if you aren't Josh any more. Me too." She fled to the salon.

Someone had put my guitar-case in the cabin for safekeeping. I opened it. Inside, green felt cradled rare Brazilian rosewood. More than anything, I wanted to play it, yet I dared not. As far as I knew, Marco Capra wasn't musically inclined. At least, I could look at mother-of-pearl flowers on the ebony fingerboard.

Even with the hatch open, it was too hot to do anything except read. I'd just unwrapped the towel and started on John Steinbeck's *East of Eden* when *he* came into the cabin and closed the door behind him.

He almost laughed. "I see you got the 'stay in character' lecture."

"I look different, huh?"

"Especially with curlers. I won't tell a soul. Ben would never let you forget it."

"Thanks for the new clobber. Clothes," I translated. *He* didn't like slang, Australian or any other variety.

He noticed that I'd removed the book's dust jacket and set it aside. "I got Steinbeck in 1976, my 15th birthday."

"I got *Doktor Faustus*, the German edition."

"Not a lot of bookstores in Rockhampton. Nick... Ron said he'd read it with you."

"'e's Mario now," I reminded him.

"Mario," *he* repeated. "You think Mario reads German?"

"Not bloody likely. Only thing 'e reads is the Sports."

"How far did you get before the switch?"

"Page 95. Took us two bloody weeks."

"Any good?"

"It's kinda dark and depressed. We talked about zeitgeist when 'e wasn't tryin' to teach me Italian."

He grinned. "His Italian was always better than mine. We could read *Faustus,* if you like?"

"I'll stick with *East of Eden*."

"It's about two families; how their lives are interwoven. Throughout, there's a kind of sad inevitability."

"So, like our family and Sal's?" The words were out before I could stop myself.

He did stop himself. "Did you read the inscription? 'Everything you have read has been, in a sense, practice for this.'"

I checked the first page. "I'm impressed."

"It paraphrases a comment by Steinbeck about his book," *he* went on. "I think my father was saying that we live our lives based on what we've already done."

I wondered where that left me. "I'm not even sure what my name is from one day to the next."

"Which is why you always have to stay in character."

I'd dropped the accent without realizing. I put Steinbeck on the bed.

"One day your life might depend on it." *He* didn't look at me, yet I knew *he* was waiting.

"I 'ear that coupla times a day; like I need a bloody 'earin' aid or somethin'."

"I know it's a pain. You'll get used to it eventually."

"Wearing contacts is a pain."

94

He picked up Steinbeck and perused the inscription. "After they tried to kill you in the hospital, we had to completely change who we were. Your dad got angry because I wouldn't get rid of some things."

"Yer books had to go, huh?"

"The books we could hide. Mostly, he worried about the music." *His* sigh lasted so long it seemed phony. "He was right, of course. Things like clothes are easy to leave behind, unless they have memories, like that 'I love NY' T-shirt of mine that you wore until it fell apart."

"What about it?"

He put Steinbeck where I could reach it. "I wore it when Nick and I went to Game Six of the 1996 World Series. October 26; the New York Yankees against the Atlanta Braves."

"You let me wear that?"

He shrugged. "You liked wearing it. Besides, your dad is the Yankees fan, not me. The difficult things to leave behind are what define you as a person. You never want to lose the people you love. The same goes for anything with real meaning to you."

"Like my guitar?"

He'd been waiting for that. "I see you managed to resist temptation."

I wondered why *he* was in such a good mood. "Bloody 'ard it was too."

"I know this is difficult for you."

There was something about the way he said it. "'e took his Fender with 'im, din' 'e?"

"It almost got him killed." One glance at my face was enough. "He hasn't told you?"

"Nope."

"A few months after the fire, he was in Sydney. One of Zagarovsky's people traced him to a guitar shop. He thought he'd get a better price if he sounded like an American rock guitarist."

"'e must'a needed the money pretty bad?"

"The man pulled a knife on him when he got to his car, stabbed him three times. He was lucky a passerby came to see what the noise was about."

"'is guitar gave him away?"

"Same as it will you, unless you're careful. What did he say about your arms?" *he* added.

"Keep them covered."

"Stay in character, always!" *he* snapped.

I jerked my sleeves down to my wrists. "Covered, see?"

"Your dad used to say working undercover was like acting. If I remember correctly, his version of acting has four As; right accent, appearance, attire, and attitude; all of the time; not when you feel like it. Keep acting and you might see 20!"

My frustration exploded. "Bloody 'ell!"

"Now you know how we feel. We've lived like impostors since before you were four." *He* opened Steinbeck again, thumbing the pages. "I didn't mean it the way it sounded. Living at Acadia Park wasn't the cover I would've picked. Sure, it wasn't a place they'd expect, but the trailer was awful."

Our trailer's air-conditioning worked intermittently, yet it was never as uncomfortable as *his* cramped little *Spray*. On the plus side, a boat had charm in abundance. It creaked under sail, and there was golden teak and polished brass everywhere.

"'ow did we end up there?"

"Norfolk had plenty of jobs, plus you needed a hospital twice a week. It made sense at the time," *he* said doubtfully. "We thought Zagarovsky would give up looking for you after a few months."

"Well, that didn't happen."

"Then, your dad emailed me about what happened in Sydney. He thought it would take another year or two. We had to stay put. Virginia got a job at Norfolk General as an orderly so she could attend nursing school for free. I needed something to take my mind off it..."

Another piece dropped into place. "You started building the *Spray* as therapy?"

"It was mostly the lure of romantic islands." *His* joke, like mine, fell flat. "It was easy for Jessie and Ben; they never knew anything else. For the rest of us..." *he* trailed off.

Deep down, I understood. "I wasn't even your kid and you guys gave up everything to help me."

For a moment, I thought *he* would nag me about 'staying in character.'

"We loved you so much it was never in question. Seeing you in the hospital was horrible. You were so small, just bandages and tubes..." *His* voice cracked. *He* turned to leave so I wouldn't see him cry.

"I wish you weren't my uncle."

He didn't look back. "Don't ever think it was your dad's fault. We've been lucky he and Sal had something in common."

"How does Sal fit in?"

He turned reluctantly. "The short version..."

"John," Aunt Vee called from the salon. He opened the door. "A cop just called on the VHF. He's on his way."

"I could go ashore?" I suggested.

97

"You need to stay out of sight. On the way here, we emptied the storage compartment under the berth, just in case. It'll be a squeeze, but you'll fit. Hopefully, there'll be enough air."

+ + +

Under the foam mattress was a storage compartment so small I had my knees in my face and a drawer rammed into my back. He was joking about running out of air. He'd installed ventilation grills in the side. The temperature was another matter. I sweated profusely as I listened to muffled voices in the main cabin. Suddenly, two voices were louder. Officer Cramer's voice was unmistakable.

"Ah, the master suite; or should I say the Captain's cabin... Not a lot of room on a boat, is there?"

"We get by." Uncle John was justifiably abrupt.

"Three adults and three kids; it's hard to believe you came all the way from the USA in this." A locker door snapped open and shut. "Almost no storage. Where did you say you left from, Mr. Walker?"

"Norfolk, Virginia. Sarah's been with us since Tahiti."

I could tell Officer Cramer was in the head, likely checking the shower. It was so small it was difficult to turn around.

"My wife wouldn't like this."

"We make do."

"Six people for two years. Bit crowded, wouldn't you say?"

"That has to do with Victor's death, how exactly?"

I grinned in the darkness.

"Just curious. Your children are taking it well."

"They cried the whole way from Cairns."

"It must've been very upsetting hearing about their cousin on the news. Normally, we try to contact the family before we release names and details. Unfortunately, your brother didn't know where you were."

"I told him our schedule when we split up."

"He said you had an argument over Victor."

"He lived with us for twelve years. We loved him like a son. It was very difficult giving him up."

"As I said, we'll keep looking. Even if he survived the explosion, given what we've already found, there isn't much hope. That piece of black cloth I mentioned earlier; I didn't want to say this in front of the others. One of our local fishermen saw him in a black T-shirt yesterday." Officer Cramer lowered his voice. "It's often impossible to locate the remains."

"Everyone knows crocs hide their kill." Uncle John sounded impatient.

"That's his guitar, right?"

"It was his guitar. It was my mother's before she died."

A finger plucked the strings. It made me angry.

"Nice sound. I bet it didn't come from a guitar store."

"Is there anything else, Officer?"

"I know how upsetting this must be for you, Mr. Walker. About the funeral; the nearest funeral home is in Tully. If there's anything I can do to help…"

"I haven't spoken to his dad yet. I expect we'll do a memorial service at sea. Victor would've wanted it."

"Right. I'd like to be there, if you don't mind."

"It'll be family and a few friends."

"I won't get in the way. If you need me, I'm a phone call away, Mr. Walker."

"I'm going to be buried at sea?" I grouched, flexing my joints. My whole body ached from being cramped up.

"It's brilliant, isn't it?" he gloated.

"It's unbelievably stupid!" Sarah gripped the dining table with both hands. "The last thing we need is media attention." She shook her head in dismay, or maybe disgust.

Aunt Vee intervened. "Mom, I think John's right this time. Zagarovsky won't believe he's dead if there isn't a funeral. We've lived on this boat for so long, a memorial at sea makes the most sense."

"A tragic demise with an inspirational service," Uncle John chuckled. "It'll be all over the TV."

"Don't I get a say?" I asked.

"You get to hide under the bed... Marco." It was his way of reminding me to stay in character.

"Actually, it makes more sense if Marco Capra is there."

He frowned at Aunt Vee. She was unbendable when her mind was made up. "Why risk it?"

"John, if it works, we'll know he's safe."

"If it doesn't, Zagarovsky will try again."

Chapter 11.

"Ahoy *Spray!*"

Sal's voice, more raspy than ever, was the last thing I expected. I left *Faustus* in solitary confinement and bolted up the stairs. After two windy days, the sea had settled, a mirror for a few fluffy clouds drifting on the tail of the front.

"Below. Now!" Uncle John growled.

I could've pointed out that it was so early no one would see me; however, he was already upset. There was no point in antagonizing him further. I quickly backed down the companionway.

"We're bereaved, remember!" he added loudly for everyone below to hear.

Aunt Vee patted my shoulder. I smelled onion on her hand.

"He still blames Sal," I said under my breath.

"And he always will, Marco." As rebukes went, hers was mild. "I better go act bereaved." Sniffling insincerity and trying not to smile, she rubbed her eyes and headed for the stairs.

"Aristotle says the hero meets a tragic end, whether from human frailty, nature, or the will of the gods," Ben read from his laptop computer. "Sound right, Grandma?"

His scribbled notes on the elements of tragedy and five Britannica volumes spread across the table. It was the same essay assignment that I had done on our first day on the Intracoastal Waterway two years earlier.

"The elements of tragedy are appropriate to the situation." Sarah sounded tense, more professorial than normal. Since sunrise, she'd worried about Zagarovsky recognizing me.

"Being eaten by a crocodile would qualify as nature, right?"

Jessie kicked Ben under the table. He sneaked a peek at me to see if I was listening.

The conversation in the cockpit was far more stimulating. Somehow, Sal had convinced the captain of the Dunk Island ferry to come alongside the *Spray* to drop off him and Angelo.

"I'm so glad you could make it at such short notice." That was Uncle John, disingenuous and not at all happy after the ferry bumped the side of his boat for Sal to step aboard.

"Sal, Angelo, thank you for coming," Aunt Vee said, still sniffling.

"I'm so sorry. When I heard what happened… Awful business; just awful. I've always had a special fondness for him." Sal actually sounded sad.

"His dad still ashore?" Angelo wasn't weepy like everyone else, just not his usual jovial self.

"The cops had some last minute questions about his boat blowing up. They'll bring him when we're ready to leave."

"Is there anything we can do to help?"

Uncle John hesitated. "Not at the moment."

"Excuse me, Mr. Walker. Is it okay if we take photos of the service?" someone on the ferry asked.

"I don't mind, just not if the kids are upset."

"No problem, mate. Officer Cramer said we can observe if we stay out of the way. His dad has to okay anything we put in the paper."

Angelo interrupted the reporter. "My nephew around? I brought him some clothes. Don't want him looking like something the cat dragged in."

"Downstairs."

102

Angelo poked his head through the companionway. He stared at me. Behind him, Sal looked into the cabin. I was about to say 'hi' when he turned away. The last time I saw him, he was pasty-pale and shaky from a minor heart attack. Now, he looked like the man I'd met in the Bahamas two years earlier, full of life with wrinkled brown skin.

Angelo tossed a gym bag for me to catch. "Here you go, Marco. Hope they fit okay." He lowered his voice. "Your dad had to guess your size."

Inside the bag were a couple of surfing magazines; underneath, a white oxford shirt, creamy chinos, and a pair of surfer-style slip-ons, no socks. I might have been going on a date with Dani instead of attending a memorial service.

+ + +

The *Spray's* anchor came up at precisely 11:00 am. Only a few minutes earlier, my father had stepped from the police launch. Officer Cramer recognized me in the bow, and gave a cursory nod. I wondered what he was thinking as we motored northeast, away from Dunk Island. A little flotilla of three yachts, the police launch, and the Dunk Island ferry trailed behind the *Spray* like a funeral procession.

Angelo came up behind me. "You look like you've got a problem."

"What's wrong with Sal?" I whispered. "He won't even look at me."

Angelo pursed his lips, making it clear he wasn't about to say. "Anyone or anything that doesn't belong, you tell us right away, Marco."

"Ain't no sport fishin' boats, that's fer sure."

"Too obvious. Zagarovsky will have someone here; bet on it." He pointed to nearby Mound Island. It was tiny, a few dozen trees on a miniature hill, and a sandy spit. "That it?"

"I reckon."

If I sounded grumpy it was because other than mumbling the obligatory, 'I'm sorry about Josh,' I still hadn't talked to my father.

Angelo surprised me. "There's no more Victor Joshua; you know that, right?"

"If this works, it's okay by me." I thought about it some more. "I'd rather not be Marco Capra for the rest of my life."

"If I was a betting man, by the end of the year you'll be someone else." Angelo brought his head close to mine. "Just so you know, you're the spitting image of Dante."

He ambled back to the cockpit, leaving me with that to think about.

+ + +

Uncle John and Ben stood side-by-side, a sad pair in matching blue button-down-collar shirts, worn only to the Sydney Opera House. It hurt to look at them, Ben blinking and sniffling, his father resting a hand on his shoulder.

The minister had a squeaky voice and a lot to say.

"We come here today, to this beautiful place, this little island in paradise, to celebrate Victor Joshua Walker, beloved son, nephew, cousin, and friend. All of us remember him with great fondness. Now that he is gone, all we have left are our memories."

Standing in the cockpit, my father was a statue of sadness. Uncle John closed his eyes. Aunt Vee and Sarah held Jessie's hands. Ben was poker-faced. Sal stood by the stern rail. He breathed deeply. I felt his eyes pass me by.

"For him, death is not the end. Our love for him will go on. Long after this day, you will see the evidence of his life…"

He went on and on. I was glad they'd put me next to the mainmast. At least there was shade. On the ferry, a

104

woman in dark sunglasses videoed all 32 minutes. Then, my father cleared his throat.

"There is a special bond between a father and his son, a bond that grows stronger over time. I shared his first three years, and his last two months. Not quite twelve years in between; I missed his growing up, yet I count myself fortunate. He was a great kid."

He looked around, momentarily resting on me. I was so hot I'd turned up the ends of my shirt sleeves and turned my wrists inward. His gaze moved onto Sal, who had yet to say a word to me. Aunt Vee, still teary, nodded encouragingly. My father took a breath, bracing himself.

"March 5th we were going to go fishing after breakfast," he said softly. "We went a few times when he was little. He liked to fish, only I was too busy to take him back then. That was why he was downstairs; he was making coffee when the boat blew up... He was talking about catching barramundi for dinner... I'm sorry. It's not supposed to be like this... I barely got to know him again. I keep wishing we had more time together. There's so much I wanted I say to him. The little time we shared... just days really; it was... it was unforgettable..."

Uncle John told a story about sending me up the mast when the gaff fitting broke.

"... The wind was howling, and it was freezing cold. The boat was heaving up and down. Lines were banging against the mast, and up he went. You'd think he'd be scared stiff because of what happened when he was three. Not a single complaint out of him. Just get it done. Afterwards, he told me about a colony of sea lions he could see from up there. Said if he had to do it again, he was going to send me a bill. He was nearly 14. I always knew he had guts; I just never realized he was that brave. I could tell a dozen stories like that."

He blinked and rubbed a knuckle in his eyes. "What I remember most was listening to him on the guitar. An hour every day, sometimes hour after hour. He didn't just play it though; he lived it. He put his soul into every note. That takes real skill."

Sal talked out of turn because Aunt Vee was crying.

"… The kid could swim like a tuna, believe me. That Hammerhead was right behind him. Biggest dorsal fin I ever saw. We got his little brother over the side of my runabout just as the shark went under. I was sure I was going see the sea turn red. The next thing I know, I'm pulling this skinny brown kid over the side, so exhausted he can barely breathe."

Sal took off his sunglasses and looked right at me, yet to anyone else he was avoiding the glare while he wiped tears from his eyes.

"And that's how I met Victor Joshua Walker. I nicknamed him Sharkbait later that day. He's still my Sharkbait."

Aunt Vee talked about my appendix operation. It was a few weeks after going up the mast, during a terrible storm off the coast of Patagonia.

"He took it in stride, except for getting a shot and not wanting to be shaved down there," she added.

It was so inappropriate that everyone laughed.

"The bigger problem for Josh was recovering afterwards," she went on. "If you knew what he'd been through when he was younger, you'd understand. He wasn't the kind of kid who stayed in bed."

She brought her handkerchief to her face and started crying. Jessie tugged on her arm to use the handkerchief. She cried to the end, dumping the first of a dozen handfuls of white flower petals over the rail.

+ + +

"Well, that went better than I expected," Uncle John said almost gleefully. He had a bottle of beer in one hand and one of Sarah's tuna and cheese canapes in the other.

"Here's to the untimely demise of Victor Joshua Walker." My father clinked bottles. "A saltie snack."

"Assuming your plan worked."

Like Angelo, Sarah hadn't said more than a dozen words during my memorial service. When the rest of us went below for food and drink, Angelo and Sal stayed on deck. I sat on the steps, trying to listen in. However, their voices were so low, I heard only a mutter. I was certain they were talking about my father and me.

Aunt Vee made of point of bringing me the platter of canapes. I hadn't eaten much since the morning before. Without warning, people we didn't know dropped by to offer their condolences. Each time, I scrambled to get into the aft cabin before they saw me.

She gave me a hopeful nod. "If Zagarovsky had someone there, I didn't see him?"

"Didn't you see the woman with the video camera?" Uncle John asked, his good mood disappearing along with the canape.

"She works for the local TV station; Mary Simmons or Simonds. The woman sitting inside the ferry; she's from the sport fisher; I'd take bets on it," my father said. "She pointed her cell phone at all of us a couple of times."

I'd thought she was rude using a cell phone at a memorial service.

"It always pays to keep your eyes open," he added, mostly for my benefit. "The people who blend into the background are the people you need to watch out for the most."

"Chameleons can be deadly, we got it," Ben joked.

"It isn't a game, Ben. Just one mistake and he's dead." Uncle John used the same stern voice with me. It seemed to be Ben's turn, now.

Ben glanced at me and didn't say a word.

"I'm not worried, John. Marco was in the shade. With that much glare, the photos she took won't be worth sending to Zagarovsky."

"How about when he tossed in the petals?"

"I would've stopped him if she hadn't already put away her cell phone. She wouldn't do that if she thought she was looking at Victor Joshua."

Uncle John's mood brightened. "Then, it worked."

"Too soon to tell. If I was Zagarovsky, I'd keep an eye on the *Spray* for a week or two, just to be sure."

+ + +

Sal, Angelo, my father, and I left on the 4:00 pm ferry back to Wongaling Beach. Like a moody teenage boy, I kept my head buried in surfing magazines. Across the aisle, they talked about the service, and poor Victor Joshua Walker.

There was a rental car waiting for us under the trees. They dropped my father and me at a motel-resort. Across the street was the caravan park entrance.

"We're heading back to Brisbane. I'll expect you at Rivergate Marina, The *Maid Marion*. It's right by the big bridge. You can't miss it." Sal still hadn't said a word to me.

"We'll be there, just as soon as I tie up some loose ends," my father said. "Any news on the passports?"

"Not yet."

Angelo passed his gym bag through the window. "You'll be needing this, Marco."

"Thanks Angelo."

108

There wasn't much inside the gym bag; Marco Capra's surfer shirt and board-shorts, three sets of Victor's underwear, Sarah's curlers, my *Faustus*. I joined my father on the footpath.

I turned back when Sal opened his window. "You took a big step today... Marco."

"Y'know I didn't choose to look like this."

"Not your fault you look like him." He almost sounded apologetic.

"I'm sorry, Sal."

"Always stay in character," my father said quietly. "You never know who's watching."

I stuck my hand through the window, wondering whether he'd shake it. "Thanks for everythin', Sal."

He squeezed my hand harder than ever. "Be careful, Sharkbait." He didn't let go of my hand; in his eyes was a glimmer of the old Sal. "Dani's spring vacation starts tomorrow," he rasped. "She and her mom will be here in a couple of days."

+ + +

My father had rented a caravan conveniently next to the toilet and laundry building. I waited outside, going in every five minutes to check the washing machines. It took 23 minutes for him to check out of the motel, divert down the beach, and sneak through the seaside entrance to the caravan park. He didn't have much, just a cheap vinyl gym bag the same as mine.

The caravan was set on concrete blocks, with flowers around the base. It was hand-painted white with metal-grey patches where the paint had peeled off. Inside was dingy. It smelled moldy. He turned on the shower. I turned on the TV. Within minutes, I was so bored that I sacrificed constantly buzzing, chilly air-conditioning for the sweltering afternoon outside.

I wandered around the mostly empty grounds, looking for shade. A handful of budget-tourists occupied the swimming pool, including a twenty-something in a black bikini, basking in a fold-up deck chair. I occupied a plastic lounge on the other side of the pool, sweating in the clothes that Angelo brought me.

"I thought I'd find you here, Marco." Officer Cramer towered over me. His face was ruddy from being in the sun.

"Now what?"

"Nice service, wasn't it?"

"Not bad."

She was gorgeous, shiny with tanning oil, one arm draped across her face to keep away the sun.

Officer Cramer blocked my sun. "His dad said you knew him from Sydney?"

"Met 'im a coupla times at Uncle Angelo's. I thrashed 'im at billiards."

"His parents said he played guitar. You ever hear him?"

Something about him said it was time to be careful. "Twice maybe."

She was sitting up, looking directly at me, likely wondering what I'd done to get in trouble with the cops.

"Any good?"

"Dunno. 'e played some prissy crap, like on public radio."

I could tell he was worried about something. "Is your father around, Marco?"

"Caravan." I pointed through the palm trees, not about to say which one. "'e's 'ung over."

That got his interest. "He's got a hangover?"

"'e thought 'e 'ad a job up 'ere, only some other guy got it. 'e was boozin' most'a last night."

She lay down again, her arm back across her face; my interrogation apparently of no interest.

"Is that why he missed the memorial service?"

"Reckon."

A bald-headed man came up behind her. Even outside the safety fence, he looked disgruntled as he scanned the pool. All I recognized was his abrupt gesture, mostly hidden by fanning his face with a folded newspaper. He beckoned impatiently.

Officer Cramer turned to look across the pool. "That your dad, Marco?"

"Reckon 'e's still pissed at me."

"No worries. I'll have a chat with him. What's his name?"

Despite all the times I said it, I still had to think. "Mario."

Officer Cramer walked all the way around the pool to the gate. While his back was towards me, I signaled to my father; he was supposed to have a drinking problem.

They talked. From my side of the pool, it looked as if they were on the verge of arguing until Officer Cramer suddenly burst out laughing. He shook his head as he walked towards his car. I ambled around the pool until he got in the car, then I hurried to catch up to my father.

"Stupid bugger," he said under his breath.

"Officer Cramer?"

"You, mate! Next time you change the narrative, bloody tell me!" His accent was born and bred Down Under.

"What did I do wrong?"

"Stop lookin' like a roo in the headlights. He asked how you got in the bloody paper, didn't he?"

"Oh!"

"Yeah, oh! It would've been nice to know you busted some car windows beforehand."

"Sorry, Dad. I forgot." I started to explain about the phone call to Angelo; how Sal told me to keep out of the news.

"Not now!" He stepped into the shade of the laundry building. "We came this close to blowing it, Marco." He grasped my shoulder, the thumb and first finger of his other hand inches from my face.

"I'm sorry, okay."

Slowly, he smiled. "Other than giving me a drinking problem, you were great..." He brought his head close to mine and whispered, "Sander."

It slowly sank in that the lecture was over. "What did you say that was so funny?"

"One of the cars was a Beemer. It belonged to your mum's boyfriend. That's why she kicked you out."

"Not that funny."

"It was to him. The clincher was I gave you twenty bucks to do it."

He set the pace to the caravan. To anyone else, he appeared grumpy, jerking the door open and all but shoving me inside as he slammed the door behind us. After a high-five, a friendly shove sent me toppling onto the couch. I threw a flowery cushion at his head.

He tossed it back and sat on the table. "I worried about you nonstop."

"Me, too. I almost didn't spot you at the pool."

"You'd think Cramer would recognize me after we spent three days together, looking for your miserable carcass."

"You look really different with your hair shaved off."

"Actually, I used hair remover. It lasts longer." He peeked between blind slats. "Survival is more than switching appearances and a fake accent. It takes behavior and psychology to stay alive; and using your wits."

Chapter 12.

We arrived at the Greyhound Bus terminal in Brisbane shortly after 3:00 pm, one day, 6 hours, and 20 minutes after getting on the bus at Mission Beach, a short hike from Wongaling Beach. Unlike my father, who'd slept most of the way, I'd spent most of the trip thinking about my family and Dani. It was all I could do to stumble through the terminal and into a taxi for the 18-minute ride to Rivergate Marina. It was as impressive as any marina I'd visited since leaving Norfolk, Virginia. Not that there were more dock spaces; instead, huge motor yachts lined the river.

I trailed after my father as he strolled along the boardwalk, undaunted by sweltering heat to look at rich people's toys on display. We rested at the end of the boardwalk, where the freeway bridge blocked the sun. The hum of traffic was a constant distraction, yet we reveled in the breeze, watching stylishly attired crews cleaning and polishing, or serving drinks and hors d'oeuvres to their upper-class owners.

"This is the life I should've had," he said dreamily. "Boring, but I can see why people enjoy it so much."

"Living on the *Spray* wasn't boring. Day after day of schoolwork interspersed with near-death experiences." I got him to smile.

"Every day's an adventure when you're living on the run." He turned around to get his bearings. "Sal said his boat was next to the bridge."

I yawned. "Maybe he meant the marina was next to the bridge."

We walked to the opposite end of the boardwalk. Hidden among smaller motor-yachts was Sal's sailing yacht, *Maid Marion*.

"Pretty spiffy, eh?" he said after I pointed it out. "Stay here till I signal." He was back in cautious mode. 'I want to have a chat with someone from my past."

He ambled down to the dock. From the boardwalk, I watched him chat with Tony, Sal's bodyguard. You respected Tony; he was lethal with or without his handgun.

After five minutes, my father scratched his back. I assumed it was the signal for me to come down the ramp. Tony spotted me before I was halfway down, not saying a word until I was next to him.

"Angelo said you looked like him." He looked me over. I could tell he wasn't thrilled to see me. "No wonder Sal got upset."

I stepped back, uncomfortable with being studied close up.

"Where's your dad?" Tony asked.

My conceited father leaned against a massive black pile artfully topped with a bright blue cone. "You blind, mate?" he drawled.

Tony peered at him. "Nick?"

"Mario Capra, now." My father held out his hand. "This here is my son, Marco."

"G'day. Nice ta meet-cha," I said in nasally Australian.

Tony beamed as we shook hands, pretending it was the first time. "No wonder Sal said it took him a day to get over it."

"Where is everyone?" my father asked.

"Sal went shopping with Angelo and Rocco. Sal hired him and his brother, Aldo, in New York. They're my cousins, from Palermo," Tony added pointedly.

"Is Marion still in New York?" However, I really wanted to ask about Dani.

"She's been back for a week. She hired a chef to take over the galley, so they're at the market, stocking up. I'm running the ship till tonight. We didn't expect you until tomorrow at the earliest."

"One of the local cops was worried I was leading Marco astray with booze and women," my father said with an amused glance at me.

Tony nudged me. "Sounds about right for you."

"I told him Marco's got a tendency to make up stuff. I think he bought it. Still, it made sense to leave the next day."

We followed Tony up the gangplank and onto the *Maid Marion*. Eighty feet long and twenty feet wide didn't seem as vast as the first time I saw it; yet it still took my breath away. Golden teak trim begged to be stroked; every line was coiled in a seaman-like manner; every porthole, window, and hatch polished to brilliant transparency. Inside was cool and invigorating, and smelled sweet and woody, like wattle blooming in the Blue Mountains, west of Sydney.

I sat on the stairs. After two days without a shower, and little sleep, I was tired and grubby. My father, on the other hand, was in the throes of boat envy. He gazed at the array of electronics in the navigation area; he perused shelves stacked with books; he scrutinized gilt-framed oil paintings; and he tried out the big creamy leather couch in the upstairs salon.

Down a half-flight of stairs, towards the bow, was the dining table and galley. It was bigger than most kitchens.

"You up for a snack, Marco?" Tony asked, taking a platter from the refrigerator.

"Can I take a shower first?"

"Sal said for you to use Dani's cabin. It's only until she gets here, then it's off limits for chick magnets."

"Who me?"

"You see any other fifteen-year-old boys onboard, let me know," Tony laughed. "You'll find a birthday present from her on the bed."

+ + +

Dani's cabin had two berths, as big as twin beds, a private bathroom, a miniature walk-in closet, and a dresser that doubled as a computer table. Everything in the cabin reminded me of her. She liked fuzzy blankets and collected zany ceramic animals in her own 'Animal Farm'. On the burnished cherry wall was a vivid cel from *The Little Mermaid,* and three pencil sketches she'd done of Anaho Bay, Nuku Hiva. She had *Wuthering Heights* and Orwell's *1984* on the shelf behind her bed. *Catcher in the Rye* was on the dresser with a bookmark inserted. There were silver-framed photos of her mother and brother, and a father she never talked about.

On the berth next to the portholes was a red T-shirt. I picked it up. On the back was a Hammerhead shark, jaws open, black eyes bulging. Beneath was 'Shark bait,' which left me wondering if Sal had a hand in choosing it.

Since January 27th , when we made a very hurried departure from my father's house, a shower consisted of a wash cloth and a small basin of lukewarm water, followed by a quick rinse-off; I didn't miss that at all. On *Maid Marion*, my shower lasted until I resembled a prune.

I dried off and returned to the cabin. The T-shirt was so big it would've been loose on my father. With only a towel around my waist, and no clean clothes; I pulled on the T-shirt. It smelled like the jasmine flowers Dani discovered when we explored Nuku Hiva. There was also a hint of orange blossom, and something else I couldn't identify.

I stuck my head out the cabin door. "Hey, I'm takin' a nap, if that's okay mate?"

"Too much excitement for one day, huh?" Tony said.

117

"He didn't sleep more than an hour or two on the bus," my father explained.

I closed the cabin door, drew the curtains, and got into Dani's bed. Her pillow smelled like jasmine too.

+ + +

Her long brown hair streamed behind her, flowing over me, enveloping me. I clung to her, bare and lean and soft... I grasped at fleeting memories to keep the dream going. Fantasies didn't cut it. I awoke, tangled up in sweaty sheets, stiff, hot, and shaky. My heart kept thumping. Then, embarrassment set in.

Red-faced in the darkness, I shuffled into the bathroom, turned on the faucet, and pulled a handful of tissues from the dispenser. All I could think about was Dani and me swimming in a turquoise lagoon, side-by-side and playful like dolphins. I'd never had a dream as powerful, or as wonderful.

I pulled on grungy board-shorts and stuffed excess damp T-shirt under the waistband. My eyes were red and I needed a session with Sarah's pink curlers. I found Dani's hairbrush in the vanity drawer and used it to make myself presentable in the mirror.

Marion rushed to hug me as soon as I entered the salon. "Marco, it's so nice to see you again."

Sal pecked on a laptop with two fingers, the same way Uncle John typed. He looked up. "Ah, my Sharkbait is finally awake and ready for dinner."

I grinned back at him. "G'day Sal."

"Marco, unless I say otherwise, you will speak Italian during meals, minus the accent," Sal said.

He was so serious I thought Tony was wrong about him taking a day to get over it.

My father stopped contemplating a glass of red wine. "It's part of your heritage. Any other time, you're Australian, mate."

From the dining table, Angelo said, "Don't worry, Marco. It won't be as bad as you think."

Marion gave me a nod to confirm. "Celia, we're ready whenever you are."

Celia was the *Maid Marion's* new chef. She specialized in the cuisine of Calabria, beginning with Focaccia al Pomodoro. It was doughy, oily, and thick with tomatoes, thyme, and garlic.

"In Sicily, this would be Sfincione, not Focaccia." Sal spelled 'Sfincione' and said it three times until I got it right. "Both can have anchovies and onions. Sfincione always has Caciocavallo cheese; the best is made from sheep's milk. Caciocavallo, Marco."

"Caciocavallo."

"Round your 'o'. Just so you know, it means 'horse cheese.' They make it in two lumps straddling a stick." He cupped his hands. "Like horse balls."

"Sal!" Marion shrieked.

"If Marco's going to carry this off, he must know the culture, everything from food to slang."

The next course was Vongole al Pomodoro Leggero, Clams in Light Tomato Sauce, served in bowls with grilled Italian bread.

I was savoring my second spoonful when Sal said, "Tell us about the bus trip, in Italian."

I struggled with my limited vocabulary, trying to sound casual as my soup got colder. My father watched, occasionally gesturing for me to elaborate. Somehow, I made it to Brisbane. To demonstrate I was truly all over the place, they engaged in a heated discussion about Italian politics, and then invited my opinion.

"How do I say 'on the head,' not 'sul capo'?"

"Sulla testa," Sal said. "'Pin' is 'testa'."

"Sulla testa di uno spillo," I said, hoping it would be enough.

He chuckled. "Quello che so si adatterebbe sulla testa di uno spillo."

My father translated. "What I know would fit on the head of a pin."

Sal summed it up. "He'd be lucky to last a day in New York."

Then, the next course arrived. Torta con Cime di Rapa e Salsiccia was broccoli and sausage pie. Sal told me how to say it before he conversed with the chef about sausage types. Angelo and my father also gave their opinions of salsiccia, whether Ciauscolo, Mortadella or Soppressata. I kept my head down, too flustered to enjoy what I ate.

Sal regarded me, rubbing his chin. I wondered if his next quiz would be to name all of the sausage types.

"Name the two cheeses you just ate and you're done for the night."

"Mozzarella," was easy. The other cheese was grated with a strong flavor. I panicked. "Not Parmesan. It tasted nutty."

"Pecorino."

"It's made from sheep's milk," I said, silently thanking Sarah. She'd bought a small piece in Papeete for a pasta recipe.

"You might last two days."

I couldn't stop myself. "Not bad for half an hour."

"Tomorrow night you will tell us everything since the last time I saw you."

"In Italian?"

120

"Ovviamente." Sal smiled. I thought it insincere.

+ + +

After dinner, Sal, Angelo and my father sipped Campari as we played Italian Monopoli. It had prices in lira, and we stopped on a via, corso, or largo instead of a street, lane, or road. I was soon bankrupt.

"Marco and I need to talk," my father said tersely.

We went upstairs and sat in the cockpit. There was a party going on, judging from the noise coming from the motor yacht at the adjoining dock.

"Now, what did I do wrong?"

"You lost deliberately."

"I ran out of lira."

"I've seen you play a dozen times."

I ignored him and hoped he'd let it go.

"You want to talk about what's bothering you?" he asked.

"Nothing is bothering me."

"If you think Sal stopped liking you because you remind him of Dante, it's the opposite."

"I'm tired of pretending, that's all!"

"Eventually, you'll stop pretending, Marco."

I let out a long sigh and resumed the accent. "I 'ate bein' some second generation Italian kid from Sydney."

"You aren't for the rest of tonight." He leaned back and folded his arms. "You want to continue that talk about your mom?"

I nodded, surprised that he'd brought it up.

"The night of the fire, I told you she practiced at the Cathedral of the Incarnation. She loved being there."

"She was religious?"

He twitched. "For her, just being alive was a spiritual experience. She affected everyone around her. The first time I saw her, I knew she was different. The way she looked at me, it was like she knew what was missing from my life."

"Uncle John said she was beautiful inside and out."

He stiffened. "Sounds like something he would say. My mom called her 'radiantly fragile.'" He went on, "Our first date, she played Handel's *Messiah* at a church off Times Square, all two hours of it. Then, we ate vegan at a Filipino restaurant. It was quite an experience."

"The food or the music?"

"The food was okay; the music was inspirational. She made Handel sound ethereal. If I wasn't already in love with her, that would've done it. On the way home, she said she saw God through music. Maybe she did. When she played, the music came alive. Her 'Hallelujah' erupted like a Divine Vesuvius."

It was an odd choice of words, yet I knew what he meant. "A sacred storm, more so than the *1812 Overture*."

He looked confused for a moment, his eyes penetrating, almost searching my mind, or his.

"You're surprised I know good music?"

"That you remember that far back." Before I could ask, he continued. "We were married the day after she graduated. I started working overtime, six days a week. As soon as we had enough money, we bought a house in Brooklyn. I spent every evening rebuilding it."

He reached over and clasped my shoulder. For the first time, I didn't feel uncomfortable.

"Then, you were born. I thought life couldn't get any better. No way were we going to take you on the subway; so we splurged on a new Mini. It was just big enough for the three of us. Every Saturday afternoon, we'd drive to the church so she could play the organ. I'd hold you during 'Hallelujah'. We'd pretend we were in a storm."

"A sacred storm."

"That's what we called it. Afterwards, we went to Central Park."

"I remember feeding the ducks." It was like looking through fog. "There was a stone bridge. We always had a picnic next to it."

"I'm not sure if it was the picnic or listening to her play the organ, but you drove us crazy every morning, asking if it was church day."

"Is that why we went to church in Norfolk?"

"I wondered about that. In one of the emails, John mentioned they took you to St. Luke's. Virginia thought it was some kind of subconscious thing because it had a big organ, same as the church near Times Square."

Chapter 13.

Angelo departed for Sydney three hours before Dani and Donatella were due to arrive from Los Angeles. I went to the airport with Sal—my father said he had something he needed to do. The L.A. flight was delayed, which meant that Sal and I waited at the airport for most of the day, the last hour with me standing in front of the exit portal.

Among thousands of strangers, I instantly spotted Dani breezing down the concourse. Long before she reached me, I realized her long hair was plaited and her suntan had faded. Even when she was so close that I could've touched the gold hoops dangling from her ears, she didn't recognize me. She kept walking even after I smiled at her. Her mother, on the other hand, abruptly stopped and stared at me.

"Dad said it was uncanny how much you look like Dante," she said quietly.

I turned red. She was about to say something else when Dani wheeled, a complete circle while craning her neck from side to side to see beyond passengers and flight crews bustling past. I might've been invisible when she looked right at me. I didn't think I was that different. She was even more beautiful than I remembered.

"Mom, I don't see him anywhere. Nonno promised he'd be here." Suddenly, her eyes went wide. "Oh my... " She slapped her hand over her mouth.

"G'day," was all I could get out.

We stared at each other, her mother like a picket fence between us. After eight months, she was two inches taller, still two inches from being eye to eye with me. Tight blue jeans made her lanky. As if her shiny black diamond-quilted vest was suddenly too hot, she unzipped. Underneath was the same silky white blouse as in her Christmas photos.

"Are you going to introduce us, Daniela?"

"Um… ah," Dani was as flustered as I was. "This is my mom…"

"I'm Marco Capra, Mum," I managed to say without making a fool of myself. "I'm pleased to meet you, Mrs… Ms…."

I blushed hot crimson, with their last name eluding me, when her amused mother took my hand, raising an eyebrow at Dani.

"Why didn't you tell me you had such a handsome boyfriend, Honey?"

"Because he's not, Mom."

"You wouldn't know it." She inclined her head, looking at me. "I can see why she never stops talking about you."

"Mom; enough already!"

Sal came up behind Dani and hugged her before smooching the top of her head.

Dani arched to kiss his cheek. "Nonno, I missed you so much."

"Not a bad catch, eh Donatella?"

"I didn't realize she had such good taste, Papa. He's positively delightful."

Dani scowled. "Mamma, comportarsi!" (behave)

Sal let her go and laughed out loud. "Il mio Gattino ha artigli." (My Kitten has claws)

Giggling, she swiveled and cat-hissed over her shoulder, her fingers clawing. "E Squali esca ha i denti."

"Be careful, Gattino; he speaks enough Italian to be dangerous."

Knowing 'kitten' was 'gatito' in Spanish, I grinned at Dani and meowed cheekily, wondering what Dani had said.

Her mother stepped in. "Keep baiting the shark and he will bite you."

It took a moment to sink in that Dani had said, 'And Sharkbait has teeth.'

"Mamma, you're embarrassing me."

Her mother shrugged it off. "Seeing as Daniela is too embarrassed to introduce us, Marco; I'm Donatella. Anything else from such a handsome young man will make me feel like a fat old lady."

"I'm pleased to meet you…"

Good-naturedly, Dani glowered at me. "Don't you dare call her Donatella."

Then, with a laugh, she gushed Italian. Her mother gushed back. People passing by gave us a wide berth until Sal took the two of them in hand. Even as we headed towards the exit, it went on and on, all three of them laughing and arguing at the very same time. I was completely confused.

Finally, Sal explained, "It seems that Dani has been teasing her mother all the way from L.A. about flirting with a man sitting across the aisle."

"It was more than flirting, Nonno."

"I was just being polite to him," Donatella said, gleefully shaking her head at Dani. "Besides, he needed cheering up."

Mother and frisky daughter resumed their Italian tirade. I was certain Donatella was teasing Dani about flirting with me when all she did was unzip her vest.

"Enough!" Sal interrupted. "Poor Marco will think we're crazy."

"Poor Marco needs to know what he's getting into," Donatella countered.

"Avere la coda di paglia," Sal said on his way into the revolving door.

I'd heard it before. My father had said it about himself—it was a nice way of saying someone had a guilty conscience.

"Like cheese on macaroni, Papa," Donatella muttered to his back.

Sal turned to look me in the eye. "I have an obbligazione with this one. It is an important word to know. You can look it up when we get back, Marco."

I was so confused, I didn't say much on the way back to the marina.

+ + +

My father returned a few minutes after we boarded *Maid Marion*. He'd been shopping for clothes for himself and surf-themed shirts and board-shorts for Marco Capra. I introduced him to Dani and her mother. I didn't expect he would kiss Donatella's hand and compliment her for having such a beautiful daughter, much to Dani's amusement.

While my father showered, I dressed in the clothes I wore to the memorial service, now freshly laundered.

"You go! I'll be up in a moment,' he called from the bathroom.

I opened the door. At the same instant, Dani exited her cabin across the corridor. She was even more radiant with her hair combed out and shimmering. She gaped back at me.

When she smiled, I smiled.

"Um... hi."

Less tongue-tied, she pointed out the obvious. "I see we were both told to wear white."

Her dress was pearl-white with creamy-gold floral embroidery all over. It flared out from a jeweled belt at her waist. It looked very expensive.

"We probably should go up," Dani added when my mouth refused to speak.

Eventually, I managed, "You're really…brown."

"Should I take that as a compliment?"

"I've never seen a brown kitten before."

"Meow." She stepped back, mischief in her eyes. "Cucciolo," rolled off her tongue.

"I'm a puppy?" I guessed. 'Cachorro' was 'puppy' in Spanish.

"You're cute and cuddly, aren't you?"

"I meant to say 'you're really beautiful', only I chickened out."

"Better Cucciolo than Pollastro," she giggled, caught my fingers, and tugged. "Come on; I want to show you off to Mamma."

+ + +

We stuffed ourselves with mouthwatering Calabrian-style pork ribs, baked in the oven and topped with tomatoes, mushrooms, artichokes, and basil. I sat next to my father and opposite Dani, both of them helping me with Italian words and phrases as I retold the highlights of my life after the bomb went off.

I was getting my hair dyed on my birthday when Sal interrupted.

"Si potrebbe durare una settimana, Marco." (You might last a week)

"I deserve more than a week, Sal," I fired back once I'd figured it out.

"Who are you trying to deceive?" My father had to constantly remind me to act like Marco Capra.

I faked angry. "A bloody week, you reckon?"

128

Donatella frowned at her father. "He's just pulling your leg, Marco."

"He knows how he's doing." Sal as much as said he was pleased with my progress. "What is 'obbligazione', Marco?"

"It's what it sounds like, an obligation."

"Indeed it is. However, my 'obbligazione' is more. It binds you, a relationship so strong you are knotted together. Now, there is something else I must address."

He sounded so serious, I had a bad feeling

"On February 17th, a certain young man, unfortunately now deceased, turned 15. He had only his father to celebrate what should've been a very special occasion. When I turned 15, my father said I'd reached the junction of childhood and maturity. If he meant I could start dating, he was a year too late."

"At 15, my dad thought I should have a job after school," my father chuckled.

"With so much at stake, a delayed celebration is better than no celebration, even if poor Victor Joshua is no longer with us. Buon compleanno, Sharkbait!"

He nodded at Marion, Donatella, and Dani. Across the table, Dani smiled shyly. They sang.

Ecco la torta con quindici candele,
una ogni anno per il suo compleanno.
Ecco la torta di crema e cioccolato,
scritto sta il suo nome col zucchero filato.

(Here is the cake with fifteen candles,
one for every year for his birthday.
Here is the cream pie and chocolate,
his name is written with cotton candy.)

"And now, to finish this momentous and joyful occasion we must eat cake and open presents," Sal teased.

Celia carried over a cream pie with chocolate and candles, and Tony lugged a big box down the stairs. Everyone watched me rip off blue paper and sealing tape. Inside, was a guitar case. I unfastened the latches, silently hoping they'd somehow managed to bring my guitar from the *Spray*.

"Hurry up!" Dani sounded exactly like Jessie.

Inside the guitar case was an acoustic guitar, creamy spruce and dark-red rosewood, with mother-of-pearl diamonds separating the frets. I ran a finger over the strings. The sound was vibrant. I picked it up, seduced by gloss and silkiness. The high notes were crisp, the mids were warm, and the lows firm. Chords had sparkle, clear and balanced.

When I glanced up, everyone was staring at me.

"It's beautiful," I murmured, picking notes from memory and comparing what I heard to my other guitar.

Of course, I couldn't accept it. I'd seen them in guitar magazines. I used to dream of having enough money to buy a top-of-the-line Taylor.

"Marco…"

I glanced at Marion. Each note was so pure it seemed to pass right through me.

"We want you to have it."

"I… I can't." I shook my head, plucking to test range and intensity, making chords to find harmonies.

"Marco, it's important to me that you accept it. You saved my life at the marina," Sal said solemnly.

"The real reason is that it makes him happy," Marion added.

"I'm not good enough for a guitar like this."

"We'll decide that after you open Dani's present."

Dani brought it out from under the table, grinning as I mouthed 'meow'. Her eyes sparkled as she handed it over. "You better like it, Cucciolo; I picked it out," she whispered.

It was smaller than a shoebox and wrapped in paper with sailing ships, with an envelope taped on the front.

"You have to open the envelope later," Dani said.

Her voice was so determined it surprised me as much as it provoked her mother's gesture of utter disbelief. Dani stared her down, much to Sal's amusement.

I ripped off paper. Inside was a guitar strap, a crimson Celtic Knot woven through suede and embedded in hand-tooled brown leather, with bronze studs and buckle.

"It's really beautiful. Thank you." I caught myself. "Grazie. Mi piace moltissimo."

Dani effervesced delight while I attached it. I knew she'd chosen it, and likely paid for some, if not all of it herself. Fingers that should've been deft, turned clumsy; she was watching; my father was offering suggestions; and Sal was reading instructions on how to take care of the belt.

"Now, we'll see how good you really are." Sal picked up two of sheets of music from the bottom of the guitar case and put them on the table. "Play one."

I didn't need the music. I played *Santa Lucia*, and segued to *Return To Sorrento*.

By then, Sal was rapt. "How?"

I wasn't about to say that I started playing Italian ballads after I met Dani, practicing the wavering effect of tremolo until it came easily. Instead, I played *Una Ragazza*. She sat spellbound. Twice, she wiped her eyes. Though it made me sad, I couldn't stop playing.

"I think the guitar found a new owner," Sal said softly.

Marion waited until I finished. "Marco, that was truly beautiful."

"Bello e affascinante," Donatella affirmed.

"Mamma, comportarsi," Dani snapped.

Donatella laughed. "Beautiful and charming is not an exaggeration, Gattino."

"Enough, Mamma!"

"Stupendo," Sal finally got in. He was hoarse, his hands fluttering like the notes. "Angelo must hear for himself."

Chapter 14.

Locked in my cabin, I practiced four songs, from the time I woke up to mid-afternoon. No schoolwork; and I even skipped lunch. My fingers were sore long before Donatella knocked on the door and announced it was time to leave. I packed quickly and carried my guitar up the stairs.

In the salon, Sal and Tony were interviewing a candidate for *Maid Marion's* permanent crew. He reminded me of the pizza delivery guy who came to our trailer in Norfolk, which wasn't reassuring.

Sal wasn't pleased. "You think you can find your way through a narrow reef with waves breaking over the boat?"

"I'd be willin' to give it a burl, mate. Give anythin' a go, I do."

Tony saw me and stood up. "You ever been up a mast in 45 knots? I'm not talking a mast like ours, any mast."

"Um, cain't say I done that."

Tony pointed at me. I thought he meant it was time to leave. Guitar case in hand, I started towards the door.

Behind me, Tony said, "At 13, he did it in pitch dark."

Sal coughed, adding, "Without filling his pants."

We were leaving the cockpit when Tony whispered, "Sorry about the slip-up. I couldn't stop myself. I hope your dad doesn't come back empty-handed; that one was a weekend sailor with around-the-world fantasies."

We started along the dock.

"Eyes down, Marco. Don't want you getting all hot and bothered," Tony joked.

Dani and Donatella were lying face-up on towels spread over the foredeck. We were halfway up the ramp, when I risked glancing back. Dani was sitting up. She waved. I waved back, gaping despite how often I'd seen her in a bikini on Nuku Hiva. She hadn't just gotten taller.

Her mother blew me a kiss, Italian style.

Tony cuffed me on the shoulder. "Down boy."

"Geez, I'm just lookin' at the scenery, mate."

"Looking's okay, but you're breathing too hard."

He didn't stop teasing until we got in the taxi to go to the recording studio.

+ + +

I played *O sole mio* three times before I forgot about the video camera and stopped thinking about notes and chords and Luciano Pavarotti's rendition. I imagined the words of the song, 'What a beautiful thing is a sunny day!' The air was fresh and clear after a storm, and a Neapolitan girl who was brighter than the sun.

Finally, the sound engineer gave me a 'thumb up' from the control room. I played *Clair de Lune* next. I'd played it often. He was happy with a single repeat.

My father wanted me to play Stanley Yates' *Cavatina*. It was meticulous, poignant, and heart-wrenching. It took four attempts before it was acceptable.

Nervously, I started into *O Cara Armonia,* adapted from Mozart's *The Magic Flute*. Segovia had played it on my grandmother's guitar. It was both playful and very difficult. I was shaking at the end; however, I'd never played it so well.

Through the glass-front of the control room, the sound engineer grinned approval and held up four fingers to show four minutes remained from my half-hour allotment.

134

For a lark, I played *Waltzing Matilda*, fingerstyle, my own version of the Australian bush ballad, desolate and sad, gradually elevating to the ending note.

+ + +

My father was just getting out of his rented Toyota when our taxi pulled up at the boardwalk.

He hurried over, leaving his passenger still getting out of the car. "How did it go?"

Before I could answer, Tony said, "He was awesome."

"So he didn't embarrass the family name?"

"The sound engineer said he was incredible for his age. I think he's heard enough guitar players to know."

My father just smiled. Behind him, Bruce McKenzie gave a friendly wave and hoisted a bulging backpack from the Toyota's trunk.

"He emailed the sound files to Sal. I bet Angelo's already listening to them," Tony added.

"Marco, how was it?" my father asked me directly.

"Not bad." My voice wavered. I was so tired I didn't want to talk to anyone, not my father, not Bruce, not Sal, not even Dani.

"I'd like to be there when Angelo sees the video," Tony went on.

My father took the guitar case from my hand. "He looked okay, I take it?"

"More like he pulled off the performance of a lifetime. Like a movie star, just as calm as can be."

My *Waltzing Matilda* was playing on the cockpit speakers when we came aboard. I hadn't realized how good I sounded until then.

Between Sal enthusing and Dani regaling me with questions about being recorded, Donatella plied me with delicacies from a platter on the table. Calabrian nduja was salami made from pig fat and cured for a year. There were paper-thin slices of salty ham and crusty bread, marinated tomatoes, big oily olives and eggplant, and ricotta calabrese.

I was still stuffing myself on Italian culture an hour later when *Maid Marion* drew away from the dock. Bruce and I coiled dock lines and stored fenders, and returned to the cockpit. Tony headed down the Brisbane River, using the autopilot to demonstrate how to steer and navigate using *Maid Marion's* complex electronics.

We were passing the massive wharves on Fisherman Island when Tony announced it was my turn to steer. Unable to say no with Dani looking on, I reluctantly took over the helm.

Tony stayed nearby. "If you weren't so nervous, Sal would put you on the payroll."

I was getting used to Tony's badgering. Still, with ships, tugs, and launches all around; I kept a finger hovering over the 'standby' button, and a hand on the steering wheel. Nearing a vast cruise ship departing its dock, I jabbed the button and veered off to port, cutting close to a marker at the edge of the channel.

"Yep, Sal should definitely hire you," Tony said.

I felt my face turn red. "Sorry, mate. I went a bit too far."

"Ya think?" Tony pushed the throttle lever, increasing our speed to ten knots, double that of the *Spray* at full power.

"Tony, there's no need to be mean to him," Donatella said sharply.

"I'm teasing the puppy," Tony said. "I would've done the same thing. When a ship's that big and the channel is this narrow, you don't just get out of the way."

"The turbulence is enough to spill the wine." Sal had been in a jovial mood since Bruce joined the crew. "You want him on the payroll; it's your call Tony?"

"You heard him, Marco. She's yours for two hours."

Bruce headed off to unpack and familiarize himself with the engine. Sal, Donatella, and my father went below to rest. They had the sunset watch with Rocco.

+ + +

With the sea breeze freshening, the decision was daunting. Tony wasn't helping, not with his feet up and arms folded, enjoying the last of the sun. Dani was asleep on the opposite seat, lulled by the steady slap of waves and engine drone.

I couldn't stop myself from glancing repeatedly at faded jean-shorts with fake stains. Her thighs were slim, already browner than mine.

"Should we put up the sails?" I finally asked, anticipating more stress and a flurry of activity.

"Thought you'd never ask, Marco," Tony drawled. My father had shared his way to remind me.

He pressed buttons on a control panel, explaining the function of each one. Electric motors hummed, raising the mainsail and mizzen sail, and unfurling the jibs. He turned off the engine and adjusted sail shapes to make *Maid Marion* accelerate in the gusts. Our speed topped out at 12 knots, the bow slicing through waves, the stern leaving a long white wake behind.

Tony went to check that everything was properly secured below. I went to 'standby' mode, following the wind and steering with my fingertips, watching immense sails overhead, straining and taut as drums. This was sailing!

Dani woke up, sat up, looking around before she frowned at me.

"Hi."

It was all I could manage without making a fool of myself—her T-shirt had thin horizontal stripes like a contour map.

"Where is everyone?"

"Um, downstairs, I reckon."

She shook the wind from her hair. "They left you up here all by yourself?"

"Um, you're 'ere," I pointed out. I turned the wheel until the jibs stopped fluttering.

Dani bounced up. "How do you know which way to steer?"

I wriggled the wheel. "A little to port, a little to starboard; it's easy." Then, I stared at her front until I had to say more. "Um, there's sort of a rhythm; like music, I guess."

She dug into her ever-present shoulder bag. "That must be why you're so good at it."

"Mostly you listen, especially at night. You can feel the wind too. When everything's right, it makes the boat surge."

She brought up her cell phone. "You look cute behind the wheel, Marco."

I smiled for her, feeling inane, inarticulate, and unworthy.

"Could you teach me to sail?"

I didn't realize she meant right then and there until she was standing in front of me, her warm back pressed against my front.

"Don't hold the wheel so tight." My hands covered her hands, breathing jasmine-and-orange-blossom-scented hair.

"Now what?"

"My uncle once told me to close my eyes and listen to the sails."

"I don't like not seeing where I'm going, Josh."

"Then, don't close your eyes. When you see the front of the jib fluttering, turn the wheel away from the wind."

She tightened her grip. "It's not fluttering, Josh."

I moved her hands, turning towards the wind. "Go up means to go towards to the wind, Dani," I said in her ear.

The jibs wavered at the front, not enough to hear, just enough vibration to feel if you concentrated. Her hands were hot and trembling like mine.

"Now, go down, away from the wind." I turned the wheel with her. "It's either up and down, or down and up. That's the rhythm."

She pressed back against me. I pressed into her back. I couldn't stop myself. It was embarrassing.

"Gattino?" Sal called from the galley.

"Nonno, I'm up here."

I drew back as Sal stepped into the cockpit. I inched away again while he looked up at the sails.

"Tony's going over some charts with Bruce," I said, hoping it was the right answer.

Sal nodded slowly, taking in the hulking hills of almost-deserted Moreton Island. I worried when his eyes stopped on me.

Dani seemed oblivious. "Josh is teaching me how to steer, Nonno."

"I didn't realize that putting you on the payroll included giving sailing lessons to my granddaughter."

Immediately, the jibs started fluttering. Dani looked over her shoulder, seeking assurance. "I go right, right?"

"Rhythm, remember. Up and down, or down and up. If it's fluttering, go down until it stops. Then, back up slightly," I said, withering under Sal's steady gaze.

She turned to port, enough that the fluttering ceased. "I'm sailing, Nonno."

Sal beamed at her and turned to me. "I just spoke with Angelo. He thinks you're a musical genius."

"Nonno, you're embarrassing him!"

"Maybe that's my intention. Marion would like you to help her downstairs, Dani."

I took over the wheel and waited, checking the chart plotter for what lay ahead and worrying about what came next. Sal delayed until Dani was in the galley.

"I had a call from New York earlier. Zagarovsky had a private room at The Tsar's Samovar last night; it's a Russian restaurant in New York."

"If he was celebrating, it means I'm safe, right?"

"He dined with nine of his Bratva buddies so it's likely; however, you still need to be careful. Very goddamn careful." More than anything, his tone got my attention.

"Sal…"

"She called you Josh! Not once, a couple of times. You didn't remind her; and you spoke like a kid who grew up in Virginia. Again and again." He pointed two fingers, and fired twice at my face. "Just one slipup is all it takes."

"What if I don't want to be Marco Capra for the rest of my life?"

He shrugged as much as saying he didn't care what I wanted. "Act like you're an Australian with an Italian

140

heritage and you might see 16. Act like a horny teenager and you definitely won't."

"I didn't do anything, Sal."

He tilted his head. "You're 15 years old, Marco; I should know better than to leave you alone with Dani." He thumped my shoulder.

"I weren't doin' nothin,' Sal. I was showin' her 'ow to follow the wind, 'onest."

"At 15, just looking at a beautiful young girl can be a problem, especially if a boy is as good-looking as you. Touching her, Marco; that's hazardous to your health."

"I didn't mean to…"

He gave a disdainful gesture, dismissing argument. "When I was your age, I asked for permission."

"I'm supposed to ask beforehand?"

"If I was you, I'd ask in Italian."

I took a skeptical breath, unsure of what I was asking for. "Si prega posso avere il suo permesso?" (Please may I have your permission?)

"Granted." Sal gave a nod towards the salon. "Donatella likes you a lot. Don't mess it up, Marco. I'm harmless compared to the Bratva; they eat their young. You still don't want to upset me."

Chapter 15.

It was 822 nautical miles from Brisbane to Cairns. It took a week to get there, stopping at four islands along the way. On the last afternoon, with our destination only two hours away, we anchored in Welcome Bay on the lee side of Fitzroy Island.

Dani and I swam ashore. Everyone else piled into *Maid Marion's* inflatable dinghy. We were about halfway to the beach when we stopped for Dani to catch her breath. I sculled around her, doing duck dives and dolphin rolls. Dani splashed in my face if I came too close. I made plaintive dolphin sounds and looked offended.

"Dopey dolphin!"

"Dolphy wants a hug."

Dani scooped water. "Bad Dolphy. Comportarsi!"

I splashed back at her, side-stroking as she floated on her back, both of us flipping leisurely towards a white sand beach and a grey-roofed resort surrounded by palm trees.

"This is the longest we've been alone since I got here," Dani pointed out.

"Tony's got eyes on me; like a flamin' 'awk, 'e is."

"Because Sal told him to keep horny Australian boys away from me."

"Not fair! 'e's my bodyguard too," I mocked, openly sneaking peeks of her bare brown middle.

"To protect you from Zagarovsky." She sculled closer. "You're safe with me."

"Right!"

She caught me looking. "You're like a kid in a candy store."

She glanced at the front of my board shorts and grinned. A moment later, she fiddled with her bikini. I got a glimpse followed by a mouthful of salt water. I gave her a head start, caught up to her before she reached the beach, and yanked off her flippers. Then, we wrestled in waist-deep water.

+ + +

"I'm goin' for a walk with Dani and 'er mum."

"Just stay where Donatella can see you, Marco." My father sounded miffed.

"Now, what did I do wrong?"

He shook his head. I followed him down to the dinghy. He hoisted the drink cooler onto his shoulder. On the way back , I confronted him again. He made me carry the cooler while he explained it to me. Now, I was offended.

"Dani and I were clownin' around, that's all."

"Sal's old time Mafia. Annoy him; he'll cut off a finger. If it involves his granddaughter, it'll be something else he cuts off."

"I got it; only I didn't do nothin'," I protested.

"Doesn't matter. From the dinghy, it looked like you were all over her."

"Bloody 'ell!" I dumped the cooler in the sand. "I'm 15; I don't need you lookin' over my shoulder all the time."

"You do until you start thinking before you act."

He stooped and took the other handle. We started off again. We were almost at the picnic table when he said, "We need Sal on our side, Marco. We're using him, same as he's using you."

"Meaning what, exactly?"

He picked out a beer from the cooler and opened it, making it clear he wouldn't explain, even after I asked him again. I wandered along the beach. Nothing made sense. I wasn't even sure if he was on my side.

I caught up to Dani and Donatella at the boulders at the western end of the beach, round granite lumps emerging out of the sand, or stacked like cannonballs. The sun turned them into giant sculpture.

We followed a track away from the beach. A sign pointed left, up the hill, to 'Secret Garden.' Straight ahead was 'Nudey Beach.' Donatella went on regardless.

"Garden, Mom!" Dani objected.

"One of you can go look at flowers, but the other one comes with me," Donatella snickered over her shoulder.

Dani and I exchanged exasperation and incredulity. I couldn't help wondering what Aunt Vee would say. She was the most liberated person in my life.

"We don't have to take off our clothes," Dani whispered, watching her mother's back.

"Probably no one there anyway," I whispered back.

"If there are, we'll leave."

We sealed our pact with a hand squeeze.

We hiked through a rainforest and coastal woodlands, clambering over smooth sunbaked boulders, carefully picking our way down narrow steps carved in rock, cooling ourselves with water dribbling from green moss.

Donatella stopped overlooking a white sand beach. "This is as good a place as any to talk." She took a small boulder for herself.

With Nudey Beach visible through the trees, Dani grew increasingly nervous. There were people sunbathing and in the water, too far away to see anything, close enough to see they didn't have clothes.

"Dani, as you know, after Dante died, your grandfather became very protective of us," Donatella began.

Dani stopped her. "It's worse than ever, Mom."

"Seeing you and Marco together bothers him, Dani."

"Because he looks like Dante?"

"That's part of it. He's also from a time when parents controlled their children's lives until they moved out of the house. For better or worse, the world has changed," Donatella said. "I want the two of you to enjoy each other's company; however, there are rules. From now on, there will be no touching in public. Is that understood?"

She let it sink in. Dani nodded. I nodded.

"In private, I can't control what you do. What happens is up to you." Donatella waved at the beach. "This is private. If you want to see each other naked, you won't find a prettier place."

Dani gaped at her, disbelief palpable. I was too humiliated to do anything except stare at ants zeroing in on my feet.

"Momma, you're embarrassing us!"

Donatella laughed. "I'm teasing, Gattino. If by chance you do find somewhere private, the no touching rule covers anything that is presently covered. Everything else is fair game, assuming it's what you want. If you don't, then say so."

It sounded like something Aunt Vee would say; however, Dani regarded her with suspicion.

+ + +

By the time we hiked back to the resort, the *Spray* had arrived, uncharacteristically anchored in the midst of six other yachts. Dani and I waved at Nature Boy, momentarily interrupting his exploration of grey-boulder' ecosystems. Jessie whooped and ran over, dragging Dani to help her forage for shells at the water's edge. Everyone else was at the picnic table, imbibing and snacking on Celia's delicacies.

After introducing Donatella, I sat next to Aunt Vee and Sarah, looking the other way to avoid Sal's gaze. It was only a minute before Jessie ran up fetch Sarah.

"Can we talk sometime?" I asked quietly.

"This sounds so serious we better do it right away," Aunt Vee joked. She put her wineglass on the table and gave me a hug. "We can always talk, Josh," she whispered in my ear.

We walked along the beach, away from Ben and his boulders.

"Is everything okay?" she asked as soon as we were out of range.

"Mostly," I ventured, calming down. "This isn't about Dad and me."

"Dani?"

"Kind of. Everyone's mad at me."

Aunt Vee came right to the point. "Did you do something, Marco?"

"I don't think I did. The first time I was teaching Dani how to sail and I got a sermon from Sal about needing permission even to look at her. I was just standing behind her, helping her steer. I thought he liked me, and he got mad. "

"You were too close to her, I expect. People have different comfort ranges."

"Since then, Tony's been watching me nonstop. He jokes about me and Dani, only it's like he thinks I'm about to do something wrong and he's warning me."

She considered it. "Anything else happen?"

I told her about swimming ashore, my father's lecture, and Donatella's response, though talking with Aunt Vee made it seem less bizarre.

"We were having fun, tussling over her flippers."

"Again, too close for comfort," she surmised.

"All we did was splash each other. I barely touched her!"

"At your age, it doesn't take much for the libido to switch on. A few splashes and things get out of control," she teased.

"That mean what I think it does?"

"You want the 'growing up' lecture again?"

"I got it the first time."

We watched Dani and Jessie prance around Sarah, urging her to go into the water with them. Finally, Sarah hiked up her summer dress and waded through the shallows. Often, the best shells hid under the sand.

"I might be wrong," Aunt Vee went on. "I think Sal's worried about losing you."

"I look like Dante, but that's as far as it goes."

"He's very protective."

I sensed she wanted to say more, yet held back. "Not what you'd expect from a Mafia boss, huh?"

She took my hand. "It often happens when we lose someone we're very close to. You're the same way. When we moved to Norfolk, I was in my last month of pregnancy with Ben. You'd sit for hours with your hand on my tummy to feel him moving around. If I as much as burped, you'd worry that something was wrong."

+ + +

The next morning, under Sal's watchful eye, Dani and I said goodbye. We hugged until Sal cleared his throat. She was blinking tears as I kissed her forehead, much the same as I'd done with Donatella.

A moment before we parted, she nuzzled my cheek and whispered, "Ti voglio bene."

147

With 'I love you' ringing in my ears, Sal cleared his throat again. Without delay, I backed away. His eyes narrowed.

Though I hadn't done anything wrong, I stammered, "B-bye G-Gattino."

I stayed on the *Maid Marion*, basking in misery while Tony took mother and daughter ashore in the dinghy. I didn't . stop waving until they reached the resort wharf.

When I turned around, Sal was watching me. I expected another lecture.

"Sei anime gemelle."

It slowly sank in. Dani and I were soulmates. It was the nicest thing he'd said to me since they arrived, and the last thing I expected him to say.

"It's safer this way," he added.

I was still puzzled when the Fitzroy Island ferry drew way from the wharf, and began the 30-minute trip to Cairns, where Dani and Donatella would board a plane for Los Angeles.

I avoided everyone and occupied the bow pulpit. It was several hours later, as *Maid Marion* and the *Spray* drifted sluggishly on Welcome Bay, when I watched a big jet ascend in the west. As it passed overhead, I pictured Dani looking out the window. I waved until my father saw me.

He came forward. "You'll see her again." He clasped my shoulder. "If it helps, I still think about your mom every day."

"I barely remember her." I omitted the accent.

For once, he let it slide. "We've been talking about what happens now."

He glanced back at the cockpit where Sal and Tony were conversing.

"Now that I ain't shark bait?"

"Zagarovsky was after both of us. He wanted to kill you in front of me, and then kill me. If you're dead and I've disappeared; what's he do next?"

"He'll keep lookin' for you."

"Very likely."

I could see the sandy bottom, so far down I'd need lead weights to get there. A giant manta ray wafted above clumps of sea grass, sending schools of black and yellow fish diving for cover.

"You're leavin', ain't ya?"

"On the next ferry. I'll be gone a month, maybe longer."

"After 12 bloody years, what's a couple of months."

He flinched. "You're right to be pissed. Tony heard from his cousin in New York that Zagarovsky's got his people looking for me."

"Then why go?"

"I have to sell the house and restaurant, Marco."

"You need the money that bad?"

"There are some loose ends I need to attend to." Before I could step back, he ruffled my hair as if I was still a little kid. "Your hair needs dying again."

"I can do it myself."

"Make sure you do it every two weeks. And keep using the contacts."

"I forgot to put 'em in this mornin', okay."

"Sal thinks you should have a choice in this," he went on. "While I'm gone, you can stay on the *Maid Marion,* if you want."

"Or?"

"Move back to the *Spray.*"

"Are you kidding?"

"I thought you'd miss them by now?"

"I get to share the world's tiniest head with Sarah, Ben, and Jessie; or I can have my own cabin and bathroom; what's to miss?"

"Be honest, Marco." As reminders went, it was deserved.

"It's lonely bein' the only kid. I like havin' 'em around."

"I'll tell Sal and Marion." He handed me two $50 notes. "Pocket money. I'll send more when I can."

"Thanks." I tucked the notes in my pocket. "You goin' to see Erin and Tanner?"

"Erin's dad is taking care of them."

He didn't elaborate. I felt awful for saying it.

Chapter 16.

From mid-morning to mid-afternoon, when the sun was high in the sky, Uncle John motored cautiously through the coral reefs and sandbars of Torres Strait, usually with me stationed in the bow as lookout. The rest of the time, the *Spray* drifted in light wind, heaved to in rain downpours, or anchored where it was safe to do so. Every day we snorkeled, catching fish and picking up shells to add to Ben's growing collection.

It was late in the afternoon when I brought up a shell as big as a Frisbee. Ben was bug-eyed as I tried to pry the sides apart.

"It's a Pinctada maxima! Big ones are really rare."

"Since when is an overgrown oyster a big deal?"

"The Torres Strait islands used to be famous for them. There might even be a pearl inside."

"If you can open it, you can have it." I handed my knife to Nature Boy.

Split open, the dull shell revealed a slimy oyster nurturing a perfect pea-sized pearl. More beautiful was the smooth lustrous interior, mother of pearl shell much sought after by the pearling luggers of the 20th century. Ben and I were still deciding what to do with the pearl when we docked at Thursday Island. Uncle John planned to stay only as long as it took to refuel.

In front of the *Spray* was a rusty homemade steel ketch, *Rock and Roll*, home port, Gibraltar. Clothes draped the safety rail, clipped with wooden pegs. A potted bean plant swung from the boom, leaves dangling over a wooden steering wheel so old it might have belonged to Captain Slocum's *Spray*. A white-haired man went back and forth from the cockpit to check fishing rods at the stern. Each time, he bumped his head on the mizzen boom. Anyone else would have moved it, or ducked. That he crossed the oceans with his boat was both reassuring, yet disturbing.

On the other side of the wharf was a small modern yacht that hailed from Stockholm, Sweden. A woman who looked like a middle-aged pixie sat in the cockpit, busily chiseling at a block of reddish wood despite the heat. At the top end of Australia, winter was only a few degrees cooler than summer. The end of April was hot and unpleasantly humid, even though the rainy season was nearly over.

She looked up, noticed me putting on the mainsail cover, and waved. I went over to talk with her before she went back to work. Anna made jewelry boxes from materials acquired during her travels. She sold them to support herself and her daughter.

"The wood is sandalwood, from India." She carefully scraped her chisel into the corners. It was so sharp it left the wood polished, machine-smooth, yet clearly handmade. "On the outside, I will use mother of pearl. To buy shell is why we are here. Elsa, can you bring the last box?"

Elsa, seven years old, scrambled up the stairs, jewelry box in hand. During our travels, I'd seen jewelry boxes at markets in Charleston, Rio de Janeiro, and small towns scattered through the Caribbean and South Pacific. They ranged from wood blocks to carved chests ornately decorated with bone, shell, and different types of wood. None of them were as striking as Anna's simple geometric box.

She gave me a sliver of sandalwood to smell.

It reminded me of Dani in a way that made my heart race. "Kinda like perfume."

"Mamma's favorite perfume is sandalwood oil with jasmine and orange blossom," Elsa said, sniffing the air.

"It was when I could afford it," Anna laughed.

I'd priced perfume online. I couldn't afford it either, not when Dani's 14th birthday was only five weeks away.

I opened the finished jewelry box. "It's really nice," I muttered, accent forgotten.

"He wants one for his girlfriend, Mamma."

I stroked wood, so warm and silky my libido reared up. Amused, Anna winked at me.

"It's beautiful." I inhaled sandalwood fragrance yet again. "Pretty pricey, I bet?"

She shrugged. "With good design, the look is expensive."

I had $97.60 left after buying Tim Tams in Cairns. It wasn't enough to buy a tiny bottle of French perfume. It certainly wasn't enough to buy a jewelry box. Reluctantly, I placed the box on the cockpit seat.

"My boat needs to be polished," Anna said.

Except for a shopping trip when we first arrived at Thursday Island, I didn't do much of anything for five days except schoolwork and work on Anna's boat until it looked new again.

+ + +

We were at anchor, sitting in the cockpit enjoying Sarah's dinner of lime-baked grouper and tomato salad, when Ben presented the educational benefits of visiting the museum on Horn Island. Horn Island was the next island over, many times bigger than Thursday Island. It was only a dinghy ride away.

I flexed arms sore from waxing and polishing. "I think we should go tomorrow."

"I'll book it after dinner," Uncle John chuckled. "I like the new you. Not half as stubborn as the old you."

"A little history, a little science; what's not to like?" I said.

Sarah and Aunt Vee exchanged questioning looks.

Jessie glanced up from rearranging salad on her plate. "He's got a reason."

"I'm sure he has." Uncle John frowned at her starburst of tomato and green pepper slices. "I expect you to eat all of it when you're done."

It was as good a time as any. "That shell I gave Ben; I want Anna to use it in Dani's jewelry box," I said. "I'll buy it back if I have to."

Ben smirked. "See; I told you he's in love with her."

Everyone stopped eating and looked at me. I tried to ignore them, scooping up Jag to feed him white flakes of grouper. I could feel my face glowing.

As soon as we'd cleared to table, I motored across to Anna's boat to deliver the good news. She'd never seen a mother-of-pearl shell that big.

+ + +

With six people crammed on board, *Squirt* rocked so much you thought it was about to tip over. Ben and I were in the bow where the bouncing was worse. After diverting around the sandbars, we headed into the tide. With the wind behind us, the waves became steep and choppy, drenching Ben and me with spray.

"Should'a gone the other way, Nature Boy," I said under my breath.

"Up yours." Ben gestured rudely; it was his idea to go the shortest way.

"Do it right, mate." I gestured in his face.

He slapped my hand away. I cuffed his head. Grinning, he elbowed my side. I splashed water in his face. He splashed back. Not that it mattered; we were already soaked to the skin. It made me realize how much I missed him.

Only Jessie saw us. Aunt Vee and Sarah were facing astern to avoid the spray; and Uncle John was busy trying to dodge the biggest waves.

Horn Island had two jetties crowded with barges, commercial fishing boats, runabouts, two big sport-fishing boats, and a solitary sailboat. Ben and I were so busy pretend-fighting we didn't notice Uncle John was heading for the beach between the jetties.

"Shoes off and get out," he directed.

Ben snapped a defiant salute.

He cut the motor and Ben and I hopped from the dinghy to drag it across stones and shells, all the way to the water's edge. Dozens of grey and white seagulls scattered, their erratic wheeling and raucous calls culled from a horror movie. Within seconds, they were back, ravaging schools of tiny fish. They were so bold we could come right up to them before they flew off.

+ + +

With some 500 residents on Horn Island, the entire town occupied only a half-dozen blocks. Houses were spread out, small and unpretentious, no different to any Australian outback town we'd seen. There wasn't much to see; two run-of-the-mill tourist resorts, a hotel, and a small supermarket. After buying snacks and refilling our water bottles, we headed off to find the museum.

The museum was a half-block from the water, a squat red building with a mini-tour-bus parked under straggly trees, along with two cars, and a rental golf cart with a white cooler stuffed in the rear. We went inside while we waited for our 11:00 am 'lunch and tour' to depart.

The air-conditioning was down for repairs; however, every window was open, muslin curtains pulled aside. A cool draft wafted scents and insect sounds from outside.

Ben grabbed a brochure from the counter display and consumed it in seconds. "In World War 2, Horn Island was strategically important because of the airfield."

"Bein' with you is like 'avin' a personal tour guide," I said.

"Listen and you might learn something," Ben fired back

"Cool it! People don't want to listen to your sniping," Uncle John grouched.

Regardless, Ben went on reading, loudly so I heard every word. "'From here, Australian and American airplanes could bomb Japanese positions.' That was why it was attacked so often."

The calamities of war didn't affect Ben. He stopped at every display and read every sign. The photos were enough for me; Jessie too. Until Aunt Vee dragged her away, she'd been poring over faded photos of the airfield after it had been bombed. Among the ruins of the field hospital, bandaged soldiers and airmen lay in foldup cots with nurses hovering nearby. Fires were still burning in the coconut trees along the beach. A plume of smoke rose from a crashed bomber; its left wing skewed out of the water.

War was hell even in a tropical paradise; heat, disease, rationing lousy food and filthy water, and air raids. Done with World War II, I meandered into 'Torres Strait Pearling.'

A man and woman were studying a display of fake pearls and mother of pearl shell. Wondering if they were going on our tour, I went the other way, drawn to a detailed model of a sailing lugger, circa 1922.

Uncle John had stationed himself in front of diving apparatus, tubes and a rope going up to the blue-painted ceiling, a canvas suit with lead boots, and a huge spherical helmet with little portholes. He gave me an amused look.

"If you went down in this, what are the chances you'd come up alive?"

After being told to 'cool it,' I wasn't in the mood. "Better than goin' down without it, mate," I muttered as I walked away.

He seemed surprised, even hurt. I didn't want that. Besides, I was sure the man and woman were listening to us. She lifted her dark sunglasses as if to examine the pearls. Instead, she looked directly at Uncle John.

I lowered my voice. "I'm sorry, okay!"

"I'm sorry too." He nodded hopefully. "I've missed your kooky humor."

"It's better this way. You said so yourself."

His jaw dropped. "I shouldn't have said that."

"But you did."

"If I hadn't, it'd be something else just as stupid." He lowered his voice to a whisper. "After the bomb went off, your safety was all that mattered."

I could tell he wanted to say more. I wasn't sure what I wanted any more. I headed for 'Torres Strait Art' in the next room. I wasn't the only person leaving; the man and woman were already at the front door.

"It bothers me when you guys fight," he said to my back.

I immersed myself in indigenous art and artefacts, not Australian aborigines, Melanesian culture like that of Papua New Guinea. The myths and legends of Torres Strait Islanders went back to when the islands formed a land bridge to Australia.

Sarah was busily sketching a tribal face mask in her journal. Aunt Vee joined us after Jessie went outside to look at 'Torres Strait Agriculture', a weedy plot of coconut palms, wild fruit trees, and root vegetables like cassava and taro.

At 10:55 am, Linda, the museum curator, announced that we should board the minibus. It had pulled up alongside the museum a few minutes earlier. Uncle John, Aunt Vee, and Sarah made a beeline for it, hoping to stake a claim on six seats together. I went to fetch Ben and Jessie. I found Ben examining the rusted remains of a fighter plane engine and sent him on his way. Jessie wasn't in the garden. I went through the entire museum, including the restroom before I panicked.

Chapter 17.

I was breathless after running to the beach to see if Jessie had gone back to the dinghy. "Not a sign. I checked the boats like you said."

"And?" Uncle John prompted, optimism lurking.

"I didn't recognize any of them, just *Rock and Roll.*"

"He's weird, but harmless." Like me, he couldn't remember the old man's name, even after he gave us a freshly caught grouper.

"I told Ben to stay at the dinghy in case she returned."

Uncle John regarded me tiredly. He'd assigned himself the job of circling the museum in increasingly wider loops. I'd heard him calling her name.

"I asked a few people on the way back too," I added. "No one saw her."

"Goddamn!" he exploded. "Where is she?"

"John, let's take this a step at a time." Aunt Vee stepped into shade of a banana tree, smearing sweat on her forehead. She'd jogged to the supermarket, three blocks away, even though it was highly unlikely Jessie would go there without asking permission. "We don't even know that Zagarovsky has her."

"You think she just wandered off by herself; or she chased a stray cat? Maybe she made a new friend and forgot the time."

"John, anything's possible in this godforsaken hole."

Sarah had stayed at the museum in case Jessie came back. "Why would Zagarovsky take Jessie?"

He glared at me. "Oh, he's got her, Sarah. She's bait for him!"

"Why take her, when I'm right here?" I asked.

"He's got a point, John." Aunt Vee hesitated, as much as saying if Zagarovsky's men had recognized me, I'd be kidnapped or dead.

"It doesn't make sense," he agreed.

"We need to contact the police, John."

"You call them! I'll look."

He turned at a noise from behind one of the two remaining cars in the parking lot. A mangy dog scraped through a pile of discarded ice cubes.

"I can't wait for some local cop to finish his lunch."

He stalked off, skirting the museum. Sarah and I trooped behind. He stopped in 'Torres Strait Agriculture.'

"When the cops arrive, I'll do the talking," he warned. "Marco, make sure you stay in character." He looked around. "She had to leave from here or we'd have seen her."

A low wire-netting fence surrounded the garden. Beyond, seldom-cut grass ended in a thicket of bushes. In the gaps were a few small metal-roofed houses and sheds.

"Did you check the sheds?" Sarah asked testily.

I was worried, too. It wasn't like Jessie to leave without telling someone.

He pointed at a shed with a white roof. "Except for that one, they're locked. It's time we knocked on doors."

"If someone took her; how did they do it?" I asked, trying to stay calm and think it through the way my father would.

He gave an impatient sigh. "In a car, most likely."

"Not possible. We'd have heard it," Sarah argued.

+ + +

Harriet Dodson was unflustered. Her questions came slowly because she wrote everything down, from our names and ages, to the exact circumstances of Jessie's disappearance.

She ended with, "Clothes?"

"She was wearing a pink T-shirt with a koala bear on the front," Sarah answered. "White shorts, and sneakers. Blue with red laces."

"Blinky Bill or another koala?"

Bewildered, Sarah gaped back.

"Was the bear on the T-shirt wearing pants, Mum?" Senior Constable Dodson queried.

"Red overalls, actually."

Uncle Ron was on the verge of shouting.

"Then, she was wearing a pink Blinky Bill T-shirt." She wrote it down before she looked up again. "If it's a favorite, it's likely she ran away."

"It wasn't a favorite," Uncle John snapped.

"Then, she's wandered off," she concluded.

"Jessie doesn't wander off!"

While he waited for her to jot down the rest of Jessie's attire, he stared at me, either blaming me, or a warning to keep my mouth shut.

When she finished writing, she plucked a green grape from a plastic bag. "I was eating lunch when your call came in."

He looked at her blankly.

"You said she's nine," she went on, grape pinched between her thumb and first finger. "Even teenagers wander off, Mr. Walker."

He took a deep breath. "I've gone to all the houses on this street, and my wife is doing the next street over. No one has seen her."

"That's my job, Sir, not yours." She popped the grape in her mouth and reached for another. "The best thing you can do is stay calm and…"

"We think she may have been kidnapped," Sarah interrupted.

"Highly unlikely, Mum. That sort of thing only happens in America. Here, the kids either run away or wander off. I'll get a search organized. Rest assured we'll find her by nightfall."

"We've been searching for two hours, Constable." Somehow, Uncle John controlled himself. "Marco's gone back and forth along the waterfront. We've walked all over town. My son is waiting at our dinghy in case she goes there."

She looked at me, a third green grape in hand. I had a bad feeling, until she smiled reassuringly. "All good steps to take, Sir. Even if she's gone inland, there's no need to panic."

"I'm not panicking."

"Mr. Walker, I'm not new to this. We had a missing child just a month ago. Little Marty Tully. The next day we found him hiding under a neighbor's house. Poor thing had been bullied by some boys from Thursday Island."

"My daughter is not hiding."

"I didn't say she was, Mr. Walker. I don't want to worry you unnecessarily; we take getting lost in the bush very seriously, even if the island is only five miles across. Unfortunately, it's crawling with deadly snakes and spiders, and a fair number of poisonous plants. The best thing you and your family can do is wait here while I round up some volunteers for a search party."

We watched her walk back to her police car, eating grapes from her lunch bag.

"You and Ben take *Squirt* and bring back the *Spray*. We'll keep searching." Uncle John grasped my shoulder. "If Zagarovsky's behind this…"

"I'll be careful. We should contact Sal," I suggested.

"Send him an email before you leave. With luck, he's still in Port Moresby."

Four days earlier, the last time I emailed Sal, *Maid Marion* was docked at the Royal Papua Yacht Club.

.+ + +

Anna waved vigorously as we raced past boats anchored off Thursday Island. I diverted from a beeline to the *Spray*, hoping she had news of Jessie. Instead, she handed over the finished jewelry box, a surprisingly large package wrapped in boring brown paper tied with string.

"We need to go, Anna. Jessie's missing," I blurted.

Anna gaped at me.

"Dad thinks someone kidnapped her," Ben shouted.

I shoved the outboard into gear, opened the throttle, and swerved away from Anna's yacht. I didn't slow down until *Squirt* slammed into the *Spray*. Ben and I jumped. He tied off the painter while I started the engine and raised the anchor.

"Take the wheel." I grabbed the jewelry box and rushed downstairs to email Sal.

+ + +

It was late in the afternoon when I steered towards the jetties, looking for a space big enough to dock the *Spray*. Ben dragged two fenders from under the cockpit seats and readied dock lines at the bow and stern. The first jetty was full, two barges loaded with building materials, another barge stacked with logs, two fishing trawlers, and a launch undergoing repair. There was plenty of space at the start of the jetty; however, the *Spray* would be hard aground when the tide went out.

I motored over to the second jetty, occupied by a barge carrying a truck and fuel drums, another fishing trawler, two sport-fishing boats, and the rusty steel ketch from Gibraltar. A policeman walked along the dock until he reached a golf cart blocking access.

I saw a chance to talk about something other than Jessie.

"There's a moron at every marina," I said.

I got a smile from Ben. "Maybe he'll get a ticket for stupidity."

The driver leisurely got off the biggest of the sport-fishing boats and sauntered over to speak to the policeman. After a few moments, the policeman pointed at the parking area at the end of the dock. He continued on, momentarily surveying each vessel before he moved on to the next.

With both jetties full, we motored on, anchoring the *Spray* close enough to shore that it gave some protection from the wind. We jumped in the dinghy, hoping we'd find everyone waiting for us on the beach. Instead, four islanders walked slowly along the shore, poking among rocks, driftwood, and trash.

We skirted mangroves and a small muddy creek that Ben insisted was the ideal habitat for a saltwater crocodile. After stomping a path through dry prickly grass to scare off venomous reptiles, we met up with Uncle John and Aunt Vee.

"I watched you anchor. You guys did a good job." He was tense, though doing his best to stay calm.

"Any news?" Ben asked for both of us.

I dabbed blood from my leg where thorns had ripped through the skin. Aunt Vee looked on, too worried to offer assistance.

"Dodson's convinced Jessie went this way," she said.

"According to the Senior Constable, 'Kids like the water.'" Uncle John's sneer was without equal.

"She's only saying what she thinks is most likely, John. There's no sign anyone took her," Aunt Vee said tiredly. She turned completely around, scanning clumps of brush and piles of trash beside the road.

"I told her Jessie never goes anywhere without telling someone." He managed a weak smile at me. "You, on the other hand, are like a dog after squirrels."

"It's all a bit dodgy, if you ask me," I ventured.

He nodded for me to continue.

"Tell him, Josh," Ben prodded.

"Go on," Aunt Vee prompted.

"We didn't talk to anyone about where we were going today. I didn't even tell Anna. After we got here, we didn't see more than a handful of people."

"A few men at the wharf, the lady at the store checkout, Linda at the museum. What's your point?" He was impatient.

"Zagarovsky couldn't know we were here."

With a warning toot, one of the sport-fishing boats departed the nearest jetty. It was white and large with a flybridge. For an awful moment, I thought it was the same boat that had followed us up the Queensland coast when it headed towards the *Spray*. However, it had high outriggers and rods set up for big game fishing. There was no reason to point it out.

"Meaning some weirdo took her?" he barked.

I didn't want to admit the possibility. "It makes as much sense as Zagarovsky taking Jessie as bait for me. Or her wandering off," I added.

"Where's your father when we need him?" Aunt Vee sniped.

165

Chapter 18.

With rain clouds looming; Sarah, Ben, and I raced back to the *Spray*. A few minutes later and it would've been too dark to see where we were going. We climbed aboard, worried, tired, and hungry. We'd eaten only snacks since breakfast. Sarah made sandwiches, Ben fed Jag, and I checked the anchor and made sure nothing would be damaged by the rain.

Below, I switched on the anchor light and checked email using Sarah's cell phone. Sal had answered my email only minutes after I sent it. His response was blunt. 'Leaving noon. MM ETA 28 hours.'

"Sarah, *Maid Marion* will be here at 6:00 pm tomorrow," I called out. I forwarded the email to Uncle John. "Tomorrow morning, I'm taking *Squirt* and searching along the shore after I drop you and Ben off at the beach."

"I'm coming too," Ben interjected. He'd been on the verge of bawling since his mother and father sent him back to the *Spray*.

"You've both come such a long way. I remember you were afraid of leaving your friends, unable to do much..." Sarah pulled off a paper towel and wiped her nose. "Now look at you. So self-assured and capable; you're like two different boys."

"I'm the same old me, only two years smarter." Ben managed to get it out with only a sniffle. "Marco dropped out of school."

I threw Jag's rubber mouse at him.

Rain splattered on the hatches. The *Spray* creaked and turned to the breeze, taking the current broadside with walloping waves. It was going to be a long, bumpy night.

+ + +

I stepped into the cockpit and stretched. My eyes burned in the bright morning light. I remembered getting up after the rain ended, talking with Sarah into the middle of the night, both of us too worried to go back to bed. My neck ached from sleeping on the settee.

All around, schools of fish darted, plopping in glimmering water, while Australian pelicans paddled on the fringes, ready to plunge. Predictably, three yachts previously at Thursday Island, were anchored nearby, including Anna's boat—sailors helped out in times of emergency. North of town, a commuter jet banked right, wheels down and flaps extended as it lined up its final approach to the airstrip. Any other time, I'd fetch a camera.

I didn't notice the sheet of paper stuck over the floor drain until I started back down the stairs. I peeled it off, tearing it twice before I realized there was writing on the other side. It was almost unreadable, printed letters smeared and fuzzy. I reassembled the pieces on the cockpit table, blinking in the bright morning light as I tried to decipher what remained.

"Sarah, I need you up here!" I shouted.

She rushed up the stairs, Ben on her heels. They crowded around, peering down. She followed each letter and smudge with her finger, muttering to herself. She might've been translating a papyrus manuscript.

"Zagarovsky has Jess, right?" Ben's voice cracked.

"It says 'We' and 'her.'" I pointed where the paper was shredded. "I'm betting that was 'have'. This is '24 hours'," I added, pointing lower.

Sarah nodded absently, still pondering smears. "I'm not certain. I think it says 'swap in 24 hours.'" She adjusted her glasses. "Unless I'm mistaken, they'll swap her for you."

She went over each line again and again, shaking her head. "It's a pity it got soaked. It must have been left here yesterday afternoon."

While she carefully placed paper fragments inside one of Ben's notebooks, and copied the legible letters on the opposite page; I sent another email to Uncle John. Ben grabbed cookies and sunscreen, and stuffed water bottles into an insulated carry-bag. Minutes later, I ran the dinghy onto the beach. Again, Uncle John and Aunt Vee were waiting.

This time, Senior Constable Dodson was with them, her police blouse wrinkled, her skirt flecked with grass burrs. She studied the remains, her brow furrowed, squinting in the sunlight.

"Could be anything," she surmised. "Something one of you wrote most likely."

"It's not ours!" Uncle John's hand was clenched so tightly his knuckles were white.

"You're suggesting someone put it on your boat?"

"There's no other explanation," he snapped.

"We didn't see it when we got back. It was too dark," I added.

Calmly, Sarah took over. "I'm quite sure it says, 'We have her.' Then, it's anyone's guess until '24 hours.' After that, I think it says 'swap her for him.'"

"Who would this 'him' be?" Dodson asked.

It was all I could do to stay in character. "'im would be me, Mum."

Dodson brushed that off with a curt shake of her head. "Looks more like directions to me." She stabbed her finger at a group of badly blurred letters. "'T I N E', that's got to be Thursday Island, northeast. It's a prime fishing spot."

"Without context, 'T I N E' could be anything. I don't know about you; I can't read the letters before it!" Sarah was justifiably abrupt.

Senior Constable Dodson looked up. "Could it have blown onto the boat?"

"Very unlikely, but yes; it's possible," Uncle John allowed.

She frowned. "Right. Well, until we're certain she hasn't wandered off; we need to keep searching."

"Let's assume for the moment my daughter was kidnapped," Aunt Vee began. "The 24-hour period is since she disappeared."

Senior Constable Dodson was unflappable. "Very unlikely, Mum. You need to be patient. She'll turn up soon. They all do."

"Assume she was kidnapped," Aunt Vee repeated. "It means we have four hours left. We need to do something besides argue."

"If you're suggesting a house to house search; we're not set up for that. I'll have to call in Thursday Island."

"You should've done that yesterday." Uncle John held the notebook in front of Senior Constable Dodson. "You want evidence? Here it is."

"Sir, we don't know it's a ransom note." She hesitated, again peering at the open notebook and Sarah's transcription. "If it is, why 'swap her for him'? It makes no sense at all. He's not even your son."

He took a breath. "Marco and my nephew were friends before he died. He's staying with us while his dad sorts out a few problems."

Senior Constable Dodson regarded me, suspicions forming the longer I kept silent.

"'e drinks too much," I said after a much delayed shrug. I made her wait for the rest. "Sometimes, 'e turns mean."

"You saying he hits you?" she demanded.

"Gets real mean, 'e does." The implication was obvious.

"What's his name, Marco?"

"Mario Capra. C-a-p-r-a."

She wrote it down. "This swap, what's that about?"

I shrugged again. I glanced around. Ben was behind Sarah, lips clamped and trying hard not to smirk.

"Bets on the 'orses; it's all 'e does."

She frowned. "So your dad gambles a lot?"

"Me mum threw 'im out 'cause of it."

"Those problems your father is sorting out, they're gambling debts, I take it?"

"Reckon."

Senior Constable Dodson arrived at the obvious conclusion. "There must be a lot of money at stake."

"Borrowed on the 'ouse, didn't 'e? Only it weren't 'nough, so me and 'im come to Queensland, only 'e got in more trouble."

"We met Marco and his dad at Wongaling Beach. They have problems wherever they go," Uncle John said.

Senior Constable Dodson wrote it down. "I can see why."

Sarah gave a disparaging grunt. "I think owing money to bookies is enough reason to kidnap someone."

"Except there isn't any proof; not with this note." Senior Constable Dodson closed her notebook.

Aunt Vee was open-mouthed.

"Sorry, Mum. I'm just being honest. If there's nothing else, we need to get back to the search."

I flashed a sideways glance at Ben. "We want to take *Squirt* and search along the shore. Jessie might've gone to see where the field hospital was and gotten lost."

170

"You've got three hours. We're going to the police station. It's on Nawie Street," Uncle John growled.

With Sarah dragging in the rear, they cautiously made their way back to the road, got into the police car, and drove off with hazard lights blinking.

Ben and I shoved the dinghy into knee-deep water, turned it around, and climbed in. I started the motor and headed east, towards the nearest jetty.

Chapter 19.

"We're checking the boats, right?" Ben asked when I slowed the dinghy to go past the first jetty.

"No point. A cop was checking them yesterday when we brought back the *Spray*," I reminded him.

I opened the throttle, heading for the next jetty. After that, I stayed close to shore. Using the map in Ben's museum brochure, we went all the way to the north end of the island, slowing down when we spotted the ruins of an anti-aircraft battery at the end of the airstrip. The field hospital was long gone. The map also showed wreckage from a B-17. If it was there, we didn't see it.

We stopped to put on more suntan lotion. I sipped water while Ben studied the map. He was sweating and his hair stuck to his forehead. I made him put on a hat.

"What I don't get is how they knew we were there?" he asked.

"I was thinking about it all night. Either one of us messed up somehow, or they just happened to be there."

"I've been wondering…" He trailed off. "What if she's dead?"

"She's not." It hurt whenever I thought about it. It didn't matter that she wasn't my real sister. "Zagarovsky wants to swap Jess for me, I'm all for it."

"Mom and Dad won't do it; you know they won't."

"We better get back." I pointed *Squirt* in the opposite direction.

"Josh… What are we going to do?"

"Keep lookin', mate. That's all we can do."

Ben sniffed and started gnawing his knuckle. "You really think one of us screwed up?"

"Most likely me. It's hard to be someone else all the time."

I took a fresh bottle from the cooler, unscrewed the cap, and handed it to Ben. He took a small drink and went back to gnawing.

"Ben, if you wanted to take Jess from the museum so we wouldn't know, how would you do it?"

"She'd never go with a stranger without making a fuss." Ben shrugged wearily. "She'd have to be unconscious, or tied up and gagged."

"Or so scared she can't move," I added.

"Not much scares Jessie."

"She's pretty tough, unlike you." I got him to smile.

"About the only thing she hates is being in my berth when the curtain's closed."

"Remember that time we played hide and seek and I locked her in the broom closet for cheating? She lost it big time."

Ben smiled again, though neither of us had smiled at the time. When we released her, she was curled up like a fetus. It took both of us to get her back to normal.

"You were so worried she'd tell Mom and Dad, you gave her the rest of your Halloween candy," Ben said, leaning out of reach.

+ + +

We were approaching the first jetty when I noticed Ben wiping the water bottle against his cheek. He was flushed and blinking, and gnawing on his knuckles again. I tried to ignore him, hoping he would stop. Instead, his arm started trembling.

"You gettin' 'eatstroke, mate?" I said, though it made no sense to keep using the accent.

173

He shook his head and whispered, "I can't stop thinking about Jessie."

"Yeah, me too, Ben."

I didn't slow down when we passed the jetties. At the last moment, I veered towards the jetty with the sport-fishing boats. On the first boat, a man stopped dragging a cooler across the foredeck and gestured obscenely. I didn't care. Time was running out.

With the tide rising, we dragged Squirt up the beach and rammed the anchor between two rocks. I left Ben standing on the beach and started up to the road. His map showed the police station two blocks away.

He didn't follow.

"Get it in gear, Benjamin," I shouted. I went back to get him.

"I've been thinking about how they got Jessie away from the museum," Ben said, stubborn and staring at the nearest jetty. "What if they put her in a car trunk?"

"No car. We'd have heard it leave."

"They put her in a laundry bag and carried her off?"

I rejected the idea outright. "People usually don't carry laundry bags around with them." However, it made me think about backpacks and suitcases.

"Didn't Sal say he'd be here at six pm?"

I stopped thinking and looked where Ben was looking. There was a white-haired man with a Floridian tan talking with an islander on the fishing trawler. Maybe it was Sal; maybe it wasn't.

"It sure looks like him," I murmured.

"There's your dad!" Ben pointed.

He was farther down the dock, looking over the barge with the truck and fuel drums. He was still bald, wearing the grass-green golf-shirt he'd bought in Brisbane.

"How did they get here?" I pondered aloud.

"By plane, of course." Ben was already on the move.

He loped down the beach. I jogged after him. Sal spotted us as soon as we reached the jetty. We skirted fishing nets, piles of rope, and slatted wood boxes stacked in rows with seagulls perched on top.

"Any sign of Jessie?" Sal asked throatily.

"No."

"Should've expected this." He faltered, glancing around. "I need to sit down for a while."

Ben and I followed him back to the boxes. He was breathing heavily, and fast.

"You okay?" I asked. His face was beetroot red.

"The heat. Long day yesterday." He mopped his forehead and sighed. "I was certain Zagarovsky gave up on you."

"We fooled him for a while," I pointed out.

"Your dad's real upset."

"It's not his fault. I messed up."

Sal looked at me oddly. "What did you do?"

"I don't know. I must've said something and they overheard."

"This isn't about you." He gestured towards my father. "It's him they're after. You're dead and buried."

I watched my father talk his way onto the nearest sport-fishing boat. He was onboard for only a few moments before he headed for the next boat, the steel ketch from Gibraltar.

"He's wrong if he thinks they came by boat. It's the first thing I checked. The cops too," I added.

At the end of the jetty, smoke billowed behind the sport-fishing boat as its big diesel engines started up. It was the same boat I'd seen leaving the day before, its outriggers as high as the ketch's mizzen mast.

"It's the only way on and off an island without leaving a trace," Sal countered.

He coughed and held out his hand. Ben handed over his bottle of water. Sal gulped the rest of it, brushing away bush flies that came too close.

"You okay?" I asked. His face was wet with perspiration.

"Angina." He pulled a pill bottle from his pocket. "This'll fix it right up."

He flipped the cap, shook out a pill, and put it under his tongue. Suddenly, he got to his feet. He teetered, grabbing the boxes to hold himself up.

"Mother of God," Sal croaked. "I've seen that boat before. It left Cairns the same time we did."

The sport-fishing boat's diesel engines roared as I bolted down the dock. I heard a rope break like a gunshot. Then, another bang as a cleat ripped out of the dock. It ricocheted against the boat's cabin, shattering the window.

My father leaped from the ketch to the dock. He grabbed my arm and yanked me back, following me down. He lay over me, pushing my face into dried seaweed and fish scales. Engine roar reverberated in my ears.

I lifted my head to see the sport-fishing boat tilting as if making a hard turn to starboard, straining against the final dock-line. In the flybridge, a woman was braced against the radar arch, pointing a handgun at us. The remaining line snapped and the boat rocketed away from the jetty, flinging water in sheets. A large white cooler slid along the foredeck and under the railing. It splashed into water churned to foam and fury.

Chapter 20.

My father and I stared at the sport-fishing boat. He cussed loudly, again and again. I just stood there, my gut churning, anger unlike anything I'd ever known, tears burning my eyes. The sport-fishing boat raced down the channel, flinging out sheets of spray, leaving a long foamy wave behind. In less than a minute it was gone from sight. Two shredded dock-lines and a white cooler bobbing against a dock pile were all that remained.

Ben came up behind us, Sal lurching, trying his best to stay with him.

"She pointed her gun right at you, Dude. Your dad too," Ben murmured.

"Means they didn't recognize either of us. That was them though. I'd know them anywhere, even with sunglasses on," my father said.

"Now what?" I could scarcely get the words out.

"Take a boat... go after them." Sal made it sound easy.

"Waste of time," my father grumbled. "We'll need a plane to catch them."

I thought we were wasting time. Sal knew what to do; he always did. I was about to say so when my father started back to the other sport-fishing boat, its owner standing in the middle of the jetty in mute disbelief.

Ben tugged my hand. "You think they've got Jessie on board?" he whispered.

I shrugged, feeling utterly useless.

"Nowhere else," Sal rasped.

Ben cussed like my father. His father would've grounded him for a week. Sal grunted agreement and hobbled off, towards my father and the owner of the other sport-fishing boat.

I moved away before Ben saw me lose it. Below, water was settling, fish back to swirling around the piles. The cooler rocked and slowly sank to within a few inches of the lid. It looked heavy, probably full of ice and beer.

Ben wandered over. He cussed again and stared down. "Going to tip over," he muttered as the cooler rocked farther to one side than the other.

On the next roll, it flipped upside down.

"Now, it'll sink. The drain plug isn't in," he pointed out.

It took a moment to sink in. I jumped. Ben was right behind me. I came to the surface with the cooler only a few strokes away. I rammed the plug back into the hole. We used the handles on the sides to turn the cooler upright again.

"Open it, goddamn it!" my father shouted.

There was a latch on the front and both sides of the cooler to keep the lid airtight. Ben and I tried all of them. Only one latch opened.

"They're jammed," I shouted up.

My father jumped in, thrust me out of the way, and rammed his thumb into the lever until it snapped open. I yanked on the center latch. He flung back the lid, releasing the stench of feces. Jessie was crammed inside, her knees forced against her chest with her head skewed towards the drain plug. She was still wearing her pink T-shirt, Blinky Bill smeared with dried vomit. She might've been dead but for her hands trembling.

+ + +

The owner of the other sport-fishing boat gave Sal the keys to his SUV before he departed in pursuit. We rushed Jessie to the Horn Island Health Centre. Sal drove, my father beside him, cradling Jessie. I could tell he was worried that Jessie wouldn't make it. No one spoke. She was pale and barely breathing. It was as if life had been drained from her. Not once did she move.

Nurse Schiff was on duty when my father carried her in. She gave Jessie a cursory examination.

"Take her in there," she said to my father, pointing to the door marked 'emergency room.'

She called the doctor at Thursday Island. Clearly, a catatonic child was out of her league.

"He's delivering a baby. He'll be here as soon as he can," she explained.

Ben went over and stared out the window. I took off for the police station across the street. Aunt Vee and Sarah were standing in front of a map of Horn Island as Senior Constable Dodson inserted push-pins where they'd already searched.

"We found her," I shouted.

Aunt Vee gaped. Sarah started to cry. I added 'alive.' and she shouted 'Yes!' Senior Constable Dodson wanted to know the precise location where we found her. I babbled something about a cooler, and took off at a run. They stayed on my heels all the way back. Aunt Vee went straight into the emergency room, ignoring 'Medical Staff Only' signs.

Within seconds of stepping through the door, Senior Constable Dodson cornered me. She peppered me with questions about Jessie. Sarah got her version from Ben until the policewoman realized he'd been there too. She called Ben over and asked him the same questions. Sal and my father watched from the opposite corner of the waiting room. They might've been waiting for an appointment, thumbing through health magazines; except my father's clothes dripped water on the floor.

Senior Constable Dodson read from her notes. "This boat with the man and woman onboard; they left in a hurry, you said?"

"They got outta there, soon as we came near," I said. "Reckon they recognized us from the museum."

"It snapped all the lines," Ben added. "It was tilted right over."

Senior Constable Dodson checked to make sure she'd written everything down. "I assume that's how the cooler fell in the water?"

"I didn't actually see it go in. There was water flying all over," Ben answered.

"How did you know she was inside?" she asked.

Ben and I glanced at each other. "We just did," I said.

Sarah put an arm around each of us. "The gods have their ways of intervening."

"Sorry, Mum; I need to hear what happened from them," Senior Constable Dodson interrupted.

"It was barely floating. A cooler is mostly foam insulation so it meant there was something heavy inside," Ben added earnestly.

I'd seen the golf cart at the museum, with the cooler in the back seat. I saw the golf cart again on the jetty, and the pile of melting ice outside the museum. I felt like an idiot.

"It was the only thing that made any sense," I added.

"How could she survive? Twenty four hours in an airtight container; it isn't possible."

"She pushed out the drain plug to get air," I said.

She regarded me with disbelief. "Right!"

"You don't know my sister," Ben said proudly.

+ + +

180

Nurse Schiff came out a few minutes later. Jessie was semi-conscious, responding erratically to stimuli.

"Poor little thing. She's in good hands." She sounded relieved.

Across the waiting room, Senior Constable Dodson targeted my father for questioning.

"Mr. Capra, you want to tell me what happened?" she demanded, notebook at the ready.

He scratched his head. "Dunno, really. I just arrived, the 9:00 am flight out of Cairns."

"You have no idea why she was kidnapped?"

He gave a shrug. "Sounds like some wacko nabbed her from a museum. I got no idea why he stuck her in a cooler for 24 hours."

"Your son said it was a man and woman who took her, Mr. Capra. It sounded to me as if he knew them already."

"I never seen 'em before," I called, sure to get his attention.

"I think he knows more than he's letting on," she said evenly, giving me a cold stare.

"Marco don't know shit from a sandwich!"

"She knows about you and me at Wongalin' Beach," I said from across the room.

I intended it to sound like he'd mistreated me, in case she brought it up; however, from the look on his face, it came out wrong.

"Mr. Capra, I asked you a question."

He looked her in the eye. "Whatever he says; none of it's true. He lies like his mum."

"I didn't say nothin' 'bout why Mum threw you out."

He glowered at me, yet a slight twitch of his thumb said otherwise.

"Marco, you need to stay out of this," she barked.

"Bloody 'ell! Ask 'im about owin' money. Go on!"

My father gave me an icy stare. I looked away. Sal started to get up, but thought better of it. He beckoned to Sarah and whispered something. She whispered back and sat down beside him. He shook his head. She whispered again. It concerned me, no doubt about it.

Senior Constable Dodson started again. "Mr. Capra, it's been suggested that the people who took Jessie may have wanted to exchange her for you; is that true?"

"Had to keep bettin' on the horses, didn't ya," I sneered, making sure my father understood.

"You ain't so big I can't wallop yer arse," my father growled, turning back to Senior Constable Dodson. "This has nothing to do with me."

"Owe a lot of money, do you?"

"Instead of asking me questions that ain't none of your business, you oughta be going after the kidnappers. They're in a sport-fisher, white with a flybridge, about 15 meters long." (49 feet)

"I'll do that, Mr. Capra. We'll resume this conversation later." Before she reached the door, she turned and nodded at me, a silent warning to him.

"You'll need an airplane to catch them. They were heading nor-east, speed 30 to 35 knots," Sal added loudly.

+ + +

"She still isn't speaking," Uncle John said wearily.

He'd been conducting his own hunt at the second of two resorts when the search was called off. He'd arrived 30 minutes earlier, and spent all of it at Jessie's bedside.

He hugged Ben. "She'll be okay, Buddy."

Ben was close to tears. He nodded seriously. "It doesn't help to worry, Dad. Coming out of a stupor just takes time."

Aunt Vee followed Uncle John out of the examination room. She took me aside. "Jessie's responding too slowly. I need you to go to the *Spray* and bring back Jag."

"Her toy cat too?"

"Good idea." She looked at me curiously. "Every time I see your eyes, it's like seeing you for the first time. I miss the old you."

"Bein' Marco's hard for me too." I choked, wanting more than anything to call her 'Mom.'

She brushed back my salt-crusted hair, kissed my forehead, and went back to Jessie.

Behind me, my father, Sal, and Sarah seemed to be in the same conversation. My father kept glancing at me. As I walked towards the door, I heard him whispering.

"Real talent is born and bred, Sarah. It's refined over a lifetime."

"That's why he needs proper training. You said so yourself."

Sal stood up. He was pale, though breathing normally. "I need some fresh air. I'm going with Marco."

I waited until we were outside. "What was that all about?"

"Your dad thinks you should go to music school; Angelo too. According to him you're the ideal candidate for Juilliard."

"Not going to happen, Sal. No money plus I'm not good enough."

We drove back to the jetty in the borrowed SUV and left the car keys under the seat.

+ + +

At 6:05 pm, Sal's *Maid Marion* tied up at the end of the jetty, the same place where the sports-fishing boat had been docked. At 8:30 pm, we sat down to Celia's Chicken al Mattone, chicken grilled under a brick. The Calabrian version was charred and basted with hot chili paste.

With the table was cleared, Celia brought out a plate of butter cookies, a platter of Italian cheeses, and three different wines. Sal entertained as he lectured on types and tastes. Under different circumstances, it would've been fun; Aunt Vee was so worried she was spending the night at Jessie's bedside.

After taking a sip of Chianti, Sarah took the bull by the horns. "After today, I think the best defense is a good offense."

"It would be if we knew where Zagarovsky lived," my father said.

"I'm all for avoiding trouble."

"Sometimes, the best thing to do is take the initiative," he finished.

Sarah hesitated. "I don't have it all figured out."

"Go with what you have."

Before she could start, Marion's cell phone beeped an incoming message. She went upstairs to get it. When she came back, she whispered to Sal, who promptly nodded to my father.

Like a Cretan at Knossos, Sarah vaulted on. "The best hiding place for something is where it belongs."

She sat across the table from Uncle John, who was savoring Gorgonzola piccante. Dani had laughed when I'd tried it for the first time. I'd gagged rather than spit it out.

"Do I have it right, John?"

He looked up as if she'd kicked him. "Ask Nick. He said it when we were still in New York."

My father took over. "You usually don't notice something if it belongs there. However, if you don't expect it to be there, you won't even look for it."

I sat up. They were talking about me and trying to hide it.

Sal mulled it over. "It works for people too." There was dead silence. Finally, he looked at me. "Since no one else is going to say it; it's why living in a trailer park in Norfolk kept you safe for so long."

"I want to hear what Sarah has in mind," my father cut in.

Sarah seemed as surprised as Uncle John looked defeated. "What if we did the opposite with Marco?"

Uncle John came to life with a disapproving grunt. "Putting him where he'll be noticed; are you crazy?"

She brushed cookie crumbs into her hand and held them out for Jag to lick off. Endless snacks and stroking kept him away from Sal, who was very allergic.

"John, what's the point of hiding him if Zagarovsky thinks he's dead?"

Uncle John brooded over his glass of Marsala. It wasn't just Sal who upset him; both Sarah and my father seemed to annoy him.

My father templed his fingers. "If he's out in the open, there's a chance Zagarovsky will realize he's been conned."

"After that, he'll have a day or two left," Uncle John murmured, so quietly that only I heard him.

"The difference is Ron and Sal will be in control. Of course, it can't look like a trap." Sarah couldn't have been more confusing.

"All I need is Zagarovsky's location." Sal swilled his glass and thought about it. "It's the last thing he'll expect."

However, I was still thinking about his earlier comment about Norfolk. "Sal, was Arcadia Park your idea?"

"It met all the criteria," he said simply.

Uncle John considered it while he gnawed a chunk of hard, salty Romano Pecorino. "It wasn't ideal."

With no answer forthcoming, I knew better than to ask again.

Sal inclined his head. "Marco, you remember 'obbligazione'?"

"It's an obligation that binds you."

"When Dante died, I told your father how to catch Zagarovsky."

I gaped at him. He was responsible for the fire that killed my grandparents.

"It's the knot between us." He continued on as if telling me to try a different fly on my next cast. "After the fire, I provided some money to make up for what was lost, and covered up your tracks." He smiled slightly. "I expected them to take you to Boston."

Uncle John had had enough. He exhaled loudly. "Taking on Zagarovsky; it's too dangerous. Count us out." He looked to Sarah for support.

She didn't hesitate. "We'll hide for the rest of our lives if we don't do something."

"I'll rather do that!"

However, I could tell my father was still considering it as he looked from me to Sal, and back again.

"It's an idea, that's all! If things don't work out, we'll try something else," he said abruptly. "Right now, I'm more interested in Marco attending Juilliard. His chances of being accepted are better if he's been in a pre-college program."

"No point unless it's top of the line," Uncle John said.

"I was thinking…" My father scratched his ear. "Angelo said Eliana Stein Academy has a Saturday program during summer. He could continue into their pre-college program."

I had an unpleasant feeling that he was sending me away, even though it wasn't me who Zagarovsky was after.

Uncle John considered it. "Do you have any idea how expensive that would be?"

"It's not an issue," my father said.

Everyone looked at me, even Ben. I looked at mahogany and maple patterns on the table.

"Marco?" Sarah asked.

"He's pretending he didn't hear," Ben snickered.

"Their courses in composition and music theory are really outstanding," Uncle John mused, as if warming to the idea. "Perhaps he could get a scholarship?"

I kept my head down. The patterns made a compass, the center an expanding star of rosewood and purple-heart.

"It's a wonderful opportunity. Sal and I will help out," Marion said distantly.

"I have the insurance on my house," Sarah offered.

"Unfortunately, summer's only a few weeks away." Uncle John paused. I could tell he'd changed his mind already. "Maybe next year. He doesn't even have a passport."

"I have their passports in the safe," Sal said.

"Forged?"

"They're good enough for the airport. Your real passports will be here in a couple of weeks," he added, sounding smug.

That should've pleased Uncle John, or at least raised a question. Instead, he exchanged a long eye-to-eye with Sarah as if he wanted to say something, but couldn't.

She took over. "I'd rather he stayed with us." She stopped stroking Jag and turned to me. "If he wants to go, I'm all for it."

Uncle John stayed on theme. "It's too late to apply. Next year; plus he'll have time to audition."

"He's already applied and auditioned; thanks to Sal and Angelo." My father smiled at Marion.

"I emailed Angelo as soon as we arrived." Marion paused, searching beside her for her cell phone. "This is what he sent back just now. 'Marion, I just got off the phone with Stein's director. Marco rated 95.8 on his audition. That's very good, btw. The class average is 92.5. No problem with school grades. They'll test him when he gets there. Unfortunately, no scholarships for classical guitar. I have an idea regarding that. Please congratulate him for me and confirm his acceptance. Summer school starts in a week.'"

I felt sick to my stomach. "Can I think about it for a while?"

+ + +

I was still thinking about it when my father came into the cabin we shared on *Maid Marion*.

"You awake?" he said softly.

I rolled onto my back.

"You decided yet?"

"Going just one day a week during summer is really expensive. I looked it up online," I added.

"If you're half as good as I think you are, it'll be worth every penny."

"What would you do?"

"This and that."

I knew a lie when I heard it. "While we're there, I want to find out what happened to Mom."

188

"We can try. Just remember, it might not be what you want," he said.

+ + +

The next morning, I was waiting for Aunt Vee to report on Jessie's condition when Dani called from New York. I'd decided during the night to tell them I wasn't going. I changed my mind as soon as I heard her voice.

Chapter 21.

At 2:30 am on Tuesday morning, my father turned on the lights, made sure I was awake, and went to shower. I dragged myself from bed and checked my email. Ben was his cheerful self now that Jessie was sitting up and cuddling Jag. Only two days earlier, it was all she could do to stare at the ceiling and stroke his flank. Now, she muttered occasionally, although she didn't make any sense.

I typed, 'Enjoy peace and quiet while you can. Give her lots of hugs from me.'

I put away my laptop when I heard the shower stop.

"Try to stay awake in there. You've got five minutes max," he said as I passed him on the way to the shower.

It was all I could do to keep my eyes open to put in my contacts.

+ + +

At 4:45 am, we boarded a Boeing 737 in Cairns. I woke up briefly as it hurtled down the runway. I gripped the armrests. Beside me, my father read my *Doktor Faustus*, seeming unaware of the roar and vibration. At 7:40 am, we landed in Brisbane; at 10:00 am we were on our way to Los Angeles. For 13 hours, we crossed the Pacific Ocean, occasionally glimpsing tiny islands far below. We arrived at Terminal 7, John F. Kennedy International in New York City at 4:40 pm, still Tuesday, May 15th.

After collecting our suitcases and my guitar from baggage claim, my father took me aside. He handed me *Faustus* with my phony Australian passport tucked inside.

"This is where we split up, Marco."

"What?"

"Not so loud! You have to trust me." He lowered his voice. "They're waiting for you outside."

"Who's waiting?"

"All you have to do is walk to the second exit." He pointed down the concourse, a stream of people dragging suitcases on wheels under overhead signs to car rentals, and ground transportation.

"This is bullshit!"

"It's safer this way."

"Why do we have to split up?"

"I need to take care of some business, Marco."

"You promised!"

"I'll look into what happened. If I find out anything, I'll let you know right away. You have my email address on your laptop. I expect to hear from you every night."

"Dad, you're creepin' me out."

"Listen to me. It's all been arranged." His eyes were everywhere except on me. "You'll be staying with them."

I glared back at him. "Who's them?"

"Think before you act and you'll do just fine," he said snidely.

After spending 26 hours in airplanes and terminals, I wasn't in the mood for mystery.

"I'll always be close, Marco. You'll be safe with them." He took my hand, squeezed firmly, and whispered, "I love you, Sander."

"I love you too, Dad." It bothered me that he kept looking around. "You really think Zagarovsky's watching the airport?"

"It's unlikely; however, there's no way to be certain without staking out the place beforehand. As far as you're concerned, you're always at risk. Avoid standing out; it's always safer in a crowd. Above all; stay in character."

"I'll try."

"Just do it; all the time, not when you feel like it. Be careful what you say and do. Sal's got Aldo keeping an eye on you, but email me immediately if you notice anything unusual."

"Who's Aldo?"

"He'll meet you outside, if not sooner."

I glared back. "I'm not leavin', not without you!"

He stepped back, pushing his suitcase out of my way, smiling and jerking his head towards the exits. "Go before one of us starts bawling."

"This really stinks."

"On the plane, didn't you say you were going to ride the subway to school by yourself?"

"Must've been someone else. I'm chicken!"

"Nah, you're the kid with guts."

+ + +

I easily spotted Dani in a shiny black Chrysler. She had her head stuck out the window, waving madly and yelling 'Marco' until I hoisted my guitar case and waved back. A man came from behind, stepping around me to grab the door handle even as I reached out. He was the spitting image of Tony, broad-shouldered, buzzed hair, a no-nonsense bodyguard. He wore a black windbreaker jacket with a black holster poking out from under his left arm. He snatched my suitcase and guitar case and all but shoved me into the car.

Giggling, Dani seized my hand, pulling me with her as she slid across the rear seat.

"Mi sei mancato tanto. Ero così infelice. Ho aspettato e in attesa da Nonno ha detto che saresti venuto a New York. Ora, si è finalmente qui."

(I missed you so much. I was so unhappy. I've been waiting and waiting since Nonno said you were coming to New York. Now, you're finally here.)

Donatella sat in the front seat, shaking her head. "Hello Marco. Would you mind telling Dani to behave? She ignores everything I say. Maybe she'll listen to you."

I had a million things I wanted to say, including how beautiful Dani was, her hair in a long shiny ponytail, a black-striped Venetian gondolier shirt, black slinky slacks, and red sandals. And her eyes, playful and alert, hazel brown, and gazing at me.

I grinned. "Comportarsi!"

"Si, comportarsi!" Dani sat up, eyes attentive, hands clasped in her lap. "I always listen to my Marco."

"No touching, Gattino."

She erupted in giggles again, squirming away so our knees didn't bump. "We're not touching, see Mamma."

The driver closed his door, glanced at the rear vision mirror, and swerved in front of a hotel minibus. He didn't slow down until we were on the JFK Expressway.

"Signore, he wasn't followed; I'm sure of it."

"Marco, meet Aldo. He's Tony's cousin, on his father's side," Donatella said. "He drives too fast, and he's much too bossy. If he tells you to do something, do it immediately. He'll take you wherever you need to go. He also knows everyone worth knowing in New York."

"And plenty of people you don't want to know," Aldo added, glancing over his shoulder. "Hi Marco."

I said 'hi' back as Dani leaned to whisper, "He's nicer than he looks."

193

I settled into sculpted leather and brought them up to date with what happened to Jessie, 10,000 miles away. Donatella read me a text message from Sal.

'Email me when he arrives. Please let him know Jessie is eating now. The local cops are out of their league, which is good. Tony heard there was a Romanian couple looking for Nick.'

"Guaranteed they're Grigore and Narcisa Florescu. They worked for Zagarovsky before he went in the slammer," Aldo said. "The last I heard they were in Boston. Probably the same couple who iced Porcello in Philly."

I didn't dare ask about Porcello in Philly.

Aldo steered with one hand on the wheel, passing every car while pointing out landmarks. It was a sleepy blur to me. I was beginning to think we'd never get there when Dani nudged me. Directly ahead was New York City.

+ + +

Dani and Donatella lived in Greenwich Village, a block from Avenue of the Americas, two blocks from Washington Park. It was a surprisingly quiet, leafy street with apartment buildings above boutiques and restaurants, and narrow houses. Their house was brick, five stories high, built right on the footpath. From the outside, it looked as plain as its neighbors.

We entered through a high wrought iron fence into a tiny courtyard filled with flowers. Beyond the gate, we might've been in Italy, a bubbling marble fountain, a bronze statue of Pan playing pipes, and rustic ceramic dishes hung on the walls. Inside the house was breathtaking. The front room was reception and waiting room for Donatella's interior design clients. Her office adjoined. Like the rest of the house; it was a study in contrasts; the suave simplicity of modern design, pottery, fabrics, and etchings of bucolic Sicily, and religious art in ornate gilded frames.

On the next floor, Dani dragged me across to meet her cat, an elegant Abyssinian she called Buffy, which was short for Buffoon. While Donatella ordered pizza, we sat on a black leather sofa, taking turns stroking Buffy. Either I suffered from jetlag or from sitting too long; I had to get up and move around. Dani stretched out, playing nose-bumps with Buffy perched on her tummy.

I roamed the kitchen. It reminded me of Angelo's house in Sydney, stark and uncluttered, as if no one ever cooked. In the dining room, black and white photos of family and Sicily decorated white walls. One photo was like a magnet.

Donatella came over. "You see how alike you and Dante are?"

I nodded. We were about the same age. There was a resemblance made stronger by dyeing and curling my hair, yet I wasn't looking at myself.

"He'd almost gotten over losing Dante when he saved you from the shark," Donatella went on. "Of course, once he realized who you were, it started all over again. Only it was worse than ever."

Uncle John said much the same thing; Sal wouldn't rest until Zagarovsky was dead.

Dani and I followed her up two more flights of stairs. The stairs kept going. Aldo lived in a separate apartment on the top floor.

Dani's bedroom was on the right, mine was on the left. We shared a bathroom.

"I want you to feel at home, Marco," Donatella said.

"What she means is if you want something, get it yourself," Dani snickered.

"What I mean is everything here is yours to enjoy; except Dani." She fixed her gaze on me. "While you are here, Marco; you and Dani will treat each other as brother and sister. Any hint to the contrary, you will move to the basement. This is New York; there are rats in the basement."

"The only rats in the basement are Mamma's underpaid and overworked employees," Dani scoffed.

Chapter 22.

On Saturday morning, Aldo gave me a cell phone, the latest model. It was black, with GPS and camera built in.

"I've put in three numbers; mine, Dani's, and Donatella's," he explained. "There's a fourth number; however, it's only for emergencies. This isn't a toy, Marco. It could save your life."

"Got it!

"One more thing, don't give out your number unless you've cleared it with me first."

He showed me how to use the phone to send my GPS position to him, and how to bring up a map so I wouldn't get lost. We used it when we walked to the subway station at Bleeker Street.

As soon as the train doors closed, he edged away, leaving me clutching my guitar case and hanging onto an overhead railing, doing my best not to fall on someone. There was graffiti on every wall, and people who thought nothing of shoving you out of the way. A lot of them got off at Grand Central Terminal. There was room to sit, yet I stood—the seats were splattered with gum globs.

People were rude for no reason, almost no one making eye contact for longer than a second or two. Dani said strangers who looked right at you were creepy. She was right. One of them was a busker who kept eyeing my guitar case. He might've been Texan, decked out in cowboy boots, grimy jeans, and checked shirt. His unkempt long hair and a floral head band suited a guitar case decked out with country rock stickers.

The busker got off when I did, at East 86th Street Station. When I turned to see if Aldo was still tagging along, the busker stepped in front of me. He dodged sideways, muttering what sounded like 'Wanna play, cowboy.'

Aldo and I abandoned the crowd of exiting passengers so he could show me what I needed to do to take the subway back to Greenwich. The next time I saw the busker, he was strumming ballads, the crowd skirting him and his open guitar case, a few measly coins in the bottom.

The Eliana Stein Academy of Music and Dance was a private conservatory on East 84th Street. We walked. Aldo followed like a puppy in training, never beside me, yet always nearby. He caught up again when I stopped at Third Avenue, no longer starry-eyed. New York's finest music school for K-12th grade was a drab four-story brownstone building with a skinny eight-story addition from an era when stark concrete walls were all the rage. Aldo said something about meeting me after school as I entered the lobby. I heard only the ethereal notes of a well-plucked harp drifting down the stairs.

+ + +

Since my guitar instructor was still in Brazil, I spent much of the morning with Deidre Sorens, Ph.D., Director of the Eliana Stein Academy. She gave me her perspective on ESA history, school rules, and procedures on the world's slowest elevator. A guided tour accompanied her educational philosophy, visiting classrooms, practice rooms, recording studio, and a concert room with seating for 300 and a massive 2,000-pipe ofrgan. In the corridors, she introduced me to teachers and students whose names I forgot moments later.

Lunch was bring-your-own, or buy prepackaged organic snacks from vending machines on the first floor. I chose carrot sticks and a five-grain bread bun with arugula and goat cheese and went up to The Terrace, a roof garden on the four-story building, most of it shaded by the concrete monstrosity. There were a hundred kids sitting at rows of picnic tables, each with an umbrella, a tablecloth, and a tray of condiments and napkins. Every kid there was either richer than Croesus, or on a scholarship.

I recognized Chadwick, the only person I'd met that morning whose name I still remembered. I sat next to him. He was pallid with mousy hair and skeletal fingers ideal for a pianist. I ate a slightly stale bun while he pointed out a few kids he liked, and doused the rest with sarcasm.

"Keung's piano. He's stuck up, but really good. Almost all the Asian kids are." Chadwick smiled blandly when Keung looked his way. "Adam Hilton, he's the redhead. He thinks he's God's cellist. Next to him is Shelley the Snot. Her mother's English aristocracy, believe it or not. She's a flute. Talented, but doesn't practice enough. All of them go to school here. The other kid is Andy Borden. She's a mean little brat, even for a violin virtuoso."

'She' was scrawny under a flimsy pastel-green button-front shirt. White frayed shorts stopped just above knobby knees. He had coltish legs that seldom saw sun.

"Looks like 'e's in grade school."

"He knows music, but he can barely read. His mommy only lets him come on Saturdays."

+ + +

I sat next to Chadwick in my first class. Professor Domenica Koch taught *Music Theory*. I needed three textbooks in addition to the two books I'd bought earlier in the week. She'd assigned reading by email so I was already behind. Worse, she scheduled a quiz every two weeks.

Composition started at 2:00 pm, Room 605, two doors down the hall. Professor Aloysius Boyle was already there. I put my backpack next to Chadwick's table and went over to introduce myself.

Chadwick called him 'Flutey'; he had a weird mannerism, fluttering his fingers as if playing a flute. He wore bifocal wire-rimmed spectacles, giving a scholarly impression while he looked down his nose at me.

"Ah, the Australian guitarist who auditioned with *Waltzing Matilda*." Professor Boyle wagged his finger. "A Scarlatti sonata; something by Villa-Lobos; anything but the theme song of convicts!"

"Um, I kinda changed it a bit."

"Well, of course you did." He threw up his hands. "It was very inventive. You had Professor del Monte salivating over your finger work."

The rest of the class trooped in. Professor Boyle clapped once and they quieted.

"For those of you who haven't met Marco Capra from Australia, he's a student at ESA like all of you. Unlike you, he's a guitarist, a surprisingly talented one. He also has considerable compositional skill, so instead of having him introduce himself, I'm going to ask him to play a song I'm sure you've all heard before. Then, he's going to play his own rendition, and you're to critique it."

I opened my guitar case. I took a few moments to adjust tuning before I launched in the opening bars of *Waltzing Matilda*. A few students smiled. Andy was in the front row. He was the youngest kid in the class by far. He sat with his arms folded on his chest, either idiot savant or doing his best to convey utter boredom.

At the end, I paused briefly. I started again, attenuating some notes, stressing other notes, capturing the loneliness and sweltering heat of the outback, the ghost of the swagman among gaunt gum trees, adjusting the timing and rhythm the way Uncle John taught me.

"Thank you for your variation of stealing a jumbuck from a squatter, Marco," Professor Boyle chuckled. "Now, your critiques. Shelley; you're first."

"His version is much sadder; however at the end, you felt if he kept playing, it would be happy again."

"Very insightful. How about a cellist? Adam?"

"His version nixes the timing. I liked it a lot more."

200

"He made good use of tempo rubato." Professor Boyle looked around the room. "Can anyone define it? Andy?"

Andy straightened up and lowered his hand. "Tempo rubato is part of phrasing, Sir."

He was tiny compared to the rest of us. His clothes didn't help. His shirt was the kind of synthetic that clung to the skin; he looked like a Charles Dicken's waif.

"It means stealing time, Sir. Frédéric Chopin did it a lot," he went on.

"Exactly. Would you care to critique, Andy?" Professor Boyle enquired.

"It sounds like the Scots are doing a funeral march in the Outback, Sir."

With more than a few students laughing, his reedy voice made me fume. It was like a little kid telling me my version was predictable and dull. Chadwick was spot on.

"'ow would you change it, mate?"

He looked around as if I'd asked the rest of the class. "Play it on bagpipes."

It wasn't that funny, yet even Professor Boyle laughed. I took a breath and let it out slowly before I went back to my seat.

Beside me, Chadwick covered his mouth. "Correction. She's a mean little bitch."

+ + +

When I wasn't studying music theory or playing guitar, Dani and I took in the sights of New York. Aldo was never far away, even when we rode the red double-decker bus back and forth, from Battery Park to the Apollo Theater in Harlem, and everywhere in between. We always sat on the top deck to look down on New Yorkers scuttling about like rats in a maze.

On Wednesday, we went to Central Park Zoo, changing tour buses at Times Square. With only two vacant seats on the upper deck, Aldo headed downstairs to find a seat. Dani and I exchanged glances as the bus started moving. She smiled in the bright morning sun. I nudged her knee with mine as I stretched my legs.

"No touching in public," she said under her breath.

"No one can see us."

Her hand glided from her lap to smack the back of my hand. "Bad puppy."

However, she gave me a conspiratorial look as her fingers stroked between my fingers. Suddenly emboldened, we held hands, all the way from 42nd Street to 66th Street, when Aldo came upstairs to make sure we got off at the right stop.

+++

Saturday, May 26th, Aldo again accompanied me on the subway. Even before we were out of the house, he lectured me on being careful, his version of how to find out if someone was following me; how to check if there was more than one person; and what to do about it. We practiced all the way to Bleeker Street.

Now aware of subway etiquette, I squeezed into an empty seat, dumped my backpack in my lap, propped my guitar case against my knees, and kept my head down. Aldo stayed farther away than the first time. He faced away, no doubt watching me in the window reflection.

We were slowing down for Grand Central Terminal when Aldo bumped my guitar case.

"Off here," he whispered, and moved on.

I resisted the urge to get up right away. When I finally did stand, I realized the wannabe-Texan busker was three seats away. Our eyes crossed when I put on my backpack. He raised an eyebrow before I turned away. I could feel his gaze like a laser dot on the back of my head until the doors opened. I stepped onto the platform, glancing behind to see if Aldo was following. I spotted him next to the busker. I waited for him to join me on the platform.

"You know him, too?" I teased.

"Next time, tell me if you've seen someone before," Aldo muttered, already stalking towards the stairs.

I hurried to catch up. "'e some kind of weirdo, huh?"

"Something like that."

He directed me into the next carriage, getting on himself only a second before the doors closed. He stayed close.

"You notice how he kept his left arm down?" Aldo whispered in my ear.

I hadn't. "Zagarovsky knows I'm here?"

"If he did, you'd be lying in a pool of blood right now. You want to see your next birthday, Marco; keep your eyes open and your wits about you."

"I thought he was a busker."

"The woman sitting across from you had a tennis racket; true or false? On your right was a Hispanic woman with a child; boy or girl? On you left was a man. Was he Jewish or Catholic?"

I shrugged. "How would I know."

"From now on, you pay attention to everyone, every minute of every day, what they wear, what they say, how they act. We'll practice on the way home."

$$+++$$

A handwritten note taped to the front door awaited me at ESA. 'Andy Borden, Marco Capra, Adam Hilton. Professor Boyle, Room 301 at 9:00 am.'

203

Chapter 23.

Professor Boyle strolled in at 8:59 am, crossed to the window overlooking East 84th Street, and contemplated leaves splashed with sunshine. A minute later, he popped out a cough drop and cleared his throat.

"This summer, the three of you will do things a little differently to the rest of the class. You will continue to work on the five elements, pitch, time, tone, shape and performance, though not individually. The goal is to understand how instruments come together. You have a question, Andy?"

Andy brought down his hand. "Shouldn't Keung be here, Sir? Piano, cello, and violin would be a better combination."

"A flute would be a step up, if you ask me." Adam was my age, punk with bristly red hair and neck choker.

"Hmmm." Professor Boyle pinched his nose. "In the Romantic era, yes. Yesterday's zeitgeist; however, suggests otherwise."

"What's zeitgeist, Sir?" Andy's voice hadn't broken during the week.

"Adam? Marco?"

When Adam didn't answer, I pounced, ready for revenge, and silently thanking my father and uncle.

"It's the spirit of the age. Literally, it means 'time ghost.'"

"Example, please?"

"The Romantic era wasn't about love, as we think of it. It was love of nature and living simply, at a time when science was taking hold. Music transcended reality through beauty and the shock of raw emotion."

Even as the words left my mouth, I realized I sounded as if I knew what I was talking about, definitely not like a kid who had an Australian surfer emblazoned across his T-shirt.

Professor Boyle slapped his thigh. "Spoken like a true Romantic. Contemporary zeitgeist would be what for music?"

Andy frowned in silence. Adam rubbed his forehead. I forgot my father's advice to stay in the crowd.

"The age of industrialization and two world wars gave us harsh dissonance and repetition of a few musical forms with little originality."

Andy looked up at the ceiling and exhaled.

Professor Boyle gave an approving nod. "The banality of modernity, of which the electric guitar is the primary icon! Next, we'll discuss learning objectives; and then the three of you will choose what to play. Nothing too difficult to begin."

Adam's hand shot up. "John Cage."

"One more thing before I forget. You'll need variations to make this work. You will do the arrangements in my composition class for extra credit. Now, what about Cage, Adam?"

Adam argued for Cage, firing off a dozen reasons why his music exemplified the age. Mostly, I kept my mouth shut.

+ + +

Adam bided his time until Professor Boyle announced a five-minute bathroom break. As soon as he left the room, Adam started on me.

"You should've backed me on Cage, Capra."

"No way am I playing Cage with cello and guitar, unless it's *Any Combination*." Andy, eyes defiant, started to get up. He'd been silent until then.

If Adam saw the humor, he showed no sign. "Cage is classic zeitgeist!"

"Cage is classic crap!" Andy shot back.

Adam held Andy down with one hand. "I rearrange Cage all the time."

Andy shook off Adam's hand. "Don't touch me!" He seemed to be quivering.

Adam flipped at Andy's collar-length hair.

"Stop touching me!" Andy snarled, jerking back. "I'm not playing Cage!"

"You got a better suggestion, wimp?"

"Beethoven's *Symphony No. 5, First Movement*." Andy voice was high-pitched, his head twitching.

"Da-da-da-dahhh!" Adam flicked again and missed. "Allegro con brio; now there's originality."

I could tell Andy hated criticism. He glared up at Adam, his lips bitter-thin until intelligence got the better of anger.

"Contemporary crap versus Romantic refinement. Guess which wins Hilton?"

"The wimp has attitude!" Adam laughed in his face.

Andy backed away until his butt hit the window. He kept his head down as if he was about to cry. His hands clenched to impotent little fists.

"How about you, Capra?" Adam added.

Andy jerked. "Can't you tell; the Australian's got nada."

He was fragile, scrawny-thin and pale, his hair two shades lighter than mine before my father dyed it.

"Borodin's *Steppes*," I said.

Andy looked up, brushing wavy bangs from his forehead. "I used to play *Steppes* with my mom..." His voice trailed off.

"Aw, he plays with his mommy. That's so sweet," Adam snickered.

Andy brooded and absently picked at his shirt. The top three buttons were missing. He was anemic underneath.

I looked him in the eye. "Beethoven's bloody 'ard to mess with."

"The same as Borodin," Andy mumbled, suffering from low self-esteem when things didn't go his way.

"I work with Cage all the time. Easy as pie," Adam interrupted.

Andy didn't give up easily. Watching him was like watching myself at the same age. "Guaranteed *Steppes* isn't scored for guitar. That's a problem."

It was like playing chess with Ben; you never knew where he was headed. "Who needs a score?"

"You ever write a score, Capra?"

"I didn't say it would be easy, Borden."

"Scoring takes a load more talent than you've got."

His eyes were green with sturdy eyebrows, intense and always moving. Sarah would've said there was a hyperactive brain inside his head.

I hesitated. "You don't 'ave to prove you're a mean little bitch. I already know, mate."

He deserved it.

Maybe it was Adam's smirk; maybe it was the shock lingering on Andy's face; I was still thinking about what we should play when Professor Boyle returned. I sided with Andy for no other reason than I felt sorry for him. He reminded me of Ben, lonely because he couldn't relate to kids his own age, and older kids wanted nothing to do with him.

As soon as Andy started playing Beethoven's *Symphony No. 5*, I realized he was extraordinary, even though I'd never played it. His focus was single-minded, and he had impeccable timing. Emotion flowed from every note. He was as good as any violinist I'd ever heard on my uncle's CDs.

Even as he played from memory, he watched me struggle with only a piano score to work with. I plucked notes and strummed chords that seemed most likely to work, usually changing my mind immediately after. He was attentive to every sound I made. When I flubbed a note, he winced. By lunchtime, I'd figured out enough that he'd stopped wincing.

I stayed behind to practice with Professor Boyle.

+ + +

I was getting off the elevator at the roof garden, when Andy blocked my way.

He looked at my lunch, tilted his head, and shook it. For a moment, I expected a scathing quip about my celery salad and rye bread roll.

He strolled into the elevator and pressed his floor before he turned around. "You don't need a score. Right!"

+ + +

Saturday classes ended at 4:00 pm. Instead of waiting for the elevator to make the return trip, I lugged my guitar and backpack down six flights of grungy fire stairs. Aldo was waiting in the foyer. He rubbed his thumb up and down on his forehead, his 'everything is okay' sign. I breezed through the front doors and turned right, a few steps behind Adam Hilton.

Andy stood at the curb beside the latest model black Cadillac. He said something to a man getting out of the

208

driver's seat. Like Aldo, his bodyguard was buzzed and buffed, and he wore the same windbreaker-style jacket.

"Get in ze car, Annie!" He sounded European.

Andy wasn't happy. He said 'yes sir' and something else before he spotted me. He waved insipidly. Before I could wave, he got in and closed the door. I saw the Cadillac again when it turned left onto Lexington Avenue. It had Pennsylvania license plates.

Aldo came up beside me while I waited for the pedestrian light. "You're walking back."

Surely, he didn't mean all 80 blocks. "That'll take hours."

"It's 4.3 miles. You need the exercise. If you get lost, use your cell phone." He took my guitar case in hand. "By the way, you're being followed for real. Spot him and we'll take a taxi the rest of the way home."

I was certain by the time I reached East 65th Street; however, proving it was difficult. I cut across to Central Park, checking at every intersection. He was there at Madison Avenue, and again at Fifth Avenue, middle-aged with a white polo shirt, blue jeans and baseball cap. I diverted into Central Park, past the Zoo and around The Pond. Once across 59th Street, he ducked into a hotel. It didn't make much sense that he'd give up so easily, so I lingered at a newsstand, remembering what Aldo had said about the likelihood of a second tail.

A few minutes later, he came out, glanced around, and began walking quickly. At Columbus Circle, he turned left on Broadway, and left again at 56th Street. He went into another hotel, not nearly as fancy. I continued on, dodging pedestrians as I checked out the hotel on my cell phone. It was 100 years old, with an outstanding restaurant. It was too expensive for a Yankees baseball cap and blue jeans.

Aldo was waiting at the corner of Avenue of the Americas, reading a business magazine. Clearly, he expected me to be there eventually.

"You might as well have worn a sign, Marco. Too much looking over your shoulder. Going into the park was idiotic. Any number of clear shots."

I felt foolish. "Who was 'e?"

"A friend." Aldo beckoned to a taxi.

+ + +

I emailed my father after dinner. It was matter-of-fact about my day, mostly how Professor Boyle's classes made me think about music, and how my playing of Beethoven's *Symphony Five* without a score impressed him. At the end, I mentioned the incident on the subway train, and Aldo's overreaction.

His response arrived within the minute.

'You were sloppy. Next time you might not be as lucky.'

Chapter 24.

Saturday, June 2nd, was Dani's 14th birthday. She was still in bed when it was time for me to leave for ESA. I drummed *Happy Birthday* on her door.

"Come in," she called. "I'm decent!"

I stuck my head around the corner. "You're awake before noon; I don't believe it!"

Her room was white with pastel accents, her bed like a picket fence with a flowery comforter and eight fluffy pillows. She read a book propped against her pillow, stroking Buffy, purring contentedly beside her.

I grinned. "I wish I was Buffy."

"You're such a buffoon." She blew me a kiss. "You're not going to be late again, are you?"

"Ask Aldo."

"Tell him to have you back here by five." It was a standing joke; you didn't tell Aldo to do anything. "The reservation is for seven o'clock."

"You decided where you want to eat?" I asked.

Donatella thought kids' birthdays were made for cultural exploration. On Monday night, while I practiced upstairs, Dani and her mother had narrowed eight restaurants down to L'Atelier, The Owl, and A Voce.

She smiled mysteriously. "No surfer T-shirts. You have to get dressed up. That's all you need to know."

"I better go. Wish me luck. I have to make up for being awful last week."

+ + +

Practicing every spare moment during the week paid dividends. I skated through Beethoven *Five,* adding passion and verve, my own variation. Professor Boyle tapped his lips. He looked at Adam.

"Are there any more complaints about a string combination?"

"Not from me," Adam said. He'd played admirably when it was his turn. "Andy maybe."

Andy had managed to miss a note, missed by none of us. Humiliated, he sat hunched before the window, his violin cradled in his left arm.

"Andy?" Professor Boyle prodded.

"My mom said it's not the combination of instruments; it's how we work together that counts, Sir."

Perhaps it was my imagination; it seemed as if Andy was less arrogant. Part of me hoped he missed more notes. I actually liked the humble Andy.

"I'll take that as no. Marco, can you stay back after class this afternoon to incorporate your variation?"

I was thinking about Andy's questionable choice of clothes when I answered, "Yes Sir."

Professor Boyle's gaze shifted to Andy. "What happened to your head?"

There was a dark bruise on Andy's forehead that he rubbed at when he thought no one was watching.

"I fell on a rake, Sir." His voice, as elusive as a flute, made him even more pitiful.

"That must've hurt." I had to say something.

Andy reached to turn his sheet music on the stand, his hand trembling on a bony wrist. His hands were like mine, dexterous with long thin fingers that could stretch to find notes and chords. His nails were chewed worse than I'd ever seen.

212

"A girl punched him, I bet," Adam whispered to me.

"I was cleaning out my horse's stable. I didn't see it under the straw."

"Poor little Annie. Stick with my version; you'll get more sympathy," Adam snickered.

Andy's eyes turned dark with anger, his voice raw. "I don't want sympathy from anyone, especially you and Capra."

+ + +

After I finished with Professor Boyle, I was running fifty minutes late. Aldo was waiting in the lobby when I came down the stairs. He caught my eye, touched his forehead with his thumb, and gestured, 'go left'. He'd parked the car halfway down the next block.

Aldo took Lexington Avenue rather than gamble. Getting stuck on FDR Drive guaranteed we'd miss our seven o'clock restaurant reservation. It still took an hour to get to Washington Park. He stopped outside the house, and I raced inside to change my clothes. There wasn't time to shower. Worse, I hadn't wrapped Dani's birthday present. I'd been too busy to even think about it.

+ + +

Cars, taxis, and busses streamed down 55th Street. Except for a giant brass samovar beside the entry, The Tsar's Samovar was obscenely red, from pompous foundation to an ornate onion dome perched on a red-tiled roof. The lights were red, the door was red; even the window frames.

"If this was on the list, I didn't see it."

I was dressed to the nines and about to go to dinner at a five-star restaurant; a low-class Australian accent was ridiculous.

Donatella chastised me with a glance. "It was Dani's idea. I'm sure we'll enjoy cabbage soup and offal," she added, giving a wink to me.

Dani nudged me. "What do Russians eat, besides cabbage soup?"

"No idea."

Dani lowered her voice. "When your grandfather was still alive, I bet you ate Russian food."

"Only for Thanksgiving. We had cabbage soup with cow tripe and roasted lamb brains."

Dani regarded me doubtfully.

Aldo looked for a break in the traffic. He'd planned to drop us off at the door until we spotted a car pulling out of a parking spot halfway down the block. Suddenly, he beckoned us on. Donatella took Dani's hand and started across the street. Dani grabbed my hand and dragged me off the curb. She squeezed, and I squeezed back. On the opposite sidewalk, we kept holding hands. Aldo looked the other way. Her mother noticed, yet didn't say a word.

Time stopped with a history lesson in the foyer. In 1917, the Bolsheviks under Lenin stormed the Winter Palace in St. Petersburg (Petrograd), ending 500 years of Tsars. Black and white photographs of sumptuous domed buildings and aristocratic sculpture adorned a dark-green wall. Beyond, gilded frames of heavily varnished Romanov princes and Baltic landscapes glowed under hidden spotlights; brocaded curtains draped every window; chandeliers sparkled overhead. In one room, elaborate samovars decorated every table; in the next room, flowers festooned from bulbous ceramic vases.

Outside a private room, two men in dark grey suits with murky sunglasses stood guard. We passed quickly, barely glimpsing mirrored walls replicating a dazzling gilded tree with fanciful glass fruit, waiters busily arranging crested cutlery and crystal goblets.

The maître d' escorted us to the Tsar Peter the Great Room. It had red leather booths, not tables and chairs. A giant painting filled most of the opposite wall, the enlightened Tsar attacking Sweden, with cannon, horse, and trusty hound at his side.

A tuxedoed waiter greeted us, handed out menus, and scurried off. I scanned the menu, growing increasingly uncomfortable in blazer and necktie, wishing Sarah was there to guide me—I didn't know Borscht from Blinchik.

Beside me, Dani chatted with her mother about the opulent pre-Communist decor. I fiddled with the plastic bag holding Dani's present. Suddenly, her fingers touched mine.

Donatella cleared her throat. "Aldo?"

Aldo smiled into his menu. "I'm off duty, Signore."

"Dani, seeing as it's your birthday; it's okay to hold hands under the table," Donatella said quietly.

"Momma!"

"It's only until we get in the car and Aldo is back on duty."

Both Dani and I glanced sideways. My necktie tightened.

"You're embarrassing Marco, Momma."

"I see it as a way to save money. Now that you're boyfriend and girlfriend, I expect you'll be sharing plates," Donatella teased.

"I'd never do that!"

"Gattino, it wasn't so long ago that I was your age. My boyfriend and I shared a hamburger and fries on our first date."

"We're not on a date, Momma!"

Donatella gave a dismissive shrug.

Dani and I started on a bowl of Borscht, red beets and dill in bacon broth, with a boiled potato and sour cream. After tasting it, Dani insisted I finish the rest. She made up for it by eating most of the Blinchik; a crêpe stuffed with duck and goose liver, with an arugula-pomegranate salad. We held hands, her left and my right, stifling giggles when our fingers entangled and one of us wouldn't let go.

Donatella and Aldo ignored our antics, providing comical, and sometimes cynical commentary about other people in the restaurant. Finally, Donatella turned her wit on our table.

"I didn't realize Marco was ambidextrous. That's a very useful talent to have, especially in a restaurant."

Dani abandoned my hand, putting both of her hands on display. Her nails were manicured, metallic silver, and lacquered, a present from her mother while I was at ESA.

"My mom can be brutal," she laughed.

Two waiters served our main courses, Russian stalwarts, Beef Stroganoff and Chicken Kiev. Then, came caviar; a tiny mound of Sevruga on glass, because as Donatella pointed out, Sevruga was the standard to judge the rest by. Dani and I made it last, one sturgeon egg at a time, sharing a beautifully curved spoon of mother of pearl.

"I'm sorry about how it looks," I said, opening the plastic bag. "I'm genetically inept at wrapping gifts." I handed over the much-traveled package.

"It's what's inside that counts," Donatella added with yet another wink at me.

Dani looked at the untidy muddle of newspaper and string. "No card, Marco?"

"Um, I kinda forgot. Happy Birthday, Dani."

She swatted my shoulder and began untying knots. Scraps of brown paper covered her lap before she reached tissue paper. She ripped it off. From upside down, my gift looked like a boring block of wood. Slowly, she turned it over. Her eyes went wide. The rectangular bottom was an undulating wave on the top. Anna had made geometric sails of iridescent mother of pearl shell incised into polished sandalwood.

"It's beautiful," Dani murmured.

She opened the lid slowly. Inside the lid was a huge shimmering piece of mother of pearl. White satin lined tiny compartments. One compartment held the white pearl I'd found. It was mounted on a thin gold chain. I didn't know how it got there.

Dani blinked, wiped away tears, and rubbed her bottom lip with the tip of her tongue.

"Once she gets her wits back, she'll thank you," Donatella said.

Dani's thumb stroked mother-of-pearl. Suddenly, she turned and leaned towards me. She kissed me. It was short and wet, and wonderful. A moment later, she jerked away.

"Momma, don't you say a word or I'll do it again. Longer."

Donatella gestured, 'who me?'

"A Swedish lady made the box for me," I explained. "I found the shell when I was diving."

"And the pearl was inside. How special is that?" Donatella enthused.

Of course, she'd put the necklace in the box. The gold chain and claw holding the pearl had Sal's fingerprints all over them.

Dani leaned back, her eyes glistening wetly, clasping her jewelry box. "Can we share a dessert too, Momma?"

+ + +

After stuffing ourselves with Crème Brûlée and raspberries, we headed towards the foyer with Aldo leading the way. Dani and her mother trailed behind, complaining about eating too much. The two guards were still outside the private room. As we passed, a waiter came out with empty vodka bottles on a tray. Inside, a dozen men sat around the table, picking at plates of caviar. Andy stood at the far end of the table. He wore the same clothes he'd worn to ESA, knee-length pants with a cord tied around his waist and a sleeveless T-shirt. Before him was a man who could only be his father. He was wimpy, like Andy, and he wore oblong glasses.

The man on his right bellowed, "Close the door!"

Andy's head was bowed and his hands were behind his back. I thought he was being punished. He glanced up and our eyes met momentarily. He looked shocked, definitely not happy to see me. His father looked right at me. Then, a guard shut the door.

The other guard stepped in front of me. "What are you looking at?"

"Nothing."

"Your parents need to teach you some goddamn manners." He was so close his spit hit my face.

"I bet it costs a bloody fortune to rent the room," I said.

His associate took over. "Is not your business." He was Andy's driver, his voice coldly intimidating like the Tsar's personal guard.

Aldo spun around. "He's a kid; calm down. He's just curious."

"That's me, curious as a cat."

"Keep walking, smart ass."

"Do what he says, Marco," Aldo said, his voice unnervingly calm.

He waited until we were in the foyer. I was sure he was going to say I'd done or said something really stupid. I felt stupid. Instead, he just shook his head. I counted myself fortunate that he hadn't seen me wave to Andy.

+ + +

Aldo shepherded us across the road, his cell phone already out. His usual unruffled demeanor was a razor's edge when he got in the driver's seat.

"What was that all about?" Donatella asked me.

"The 'ell if I know."

"I just saw someone, Signore. I need to email the boss right away," Aldo muttered, typing text with two fingers.

Chapter 25.

Adam Hilton skirted his friends of the previous week and made a beeline for the tables looking over 84th Street. From there, you could look down on the Upper East Side; people shopping in classy boutiques, savoring coffee with liqueur at La Martinique, or walking their poodles.

Very likely, Adam spotted Andy opposite me, as far away as he could get and still be at the same table. For some reason, Adam went out of his way to pick on Andy. I kept my head down and picked at my plate.

Adam leered over me. "Tasty lunch, Aussie?"

'Healthy Salad' was spinach and dandelion leaves, purple kale, and romaine lettuce sprinkled with parmesan cheese.

"Weeds are good for you, mate."

"Should've got eggplant fondue." Adam stepped over the seat and sat down. "How did you do on Domenica's test?"

"I messed up the melodic minors scale." I sopped up balsamic dressing with kale shreds. "You reckon Boyle liked how we sounded today?"

Adam forked through eggplant, searching for crumbs of feta cheese. "Talented young musicians must learn to critique themselves before their heads get too big.'"

It was a passable Professor Boyle impersonation.

"What did you expect him to say? We sucked because one of us wasn't up to scratch?"

Other than a subdued 'hi' when I came into Room 301, it was the first thing Andy had said all morning.

Thinking he might've meant me, I leaned over the table, licking my lips. "'ow about I 'old you down and eat your lunch?"

Andy shifted back, taking his half-eaten sandwich with him, peanut butter and jelly on rye bread.

Adam dangled the remaining half-sandwich, still in the plastic bag. "Your mommy make your lunch, Borden?"

"I did," Andy snapped. He snatched and missed. "Give it back!"

"Calm down, girlfriend!" Adam opened the bag, slid out the sandwich, and lifted a corner. "Weird looking jelly."

"It's cherry, asshole."

"You'd know."

Andy was more than worked up, and redder than his collar. It bothered me enough to intervene. "Stop pestering him, Adam."

"Now, you're sticking up for the fairy?"

Andy looked like he'd been slapped. He glared at both of us, hatred in his eyes.

"'e's awesome on the violin, mate. That's what counts."

"You sure about that?" Adam dropped the sandwich on the table, and the subject.

I went back to searching through Healthy Salad, asking myself what Adam meant. Any way I looked at it, it was mean. I was no closer when Keung called for Adam to play chess.

"You want me to leave, too?"

I looked up and Andy immediately glanced away. "Now, what do you want?"

"I don't need you to stick up for me,' he muttered.

"I wasn't. Just 'ow old are you anyway?"

Suspicious, Andy stared back. "I'll be 12 in August."

"My cousin turns 12 in September," I said, thinking how wimpy Andy was compared to Ben. Then, it struck me; a single word and I was on the way to blowing my cover.

"What's he like?"

"Kinda like you; 'e's been takin' 'igh school science for a year."

"Meaning what?"

"'e's so bloody smart, it's near impossible for 'im to make friends," I said.

"What's your reason?"

+ + +

Professor Boyle kept the three of us back after Composition. He began by stroking his struggling goatee.

"After this morning's class, I met with Director Sorens to discuss the String Theory project. She wanted to know if you're ready to perform for the ESA Foundation at the end of the month."

He pinched saggy skin under his chin, waiting for one of us to say something.

Andy slowly raised his hand. "What's the String Theory project, Sir?"

Professor Boyle did his fluttery 'flutey' thing. "One of our Board members wants to set up a scholarship just for Strings. Director Sorens and I thought it should sound avant garde. Donors want to be cutting edge. What you'll be doing is very innovative; at least, we'll tell them it is."

Bewildered, Andy didn't ask.

"The three of you are the top candidates, so it only makes sense that you participate in the kick-off brunch. You'll play a half-dozen pieces."

"Six by the end of the month?" Adam queried.

222

Professor Boyle fluttered again. "Now, we want to demonstrate interaction and individuality independent of style and era; a string-spectrum, if you will. Of course, you'll be closing with selections from Beethoven's *Symphony Five*." He pulled a scrap of paper from his vest pocket. "We'll start with the Telemann sonata for Baroque. Romantic, you'll be playing Massenet's *Meditation* in full. There's no better fundraiser. Then, each instrument in solo. Director Sorens thought violin should be something to show off Andy's quick bow arm."

Andy frowned momentarily. "My mom and I have been working on *Caprice No. 24*, Sir?"

"Way too hard, dear boy. I suggest Dinicu's *Hora Staccato*, you have agility not strength. Adam will select from Bach's *Cello Suites*. And for guitar, I'm open to suggestions."

"Granados' *Andaluza*," I said.

Professor Boyle smiled. "Excellent. Then, we'll segue to Modern before the finale."

"Something by Cage?" Adam interjected.

"Too avant garde. Desmond's *Take Five*; everyone likes it. It'll loosen the purse strings too. Now, about the brunch. It's Saturday, June 30th, on the Terrace, weather permitting. I'll meet you in the foyer at ten sharp."

"What about clothes?" Adam asked.

"It's about innovation, not fancy dress; school uniform will be fine. Black slacks and long-sleeve white shirts," Professor Boyle added for my benefit. "You'll be done by eleven. Afternoon classes won't start until two. Bring something to read because you'll have three hours to fill in."

+ + +

Aldo wasn't waiting in the foyer. I was only ten minutes late. I wandered outside, scanning both sides of the street. No sign of Aldo. I started down the street, thinking he'd come by car and had managed to find a parking spot. By the curb, Andy chewed a thumb nail, his eyes on the move constantly.

"What were you doing at The Tsar's Samovar?" he asked when I passed him.

"Birthday dinner, mate. You?"

"He has business meetings there once a month."

"Your dad didn't order enough seats, huh?" I teased.

Andy's mood darkened. He looked past me, clutching his violin case to his chest.

"The food was bloody good." I planned to segue to eating Blinchik with Dani.

"I wouldn't know." Andy turned away.

"You sounded bloody good today."

He saw me over his shoulder. "Is bloody good how Australians say outstanding?"

"Outstanding is bonza. Bloody good's like okay."

"Hmmph."

Andy stepped back as his black Cadillac swooped in. He opened the rear door and got in.

"Actually, you weren't bad today. That's a step up from bloody good," I said before his door slammed shut.

A moment later, the Cadillac surged away, disappearing into the traffic. When I turned to continue my search for Aldo, he was standing right next to me. That was creepy.

"He's rich," Aldo said indifferently.

"He's weird."

"And you're dead." Aldo shook his head. "This morning we worked on your being aware of your environment; were you paying attention, or thinking about Dani?"

I shrugged in silence.

"No one ever gets this close to you, not without the alarm bells going off."

"I was looking for you."

"Next time, use your cell phone." He looked around. "Thank God your father isn't here to see." He stopped. "Okay, time for leapfrog."

Leapfrog was two people taking turns tailing a target. We practiced on Lexington, getting into position, pausing when a target began moving, keeping a minimum distance of 100 feet, signaling to each other, and switching the tail back and forth.

At 68th Street, we crossed to Park Avenue. We waited at the lights, Aldo standing beside me. Someone bumped hard into my guitar case. As I turned, the pedestrian beeper started. People pushed around me. I thought I saw my father on the other side of the street. Aldo was gone.

Chapter 26.

My feet hurt. My shoulders ached. My arms felt like they belonged on an orangutan. I was pissed.

"You bloody left me there!"

"You needed a lesson!" Aldo snarled back.

With a hand on my shoulder, he pushed me into the courtyard and closed the gate.

"Keep your voice down. I've warned you twice about staying aware. There won't be a third time. You need to scan nonstop. Everyone is a threat. Everyone, Marco! Even the kid you were talking to in the street."

"Andy? You're kiddin'. He's the definitive wimp."

"This isn't a game. Zagarovsky wants to kill you. He's the same as Sal. He'll never stop."

"I know that." I stuck out my hand. "Can I have my wallet back?"

Aldo sat beside the fountain, trailing his fingers through tiny floating leaves. "I made you walk all the way back for a reason"

"I figured."

"Why didn't you call?"

"The same man as two weeks ago tailed me from 68th. I ditched him at 55th. He went back to the same hotel on 56th Street."

Aldo laughed.

"What's so funny?"

He shook his head. He shifted his gaze, peering through ivy swathes on the fence. An old woman in a man's overcoat shuffled along the opposite sidewalk, tapping her umbrella each time she took a step forward. She was dirty and unkempt, one of the homeless people who plied the streets of New York.

Aldo looked up at the windows above the courtyard. "Go see Dani. She's worried sick."

+ + +

Professor Boyle was waiting in the foyer with Andy when I arrived five minutes early. At 10:00 am, Adam strolled through the doors. We took the elevator to the 5th floor and went out to the Terrace. Perhaps thirty people were gathered in small groups around little round tables, enjoying brunch delicacies, orange juice, champagne, and coffee.

With instruments in hand, we skirted the crowd. Most people smiled at us; a few even waved. Professor Boyle helped us get set up.

"Don't worry about them. Just imagine they're not here. I want you to play with panache. Let's shake the money tree. Andy, where's your sheet music?"

"It's on the stand, Sir."

"Of course it is!" Professor Boyle fluttered. "Isn't your shirt too tight?"

Andy's shirt had tucks in the sides and back, fitting him so closely you could see his shoulder blades.

"No Sir." His face was ashen.

"Right! Well, tune up as quiet as church mice while I tell Director Sorens you're ready."

Adam bided his time until Professor Boyle was out of earshot. "Mommy's boy is wearing a girl's shirt."

Andy's head snapped up, his lips sealed shut. He shook his head slowly. Gone was the wishy-washy little kid.

"Did Mommy want a girl instead of a boy?" Adam went on, oblivious to Andy's feelings.

I sensed someone approaching from behind. "Leave him alone, Adam."

Andy's lips barely moved, whispering the carnal cussword before he opened his violin case. Instead of his battered practice violin, he'd brought a much better one. Right away, I knew it was exceptional, golden maple and spruce, and hand-crafted like my grandmother's guitar. His bow glided across the strings as deft skinny fingers straddled the fingerboard. The sound was stunning, powerful and brilliant. It made his practice violin sound tinny.

"Boys, I'd like to introduce you to Angelo Romano, the longest serving member of the ESA Board, though nowadays he works remotely," Professor Boyle announced. "This is Adam, our best cellist; Marco's our guitarist, and young Andy is tuning his luscious Hochstein."

Angelo looked the three of us over, giving no sign he knew me from Adam, or Andy. It was all I could do to keep a straight face as I said 'G'day' and shook hands with Angelo. He asked me whether I'd seen the rats in New York's subways. He teased Adam about joining the U. S. Marine Band with his 'buzz-cut'. Andy, he largely ignored.

"We'll talk later," he whispered to me as Director Stein began her welcoming remarks.

+ + +

"Simply outstanding!" Angelo declared, applauding again. He nodded at Professor Boyle. "Three of the most handsome boys in New York, playing superbly. What more could we ask for besides one million dollars?"

Already, donors and Board members were gathered around the tables again, replenishing plates with mouthwatering appetizers. I was famished; I'd skipped breakfast so I wouldn't be late.

"It's time to wheedle a few more bucks from the patrons," Angelo went on. "Adam, you'll go with Director Stein. Andy's with Professor Boyle. Marco, you're with me.

All you need to do is smile, talk a little about yourselves and your instruments, and how much you enjoy ESA. They're already eating out of your hand."

We went from one table to the next, shaking hands, smiling, and being fawned over by wealthy New Yorkers. I salivated over chocolate croissants, baked brie in pastries, toast with foie gras, creamed escargot in mushrooms, truffles with goat cheese on crackers… and starved.

After ten minutes, Angelo nudged me towards the garden, an assortment of plants from palms to petunias in black and white pots, some as large as oil drums.

"Did Sal and Marion come with you?" I asked.

"Marion's still in Australia. Sal wanted to come. I wouldn't let him; he's on a diet for his heart. Plus, he has some business to attend to today."

"Meaning Zagarovsky?"

Angelo extricated a withered frond from a potted palm. He pushed a finger into the soil and grunted, "Needs water… You need to know Sal wasn't always like this. I watched him change the day Dante died," he said softly.

"Terrible?" I ventured.

"Worse than you can imagine." Angelo let out a sigh. "Faro shot him in the chest deliberately. I watched him bleed out in Sal's arms. It was like both of them were dying."

"It must've been awful." There was nothing else I could say.

"Two days later, I did something I shouldn't have." Angelo crumpled the palm frond. "I'd met your mom when I was looking at organs for ESA's concert hall. She played at a church off Times Square on Saturdays. You ought to check it out, a superb Aeolian-Skinner, over 2,000 pipes. Anyway, you and your dad always went with her. There was a rumor he was in the FBI. You were sitting in his lap when I told him to see Sal. He went later in the afternoon."

"My father said he put Zagarovsky in prison for 25 years."

"What happened to the accent, Marco?"

I shrugged. "How come he got out so soon?"

"There was no proof he ordered Dante's murder, so they charged him with racketeering. When they released him nine years later, Sal was furious. He told Tony to find out if Zagarovsky had a son; and if he did, to kill him."

"Can't say I blame him."

"He'll do whatever it takes to kill Zagarovsky. He'll take vengeance to his grave."

+ + +

I gave Andy a friendly high-five in the elevator. "Bonza job, mate."

"You were bonza too," he said shyly.

He wasn't shy when he stole the show with *Hora Staccato*. Dinicu based it on a Romanian dance. It required frenzied fingerwork for the bow's staccato, both up and down. Not only could my fingers never move that fast, every note Andy played was crisp and vibrant. He had total control of the audience for three minutes. My Spanish dance was dull by comparison, even though I loaded it with emotion.

"We can go to the Central Park Zoo," Andy suggested brightly.

I stepped out of the elevator the instant the doors parted. "We aren't goin' anywhere, mate."

I strode for the front door, feeling relieved when it closed behind me, and Andy was still in the foyer. With my cell phone in hand, I turned right, thinking I'd go to Central Park and look for the pond where I went with my parents when I was three. Andy caught up before I reached Lexington Avenue. He stayed a few paces behind all the way to 5th Avenue.

I confronted him while we waited for the lights to change. "You must like bein' an ass, mate?"

For a moment, I thought he might burst into tears. Then, the mean kid reappeared. His lips barely moved.

"And a potty mouth too." I stepped off the curb.

Andy dropped back as we weaved through the crowd outside the Metropolitan Museum of Art. I was sure I lost him when I skipped the lights at 79th Street, dodging taxis and cars before turning into Central Park.

The next time I saw Andy, I was at Bethesda Fountain, overlooking The Lake while I searched the Internet for 'church', 'organ', and 'Times Square.' He dawdled on the promenade, pretending to look for turtles.

At a brisk pace, I walked The Mall. Aldo said being tailed and not revealing it was easier than tailing someone and not being seen; and he was right. All I had to do was not look behind me too often. However, I was mean; I walked fast enough that Andy had to jog to keep up.

I headed towards the zoo, no doubt raising his expectations until I diverted towards The Pond, across Gapstow Bridge, the stone arch I remembered from the duck-feeding days of my early childhood.

+ + +

Andy followed me down 7th Avenue. I stopped at Carnegie Hall. I thought it overrated from the outside—it looked like the progeny of an Italian Renaissance palazzo and a department store.

He came up beside me, panting. "My Mom played there the year before I was born. Not the big hall, the Recital Hall."

"How cool is that," I said, turning to stride on.

"Do you have to walk so friggin' fast?"

I kept walking, as fast as I could go and not jog.

Andy ran to catch up. "How much farther?"

I halted abruptly at 56th—there was a cop car parked at the corner.

"You think you can last ten more blocks, wimp?" I said, looking down.

The top of his head was below my shoulder. His hair was sweaty and tangled. The pedestrian light took forever to change. By the time it turned green, I felt like a heel.

+ + +

My cell phone took us right to Saint Mary the Virgin on West 46th Street. Grey gothic was the antithesis of gaudy Times Square. It was dreary, dirty stone with little embellishment, scuffed wooden doors a few steps up from the sidewalk.

Andy confronted me. "We walked halfway across New York to see a friggin' church?"

"I didn't ask you to come, mate," I said.

He replied with his favorite expletive, which he thought was hilarious.

"Soap won't cut it. You need toilet bowl cleaner."

"You need an exorcism. Is that why we're here?" he shot back.

"I came here with my parents when I was younger. I'm goin' in. You can wait or go back by yourself."

Inside, Saint Mary the Virgin soared to the heavens. Lofty stone walls glowed like amber, separating vivid stained glass windows. It ended in a glorious semicircular apse with cobalt-blue vaulting, gold stars glittering like the heavens in faraway places. If there was an organ, I couldn't see it.

Andy tugged on my arm. I turned to see what he wanted.

"This is worth coming to see," he whispered.

Organ pipes framed a rose window, filtering misty light like a halo. It went from one side of the church to the other. I wandered down the aisle, gazing up. After I was born, my mother had played it almost every Saturday.

Suddenly, I felt worn-out. There was smoke in the air, and the smell of incense. I sat in a pew where I could look up at the organ. Andy meandered, beholding religious sculpture like a kid in an art gallery. It was tranquil, yet gloomy, until I imagined 'Hallelujah' booming over the congregation, a Divine Vesuvius as my father called it.

"Would you like to see the organ up close?"

I turned at the voice. He was tall and lanky, and nearly bald. He wore black with a white collar.

"I'm John; or Rector Davies if you prefer." He had busy brown eyes.

We shook hands as I mumbled my name.

"Take the stairs on the right," he went on. "All we ask is you don't touch anything."

"My mom used to play the organ here." I hesitated, fake accent forgotten, uncertain why I'd walked fast for an hour.

"No doubt she did. Lots of organists play our organ."

Behind me, a bucket banged on the floor. The cleaning lady made a final sweep dusting around the altar.

"I've got a doctor's appointment tomorrow, Rector. Mrs. Andrews will be here instead," she called.

"Thank you Elaine." He waved.

She picked up her bucket and mop, and left.

"She's a lovely lady," he said quietly. "She's been helping out ever since her husband was killed in Iraq. It helps to keep her mind off it."

"My mom stopped coming when I was three," I added.

233

He tilted his head as if he hadn't heard properly. "So about twelve years ago. That's a long time."

"I was wondering if anyone remembered her."

"Unfortunately, I've only been here for four years," he said.

"My dad said she saw God through music. She loved to play Handel's *Messiah,* all two hours of it," I added.

"Did you know Handel wrote 'SDG' on the bottom of his manuscript? The Latin is 'Soli Deo Gloria. 'To God alone the glory.'" His voice was reassuring, his eyes serene, rekindling my spirits.

"I've always wondered if 'Hallelujah' was divinely inspired."

He smiled a little. "Not many people your age would say that. If anyone remembers her, Doctor Grace will. He's Rector Emeritus. However, he's in Haiti for the week. If you come back next Saturday..." A moment later, his eyes narrowed. "Your mother, was her name Emma Lund?"

I didn't remember my mother's name; yet I nodded, my heart thumping wildly.

"I'm so sorry, my child. Doctor Grace told me what happened. It must've been awful for you and your father."

He sat in the opposite pew, leaning to close the distance between us. I could tell from his eyes he knew what happened to me. He even glanced at my shirt sleeves, buttoned at the wrists, though still enough skin showing to see wrinkles.

He took a breath and sighed. When he looked up again, I was certain he was holding something back.

"I was wondering when someone would come to see me again."

His soft voice should've calmed me, yet my mind raced ahead—I wasn't the first to ask about her.

"My first year here, he came to see me," he went on. "Poor man; I can't imagine how he survived; his daughter and her husband, and his own wife, all of them disappearing the very same day. I'm sure he hoped they'd contact him again; that's why he told me where he was going."

"Where?" It was all I could do to get out the word.

"I wasn't to tell anyone unless I was certain their heart was in the right place. In your case; I'm positive. Myrtle Beach, in South Carolina."

I'd been to Myrtle Beach, the rear-end view as we motored south on the Intracoastal Waterway canal. All we saw were the backsides of motels, fast-food restaurants, amusement arcades, and strip malls.

"He was highly educated, not the sort of person who'd go there, even for a vacation," he went on.

"He used to be a professor of archeology, here in New York," I said.

"He said they might've gone south after leaving New York; however, that wasn't why he was going to there."

"It's the least likely place," I said.

"That's exactly what he said."

He stopped abruptly. I turned to see what held his attention. Andy sauntered down the side aisle, captivated by radiant colors as sunlight lit up the stained glass windows.

"Your brother?" he asked.

"We're in the same summer school program."

"Is he always so dreamy?"

"He's usually…"

I caught myself when Andy reached slowly towards a Madonna and Child statue framed in an arch decorated with a dubious fruit cornucopia. Abruptly, he snatched back his hand.

"He's wound pretty tight," I said, relieved.

Rector Davies smiled oddly. "It's been my experience that Our Blessed Saint Mary affects people. Perhaps it's the incense. The distressed and angry become calm and thoughtful."

"Can I leave him here for a few days?"

"I'm sure someone would miss him."

Andy remained rooted to the spot, gazing intently at the statue, his shoulders hunched, enthralled yet dejected.

"Be kind to him. He's encountered too many problems."

I nodded absently. Still, Andy stared up. I went back to worrying he'd do something bad until he jammed his hands in his pockets. I took a last look at the organ before I stood up.

"I guess we better get started back. Thanks for telling me about him."

"Please be careful." Rector Davies hesitated. "He was afraid they'd find him. Not his family, someone else. He wouldn't say who."

Andy was still in front of the statue, so transfixed he didn't hear me until I was beside him. Then, he jerked away as if he was scared I'd touch him.

"That's about the ugliest thing I've ever seen," I jeered.

"Why is all the fruit around it?" Andy murmured.

"Symbolic, I guess. God's bounty, something like that," I ventured.

"Last year, I made a horseshoe with fruit for my horse."

With an hour before classes started, I headed for the front door. "Lots of apples, huh?"

"My horse and I eat a dozen apples a day." Andy grinned all of a sudden. "It was a birthday present so I wanted it to be special. There was a peach, two pears, three bananas, and an orange, and lots of fresh grass."

I pulled him aside as an old woman in an overcoat tottered past. She was dirty and smelled sour. Her gloved hands trembled so much she had difficulty holding her folded-up umbrella.

"Did your horse like it?"

Andy's good mood vanished. "Would've. He threw it away and said I wasted his money."

"Your horse got a name?"

He ignored me.

+ + +

We were at 49th Street, window-shopping a music store, when I realized we'd never get back by 2:00 pm if we walked the rest of the way. I coaxed Andy into the New York Subway for his first-ever ride.

Chapter 27.

I was right on time when I breezed out of the elevator. Aldo acknowledged me with a grim stare. A slight flick of his head and a finger to his nose as I went by, was enough to know I'd screwed up. He caught up to me before I reached the car. He jerked open the passenger-side rear door.

"Dani and I came by today. She wanted to go to lunch to celebrate."

"I went for a walk."

"What on earth were you thinking, running off without telling me? Not even a goddamn text message to say what you were doing!"

When he sounded like that, it was better not to argue. "I didn't think. I'm sorry."

The lecture started as soon as he closed his door. This time it wasn't about me about being careless, or not paying attention. One bad decision could kill me, taking a risk when there was nothing to gain, not planning ahead, thinking before acting… He went on and on.

"You even listening to me?"

"I'm listenin'."

"Your old man will be furious when he hears about this," he threatened.

"I want to find out about my mom. 'e's not doin' anything."

"The hell he's not! He was at the morgue repository all day."

"Doin' what?"

"Going over their records." Aldo braked hard and turned onto Park Avenue. "You want to know what he was doing, Marco? He was looking at bone fragments in case they missed something 12 years ago."

I took a breath and skipped the accent. "I need to see him about today, Aldo."

Aldo glanced over his shoulder. "You have a bad day? Miss a note, maybe?"

I flipped my middle finger. "I went to the church where my mom played the organ."

"Aw, poor Marco. Did it make you sad?" When I didn't answer, he went on. "He's spent the last three days looking at his parents' remains. You know what that's like?"

"I need to talk to him really bad, Aldo."

"I doubt it's that important."

"I think it is. If you won't take me, I'll go myself."

"Good luck finding him."

"I'll start at the hotel on 56th."

Aldo laughed. "Dani called you a doofus; but there might be hope yet."

+ + +

My father was in room 509. He opened the door when Aldo knocked three times. Since I'd last seen him, he'd stopped shaving his head. He hadn't shaved his face either, not for a day or two. Now, bristle-haired and stubbly, he confronted me with stubborn silence.

"Hi," I said as cheerfully as I could under the circumstances.

"I was wondering when you'd get lonely."

I smelled beer on his breath and mumbled, "I'm glad to see you too."

Aldo pushed past me. "He ducked out today while I was meeting with Sal."

239

My father thumped his forehead. "Of all the stupid things to do!" He strode across the room to the window, and yanked back the curtains, looking down.

Before he could say more, I said, "I went to the church off Times Square. Saint Mary the Virgin."

He spun around, scowling. "If Zagarovsky has people on the lookout, guaranteed it'll be there."

"I'm dead, remember?" I didn't give him a chance to react. "There were only three people inside."

"It only takes one," he grumbled.

"I talked to the rector, John Davies. He's been there four years. There was a woman cleaning the floor. She paid no attention to me. An old woman with the shakes came in as we were leaving."

"She look at you?"

"She walked right past me. She wasn't following me. She was homeless." I didn't mention Andy.

"He's real confident for being so sloppy," Aldo grouched.

He sat at the table, pulled his pistol from his underarm holster, checked the slide, and put it back in the holster.

"Exactly what did you tell the rector?" my father demanded.

"My mom used to play there. He brushed me off until I told him she played *Messiah*. It must've made a difference because he asked if Emma Lund was my mom."

Aldo and my father exchanged glances.

"I looked him up on the Internet on the way back to ESA," I continued. "He's been at Saint Mary for four years. Before that he was in Washington DC for six years, and before that he ran a mission in Africa."

My father flipped at the curtains. They were striped like the wallpaper, seat cushions, and carpet. Only the bed cover escaped.

"Why didn't you tell me her name?"

"I didn't want you running around New York by yourself, trying to find out what happened," he said.

Aldo took over. "You risked your life and got a name! Big deal!"

"How about he said someone came to see him about four years ago?" I protested. "I think it was Sarah's husband."

"You think!" Aldo barked.

"Aldo, let him finish," my father interrupted.

I told them almost word for word what Rector Davies had said.

"Myrtle Beach; it's possible, I suppose, especially if Sarah hinted we were going south," my father allowed.

He went over to the table and sat down before his laptop. "If Thom had to leave, he would leave a trail, just in case. He was like that."

"Damn stupid is what that is," Aldo grumped even as my father typed.

"There's no address listed for Thom Ryder at Myrtle Beach. Maybe he changed his name."

"There's one more thing," I began. "It might be important, though it's probably not."

For a moment, I worried my father would tell me to be quiet. He looked up from his laptop. "Go on."

"When we were in South Carolina, we stopped at a sculpture garden. I met this old guy. I should've told Uncle John, only I didn't realize it might be important."

My father swiveled in his chair, laptop forgotten. "What happened?"

"The day before, we went through Myrtle Beach; it couldn't have been more than 25 miles away. We went really slowly on the Waccamaw River because it was so pretty."

"I'm missing something here."

"He said Zagarovsky ruined his life."

He gaped at me. "You're sure?"

"Pretty sure. It was two years ago. I never heard the name before so it didn't mean anything."

He picked up the complimentary pen and tapped in on the desk. "This old guy, describe him."

"I don't remember much. He knew all about the sculptures. He quizzed me about one of them. It was from one of the Ancient Greek stories Sarah told me. Actaeon, I think."

He doodled on the complimentary writing pad. "Anything else?"

"He was nice, kind of funny. He joked about a nurse's aide coming to find him."

"Meaning what exactly?"

"He came on a bus from a nursing home."

"Gotcha!" My father turned back to his laptop. "He wouldn't have an address if he was at a nursing home," he said to Aldo. He started typing again. "I count ten in Myrtle Beach, another seven on the outskirts."

"A couple of days to check them out," Aldo said.

"I'll go tomorrow," my father decided.

I wandered over to the window. There was a storm brewing, the sky already dark, debris swirling in the street below, pigeons heading for cover.

"I'm going too."

"After today, you're with me nonstop, Mister," Aldo barked. "I'm teaching you how to stay alive if it's the last thing I do."

"We can teach him in Myrtle Beach," my father said quietly. "Any news from the *Spray,* Marco?"

I knew he would ask eventually. "I got email from Uncle John two days ago."

"How's Jessie doing?"

I took a breath. "He said she's doing okay."

"An Australian would've said 'not bad.' What else?"

"They've gone back to Cairns."

"So you think she's not okay?"

"They're taking her to therapy. She has nightmares, and she's wetting the bed every night."

"No wonder you're worried. I'm sorry."

I sighed. "I know what it's like for her."

He looked uncomfortable. "Anything else?"

"Uncle John said Ben's taking over as big brother."

"You have a problem with that?"

"I should've stayed in Australia. Jessie needed me."

He sat on the bed. "I know this is difficult for you."

"You have no idea! I used to have a family who loved me!"

"So did I. I'd like us to be a family again."

"Yeah, you and me against the world."

"Is that so bad?"

As much as I wanted to say 'yes', I'd gain nothing by annoying him.

Chapter 28.

At 6:50 am on Sunday morning, I lugged my guitar and backpack down the stairs. As soon as Dani heard me, she raced out of the kitchen. She was barefoot, still in her favorite pink and grey Cheshire-cat pajama pants. Even that early in the morning, she was radiant, bright-eyed with her pony tail bunched up in a neon-blue scrunchie. She was as brown as she'd been after 10 days in sunny Australia.

I smiled and tried my best not stare at her pearl and gold chain dangling around her neck. It drew my eyes to her flimsy T-shirt. It was obvious she wore nothing underneath.

"I thought you were still dreaming," I teased.

She giggled. "It's you who's dreaming, Doofy."

I was Doofus ever since I forgot my front door key and had to wait in the courtyard for two hours for her mom to arrive.

I grinned back. "I better leave before your mom wakes up."

"She's in the kitchen, making you breakfast."

"There isn't time. Aldo said he'd be back to pick me up at seven o'clock."

"Marco, he can wait a few minutes. Get your butt in here, pronto," Donatella called.

With a mischievous grin to match the cats on her pants, Dani grabbed my backpack and slung it over the newel post. She dragged me into the kitchen. Sal sat at the counter, sipping coffee.

"Every trip should begin with cappuccino e cornetto," he said, patting the stool next to him.

His 'cornetto' was an oversized chocolate croissant drizzled with chocolate sauce and powdered sugar. There were six on a plate.

"Hi," I said nervously, not about to remind him he was supposed to be on a diet.

"Aldo told me about yesterday."

"I screwed up pretty bad, huh?"

"He's right to be angry. Needless to say, we've got someone keeping an eye on the church." He added sugar and stirred his cup. "Angelo means well, but he has a habit of getting involved in things he doesn't fully understand."

"So do I."

Sal chuckled. "Next time there's bait put in front of you, don't bite right away. You're smarter than that."

"I wondered if I was being set up."

"Next time, trust your intuition. The priest you talked to; trustworthy or not?"

"The rector; trustworthy, I guess. He didn't say very much until I talked about music. I think he was being careful."

"Nervous? Calm? Worried? Curious?"

I thought about it. "Worried mostly. He knew what happened to me."

Sal looked at his watch. "Donatella, can you put some coffee in a travel mug for him? Dani, if you put a cornetto in a bag, I'm sure he'd appreciate it."

"I guess I shouldn't tell my dad about Angelo?"

"Trust your intuition." He thumped my shoulder. "From now on, Doofus, follow Aldo's instructions exactly."

His tone and the way he looked me in the eye said far more.

"What happened?"

"The couple who took Jessie, the Florescus; Tony heard they've been back in New York for three weeks. It's possible they figured out Marco Capra. You need to be very careful."

+ + +

Dani and Donatella escorted me downstairs. Donatella stayed on the porch. She gave me a quick hug and said 'good luck and be careful.' Dani waited in the courtyard while I carried my backpack and guitar out to Aldo's Chrysler. He gave me a friendly scowl and put my guitar in the trunk. I tossed my backpack on the backseat and hurried back to say goodbye to Dani.

"You've got just enough time for a quick good-bye hug," Donatella announced.

Dani jumped in front of me, wrapping her arms around my back as our fronts came together. She was warm, and soft, and firm. I got excited even faster than when she kissed me in the restaurant. I felt her moving against me, our bellies pressed tight, her pajama pants squeezing against my shorts. Her hair tickled my cheek, her breath burning my neck.

"Ding!" Donatella called.

We parted reluctantly, my heart pounding. Each breath was an effort.

"That was not a quick hug," Donatella snickered.

"Momma! Comportarsi!"

"I'm not the one misbehaving, Gattino."

Dani's eyes darted down. When she looked up, she smirked. "It's Marco who's misbehaving," she said under her breath.

Donatella heard her. "You need to go upstairs right now!"

Dani grabbed my hand and squashed my fingers. "Call me every night; and be careful." She pirouetted and bounded up the stairs, whispering as she passed her mother.

When I finally got the guts to look at Donatella, she smiled. "Don't be embarrassed, Marco. I'd be worried if you didn't misbehave every now and then."

+ + +

My father sat in the front passenger seat, Yankees baseball cap on his head, busily reading from the laptop computer in his lap.

"You're five minutes late," Aldo grouched when I closed the door.

"I had to say goodbye to Dani."

"Accent!" my father said sharply.

Aldo backed up and pulled away from the curb. Under his breath, he said, "You go looking for trouble, trouble will find you."

We were at the entrance to the Belt Parkway when I noticed Aldo staring at the rear vision mirror.

"Black Caddy, about five cars back," he said calmly.

My father kept reading. "We pick up a tail at Donatella's?"

"Too soon to tell. Might be going to church."

Aldo accelerated onto the Parkway, fast enough that I gripped the door-pull, my back squashing the seat.

My father glanced over his shoulder. "Make sure your seatbelt is tight. This isn't some Mafia muscle-car; it's a brute."

"Sal said the Florescus are 'ere in New York," I said.

247

"I know." He sounded as if he didn't need the distraction.

When I looked through the rear window, the black Cadillac was far in the distance. I sent an 'ILU' text to Dani, and tried to read *Faustus* without resorting to the dictionary for every word.

That early on Sunday, the roads were near uninhabited. It was only a matter of minutes before we raced over Verrazano-Narrows Bridge.

Philadelphia, Baltimore, and Washington DC were far behind when we stopped for fast-food and fuel at a truck stop near Fredericksburg, Virginia. When we got back in the car, my father passed me his laptop and a notepad.

Over a hundred file and folder icons littered the screen. Some were obvious, like 'FBI Reports June 1995' and 'Autopsy-nurse'. Others were cryptic, like 'Z-Surv-6-7'. My father had been busy in New York.

"I've listed the nursing homes by likelihood," he said. "See if you agree."

I went down his list, examining each entry he'd made with information he'd gleaned from the Internet. Without knowing how he prioritized, his rankings were meaningless.

"'ow old is Thom?" I asked.

He had to think about it. "By now, he'd be in his mid-80s."

"Would 'e want a retirement village, assisted livin' community, or a nursin' 'ome?"

"Thom would want none of the above, plus he hated resorts. That's what makes it so difficult."

"So where would 'e go?"

"He used to talk about moving to a Greek village so he excavate in his backyard."

"Not many ancient ruins at Myrtle Beach," Aldo quipped.

"Would 'e prefer close to town, or somewhere rural?" I asked.

"If he was hiding from Zagarovsky, it'd be smart to choose town. Thom would rather have classical architecture."

Where would a professor of archeology like to live when he was so old he needed assistance? Not a Greek village. Not close to the ocean, or the supermarket. I tore a sheet of paper from his notepad and used *Faustus* for a table to make my own list. Ten minutes later, I ripped off another sheet, and started again.

About six lists later, we sprinted through Richmond, Virginia, where Sarah had lived before her house burned down; and the turnoff to Norfolk, where I'd grown up in the care of my uncle and aunt. It struck me that I was missing a clue that was right in front of my face.

I had a short list of five when we zipped into the first rest stop in North Carolina. My father had two of them in his top five. We walked through the parking area to stretch our legs.

"If 'e's anythin' like Sarah, 'e'd want to be close to a library," I began.

"Books are the key," my father agreed. "He had a huge collection. In the thousands!"

"What did 'e do with 'em, you reckon?"

"Good question. That's why I focused on assisted living. There's usually a lot more space."

"I wish I'd known that," I grumped. "All of mine are close to the library, except one. Myrtle Woods 'as its own library."

"You sound like a bloody Cockney! Your accent needs to be more nasal. Pay attention to keeping the tone flat and how the words slur. And another thing; you're getting the vowels wrong. The 'a' should be more 'y' or 'e'; and 'i' is 'oi'."

"I'm doin' me best, mate."

"While you're doing your best, drop the 't' and 's' occasionally. And your 'r' needs work too. It's lazy, or non-existent, unless you're joining words together."

I felt like I'd been slapped over the head with phonetics.

"No worries, mate. We'll work on your accent after dinner. By the way, Myrtle Woods Retirement Village is on my list too. It's Greek Revival. We'll go there first thing on Monday."

I snoozed the rest of the way to Myrtle Beach. I felt safer with my father driving at the legal speed limit.

Chapter 29.

At the end of a magnolia-lined drive, Myrtle Woods Retirement Village might have been a plantation. It was antebellum style, a white, two-story building with deep, shaded verandahs enclosed by columns stolen from Ancient Greece.

"Not too shabby." I made an extra effort to get the accent just right.

"We might be lucky," my father said. "In case we are, take out your contacts. We don't want to confuse him anymore than he already is."

He went inside by himself. I waited in the shade of a southern live oak, draped with Spanish moss. Aldo carefully scraped bug remains from his windscreen.

"How fast can it go?" I asked, working the stiffness from my legs.

"Fast enough." He kept cleaning the glass.

"I'm sorry about yesterday. It won't happen again."

"It better not... I've had it up to one-seventy."

At least we were talking.

"I only wanted to find out what happened to my mom."

"So does your dad, except his first priority is keeping you alive." Aldo straightened and looked around. "Even if we find him, there's no guarantee he knows anything."

My father came down the stairs, his 'thumb up' a good sign.

"Thom Ryder missed breakfast. Apparently, that's not unusual for him," he said, his tone sarcastic.

"He's really here?" I asked.

"Look around you. As soon as we turned into the drive, I knew he'd be here. Most people are very predictable. Of course, you didn't know him. He loved Ancient Greece, same as Sarah."

"I can't believe it would be this easy."

"How many more times do I have to remind you about the accent?" He shook his head. "Actually, it was too easy. That's the problem."

"Set up?" Aldo queried.

"No way of telling. He's been here for four years. He visits his other kids a couple of times a year."

Aldo shook his head. "Sloppy!"

"Maybe he's been lucky. He's in a villa, Egret Cottage, overlooking Turtle Lake." He waved vaguely right. "Somewhere over there, past the golf course."

+ + +

Aldo parked in the visitor space, and my father and I walked down a cracked concrete path. Egret Cottage was the second villa of six, all with spacious verandahs overlooking Turtle Lake. It was a tiny pond, gloomy in shade and smelling swampy.

My father knocked on the front door while I scanned for alligators lurking in the pond.

"Just a moment!" came from within.

We waited a minute before he shuffled to the door, still in pajamas, his robe open in front. He confronted my father through flyscreen mesh. Behind him, books were piled waist high against the wall.

"What do you want?" he spluttered between coughs.

Eager to know if he was the man I met two years earlier, I came closer. He saw me, and coughed until he cleared his throat.

252

"I wasn't expecting visitors." He sounded relieved. "May I help you?"

My father's smile was genuine. "Hello Thom. It's good to see you."

He blinked rapidly, craning his neck to peer at my father. "Nick?" He shook his head. "It can't be; not after all these years."

His hand shook as he pushed back the screen door and cautiously stepped over the threshold. His hands, blotchy the first time I saw him, were darkly mottled. Suddenly, he seemed more relaxed. He grasped my father's hand, trembling, his eyes scrunched up like he was going to cry.

"Sorry about taking so long. I was reading in bed. My damned knee brace wouldn't go on." He frowned at me.

I'd hoped he'd remember meeting me at Brookgreen Gardens. Two years wasn't that long ago.

"Who's this, then?" he demanded.

My father nodded as if to say 'keep your mouth shut' as Thom peered at my face, tilting his head from side to side. He reached for my hand. His hand was cold and bony, and not very strong. After a moment, he turned my hand over.

He saw my forearm and gasped. I looked into startled eyes, hazel-brown like Ben's.

"Alexander Victor!" A smile slowly appeared among wrinkles. "I must say, I didn't care for Victor; though Alexander was perfect. *Alexein* and *Andros* in Greek; it means 'Defender of Men'; but I'm sure you know that."

I grinned back at him. "My dad's side of the family names their kids after Russian composers."

"We should be glad he didn't call you Vladimir."

I agreed wholeheartedly. "I met you at Brookgreen Gardens, Sir. It was two years ago."

"And you were as blond as Philip of Macedonia's son. Of course, I wondered afterwards. The likeness was remarkable, even after... all this time."

"I recognized him the moment I saw him," my father said quietly. "he's got his mom's eyes."

Thom coughed again, finally releasing my hand to find a handkerchief in his pocket. "Enthralled by Actaeon, you were; and you knew all about him, and Diana too. That'd be my wife's doing, no doubt."

I sat in the porch swing while my father and Thom took the chairs. They talked about New York, about dinner parties and Christmas festivities at my grandparents' house on Long Island, about Ben and Jessie, and Thom's other grandchildren, not a word about the fire. I felt light headed, as if everything would finally be right.

"What made you come here, Thom?" my father asked directly.

Thom mumbled something. He pressed a tobacco-stained thumb into his temple, kneading as if pressure on his skull would clear the haze of age, or stop memories from returning.

"Thom?"

"They came to the house one night. Quite late. It was after eleven. They pretended to be nice so I let them in. It was very stupid of me," Thom muttered. "They wanted to know where you were. I told them I didn't know."

"Who were they, Thom?"

"A nasty little man in a purple pimp shirt, and his friend. Shorty did most of the talking."

"His name is Mogilvich. He's dead," I added.

Thom stared at me. "He didn't scare me as much as the other one," he went on. "He didn't say much. All muscle, no brains."

"If he wore all black, it was probably Barkov," I said.

254

"He kept looking around my living room. We had a Hadrian bust in the bay window, a decent copy of the British Museum's marble. He said it was superb, but I could tell he was pretending to be classy; he'd cut your throat in a New York second," Thom said.

"He burned down my grandparents' house, and Sarah's too, when she lived in Richmond."

"Marjorie changed her name," my father explained.

Thom didn't seem to care. "In Richmond? I'm not surprised she was next door to Charlottesville. She was always fond of Jefferson's university." He coughed and spit over the rail. "Barkov; is he dead too?"

"Tony took care of him too," I said.

My father just smiled.

"Good riddance! He smashed Hadrian. My knee..." Thom closed his eyes momentarily. "There was another man waiting in the car. Faro, they called him. Is he dead?"

"Yes," I said.

"After what they said he would do if I told anyone..." Thom caught himself. "May the gods have no mercy."

"Thom, what was Faro going to do?" my father asked.

Thom staggered to his feet, clutching his robe. "I'd best be getting dressed. I have a lot to do today. Thank you for coming to see me."

My father and I looked at each other.

"Thom, what was he going to do?" My father was firm yet gentle.

Thom shook his head, inching away until his back hit the verandah handrail. "Not in front of the boy."

"Thom, we need your help. We're trying to find out about Emma."

255

"They said he'd send them in the mail." He grated knuckles against his brow. "There's nothing else I can tell you."

"Thom, please? Anything you can tell us..."

Thom turned away, silent, staring at the pond, gripping the rail with bony knuckles. His other hand trembled.

Hard-hearted, I couldn't hold back. "You told them your wife might be at Charlottesville, didn't you?"

"I didn't say anywhere close to Charlottesville, just in case," he murmured. "I said you'd go south, North Carolina most likely. It made sense at the time. I couldn't say South Carolina. She always talked about how much fun we had."

"You mean when we took that vacation together in 1995?" my father asked.

He faced my father, eyes blinking. "I had the time of my life. Babies on the way, and your little giggle-head Cupid running around. No wonder she wanted to be a grandmother."

"What else did you tell them, Thom?" My father was pitiless.

"Nothing." He regarded me sadly, slowly shaking his head. "Please don't hate me, Alexander?" When I didn't respond, he turned to my father. "Nick, I had to tell them, not because of what Barkov did to me. After he showed me... Emma... With so much at stake; there wasn't a choice."

He's startled my father. "What about Emma?"

"Emma?" He choked on a cough. "Emma?" he repeated when he got back his breath. "It isn't just her. I don't know what else I could've done. I'm sorry. I'm so, so sorry."

Thom would not say more, no matter how hard my father pressed.

Even though he didn't have email, I wrote Sarah's email address on a piece of paper and gave it to him.

Although he didn't seem very interested, my father promised to send Sarah his address and phone number. We said goodbye. I could hear him coughing almost all the way to the parking lot.

"He's really sick," I said.

My father nodded absently. "Not for much longer, I'm afraid."

"Can't we do something?"

He sighed, looking back at the villas around the pond. "None of this is his fault, though he blames himself. Hopefully, Sarah can convince him otherwise."

We didn't speak until we were back in the car.

Aldo switched off the radio. "From your miserable faces, I assume it was a waste of time."

Encountering his eyes in the rear-vision mirror, I stared out the side window. A woman was viewing the begonia beds, peering at large variegated leaves and splashes of color before she resumed her stroll towards the pond.

"Zagarovsky's people paid him a visit four years ago when he lived in New York," my father said. "Whatever happened, he's still scared to death."

Aldo started the engine, turned on the air-conditioning, and closed the windows. "You think Zagarovsky's got someone watching him?"

"Very likely," my father said.

"We came all this way for nothing at all," Aldo surmised.

The woman watched us drive past, though she probably couldn't see any of us through the dark-tinted windows. I looked right at her; coal-black hair and glasses to match. She was too young to be a resident.

My father turned to take a last look at the villas. "It wasn't for nothing. He knows something about Emma."

Chapter 30.

Sal came to dinner on Friday, July 27th. It was Donatella's birthday, and Dani cooked dinner; meat lasagna and Caesar salad. She was in the kitchen whipping cream for raspberries in Chambord, when I finally got the courage.

"Um Sal... Donatella... I need to ah... ask you something."

Donatella stopped browsing *Architectural Digest*. Sal put aside *The New Yorker*. Now, I had their attention; I wasn't sure I wanted to go through with it. From the kitchen, Dani gestured impatiently.

"Um... back in Australia, Sal, you said I should ask for permission." I took what I hoped was not my last breath. "SipregapossoavereilpermessodiprendereDaniacena?"

(Please may I have your permission to take Dani to dinner?)

They laughed. It took a moment to sink in that they weren't laughing at me. Donatella whispered something to Sal and smiled at me, not unkindly, affectionately.

"A dinner date?" Sal queried.

I nodded cautiously. "Saturday after summer school, if I could, Sir?"

"You want to take my granddaughter out tomorrow?"

"Yes Sir. Somewhere safe, so I don't need Aldo."

He rubbed his chin. "What do you think, Donatella?"

"I think he's too young for Gattino." She was teasing; I could tell from her eyes.

"Too much, too soon. A walk in the park might be allowed; 15 minutes, with Donatella as chaperone," Sal pronounced.

"Dani and I have already spent hours and hours together when she's working downstairs," I reminded him.

Dani nodded agreement and ducked out of sight again. However, Sal was far from convinced.

"We rode the bus all over New York when I first arrived."

"A date is different. It's like chalk and cheese. A date is romantico. A hot-blooded boy and a beautiful young girl; smoochy, smoochy is inevitable."

I stood, red faced and fuming. "I'm sorry I asked."

"I surprised Dani hasn't taught him how to negotiate?" Donatella remarked as I started towards the kitchen.

The New Yorker had polar bears and penguins on the cover. It inspired me.

"Three hours at Central Park Zoo, no Aldo, and we don't want a chaperone."

Sal counted off his fingers. "First, Aldo isn't negotiable. Second, you will have a chaperone. Third, a girl's first date must be special. The two of you have already been to Central Park Zoo. Fourth, two hours is quite long enough."

I confronted Sal with my most determined look. "Aldo, if he keeps his distance; three hours; we'll go somewhere else; and does the chaperone have to be Donatella?"

Sal chuckled. "Gattino has definitely trained you."

Donatella took over. "A third person tagging along will be ample, Marco. Perhaps a friend from your music school? I'm not sure I trust any of Dani's friends not to leave the two of you alone."

I nodded. "What if we rented a rowboat?"

"Sunset on Central Park Lake. That's rather cliché, don't you think?" Sal jeered.

"I think it's sweet!" Donatella interjected. "They could eat at the Boathouse Cafe afterwards."

"One hour rowing, an hour in the Cafe, an hour travelling; back here by eight o'clock at the latest; is that fair?" Sal inquired.

It wasn't; however, it was better than sitting in the living room, acting as if Dani and I were brother and sister. I nodded and escaped to the kitchen. Dani beamed; she'd heard every word.

"I could ask Chadwick, only he'll tell everyone, and probably make fun of me behind my back," I said as quiet as a mouse in the pantry. "The other option is Adam Hilton."

"Even his name sounds snooty," Dani whispered.

"He patronizes everyone, including the professors. Shelley's even worse. There's always Andy Borden," I joked.

Although Dani had yet to meet any of the students from ESA; she knew all about Andy Borden. She called him my 'nemesis.' More rival than enemy, he went out of his way to antagonize me.

"I want to meet the violin boy wonder," she snickered. "He'll be like a little brother tagging along."

"No way!" I was adamant.

"Someone has to keep your ego in check," she teased.

"And your libido, hopefully," Donatella said from the doorway. "It's such short notice; you should call him tonight, Marco."

I called directory assistance. There were hundreds of Bordens listed in Pennsylvania. I spent five minutes trying to persuade the phone lady to tell me if any Bordens lived on farms close to New York.

"I'll ask him when I see him in the morning," I said.

"Let me know if he can't make it. Dani can beg one of her friends."

260

"He better say yes," Dani said. "All my friends are in Europe."

"Poor thing; you never go anywhere," Donatella mocked. "If it works out, Marco, I'll talk to Aldo about keeping his distance."

+ + +

Saturday morning, I waited outside ESA for Andy's black Cadillac to arrive. At 8:59 am, it swerved to the curb. Andy scrambled out with his violin case and backpack. He said something to his driver and slammed the car door.

"You stalking me?" he asked when he saw me.

I followed him in. He was wearing girly clothes again. I almost didn't ask him; however, it was either him or the conceited Chadwick. I told him I was renting a rowboat after summer school, and he was invited.

"I would've called last night, except I couldn't get the number from directory assistance," I ended.

"It's unlisted."

"You want to come?"

He backed up, blocking the foyer. He was angry, like I'd made fun of his clothes.

"Sorry I asked, mate."

"Capra, you're so full of crap."

I walked on, leaving Andy to be pushed around by late arrivals to orchestra practice. I was still fuming in the elevator, and hoping the doors would close before he arrived. He made it with a second to spare, occupying the opposite corner and glaring at me. I stabbed '3'.

"You're in a foul mood this morning," he said.

"You're not, mate?"

"I'm not your mate, and I'm tired of your bullshit," Andy snapped. "You didn't want me tagging along when you went to the church."

"Thought you'd enjoy a row on the lake. My mistake. I reckon Chadwick will do just fine."

"He's an ass, only it insults equines!"

I smiled; Andy could be amusing when he tried. "Speakin' of equines, you never told me your 'orsey's name?"

He looked at me suspiciously. "Fanfare."

The elevator hadn't budged. I pushed '3' again, hoping it would come back to life. "Boy or girl?"

"She's a brood mare. I ride her all the time, except when she's about to have a foal. Her tummy gets too big for a saddle."

"Lucky you! I've never been on a 'orse."

The elevator lurched, beginning a slow ascent. He clasped his violin case against his chest, his chin resting on the narrow end. I made a sourpuss face that even Ben would've laughed at.

"What's wrong with you?" he demanded.

"I was goin' to ask you the same question."

"My dad makes me watch her being bred," he confided. "He just told me they're doing it again next weekend. It's gross."

He looked so miserable, I felt sorry for him. "You get a new foal at the end, though."

He glanced up, a slight smile forming.

I took advantage. "Sure you don't want to go for a row, mate?"

"I can't. It's Samovar night. I have to be outside ESA at 7:30 so he can pick me up."

262

"You 'ave to 'ang around for three and a half hours?"

Andy shrugged. "I read in the foyer until the guard locks the front doors."

"Then what?"

"I sit on the steps. People keep pestering me; that's the crappy part. There's this one guy; he always stares at me until I tell him to eff-off."

"What if you're back 'ere by seven?"

"My dad'll never let me go."

"You always tell 'im everythin' you do?"

It took the rest of the ride to the third floor for Andy to think about it.

"Count me in," he announced, as cheerful as I'd ever seen him.

"We're goin' right after school. You can leave your stuff in our car."

"We?"

"I'm bringing my girlfriend." I hadn't told him about Dani.

In an instant, his mood changed to glum. He didn't say a word to me during class, and he avoided me on the terrace.

Chapter 31.

The instant Professor Boyle's Composition class ended, Andy bolted from his seat, likely his first time being the first kid out the door. With a sinking feeling that he'd changed his mind, I trooped out with the rest of the class. He wasn't waiting at the elevator. All the way down, I considered options, none of which would convince Aldo to let Dani and I go rowing alone.

Andy was at the reception desk, telephone to his ear. He didn't say much, just an infrequent 'uh huh.' He appeared even more despondent when he returned the phone to the receptionist. He picked up his violin case and walked wearily away from the counter. He was blinking tears when I came up beside him.

"I called my mom to see if it was okay," he murmured.

"And?"

"Some days she gets really sad." He looked up; his red, wet eyes made me pat his shoulder.

"We all 'ave bad days, mate."

"She wouldn't stop crying. It's always the same thing, only she never says why."

I stopped patting. "Some people are like that."

Andy sniffled, oblivious to my hand. "I bet your mom is normal."

"I don't 'ave a mom. She died when I was three." It was out before I could stop myself.

"Marco... She's...She's... He says she's... She's..." His voice cracked.

I let go of his shoulder and stepped back. "You ready to go for a row, mate?"

"I'm not dumb. I know you don't want me tagging along on your date."

"'owzabout I drag you outside and you ask 'er?"

+ + +

Aldo had parked in the loading zone. We loaded our instruments in the trunk and got in.

"Andy, meet Dani and Aldo. This is Andy."

Aldo gave a friendly nod from the front seat. Andy and Dani smiled at each other, both shy, both murmuring 'hi'. With me sitting between them, I expected the ride to Central Park would be mumbles and whispers. I never realized Dani always wanted a horse. I thought they'd never stop talking about clumsy foals, putting on a saddle when the horse wouldn't stand still, and mucking out stables. They followed me to the boathouse, Andy going on about watching Fanfare give birth to her foal a year earlier.

Our rowboat was identical to every other green and white rowboat on the dock, yet Andy had named it *Boatie* before we got in. I put him in the bow as lookout. With Dani in the stern, I pushed away.

Dani sang *Row, Row, Row Your Boatie*. An elderly couple in the next boat clapped. Still, I skipped the oar tip across the water, trying to splash her. She skewed out of the way, unbalancing the boat, brown curls tumbling down her back. Then, she stretched, arching over the stern, her arms making a halo, grinning and golden brown in the sun. I grinned back, doing my best not to stare at her shirt; the front buttons pulled tight. It had very short sleeves like Andy's.

"Bad puppy! Comportarsi!"

"What's comportarsi?" Andy asked.

"Behave," Dani and I said together.

"No splashing allowed, huh?"

Dani and I took turns making faces at each other and laughing.

As I sculled towards Bethesda Fountain, I spotted Aldo in jogging clothes, lurking on the terrace of the Loeb Boathouse. The end of July was hot, as good an excuse as any to head for the shade on the other side of the lake.

"How do you know how to row?" Andy hung over the bow with his butt in the air, tempting carp with his fingers.

Dani smothered a laugh. I wasn't about to say I learned to row a mile off the coast of the Dominican Republic, after her grandfather made my uncle dump his outboard over the side of the dinghy.

"My dad taught me, mate." It wasn't too far from the truth.

"He teach you anything useful?"

Dani gave me a questioning look. I shrugged.

"Yeah. Lots of stuff."

I'd rowed past Bethesda Fountain and turned towards Bow Bridge before Andy twisted around and sat on the seat.

"You see any fish worth catching?" I teased.

"I've never been fishing. My dad mostly ignores me," he said wearily.

"'e takes you to The Tsar's Samovar with him, mate. Gotta mean something," I said.

"You don't understand. It's not like that."

It was easier to let it go than get involved in his life.

Dani took the opposite approach. "Is he mean to you?"

"I could live with mean. He hates me."

I didn't believe him for a moment. "That why he sends you to ESA with a chauffeur every Saturday?"

"He only does it to upset my mom. She says he's not my real dad because I have her last name; only he is. I snuck into his office and found my birth certificate. Biggest mistake ever."

It was too odd to comment; and the way he said it made me uneasy. I kept rowing, the sun hot on my back. Dani nudged my knee. I glanced over my shoulder. Andy was squinting into the sun.

"You want to go blind, you drongo?"

"What's a drongo?"

"A kid who's so stupid he looks at the sun." I jerked forward on one oar and backward on the other, spinning the rowboat around.

"What if I want to be blind?"

"No one wants to be blind."

Andy glared at me. "Maybe I've seen stuff kids shouldn't see."

"Nothing is that bad," Dani said.

Andy sulked all the way to the bridge. Only when I headed back to the boathouse did he resume speaking to us.

+ + +

"I'll wait out here," Andy insisted.

"It's my treat, mate," I said.

I was hungry. The mushroom and mesclun salad I ate at noon lasted to Composition. I was ready to find out what the Express Café had to eat.

"If you're worried about spoiling your appetite, you don't have to eat," I added.

He looked at me like I was out of my mind. "I'm not hungry."

"At least have something to drink, Andy," Dani said.

He caved; and we waited in a line that stretched out the door. Ten minutes later we were seated on the patio, each with a hamburger, a drink, and a side order of fries. For a kid who claimed he wasn't hungry, Andy devoured his burger in record time.

"I guess you were 'ungry after all, mate?" I teased.

Andy licked mayonnaise from his fingers. "I thought you wanted me to leave."

Dani erupted in giggles. "No way. You're like Marco's little brother."

"Except we don't look anything the same."

"You should've seen him in Australia…" Dani caught herself in time. "He ate a hamburger and fries in about thirty seconds."

"I was deprived of junk food," I joked.

"My dad doesn't let me eat American food."

"What do you eat when you go to school?" Dani asked.

"I don't go to school."

"You're home schooled?" I almost added 'like me.'

He gave me another 'I was out of my mind' look, gobbled French fries, two at a time, and said 'yummy'.

"I'm not sayin' it's a bad way to learn, mate. I 'ave friends who are 'omeschooled," I went on, warming to Andy's quirky manner. "They're sailing around the world."

+ + +

Aldo parked in the loading zone, outside ESA, with a few minutes to spare before Andy's father was due to arrive. With Andy's violin case in hand, I accompanied him to the stairs.

"It was fun. I like Dani a lot. She's really nice," he confided.

"I reckon there are worse ways to spend a few 'ours."

"Thanks for inviting me."

He delved into his backpack, hauled out a hand towel, and spread it over the step.

"Don't want to get your pants dirty, huh?" I teased.

"I did once. Another big mistake," he mumbled.

He sounded so unhappy, I sat beside him. "What 'appened?"

"He made me take my pants off."

It sank in slowly that he meant at the restaurant.

"It was two years ago, a week before Christmas. He was in a really good mood because something was going to happen later that night." Andy fiddled with the latch on his violin case. "He hit me with his belt, right in front of them," he whispered. "He didn't stop until my legs were bleeding."

"Now, you're makin' it up."

One glance was enough to know he wasn't.

"Getting my pants dirty was just an excuse. He did it because he wasn't there to see it happen. He calls me his whipping boy."

I didn't know what to say. I put my arm around his bony back.

He trembled, staring at his knees. "I hate being small."

"Being small doesn't mean you're weak."

He pushed hair from his eyes. "I look like a girl."

"Why don't you do something about it?"

"I can't. He buys my clothes."

A moment later, he shrugged off my arm, shaking his head. I was afraid he was going to start bawling. It made me want to hug him even more. When I tried, he scooted sideways until he reached the edge of the towel.

"You really don't like bein' touched, do you mate?"

+ + +

I remained seated when the black Cadillac pulled up behind Aldo's car at 7:45 pm. Immediately, Andy jumped to his feet, his violin case in one hand, his backpack in the other.

"Ciao! Ci vediamo! It means so long!" I called.

He spun around, his eyes lit up. "Poka!"

I grinned and played dumb. "What's poka?"

He waved. "It's Russian. It means see you later."

As he ran, the passenger door swung open. Andy hopped in, and the car departed with a howl. It took longer to change a tire at a NASCAR race.

I wandered across to the Chrysler and got in.

"What's their big hurry?" Aldo asked.

"Running late, I guess. They go to The Tsar's Samovar once a month," I added, wondering if that was where Andy learned his Russian.

Aldo muttered under his breath. He called Tony on his cell phone, something about letting Sal know.

"He's one weird little kid," I confided to Dani.

"He's really cute." Dani lowered her voice too. "Is he gay?"

"How would I know?"

"He's wearing girls' clothes," she whispered.

"It's because of his dad. I think he goes out of his way to be cruel to him and his mom."

270

Chapter 32.

Wednesday afternoon, just like every other day of the week; I holed up in my bedroom and practiced my guitar until dinnertime. I was going through chords when Dani shouted up the stairs from two floors below.

"Andy's on the house phone, Marco."

Wondering how Andy got hold of Donatella's unlisted phone number, I carried my guitar to the desk and poked at the speaker phone button.

"I got it, Dani." I heard the kitchen phone click.

"Marco; hi. It's me, Andy." He sounded like he sang for a boy choir.

For a lark, I said, "Privyet!" (Hi)

"You know Russian?"

"A friend back 'ome taught me a few words, mate," I lied. "'owzabout you?"

"My dad; he mostly hires Russians. Um... Dani said you were practicing. I can call back later, if you want?"

"I can take a break."

I played my variation of the chord progression from *Sweet Home Alabama*, focusing on the flat seventh. I wanted Andy to hear it.

"You can mess up just about anything, Capra."

I laughed. "You ain't heard nothin' yet."

"Um... Marco... I wanted to thank you for taking me rowing. Um, and for dinner too."

"It was a burger 'n fries, mate. No big deal."

"I really enjoyed it." Andy sounded flustered.

"You looked at Boyle's assignment yet?" I asked.

271

"I want to do the Adagio from Beethoven's *Piano Sonata, Opus 78*. It's only four bars, but writing's a bitch."

"You need 'elp?" slipped out of my mouth.

"I can mess it up by myself."

"You 'ave to analyze it to death," I added.

"So I blow it," Andy grumped. "Um, Marco..."

This time, when he hesitated, I was sure someone was coaching him in the background, probably his mother.

"Yeah?"

"My dad said I should invite you... this coming Saturday, after school... It's my birthday this week... Tomorrow..."

"Happy birthday, mate."

In the background, a man said, "Tell him he'll be staying overnight."

"Um, you need to stay overnight," Andy muttered. "Is that okay?" He paused. "It's too far to drive back."

"Where are you 'avin' your party?"

"It's not a party." Andy stopped abruptly. "We're in Pennsylvania. I live on a farm..."

"I'll come if it means I get to ride a horse."

I expected a wisecrack from Andy. Instead, I heard the same voice giving Andy instructions.

"Someone will bring you back on Sunday," Andy repeated.

"I've got someone who can drive me," I offered.

"It's hard to find, even in daylight," Andy said swiftly. "It's two and a half hours from New York. This way I can ride with you."

"I need to ask. Can I call you after dinner?"

"Um… I'm not allowed to give out the number. I'll call you at nine o'clock. Poka!"

"Poka, mate."

With two solid hours of practice remaining, I stole another ten minutes to call Aldo. Aldo wouldn't say yes or no, though he did offer to call Sal and my father.

+ + +

Sal called Donatella while we were in the kitchen, cleaning up after another of Dani's lasagna dinners. After a minute, he asked her to switch on the speakerphone.

"Marco, what's the deal with this kid?" Sal began.

"He's in my class at ESA. He wants me to stay over at his parents' farm on Saturday night," I explained.

Dani whispered, "Lucky you. I bet you'll go riding."

Before I could say it was a certainty, Sal said, "You told Aldo it's in Pennsylvania. Where exactly?"

"I'm not sure. He said it's hard to find."

"You don't have an address! Are you out of your mind?"

I took a breath. Donatella gave an encouraging nod.

"He's going to call back, Sal. I'll get the address then."

"He's really sweet underneath, Nonno," Dani said.

"I assume that's loaded with meaning." Sal was seldom sarcastic.

"He has a likeability problem, Sal," I replied.

When he didn't say anything, I thought he hadn't heard me.

"It's risky," he said finally. "It better be worth it."

I picked up on the change in tone. "The way he talks, his home life sucks. He needs someone he can talk to," I added.

Sal chuckled. "Now you're a child psychologist."

Dani smiled at me. "Nonno, when you see them together, they're like brothers."

"Well, that's a game changer!" Sal's voice was too muffled to hear what he said next. "In case there's a problem, Tony wants you to use that GPS thing on your phone as soon as you arrive."

"What about my dad?"

"He's incommunicado. He's following up on your Myrtle Beach trip. I'll clear it with him; don't worry. You need to take the kid a present?"

Dani nodded excitedly. "He ought to get him something for his horse, Nonno."

"Yeah, a helmet, in case he falls off. There's a tack shop on 24th. Aldo can take you tomorrow."

+ + +

Andy called back at nine o'clock while I was doing the Composition assignment.

"I can go, mate; only I need an address and phone number," I said right away.

"Um, we don't have an address. We're in the middle of nowhere."

"No address, no me, mate."

"I'll go ask. Be back in a minute." He sounded tired.

I could hear Andy's voice, too muffled to understand, yet something told me he wasn't far away, like he had his hand over the receiver.

"I got directions. You take I-78 West to Hamburg, and then Route 61 towards Pottsville."

I grabbed a pen and wrote in the margin of my score for *Piano Sonata No. 24*. "Pottsville; that must be a fun place?"

"It's okay. I've been there a few times. After you cross the river the second time, you turn right. We're off River Road. You turn left at the third bend after the church. Our gate is the fifth one you come to."

Tired of writing directions, I asked, "What's the address for mail, mate?"

"We don't get mail. They pick it up at the Allentown Post Office."

"How about a phone number?"

"I didn't ask. He'll change his mind for sure if I piss him off. Um, Marco, about Flutey's assignment..."

"It's not 'ard, mate."

"I'm not very good at writing. Maybe if I read what I've got, you could tell me how to fix it so it makes sense?"

Chapter 33.

The black Cadillac was parked outside ESA, across the street. Andy's chauffeur beckoned impatiently, the trunk already open. Despite constant traffic crawling down 84th Street, we hurried over, weaving among cars.

It was hard to miss him, sitting with his back to a trashcan, the same busker I'd seen in the subway on my first trip to ESA. He played like a Texan cowboy, picking notes and strumming chords from Kenny Rogers' 'Gambler.'

"Get in on ze curb side," the chauffeur grumbled, slamming the lid as soon as our instruments and backpacks were in the trunk.

As I stepped onto the curb, the busker segued to 'Little Red Rooster' with a country twang. It was so unexpected, I turned to look. The busker had swapped his headband for an unlikely Yankees baseball cap. My dad winked once and switched back to Kenny.

Andy came up beside me and whispered, "Sometimes, I think about running away. I could be like him and play my violin."

"You'd die of starvation, mate."

Before I got in the car, I glanced back and gave the Aldo-okay-sign.

+ + +

Andy's chauffeur stopped for gas at a convenience store in Hamburg. It was the third time he'd stopped during the drive from New York. The first time was when he got in the wrong lane for the Holland Tunnel. He drove around the block and pulled into a loading dock, his eyes glued to the rear vision mirror for at least two minutes. He stopped again in Allentown; he said to pick up mail; except the post office was closed that late on Saturday.

"The closer we get, the more he worries about someone following us," Andy confided.

It was like watching Aldo with his Chrysler, checking the tires and under the hood, all the while scrutinizing every car that came past.

"Your dad must be really important," I said.

"He never talks to me about what he does." Andy stared through the windscreen. "Those are the Blue Mountains up ahead."

Compared to Patagonia, with fjords and magnificent glaciers reaching up to snowy pinnacles, Andy's mountains were a wall of very long, low hills covered with trees.

"Geologically, we're in the Great Valley Section. German immigrants settled here in the 1600s. They spoke Deutsch, so they became known as the Pennsylvania Dutch," he went on.

"Thanks, Ben."

"Who's Ben?"

"My cousin in Australia." It was out before I realized.

"He's the smart kid, right?"

"What 'e is, is an encyclopedia with bare feet."

Andy looked around to see if his chauffeur was still pumping gas. "You like him a lot, huh?"

I was sure they'd be friends. Not right away; they were like chalk and cheese; it would take a while to accept each other's quirks.

"What's to like? If e's not asleep, e's reading. Still, 'e kinda grows on you," I mused aloud.

"The same as me, except I wear shoes and don't read worth shit."

Andy clammed up when his chauffeur got in. I watched farms pass, painted red or white, with massive barns and silos. After crossing the river, we turned left off Route 61, though not onto River Road. I was thinking I might've missed the sign, when we turned left again, still not River Road. We passed a white clapboard church and turned right, not left at the third bend after the church. Immediately, I panicked. I stuck my hand in my right pocket, tugged out my cell phone, leaned forward, and slyly put it behind my back as I pretended to scratch.

"Much farther, mate?" I asked.

"A few minutes."

Andy might've been scratching his neck as he plucked at his shirt buttons.

"I have to look the same as I left," he whispered.

I kept my opinion to myself. With my left hand now behind my back, I relocated my cell phone, jamming it between my thigh and the side of the door. There, the chauffeur couldn't see it in the rear vision mirror, even if he adjusted the angle. I flipped it open and felt the buttons until I was sure my fingertip touched the right one.

All of a sudden, I sensed Andy was staring at me. He'd undone the first three buttons and put on a silver chain, as tight as Adam Hilton's choker, and as thick as a dog collar.

I looked out my window. "That hill got a name?"

"Hawk Mountain. My dad hunts there all the time. I went with him once."

I had an uncomfortable feeling it wasn't a father and son bonding experience.

"He was after an escaped prisoner," Andy said quietly. "The dogs ran him down..."

"What did he say about keeping your mouth shut?" the chauffeur snarled.

Andy's lips formed a silent vulgarity. He sulked to the next turnoff, while I tried to press buttons and see the tiny screen without drawing attention. Mostly, I hoped Dani wouldn't call me while my phone was switched on.

Andy didn't say a word until a white rail fence began. Meadows of thick long grass came right to the narrow road. Instead of fields of corn and free-range Friesian and Holstein cows, there were sleek brown horses in fenced paddocks.

He leaned and pointed out my window. "The two horses by the trees are Hanoverians, like my horse. They're mostly friendly, but you still need to be careful until they know you."

Another horse cantered beside the fence, wheeling back and forth, stamping its hooves, shaking its head aggressively.

"That's a stallion," Andy added. "He's mean, but not like Grusha. He's a Russian Don. The Cossacks rode them. He's really dangerous. He goes crazy with noise." He lowered his voice. "When we get there, follow my lead. My dad's weird about visitors."

I gave him a doubtful look. "Some kind of spy, is 'e?"

Andy didn't get it. "He hunts and breeds horses because that's what European nobles do," he whispered.

"You sayin' yer dad's a prince?"

"He thinks he is. The other horses are all thoroughbreds, not race horses, field hunters," he added, a little louder.

"Your friend got a cell phone, Annie?"

Andy jumped. "I guess."

The chauffeur met my eyes in the rear vision mirror. "You got a phone, kid?"

"You need me to make a call for you?"

"Don't be a smart ass! Hand it over."

Like Jag with a seagull, my hackles went up. "Why?"

"Annie?" the chauffeur growled.

"You'll get it back tomorrow, Marco," Andy peeped.

"Don't want you losing it, do we Annie?"

"My dad says cell phones bother the horses."

I shot him an icy look. "I'll turn it off, mate."

"Did Annie tell you being on a farm's dangerous? People get hurt. Stuff gets broken." The chauffeur laughed. "Everything's safer this way; trust me."

Andy kept his head down, peeking sideways as I checked my right pocket. Then, I held up my cell phone as if it had been in my left pocket all along.

"Can I check my messages first?" I asked sweetly, glancing down. There was one bar of signal strength.

"Tomorrow! Turn it off!"

"Cool! I got a message from my girlfriend," I stalled, pressing 'send' again.

"Turn it off, now!"

"Okay! I'm turning it off. It's off, see?" I held it up.

He reached back and grabbed my cell phone and shoved it in his jacket pocket. Andy gave a timid shrug.

The white rail fence turned into an unruly hedge so high you'd need a ladder to see over it. The entrance was imposing, brick pillars on either side, topped with carved stone urns. Massive wrought iron gates embellished with flowery curlicues opened automatically as the Cadillac approached. A guard stepped from the gatehouse, looked through the driver's window, and waved us on. Ahead, tall poplar trees lined the avenue all the way to the house in the distance.

I'd never seen a house like it, two stories with a Mansard roof, elaborate dormers with circular windows and multiple chimneys. Below an ornate cornice, balustrades and French doors punctuated walls the color of egg-yolk with white stone pilasters. Either side of the front door, Greek-style caryatids supported a balcony. It might've been a movie set, perhaps a chateau for Marie Antoinette. There was even a fountain in front with water jetting from the mouth of a rearing stallion, and splashing into an octagonal pool.

"He built it to look like the Imperial Dacha at Peterhof," Andy whispered. "It's all fake; the walls are stucco and the statues are plastic."

Still, I revised my opinion of Andy; living in a Baroque-style mansion, he was in the Croesus category of ESA students.

The chauffeur bypassed the brick-paved parking court intended for visiting dignitaries, and took us around back. Apparently, pilasters, French windows, and balustrades became wasteful beyond the corner. Only the cornice continued, plain yellow walls punctuated by inconsistent aluminum-framed sliding windows.

"He never finished it. My mom said while he was away, he got tired of pretending he was a Romanov," Andy whispered.

The rear court was bitumen. A chain-link fence enclosed runs, two kennels, and a few dozen coondogs.

"Your family really likes dogs, huh?"

Andy returned an unfriendly look. "They're okay if you don't mind the smell."

On the far side, a single-wide trailer blocked the view. Opposite the house was a new-looking seven-car garage. Except for roller doors, it was a single-story version of Baroque architecture. The chauffeur stopped the car in front of the trailer.

Before he got out, he looked back at us. "Go in and wait for him."

Andy got out without saying a word. He took his violin case from the trunk and waited until I got my guitar before he closed it.

He looked to the heavens after the chauffeur went into the trailer. "He's a creep. His wife's even worse."

I shifted uneasily. "It's really pretty here."

"Over by the pond is the original farmhouse. I like it better."

The farmhouse was old and unpretentious with ivy-covered stone walls, little multi-paned windows, and a slate roof. It looked onto a garden and an apple orchard beyond. On the nearest side, the glass-roofed conservatory belonged to a well-to-do farm, unlike the drab single-story metal building stuck on the other side.

"Kinda lopsided," I observed.

"They added the studio while he was away." Andy was as distant as the mountains as he started towards the house.

+ + +

We took turns using the restroom off the utility room. When Andy came out, he'd swapped frayed red shorts for blue bib overalls. He still wore the same flimsy shirt. Before I could ask, he made a beeline for the refrigerator.

"Want some Amish milk? It's from the cows we saw on the way in."

He reminded me of Ben when we left Norfolk; he poured two glasses from a glass pitcher, so afraid of spilling a drop that his hands trembled.

"You think I'm weird," he muttered, not looking up.

I wasn't sure if he was asking or stating a fact. Andy smacked his lips between sips. I drank half the glass in a gulp. It coated my tongue like whipped cream.

"Musical geniuses are s'posed to be weird, mate," I joked.

Andy wandered over to the window. It overlooked paddocks, a huge gambrel-roofed barn, and the pond.

"Most people don't like me," he said without looking at me.

"Face it, Maestro; you are kind of aloof."

"I can't help it. I get mad when Adam treats me like he does. It's not like I have a choice." Andy spun around.

His father stood in the doorway. He cocked his head at me. Our eyes met and a slight smile appeared. It was uneven, like there was something wrong with his mouth.

"Are you going to introduce me to your friend, Andryusha?"

For no reason, Andy glared back at him. "Marco, this is my father, Mr...."

"I'm Stan!" He directed another lopsided smile at me. "It's easier to remember than Stanislav." He stepped around the island bench and we shook. "It's a pleasure to meet you, Marco."

He stared at me as I mumbled, "G'day Sir."

He wore creamy, stretchy breeches tucked into black-leather riding boots, a black-satin flowery vest, and a matching cravat. Even his handshake was pompous.

"You're best friends, according to Andryusha."

"We're in some of the same classes at ESA; that's all," Andy interrupted.

"We're both Strings. We play together," I added.

There was no mistaking Andy's father. He was thin and pale, with wimpy, wire-framed rectangular glasses. He looked as harmless as Andy.

"I'm sure you do. You play, let me guess, the cello?"

"Guitar, Sir."

"A Segovia with my violinist! Even better! The two of you must perform for me. I know; 'Somewhere My Love' from *Dr. Zhivago*. It's very romantic, isn't it Andryusha?"

Andy looked pathetic. "He wants to see Fanfare. I thought we could go riding before dinner..."

"Andryusha has a behavior problem. He doesn't do what he's told. He's not like that at music school, is he?"

Andy scowled back at him. "Please don't call me that."

"That's what I mean. I call him by his proper nickname and he's rude for no reason. He'll apologize, if he knows what's good for him!"

"I'm sorry."

"Your mother called you Andrei. Don't blame me for your nickname," his father went on.

He walked to the window and stopped before Andy. He was short compared to my father, yet he towered over his son.

"Andrei means manly." He looked down, slowly shaking his head, his stance deliberately domineering as he flicked at Andy's miniscule shirt sleeve. "She certainly got that wrong, didn't she Andryusha?"

Andy glanced at me, at the end of his tether. Even as I considered what to say that wouldn't make the situation worse; he caved.

"Mom can't help being how she is."

"And neither can you." Without warning, his father flicked again at his shoulder, hard enough that Andy flinched. "From what you're wearing, you must not want to show your friend your horse."

Meekly, Andy looked down his front. I hadn't noticed he'd exchanged his sneakers for scuffed leather shoes. He looked up slowly.

284

"What's the rule, Andryusha?" his father barked.

"I wear overalls in summer," Andy murmured.

"Take it off!"

"Do I have to?"

His father snapped his fingers. "Do you want to show him your horse, or not?"

Andy groped at the metal buttons on his overall straps, his left hand clasping the bib so it wouldn't fall down. Awkwardly, he jerked up his shirt, fumbling with the buttons. Underneath, he was white and skinny. His shirt dropped to the floor, leaving his arms wrapped across his front, nervous fingers bungling the strap buttons.

He was so embarrassed, I looked the other way.

"Now, go to the stables and get the mare calmed down and ready for Grusha..." His father looked at his watch. "It's 6:45. We're breeding her at seven sharp."

"You said tomorrow morning."

"I changed my mind, Andryusha. No time like the present when something's important."

Andy gave a pitiful shrug. "Come on, Marco."

"He needs to practice 'Somewhere My Love.' I'll bring him down in 15 minutes. You want to get it right, don't you Marco?" His laugh was as insincere as his cockeyed smile.

Under his father's steady gaze, Andy backed away. His father waited until the door closed behind him.

"Let's go to my office. You don't want to be disturbed while you practice."

I followed him, guitar case in hand, through the dining room, and into a library that belonged in a mansion. He went over to a cabinet, took out a bottle, and poured himself a glass. I looked at book spines and paintings on the walls, copies of works I'd seen at New York's Metropolitan

Museum of Art. There was a photograph of Andy sleeping on a red-velvet divan. A shimmering silk shawl covered his scrawny mid-section. He looked about six or seven.

His father came up behind me, glass in hand. "I keep it there to remind his mother. It was taken the day I got back."

I nodded absently. Something about the photo didn't seem right; not feigned, surreal.

"I'm glad you decided to pay us a visit," he continued, sipping and swilling his glass. "Poor little Andrei. He's very upset about Grusha and Fanfare."

"Why?"

"Grusha's well-named. It's Russian for wild horse. You'd like to see him mate with Fanfare, wouldn't you?"

I shrugged.

"You're not weak like Andrei."

He leaned against a dark-burled-walnut desk. I was sure he was waiting for me to say something bad about Andy.

"You realize why he's the way he is, don't you?" he prompted.

I wondered what he expected me to say. "'e's a bit different."

"Different?" He laughed and gulped from the glass. "That's one way to put it."

"'e's small for his age," I added, skirting the obvious.

"Ah, you've noticed he doesn't eat much. It's all quite worrying." He scratched the back of his head. "Poor little thing; he was born six weeks premature. Both he and his mother nearly died. The house dwarf kept them alive."

"'e's the most talented kid at ESA."

"Coming from you, that's a compliment he doesn't need to hear. He told his mother you were a genius."

286

I should've backed off. Instead, I blurted out, "I've never 'eard anyone play the violin like 'im."

"It's her doing. She taught him while I was away. Of course, I soon put a stop to that. He still sneaks off to see her." He took a long drink from his glass. "Imagine how she feels when her precious little boy goes off to Stein; how much it must hurt that he needs me more than her."

It made no sense, yet I had to respond. "'e's a sweet kid underneath."

He grunted. "Sweet; that would be him."

It angered me that he didn't seem to care about his son, one way or the other.

"Sometimes, I let him play with her; a little reward if he's worked hard," he went on. "I was listening in when he told her about the performance last month. You're quite the composer, I hear. Of course, she has no idea. Growing herbs is all she's good for. Now you're here, we'll see what she remembers." He peered into his glass, swilling before he looked up. "What I want to know is, do you know why you're here?"

"Um, Andy turned twelve on Thursday?"

His father grimaced. "You're determined to convince me, aren't you?"

I turned back to the books. Every book appeared untouched, case after case of matching gilt titles and authors, the spines lining up perfectly.

"Of what, Sir?"

"Your little ruse worked, except for one small detail." He waited for me to ask. I read book spines to annoy him. "We figured it out when there was no sign of your father?"

I confronted him, exceeding my personal best to convey confused. "Me dad's in Australia."

"You expect me to believe he lets you roam like a free-range chicken?"

"I'm stayin' with a friend of..." At the last moment, I changed my mind. "Me mum knows 'er from work."

"She's your mother's friend?" he sneered. "Not according to Narcisa."

I shrugged back, trying to place a name I was sure I'd heard before.

"Unfortunately, there isn't time for you to meet her before we go to the stables. It's a pity. Andrei hates her even more than he hates Faro. " He laughed again. "You'll have to tell Andryusha we talked about Faro. It'll really upset him."

"Why don't you like him?"

"You haven't figured it out yet? Now, I'm surprised. Start with whose son he is."

"Yours, of course."

He looked at me with disbelief. "You think I'd father a runt like him?"

"Andy said 'e saw 'is birth certificate..." I stopped too late.

"He swore up and down he hadn't! Of course, he lies all the time, but he can't fool me."

He picked up a riding crop from his desk. It had a braided black leather grip with a wide tab on the other end. He slapped it against his boot before he flipped it in my direction.

"When he lies, I whip him with this. Twenty times for each lie. Double if he defies me."

He whacked the whip on the desk, a resounding crack that made me jump.

"That time, Andryusha lied twice, and he defied me."

He flicked at the photograph so there was no confusion. No wonder it was creepy.

"The flap on the end is the keeper," he went on. "It keeps the horse's skin from being damaged. He would've bled otherwise. The poor little thing was still black and blue. He was so worn-out, he fell asleep on the divan."

I stared at the photo. "That's awful."

"You think his punishment exceeded the crime?"

I couldn't face him. "What's the big deal if he sees his birth certificate?"

He emptied the glass. "He knows his mother's a nut case. That's why having a father is a big deal to him."

"It doesn't explain what's so important about his birth certificate."

"I had Barkov give a thousand bucks to the records clerk to put my name on it." He rubbed his thumb and first finger together. "I did it to make her crazy. Plus, I might need proof one day; you never know how things will turn out."

He strolled to the other side of his desk and opened a drawer. He shuffled though a sheaf of papers before he selected a manila envelope. He extracted a single page and dangled it in front of me, close enough to read.

"Unfortunately, she was cunning enough to use her married name instead of her maiden name," he said.

"Why would it matter?"

"Andrei's last name is Borden." When I didn't ask, he said, "I think it's time you met Mommy."

Chapter 34.

Andy's mother was working in the greenhouse. I could see her like a wraith wrapped in white, hunched over plants, picking them up and putting them on a bench. A moment later, she changed her mind and put them back on the floor.

The path branched, continuing around the pond to the original farmhouse, or right to the orchard. I followed him left, into the garden. Hollyhocks grew in untamed profusion. He unlocked the greenhouse door, and opened it for me to enter. He locked it behind him, and checked to make sure. It was strange, as if there was something growing in the greenhouse he didn't want people seeing; yet all I could see was row after row of parsley, chives, and basil.

I felt sick as soon as I saw her. She held a tiny plant in a pot, looking at it closely, her hand shaking so much I was certain she'd drop it. She jerked her head erratically. Her hair was long, silver blond like Andy's, and as straight as mine.

My lips barely moved. "Tushka."

She turned slowly, crying so softly that I barely heard as her fingernails scraped the pot.

He jabbed me from behind with the knob-end of his riding crop. "Say hello!"

"Mom… It's me."

She looked at me blankly, her hand still twitching as she said very softly, "Who are you?"

"Tushka," I whispered again.

"Did you come to see my San-boy? He's not here right now."

"Don't you recognize him, Emma? He's wearing contacts and his hair's been dyed; but he's still your son."

Her voice didn't change. "I'm afraid you've missed him. He's visiting with his grandparents."

He stuck his thumb under my chin and forced my head back. She peered at my face momentarily. She had my eyes, blue like the sky near the horizon.

"They had to move because there was a fire at their house. I don't have the phone number yet," she went on.

I shoved his hand away. "Mom, I need you to look at me. Please?"

"Andrei said his friend, Marco, played the guitar at a party. Is today Saturday? I have to play at a wedding on Saturday."

I had an awful feeling. "Mom, it's me; Alexander."

"They let me watch until Peter arrived."

"I was in the house, Mom."

She shook her head. "Luckily, my San-boy was at the pond with his father. He likes to watch the ducks."

"He's Nicholai Borden's son, same as Andrei." Calmly, he laid his riding crop on the bench. "Your brother-in-law went in and saved him." Without warning, he grabbed my right wrist and ripped my sleeve past my elbow. "The whelp should've died."

"Did he have an accident?"

"Stupid woman! This is Alexander!"

She stared at my forearm, her eyes still vacant. "Alexander's arms aren't wrinkled like that. He'll be four in February."

He smirked at me. "We'll be sure to have a party, invite all his friends and family, especially his father."

"It'd be nice if Andrei saw his father more often. Maybe he could come, too. Mr. Mogilvich said he lives in Australia."

291

"Why do I bother! I kept her and your miserable brother as insurance," he snarled at me. "And entertainment for Faro, as it turned out," he chuckled, jerking my arm back.

I gritted my teeth. "Sal shot him in the head."

"It's a pity Barkov didn't get you two years ago. Do you know how much money I wasted looking for you?"

"A lot, I hope."

"I wonder where Andrei is?" she said, looking around the greenhouse. "He said his friend composed. My father-in-law is a composer, too. Alexander Borden; he's very talented."

He shook his head and sighed. "Sad isn't it? On the plus side, I saved two million bucks with Andryusha bringing you here."

"That's a lot of bucks."

"It's what you're worth dead." He oozed satisfaction. "And to think were under our noses since May, staying at her house. You even fooled Grigore every Saturday."

"My San-boy has beautiful blue eyes," she murmured.

All of a sudden, the splinters that made up my life fitted together. I put my fingertip to my right eye, pinching the contact lens against my thumb. I'd never wanted it out so much. I flicked it onto herbs and desperately worked the other lens into position.

"Then, Narcisa spotted you at the church with Andrei," he went on regardless. "You couldn't visit that old fool in Myrtle Beach fast enough. That was the final giveaway."

"Mr. Mogilvich said I didn't care about my baby." She stuck her forefinger in the pot. "Basil can't be too dry or too wet. I couldn't feed him. He got sick when he drank cow's milk," she went on. "San-boy is safe with Nick's parents. Have you seen Andrei's Fanfare? He's very pale without his clothes on…"

Without contacts, I stepped in front of her, her finger still probing the soil for moisture. She looked longer, yet still unconvinced.

"Mom, I'm San-boy. You and Dad called me Alexander Victor. You haven't forgotten me; I know you haven't. I knew you the instant I saw you."

"What, no silly Australian accent, Marco?" Zagarovsky sneered.

"You're Andrei's friend, Marco," she muttered. "Mr. Zagarovsky, do you remember if I watered today?"

I turned on Zagarovsky. His right cheek bulged like he had an all-day-sucker in his mouth.

"Don't blame me. She was crazy when Dmitri brought her here." He examined manicured fingernails, then back to slapping his riding crop against his boot. "Watching her son burn to death was the likely cause, don't you think?"

I tried again. "Mom, you sang me to sleep every night about San-boy and Tushka. You were a bird that helped me find children who couldn't go to sleep."

"You're wasting your time. There's nothing but slush in her brain from twelve years ago." Zagarovsky smirked. "Narcisa loves tormenting her in front of Andrei. It's really quite funny to watch."

My mother picked up a larger pot and gave it the moisture test. "It's dry too, Mr. Zagarovsky. I must not have watered this morning and forgotten."

He smirked at me. "Emma can't remember what she did this morning, let alone yesterday. Still, I'm sure when she sees you die, it'll prompt a few memories. Now, her darling Andryusha dying; that'll drive her completely insane."

I looked him in the eye. "Everyone at ESA knows I came here," I said.

"That's so unoriginal, Alexander. I'm sure they'll be very sad when they hear about your terrible accident." He looked at his watch. "Five minutes past seven. Poor little Andrei's probably already dead."

Words weren't there when I needed them most. I resorted to my father's two favorites. Before the words left my mouth, she hit him with the pot. It was a glancing blow, and not hard enough. Still, he dropped his riding crop and fell back on the bench, sending pots crashing and squashing herbs under his butt.

My mother was as shocked as he was. She was so pale she might've never seen sun. She trembled like a leaf until he staggered up, blood trickling from his forehead. With him blocking the way to the garden door, she grabbed my hand and shoved me past her. I bolted for the other door. It opened into a sunny breakfast room, bright yellow walls, a floor of black and white marble squares, French doors opening onto a patio, glazed pots of orange trees along the edge, the hollyhock garden and orchard beyond.

I tried both doors before I gave up.

"I'll see to you later! They die first, then their father," Zagarovsky shouted behind me.

I didn't hear what he said after that; my mother screamed. "Alexander, run!"

I ran through the kitchen, passing a large dining table with a tall silver vase of hollyhocks in the center. The entry foyer promised escape; however, the front door was locked. The next room was an office with blinds on the windows, computers and files covering desks, a huge olive-green safe in a corner, and a wood-paneled door in the opposite wall.

"You can't get away this time, Alexander!" Zagarovsky shouted.

I barged into a parlor from the 19th century, with brocaded curtains draping windows that weren't real. Frumpy Victorian chairs surrounded a card table with a yellow glass lamp. I crossed a burgundy-and-blue Persian carpet, skirting a love-seat and a red-velvet Turkish divan separated by a gilt-frame mirror, and two tripods with video cameras.

After that was a room stripped to bare blue walls with paint-splattered drop cloths on the floor, a sleazy motel room with a messed-up bed, and a basement made into a functional dungeon. Brick-pattern wallpaper gave it away.

I'd all but given up hope of escaping when I opened the next door. The room was stuffed from floor to ceiling with props. Someone had left open the loading dock door.

Chapter 35.

Before I was halfway to the barn, I could hear a horse neighing; interspersed with shouting from the other side of the main house. Several cracks followed, like tree branches breaking. When I turned to look, Zagarovsky had come out the front door of the farmhouse. He headed my way, although taking his time. I thought he was shooting at me until a flock of ducks burst from the bulrushes at the far end of the pond. They disappeared into the brush, flapping madly.

I didn't stop running until I reached the barn doors. There was no sign of anyone, just two blue tractors, an assortment of farm equipment, and benches and shelves littered with tools. My panic seemed pointless when I realized I smelled hay in the loft, not horses in stables.

The stables were in the next building. It was as wide and long as the barn, not as high so it couldn't be seen from the house. A set of sliding glass-and-wood paneled doors opened into a long aisle lined with stables. Still an hour before sunset, clerestory windows diffused a golden glow over the wood posts and beams holding up the roof. Compared to the barn, it was spotlessly clean, even the brick floor.

Each stall was fit for a regal racehorse, walls of varnished wood planks below and metal grating all the way to beams overhead. The grating curved down in front so that horses could hang their heads over. The first horse gave me a nosy stare, likely sizing up my equestrian experience. I'd never been so close to a horse. Despite huge soulful eyes, it wasn't friendly. Its nostrils, like vacuum cleaner nozzles, snorted a warning to stay clear.

Now wary of anything with four legs, I passed bridles and reins dangling on pegs. When one horse whinnied next to my ear, I jumped, bumping into a saddle on a stand. With my heart pounding, I walked on. I was three stables from the end of the aisle when I heard Andy's shrill voice.

"How do you know my dad, Sal?"

Though it didn't make sense, I breathed a sigh of relief. Still, instinct made me keep my mouth shut and stay out of sight. I squatted behind a hay bale standing on end.

"We were in the same business a long time ago," Sal said unemotionally. "How old are you, Andy?"

"I turned twelve on Thursday."

Across the aisle, a chestnut with a golden sheen plunged against the railing, snorting, kicking straw under the door. It had black threatening eyes. Its stall had thicker bars than the other stalls. There was no curve in front; the grate went all the way to the beams overhead.

"My son died when he was 14," Sal said.

I inched closer, avoiding a pitchfork that someone had propped against the stall wall. I peeked through the grate. Andy vigorously brushed his horse in small circular motions. Doing it right seemed very important to him.

"That's hard work for someone your size," Sal said.

"Brushing settles her down. I don't usually do it this fast, only I'm in a hurry today." Andy looked up abruptly. "I'm sorry about your son."

"If he was still alive he'd almost certainly have kids of his own by now," Sal went on. "You get to be my age, and you need grandkids to keep breathing."

Andy wiped his brow and straightened, taking a few moments to catch his breath. He looked across the aisle. The other horse snorted and slammed against the stable door.

"You have Dani. I like her a lot."

"Not as much as Marco does; am I right?" Sal said.

Andy smiled, keeping his opinion to himself as he brushed his horse's tail.

"She could do worse for a boyfriend," Sal went on.

I decided to wait a little longer before I made my presence known.

"When we went rowing, it was fun watching them tease each other," Andy conceded. "When I was little, my mom used to say guitar players are very romantic."

Sal said something, but the horse next door banged into the stall wall hard enough to make the posts shudder.

"What's his problem?" Sal asked.

Andy kept brushing. "That's Grusha. He shouldn't be in here."

"He wants to be outside, running around huh?"

"What he wants is my horse."

"Why?"

"He's a horny stallion. She's in heat. Go figure."

Sala chuckled. "If Dani's guitar player is anything like Grusha, I better keep an eye on them."

Unamused, Andy scratched around his horse's ears. "She said I could be his little brother, except we look nothing the same."

Fanfare rammed her muzzle against his chest and buffeted him in return. Andy grinned and scratched harder, raking his fingers along her nose.

"A man who worked for your father shot my son," Sal said quietly. "Maybe you know him? He went by Faro."

"It's from how he shuffles cards. His real name is Maxsim Volkov." Andy stopped scratching. "You said went. Is he dead?" He sounded hopeful.

Sal nodded slowly. "I take it you didn't like him very much?"

"He wouldn't leave me alone."

298

Sal stepped back as Andy unfolded a three-step ladder. He hopped onto the top tread and began making short straight strokes, brushing his horse's neck and withers.

"Your father told Faro to shoot my son in the chest." Sal's voice cracked. "He wanted Dante to die slowly. I'm not that cruel."

Andy's brush banged on the floor, loud enough to make his mare lurch away. I started forward, not seeing Sal's handgun until I reached the stable door.

"Sal!"

Sal glanced over his shoulder. "Stay there, Sharkbait!"

He turned back to Andy, frozen on the ladder. He lifted the gun to point at his head.

"Sal, you're scaring him!"

"Actually, you need to leave," Sal snarled.

"You need to stop!" My voice sounded like someone else's.

"This doesn't concern you." He was as cold as the icy wind of Cape Horn.

I stepped closer. "Killing him won't bring back Dante!"

His finger tightened on the trigger. "It'll make me feel better."

Andy scrunched his eyes.

I panicked. "If he said he's Zagarovsky's son, it's not what you think, Sal!"

"He's Zagarovsky's spawn. That all that matters."

"What matters is he's my brother."

One more step and I stood between them. I glared at Sal, not believing he'd shoot my brother. Behind me, I wedged a quivering Andy against his horse.

"Don't lie; not to me."

"I'm not making it up, Sal."

"You're making this harder than it needs to be. Move out of the way."

I edged aside. "You're no better than Zagarovsky."

Sal wavered. He lifted his gun, grinding his thumb against his forehead. I exhaled. Suddenly, his gun was back, pointing at Andy, his hand steady.

"Get out, now," he rasped.

I shook my head and hoped I was right. "I saw his birth certificate, Sal. His name is Andrei Nicholas. Nicholas, Sal!"

Sal's hand didn't waver.

"He was born on August 2nd, 1995. His mom's name is Emma Borden. Sound familiar?"

Sal lifted his left arm. For a moment, I thought he was going to shove me out of the stable. His trigger finger twitched, ready to pull. I put my arm around Andy's shoulder and pulled him behind me.

I braced myself. "Remember the kid you dragged into your dinghy? Doesn't Andy remind you of Dante, too? Dani picked up on it right away."

After a moment, Sal covered his face with his left hand. Slowly, he put his gun in the feed bucket, slung by straps from the top railing. He mumbled something about Dante as he turned away.

I wanted to shout, 'He really is my brother.' I watched him all the way to the door. I felt Andy trembling next to me, whimpering, his hand grasping at mine. At the last moment, Sal stumbled, clutching the side of the door. Andy needed me more.

"Who is he?" Andy murmured.

"Sal... he used to be a friend. He's not like he was when I first met him. Now, he's all about getting even."

"Why does he want to kill me?"

"He's got his reasons, only it's not going to happen. I remind him of his son too much. Both of us do."

He considered it momentarily, and shrugged doubtfully. He jumped from the ladder, scooped the brush from the floor, and returned to brushing his horse as if nothing had happened. He was so skinny his loose overalls slapped bare skin as he worked. He was wiry and agile; and so focused that nothing got between him and his horse.

I planted my butt on the railing, and wondered if being single-minded was his way of dealing with difficult situations. I wanted to talk about us being brothers; instead, he crouched underneath Fanfare to brush her belly. I was thinking I ought to find out what Zagarovsky was doing when Andy stuck out his head and frowned up at me.

"I can't believe he bought it when you told him we're brothers."

Chapter 36.

"When you've finished chatting, bring the mare over here. We'll breed her in Grusha's stall," Zagarovsky growled.

I hadn't heard him come up behind me. Andy stopped brushing Fanfare's front legs and scrambled to his feet.

"Dad, last time it was in the barn; and she still got hurt," he squeaked.

"Out! Now!" Zagarovsky slammed the stall door back on its hinges.

"Dad, please. It's not safe in a stall. She can't get away if he loses control."

"You want me to come in there and get her myself?" Zagarovsky slapped his riding crop on his boot.

Andy stood his ground, one little fist clenched, the other hand still holding the brush. "You think you're so high and mighty, but you're not. Mom told me you were in prison. That's why you're so mean to us."

"What happened the first time you defied me?" Zagarovsky cracked his crop against the wall.

Andy glared at him, his bottom lip pushed out. "I hated you afterwards. I still hate you!"

Zagarovsky stormed into the stall. He shoved Andy up against his horse and waved the riding crop in his face. All of a sudden, he flicked the keeper on Andy's cheek, just once. Andy cringed and whimpered and tried to jerk his head away.

"Poor little Andryusha. I barely touch him and he cries, just like his crazy mother."

"You coward!" I said loudly.

Zagarovsky spun around, his riding crop raised. "One more word out of you, and you'll beg for mercy, the same as he did when he was eight."

"Dad, I'll bring her," Andy murmured.

"Tell him, Alexander!" Zagarovsky said.

Eye to eye, I confronted my brother. "Andrei, he's not your father. He faked the birth certificate."

"Finally, the truth comes out," Zagarovsky mocked. "You're no son of mine!"

Andy's face crumpled. "Mommy said... I thought... she made it up... When she cries...It's all my fault..." He sniffed and smeared his face with the back of his wrist.

"You want me to give you something to cry about, Andryusha?" Zagarovsky smacked the crop on the stall door.

Andy shook his head. "Be quiet, okay?" he whispered to me. "You'll just make it worse."

Zagarovsky stepped back. Meekly, Andy untied the halter and led Fanfare out of her stable. Across the aisle, Grusha neighed and stomped, walloping the stall sides and frantically tugging on the halter.

Andy waited a moment. He lifted the latch and cautiously opened the door. Grusha snorted, shaking in fits, hooves clouting aside straw and rubber floor mats.

"Okay boy. Grusha, calm down. I'm not going to hurt you." Andy's voice wavered. "You know me, Grusha. I bring you apples all the time. Calm down. That-a-boy. He's a good boy, isn't he Fanfare?"

Grusha backed off, still uneasy, still snorting. Andy glanced back at me as he inched through the opening, pulling Fanfare behind him.

"This time, Grusha, you're going to be really gentle with her," Andy crooned.

Zagarovsky snorted, his riding crop at the ready. "Stop wasting time and tie her in place."

Obediently, Andy tied Fanfare's halter to the opposite railing. "This is really a bad idea."

Zagarovsky closed the door and locked the latch. "Now, undo him."

"No way!" Andy jumped out of the way as Grusha lurched at Fanfare.

"Don't worry; I'll let you out before the fun starts. One... Two...," Zagarovsky said, raising his voice.

"Don't! It's okay, Grusha... Alright, boy. I'm going to let you go." Andy crept closer to Grusha.

"I don't have all day, brat!"

Andy fumbled at the knotted halter. Grusha wheeled around, nearly crushing him against the wall. Andy ducked under Fanfare and tried from the other side. I reached for Sal's gun in the feed bucket. It was heavier than I expected, no plastic, high-tech pistol like Aldo's Glock.

"Please, open the door," Andy begged. "I'll finish undoing it from the next stall, I promise."

"No wonder Grigore calls him Annie," Zagarovsky sneered.

He slapped his boot with the crop, again and again until Grusha reared up, whipping his head, straining against the halter until it broke. Fanfare whinnied, barging into Andy. For an awful moment, I thought Andy was crushed against the wall. He scrambled out from underneath and squeezed himself into the corner as Fanfare lashed out with her rear hooves.

"Do something!," I shouted.

"Let me think about it." Zagarovsky scratched the back of his head. "You could call 9-1-1; but it'll take them a half-hour to get here."

Grusha wheeled, snorting and tossing his head at my terrified brother.

Zagarovsky slapped his boot loudly. "Why don't you go help him?"

I glared back at him. "You want Grusha to kill us."

"Until I met you, the plan was for the champion swimmer to drown trying to save his young friend in the pond. Mundane, yet believable; Andryusha can't swim to save his life. Two boys being stomped to death by a raging stallion is much more exotic, don't you think?"

Grusha stomped a hoof in anticipation. I brought the gun from behind my back and pointed it at Zagarovsky's head.

He smirked asymmetrically. "You're the same as your brother. You're chicken."

His smirk disappeared a moment before I pulled the trigger.

Immediately, Grusha reared up, front legs clawing, hooves crashing on the wood railing. Andy sprang from the corner, grabbed two bars of the grates and hauled himself onto the stall door. He stretched up as far as he could, the top of the door still out of reach. His feet flailed, his shoes unable to grip the smooth steel bars.

I dropped Sal's handgun on the hay bale, and reached through the grating for Andy's left foot to give him a boost. He'd be lucky if he weighed 70 pounds, yet he was so frantic I couldn't budge him. I grasped his other foot. Andy got the idea and stopped struggling. I heaved him higher. In an instant, Grusha pivoted, slamming a hoof where my right hand and Andy's left foot had been moments earlier.

I boosted him up as high as I could. Suddenly, the load on my wrists diminished as Andy hauled himself up to the overhead beam. Grusha reared again, hooves smashing against the grate, against Fanfare. Andy's shoe came off, smacking Fanfare. She whinnied, backing up against the stall door. There was blood smeared over her haunch. Andy screamed.

He clambered onto the beam, looking down at the raging stallion in the stall. As soon as he caught his breath, he let loose a stream of cuss words.

"We get out of here, the first thing I'm doing is washing out your mouth."

He mouthed, 'eff you,' yet the spark in his eyes said otherwise.

He dragged himself along the beam, clenching his teeth when he moved his right leg. Grusha shoved the mare against the door. Andy jerked up his left leg, and gripped the beam. With each frenzied lunge, the stall shuddered so much that he almost toppled off.

I slammed down the door latch and pulled out the locking bar an instant before Grusha reared again. The stall door flew open. Grusha shot out, bucking and kicking like a horse at a rodeo. For a moment, I thought he was coming for me. Instead, he bolted down the aisle and out of the stables.

When I looked up at Andy, I saw blood streaming down his ankle, his overalls ripped to the knee. All I could do was watch until he reached the next stall.

"I'll get the ladder," I said.

"Behind you," he gasped.

When I turned, Zagarovsky was standing up. His left hand clutched his chest. Blood seeped through his fancy paisley vest. He tottered towards me, dragging the pitchfork with his free hand.

"You're..." He shuddered and swayed. His head lolled and spit drooled from the corner of his mouth.

I stared back at him. "I'm what?"

He lifted up the pitchfork, turning it end to end, stopping when the long curved prongs poked my chest.

"You're... you're dead."

His head twitched at a strangled cough from behind him. I hadn't expected Sal to return. Casually, he picked up his pistol and aimed at Zagarovsky.

"This is for Dante," he rasped. He pulled the trigger twice. "This is for Ben.. And Jessie.. Andrei.. This is for Emma.."

A Beretta 92FS magazine held 15 9mm bullets. I thought Sal was going to stop at my mother. He used 14 of them before he finished with me.

+ + +

He tossed the gun aside and grasped the grating to steady himself. "Sharkbait... you okay?" he wheezed.

I ignored him. I dragged the stepladder over to the stall wall. Sal flinched, rubbing at his left shoulder, his arm hanging useless. I ignored him and helped Andy climb down from the beam. I made him sit on the hay bale so I could look at his leg. I peeled back his overalls to his knee. There was an awful gash down his calf.

Sal looked from me to Andy, long and hard. "The kid's got guts. He must be your brother."

We had his leg bandaged before my father, Tony, and Aldo arrived at the stables. They'd gone to the house, expecting to find me there.

307

Chapter 37.

By 9:00 am, the mid-September sun scorched northern Queensland. The bright-blue sky was amazingly clear over turquoise water; only a few puffy white clouds stood guard over bluish mountains that came right down to the sea. At the junction, bands of color stretched to the horizon, verdant green rainforest, a skinny yellow ribbon of beach, and palm trees mixed with white, eco-friendly tourist architecture.

I returned to my dictionary, plodding through *Faust* by translating German. It was laborious, ten minutes to get:

'To allow only the kind of art that the average man understands is the worst small-mindedness and the murder of mind and spirit.'

As the words sank in, I realized why my father wanted me to read it. He was challenging me to learn for the sheer delight of knowing more. Especially, he was daring me to think for myself, to get rid of my preconceptions. It made me think about Adam Hilton and John Cage; and the camp I was in.

"He's really your little brother."

I glanced up again. Ben slathered his arms with sunscreen. He would be 12 in three days. He was fractionally taller than when I saw him in May, still in pestering mode.

"Unless you tested our DNA since the last time you asked," I replied.

It struck me that Ben hadn't asked. I looked where he was looking. Andrei straddled the bowsprit, bony pale legs dangling as he showed Jessie how to ride a make-believe horse through wavelets lapping the bow. Three years and five days separated them, yet they carried on like twins.

"He's making progress," I thought aloud.

"Mom told Dad he's so far behind at school it'll take years for him to catch up," Ben confided.

"You'd be behind, if you didn't have a teacher from the time you were eight." However, it bothered me that Andrei and Jessie read the same books.

Ben nodded sagely. "Last night, I got him reading about horses in the Britannica."

"Don't overdo it. Be patient with him."

Nearly every day, my father gave me similar warnings.

"Mom said he's very fragile, even though he acts tough." He hesitated. "He got upset over not knowing what an ungulate is. I told him horses were *Perissodactyls*; odd-toed ungulates. For no reason at all, he started crying."

"He hates not knowing stuff. He needs you more than you know, Ben."

"I tried to explain how species of a genus are related, like horses with zebras and rhinos. He didn't even know what a tapir is. He told me he's never gone to school." Ben wiped a sunscreen-coated finger in his eye and blinked. "We're his only people-friends; that's what he said last night. Kind of hard to believe."

Although I wasn't supposed to talk about what happened to Andrei; Ben needed to know some of it. I figured with Andrei hanging off the end of the bowsprit, he was far enough away.

"From the day of the fire, our mom was a prisoner at the farm," I whispered.

"So was he…" Ben gaped. "That's awful."

"It was worse when Zagarovsky got out of prison. He wouldn't let Andrei see her." I wasn't sure how much farther I should go. Some things were better left alone.

Fearless, Andrei scooted along the bowsprit to the very tip, showing off by holding on with his legs, his arms outstretched for balance. I was about to call 'stop' when he flipped. Much to Jessie's amusement, he hung upside down, swaying to and fro.

Ben bumped my fist. "It took six months before I did that. He's been on the *Spray* for all of three days."

"It's amazing," I agreed.

My brother never had a childhood. If he wanted to eat, he had to work in the stables, grooming, washing, polishing, sweeping, and feeding the horses. Zagarovsky's employees made sure he was mostly shoveling horse dung.

"Jessie's progressing too." Like his mom, Ben didn't overstate.

Andrei's monkey-like antics and pretending to panic made Jessie laugh even harder.

"I better go save him." I put *Faustus* and the dictionary aside. "I'm counting on you, mate."

Ben grinned. "He'll catch up to you by Christmas, if I have anything to do with it."

Andrei plopped into the water before I was halfway to the bow. I flung myself over the lifeline. He was spitting out seawater when I surfaced beside him. A splash in my face and a curt shake of his head made it quite clear he didn't need help. Little by little, he dogpaddled towards the stern ladder.

Jessie looked down at him. "If you want, Josh can teach you to freestyle."

Andrei gave me a grim glance.

"He taught me," she added. "He makes it easy. The worst part is holding your breath when your face is in the water."

He gave another shake of his head, not so abrupt.

"You taught me how to ride Fanfare," I reminded him.

"It was more like how not to fall off."

310

He relented and I side-stroked next to him, lifting up his butt and telling him to kick harder as we swam around the *Spray*. He cussed when water got in his mouth. We were going to have to work on 'language arts.'

+++

Our father was lounging in the cockpit when we climbed onboard. He gave me the parental wink of approval and tossed a dry towel at Andrei. Gooseflesh covered him despite the heat.

"I just got off the phone with Sal," he said. "I would've called you, but Dani was doing homework. She said to say 'hi'. I told her you'd call her in an hour, 9:00 pm their time," he went on.

Ben and Jessie babbled in the background. They thought any news about Dani was life-changing for me. Andrei dabbed at wet skin, mostly trying to get warm by wrapping the towel around himself. It was difficult to know what he thought about anything. He'd survived by blocking out the world around him.

"Sal say anything about Mom?" I asked.

"Donatella spent most of the day with her. She didn't say much."

"That's not good."

"Remember what I said about baby steps, Sander?"

He pulled my shivering brother onto the cockpit seat and hugged him. It was the first time that Andy hadn't jerked away.

"I want her to have more good days than bad days," Andrei murmured.

Dad glanced at me. He smoothed back long wet hair. "We all do, Andy."

"One of us should've stayed with her," I said.

He looked up quickly. Our eyes locked. It was the one thing we disagreed on.

"We need time together," he said, his tone a warning to me.

I looked away, not about to admit he was right. Day in, day out, the stress of seeing her slow recovery was taxing. It was worse for Andrei. He had nightmares.

"We need time together," I repeated, emphasizing 'we' so he knew I was including our mother.

Andy picked up. "Not in New York. Here."

"I like it here too, guys; however, it would take a lot of money."

"Uncle John said we can stay as long as we want," Andy said.

I tried not to laugh. I couldn't stop myself. "Andy, the *Spray's* too small. Five of them, plus four of us is nine people."

"Jess and I figured it out. There are six beds; two more converting the dining table. I'll sleep on the floor."

"For a few days, sure…"

+ + +

When I finally looked back, my heavy-eyed brother was snuggled in the towel, my father gently stroking his side. He had a satisfied smile, like a contented cat in the sun.

Dad waited until Andrei dozed off.

"Sal's been looking into Zagarovsky's operation," he began.

I didn't like the sound of that. "He'll probably take it over. That's the mafia; once in, never out."

"I asked him to find out what Zagarovsky meant when he told you he saved two million dollars. After the

312

Florescus came back from Australia, he moved four million dollars in cash to a bank vault in Singapore. The most logical explanation is it's some kind of reward."

"For killing us?"

He shrugged rather than admit it. "Sal had some good news about Andy though," he added. "Because of the birth certificate, he inherits everything," he said quietly.

"How much?" So much for my brother being asleep.

"Sal thinks about eighteen million."

Andy's eyes opened wide. "That's a shit-load of money."

The End

The Walker Family's *Spray*

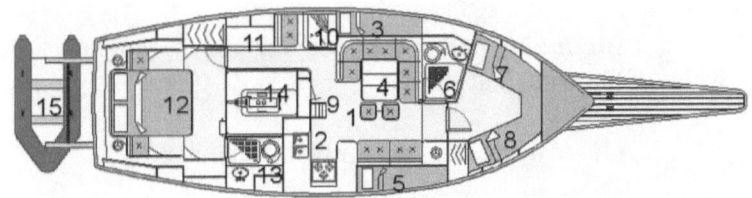

The *Spray*, modeled on Bruce Roberts-Goodson's Centennial Spray 38 ©, which is based on Slocum's *Spray*. Reproduced with permission.

1. Salon

2. Galley

3. Josh's berth, and storage

4. Dining table

5. Ben's berth

6. Head

7. Grandma's berth

8. Jessie's berth (*Encyclopedia Britannica* under)

9. Companionway stairs

10. Chart table (secret compartment underneath)

11. Storage/workshop

12. Parents' cabin

13. Parents' head

14. Engine room

15. *Squirt*

Glossary for sailing beginners

Abaft : a seldom used expression for near or towards the stern, often from a given reference point, such as 'abaft the beam', meaning back from the beam.

About : to change direction of the vessel by passing through the oncoming wind (tacking); e.g. to go about.

Adrift : not under sail or engine power, moving at the whim of the wind and sea.

Aft : towards the back or rear of the boat.

Aground : stuck on the ground, a mud bank, sand bar, or worse (rocks or coral).

Ahead : to go forward, or what is ahead of the vessel.

Aloft : anything above the deck and cabin, to go up the mast/into the rigging.

Anchor : a heavy metal 'claw' designed to grab hold of the sea floor and keep a boat from moving.

Anchorage : a place protected from wind and waves, with bottom conditions suitable for anchoring.

Apparent wind : combines both the true wind direction and the boat's speed and direction.

Astern : pass to the rear of a boat, as in to 'go astern', meaning to go behind the boat, or to leave astern.

Autopilot : a computer-controlled mechanical or hydraulic-powered device to steer the vessel. Often connected to a chart plotter.

Avast : To cease and desist. 'Avast there, mates,' if said with a pirate accent, means 'stop screwing around, guys.'

Backstay : the wire cable running from the back of the boat (stern) to the top of the mast.

Batten : a wood or fiberglass strip inserted through the leech of a sail, sometimes extending as far as the luff, to improve sail shape, support the leech, and prevent fluttering.

Beaufort scale: a 0-12 scale of wind strengths (calm through hurricane) and identifying characteristics. For example, Force 6 is a strong breeze, 24-31 mph or 21 to 27 knots. Expect to see long waves with foamy crests and some spray.

Beam : the width of the boat, or a direction, as in 'off the beam' meaning perpendicular to the vessel. Replaces athwart.

Bearing : the direction to something, usually relative to the boat or a chart.

Bear away : to turn away from the current direction usually with respect to the direction of the wind, also 'bear off.'

Beating : to sail as close to the wind as possible.

Becalmed : when the vessel is motionless because of lack of wind.

Below : under the deck, as in 'to go below'.

Berth : a nautical bed, usually narrow, sometimes wet. The expression 'to give a wide berth' is not about a captain's generous berth allocation, but to avoid something (another vessel) by a wide margin. Also, berth refers to where a vessel is normally docked.

Bilge : the part where the side of the boat turns into the bottom of the boat, also the bottom of the boat where smelly water gathers.

Bimini : a sun cover of canvas stretched over the cockpit, and supported by a metal frame.

Binnacle : a stand or support for the ship's compass.

Bitter end : the last part of a line or anchor rode.

Boat hook : a sometimes-extensible pole with a hook in the end to catch things like mooring lines, pets, and hats when they drop in the water.

Bobstay : a wire running from the bow to the end of the bowsprit to relieve the load from the forestay.

Bollard : a hefty short post typically attached to the dock. Used to secure boats.

Boom : the stick attached near the bottom of the mast allowing the sail to pivot with the wind.

Boom vang : a system of ropes and pulleys, or a spring-loaded rod used to stop the boom from lifting up.

Bosun's chair : a canvas seat used to hoist crew up the mast to make repairs.

Bow : the front part of the boat.

Bowline : a temporary knot, easy to tie, and untie after being loaded. See http:// en.wikipedia.org/wiki/Bowline.

Bow line : the rope connecting the bow to the dock.

Bowsprit : the 'stick' extending from the bow, allowing the boat to carry more sail, not to be confused with the anchor roller.

Bridge : the elevated position from which a boat is steered, or an overhead structure requiring care to go under.

Broach : when large waves and/or strong wind cause a vessel to lose control and turn sideways, often heeling dramatically, with a chance of rolling over.

Bulkhead : a vertical partition in the cabin providing stiffening/watertight compartments for the hull.

Buoy : a float used to mark a position or thing.

By and large : a common expression of nautical origin, meaning a vessel performs well going into the wind (by) and with the wind (large), so all possible points of sail.

Capsize : to turn the boat over by 90 degrees, or more. Not recommended!

Cast off : to let go mooring or dock lines so the boat is free to move.

Catamaran : a boat with two hulls side by side.

Chaffing wearing of lines against things causes them to fray and eventual fail. Prevented by chaffing gear, for example, covering the affected part with hose, canvas, or leather.

Chart : a map used on a boat, showing details of the coast and what is under the surface.

Chart plotter : an integrated computer and monitor that presents navigation charts and the vessel's location. Enables courses to be plotted as routes, or tracking of the vessel's movements.

Cleat : a fitting for preventing ropes from moving. For example, a dock cleat.

Clew : the corner of a sail furthest from the bow.

Close-hauled : to sail as close to the wind as possible. Requires hauling the sails in tightly.

Coach house : part of the cabin projecting above the deck, often with larger windows.

Cockpit : a somewhat protected area for sitting and steering, usually lower than the deck.

Come about : to change direction by passing through the wind.

Companionway : the entrance to the cabin, usually as stairs from the cockpit.

Constant bearing-decreasing range (CBDR) occurs when one vessel maintains a constant bearing relative to another vessel, while the distance between them (range) decreases. This is a collision course.

Course : the direction that is a boat is to be steered. Course over ground (COG) is the actual course after including the effect of wind, tide, and current.

Current : a flow of water from one area to another (not a tide, where the water flows back).

Cutter : a single-masted boat with two jibs. Also a fast motor boat often used by the Coastguard.

Davits : a small crane or spar used to lift things, such as a dinghy or outboard motor.

Dead ahead : directly in front.

Dead reckoning : is the process of using estimates of direction and distance traveled, and sightings of landmarks to determine a vessel's position.

Dinghy : a small open boat. Some dinghies can be inflated.

Dock : a place to tie up a boat for a period of time and walk on dry land, also a pier or wharf. To dock means to tie up at a dock.

Dodger : a see-through screen with a hood at the front of the cockpit to deflect wind and waves.

Draft : the minimum depth of water a boat requires in order to float.

Drogue or sea -anchor is a device towed through the water to slow down a vessel. Can be a parachute, a long length of rope, a large cone, or a series of small cones attached to a long line.

Fathom : six feet.

Fender : an inflated cushion between boats, or a boat and the dock to prevent damage to the hull.

Fiberglass : a durable, strong composite of polyester resin and layers of cloth made from glass fibers. Used for the vast majority of boats manufactured since the 1950s.

First rate : an expression derived from the top-of-the-line sailing warships (100 guns) from the 1600s through 1800s.

Flare : a pyrotechnic/firework, either hand-held or fired from a gun to draw attention to a vessel in distress.

Following sea : waves from astern, going in the same direction. Under certain conditions, the vessel can surf the wave, picking up considerable speed and a chance of losing control. Waves that overtake the boat can be especially dangerous if the wave is breaking.

Foot : the bottom of a sail.

Fore : forward or front, as in fore-deck (the deck between mast and bow), and fore-peak (the cabin squashed into the bow).

Forestay : the wire cable from the top of the mast to the front of the boat.

Forward : toward the front of the boat, as in "Go forward and drop the anchor."

Frames : ribs that form the hull's shape, typically used in wooden boats.

Furl : to reduce a sail's area. Jibs and genoas are typically wound around the forestay. In a similar fashion, mainsails may be furled inside/outside the mast, or inside the boom. The alternative is storing the mainsail along the boom by folding the sailcloth.

Gaff : an oblique stick attached near the top of the mast. Used to hold the top side of a four-sided sail, while allowing it to pivot with the wind direction. Also a pole with a sharp hook on the end to assist in bringing fish aboard.

Galley : the kitchen in a boat.

Genoa : a large, powerful jib overlapping the mainsail.

Gooseneck : a fitting connecting the mast and boom, allowing the boom to swivel.

Grounding : an ill-advised contact between the boat's hull or keel and the bottom (ground). Also used in lieu of 'bonding', a process of electrically connecting all metal (engine, thru-hulls, etc.) and the top of the mast to minimize damage in the event of a lightning strike.

Gunwale : the edge of the side of the boat and the deck.

Gybe : the process of changing course and/or repositioning the sails from one side of the boat to the other with the wind coming over the stern. A dangerous maneuver if the wind is blowing hard. Can occur accidentally if not paying attention.

Halyards : 'ropes' used to hoist and lower sails.

Hank : a metal or plastic hook/device to connect a sail to a mast track or forestay.

Hatch : an opening in the deck or cabin roof to allow light and fresh air to enter.

Head : the top corner of a sail, , to 'head up' is to sail closer to the wind or into the wind also a nautical toilet.

Heading : the direction the boat is going in.

Heave to : to stop the vessel by sheeting the jib to one side and locking the rudder in the opposing direction.

Heel : the vessel leans sideways, induced by the wind's sideways force on the sails.

Helm : the steering wheel, as in the command 'take the helm'.

Jackline : a continuous line running from the bow to the stern for crew to clip on to when moving about on deck. Essential when conditions are dangerous and/or there is a risk of falling overboard.

Jetty : a stone wall projecting from the shore to protect boats in a harbor. Also a quay.

Jib : a triangular sail in front of the mast, with one side usually connected to the forestay.

Jury rig : using whatever is at hand to make a temporary rig in the event of dismasting.

Keel : the very bottom of the boat, usually cast from lead. A sailing boat's keel functions to keep it upright.

Ketch : a vessel with two masts, the tallest one in front and a shorter one behind.

Knot : a speed equal to one nautical mile per hour (1.15 mph or 1.85 kilometers per hour).

Latitude : a geographic coordinate (distance) measured in degrees north or south (up to 90°) of the equator (0 degrees).

Lazy jacks : 'ropes' from the mast to the boom to keep a sail from falling to the side .

Leech : the aft or trailing edge of a sail.

Lee : the side sheltered from the wind, leeward is the direction away from the wind. A lee shore is on the side of the vessel opposite the wind. Being blown on to a lee shore during a storm is a good reason to be safely tied up at dock, or a long way offshore.

Life raft : an inflatable, usually covered raft used as a last resort when the vessel sinks.

Line (s) : there are no 'ropes' used on a boat. They are lines, unless specifically purposed as halyards, sheets, outhauls, downhauls, boom vangs, etc. Also see 'rode.'

Log : a record of a boat's operation with courses and events, also a device to measure speed.

Longitude : a geographic coordinate (distance) measured in degrees east (up to +180 degrees) or west (up to -180 degrees) of the Greenwich meridian (0 degrees).

Luff : the forward edge of a sail, also to head into the wind until the sails invert in shape and flap, sometimes very loudly.

Lying ahull : with sails removed, the vessel rides out a storm at the mercy of the sea while the crew cowers below.

Mainmast : the tallest mast.

Mainsail : the primary sail attached to the mainmast.

Mainsheet : line used to haul in the boom to adjust the sail's shape to wind conditions and direction.

Mizzen : (mast or sail) the mast or sail closest to the stern.

Mooring : attaching a boat to a sunken weight, or a dock.

Nautical mile : approximately one minute of latitude, or 6076 feet, 1.15 land miles, or 1.85 kilometers. Note that definitions of length vary. For example, the *American Practical Navigator* defines a sea mile as an "approximate mean value" of 6,080 feet; the length of a minute of arc along the meridian at latitude 48°."

Navigation : the process of way finding, from the current position to another position, conducting a boat from one place to another.

Oar : a rowing device connected to a dinghy and used to move it (not a paddle, which is used on a canoe).

Outboard : a detachable gasoline-powered motor mounted on the stern.

Painter : a line attached to the bow of a dinghy for tying up or towing.

Pier : a dock extending out from the shore.

Piling : a wood (or concrete/steel) pole driven into the bottom.

Pitch : the bow-to-stern up and down movement of the boat caused by waves.

Plane : when a boat lifts onto the surface of the water, rather than pushing through it. Most sailboats are displacement vessels, meaning they displace their weight in water and do not plane.

Port : the left side, identified with a red light at night. Also a harbor, a nautical destination.

Portlight : a waterproof window in the side of the cabin.

Pulpit : a safety railing at the bow, made of metal pipes.

Reaching : to sail with the wind off the beam, (ranging from 60 degrees to 160 degrees). A close reach has the wind forward of the beam, while a broad reach has the wind aft of the beam.

Reef : to reduce sail area by lowering the sail and tying up what is not used.

Rigging : the various lines, stays, and shrouds needed to support the mast and operate the sails.

Rode : the anchor rope or chain.

Roller reefing : used to reduce the sail area by winding the sail around the boom.

Rudder : the board attached to the steering wheel or tiller which causes the boat to change course.

Run : to allow a line to move freely, also a direction of sail, such as running before the wind.

Running backstay : is an adjustable wire used to hold the mast from the rear, employed during severe wind conditions.

Safety harness : a harness made of webbing (or incorporated into a life jacket) enabling a crew member to be secured to the vessel during hazardous conditions.

Schooner : a sailing boat with two masts, the mainmast behind the first or foremast.

Scupper : a drain from the cockpit, or to enable water to leave the deck through the gunwale.

Sea anchor : see drogue.

Seat locker : a locker under the seats in the cockpit.

Seacock : a shut-off valve below the waterline; sometimes mistakenly called a thru-hull, which refers to a mushroom-shaped fitting penetrating the hull, and attached to a seacock.

Secure : to make fast.

Seasickness : motion sickness caused by the rocking action of the boat going through waves. The primary symptom is nausea, aka puking one's guts out.

Self-steering : a mechanical system of levers , gears, and wind vane to make course corrections via the rudder so that the vessel maintains a constant relationship to wind direction.

Sheets : 'ropes' used to control the angle and fullness of the sail, attached to the jib clew, the bottom corners of a spinnaker, or the end/middle of a boom.

Shroud : a wire connecting the top of the mast with the side of the boat. There may be several shrouds per side.

Slack : the opposite of secure, something not secured, to loosen. Also slack tide, when there is no water movement.

Sloop : a boat with a single mast, one jib, and a mainsail.

Spinnaker : a large, lightweight, usually colorful sail used when the wind is coming from astern to off the beam (perpendicular to the vessel).

Spring line : a line usually from the middle of the boat to a forward or aft dock cleat.

Stay : a supporting wire connecting the mast to the bow (forestay) or stern (backstay).

Staysail : a sail fixed to a stay, for example, a cutter rig has an outer jib and a smaller jib attached to an inner forestay.

Squall : a violent wind that arrives suddenly, often with rain.

SSB Radio : single-side band modulation radio, similar to Ham radio, used for medium to long-range marine communications with fixed channels and frequency selection. Range depends on environmental/atmospheric conditions.

Stanchions : metal pipes secured to the gunwale, holding lifelines to prevent crew from falling overboard.

Starboard : the right side of the boat, associated with green (e.g. navigation lights on the vessel and buoys).

Stern : the rear of the boat.

Stern line : a rope used to tie the rear of the boat to the dock.

Storm sails : very rugged, small sails (aka storm jib and trysail) used to replace larger sails in the event that severe winds make reefing or furling insufficient.

Stow : to put things in their proper place, not to be confused with 'Stow it', a rude expression comparable to 'shut up' or 'get over it.'

Tack : the bottom, forward corner of a sail; also changing direction when going into the wind.

Tide : a periodic rise and fall in water level caused by the gravitational pull of the sun and moon, and the rotation of the earth. Tides vary by location, ranging from a few inches in lakes to many feet.

Tiller : a handle attached to a rudder or outboard motor to enable steering.

Trim : the balance of a boat achieved by distributing the weight fore and aft. Also to adjust the shape of the sails for better performance.

VHF Radio : very high frequency two-way radio (marine application broadcasts in the 156.0 and 162.025 MHz range) with international-standard channels. For example, 16 is the hailing and distress channel. The range is 'line-of-sight' and varies depending on signal strength, antenna, environmental conditions, and obstructions. US Coastguard transmissions exceed 60 miles, while a typical sailboat range is between 10 and 30 miles.

Wake : the disturbance of water caused by a boat's movement.

Winch : a metal cylinder turned by ratcheting gears and a handle to give leverage, used to hoist or pull in the sails.

Windlass : a device for raising the anchor; may be electrically powered.

Windward : generally the direction the wind is coming from. For example, going to windward is to sail close-hauled.

Yawl : a two-masted vessel, the mizzen mast being much smaller and farther aft than that of a ketch.

About the Author

Neil Barry lives aboard his 50-foot sloop, *Imagine,* cruising the East Coast of the U.S., the Bahamas, and points south. Born in Sydney, Australia, he began sailing at 12 years old. While studying architecture in college, he graduated from 12-foot boats to crewing on racing yachts on Sydney Harbour and offshore.

In 1977, he took time off from sailing to attend graduate school, travel the world, raise a family, and build a career as an academic. His next boat arrived 13 years later, a 28-foot cutter that he finished from the bare-hull stage. He sailed with his family on a small man-made lake in Indiana for 17 years before the ocean called again.

Imagine **under sail (a beam reach) in the Abacos, Bahamas, 2015. Copyright: Neil Barry**

After 30 years as a professor, Neil Barry recognized the need for a new kind of novel, one that stimulates learning, creativity, and critical thinking, while providing entertainment. His *Chicken of the Sea* series combines real places, things, events, and situations with fictional people and an engrossing, believable plot. Readers can use today's digital technology to explore the 'real' world of Victor Joshua Walker, beginning by visiting neilbarrybooks.com.

The author at the wheel, and his trusty dog, Sienna, in his lifejacket. Copyright 2015, Kathryn Ellis, Author

www.ingramcontent.com/pod-product-compliance
Lightning Source LLC
Chambersburg PA
CBHW050543260626
47157CB00002B/410